Entangled Lives

A Generation, in Rebellion for a Better World

M.S. KIA

M.S.KIA

Entangled Lives

A generation, in rebellion for a better world

To the family of all those whose loved ones died in the fight for a better life for all

Truth does not care what we think of it.
Anne Michaels, Fugitive Pieces.

Forgetting, I would even say historical error, is
an essential factor in the creation of a nation.
Ernest Renan, What is a Nation?

But truth belonged to someone once and to
everyone now.
We should care for truth.

And forgetting.
And history.

Foreword

Timeline

June 1953 CIA coup against Mohammad Mossaddeq. Shah returned to the throne.

Jan 1963 Shah announces his "White Revolution".

June 1963 Uprising in the bazaar. Khomeini is arrested and deported to Najaf, Iraq.

April 1965 Assassination attempt on the Shah in the Marmar Palace.

1965 Founding of Mojahedin Organisation (PMOI)

1967-69 Founding of Fadai' Organisation (OIPFG)

Feb 1968 Bijan Jazani and Abbas Surki arrested.

Feb 1971 Fadai' attack the Siahkal police station and the beginning of the guerrilla war.

1973 Mojahedin split, the Marxist faction later becoming the Peykar organisation.

April 1975 Bijan Jazani and others shot on the hills behind Evin.

June 1976 Hamid Ashraf and the entire Fadai' leadership killed in shoot-out.

Oct 1977 Ten days of poetry reading in Tehran's Goethe Institute.

Jan 1979 The Shah leaves Iran.

Feb 1979 The Shah's regime collapses and the Islamic Republic declared.

Aug 1979 Khomeini orders all-out attack on Kurdistan on anniversary of the CIA coup.

Feb 1980 Final attack on Turkaman Sahra.

May 1980 Fadai' Organisation split into Majority and Minority.

i

June 1980 Explosion in Headquarters of the Islamic Republican Party, mass arrests and start of repression.

Sept 1980 Iraq attacks Iran.

July 1988 Khomeini signs UN Resolution 598 ending the Iran-Iraq war.

Aug 1988 Massacre of political prisoners across Iran.

Preface

This is the story of a generation of young men and women in Iran who rose out of the ashes of the CIA-engineered coup that, having overthrown the elected government of Mohammad Mosaddeq, destroyed the only large left-wing organisation in the country with deep roots in the working class and intelligentsia of Iran, the Tudeh Party. A post-coup silence of the graveyard settled over a country ruled by an absolute monarch and his brutal secret police force, SAVAK.

Out of the ruins that was the Iranian left, a generation that found itself suffocating in the stultifying air of the Shah's so called 'White Revolution' took the only course that they thought possible: armed struggle. They were idealistic, they had only a superficial knowledge of their country and of history. They made many mistakes, but fearlessly and single-mindedly fought for a better future that they knew they might never witness. This was a generation of the left that made my country breathe.

Theirs was a spontaneous home-grown movement formed by the gelling together of numerous small groups. They had the courage to want a better world, and the courage to fight for it, foregoing love, family, and comfort. Hundreds of men and women were hunted down by the CIA and Mossad-trained security forces, killed in street battles or imprisoned, tortured, and executed.

Theirs was a lonely struggle.

But their selflessness became an inspiration for the revolutionaries that rose up, became a mass movement and overthrew the Shah only to have to fight a new adversary. No sooner had the dust settled after the overthrow of one despot when the new regime showed its true totalitarian face in the guise of a brutal theocratic absolutism.

Utterly betrayed by the death of a revolution whose main slogan was *'Independence'* and *'Freedom'*, that generation were joined by their younger sisters and brothers to fight for freedom and equality once again. This was to be yet another, and this time even greater, broader, bloodier, and more savage bloodletting and suffering.

Entangled Lives is a story of young men and women who, despite their differences, are part of the same narrative – the quest to release the entire potential of their country. Many died in their prime. Others spent years behind bars. Some went mad. A few survivors left memoirs.

Entangled Lives is is the tale of two men and a woman, as recounted to me by them or by people who knew them well. I too was a close friend and a witness to their struggles. I too had spent over a year in the prisons of the Islamic Republic. Wherever available I have let them speak in their own voice. The two who have survived their ordeal have seen and approved the final manuscript. I take full responsibility for any other inaccuracies or misquotations. Theirs is a true story that mirrors their generation. For the story of the Fadai' urban guerrillas I have consulted published works and spoken to former activists and fellow prisoners.

I have fictionalised some of the actions and dialogues to make it into a semi-coherent story. Some of the speeches are a near-verbatim translation of what was related to me. Like all memories one must allow for the erosion of time. Two of the main female characters (Jina and Azadeh), while based on real people, were neither directly interviewed by me, nor had the opportunity to have an input into the narrative and should be treated as purely fictional figures. Details of the security police's trap for the Fadai' in spring-summer of 1977 has been taken from an ex-SAVAK agent (Parviz Mo'tamed – PM in this story) in an interview published on the web and has to be approached with extra caution – it contains numerous improbable boasts.

All the dead retain their original names (a list of names is provided in appendix 2). Most of the living actors in this real-life drama have been given a pseudonym. Dead or living they deserve their story to be heard.

Acknowledgement

I would like to thank the people without whose help this manuscript could not have been written. Firstly, I thank Ahmad (not his real name) for taking the time to recalling his memories, some of which could not have been easy and took him back to truly dark places and dark times. I am also indebted to Nayyer, (not her real name, on whose published autobiography in Farsi, I based her chapters), for reading and correcting many mistakes, and for encouraging me to continue. I thank Shahla (a pseudonym) whose recollections were vital for some of the chapters on Changiz and my very dear friends Azar Sheibani and Hedayat Soltanzadeh for filling the gaps in Changiz's earlier life.

I am grateful to my lifelong friends, Charles Fox, a man of so many talents and who knows Iran, for reading and commenting on the manuscript and encouraging me to have it published; Jonathan Miller for his encouragement after reading the manuscript on his phone, his laptop misbehaving; Shirley and Humphry Hodgson, who I met in Shiraz all those years ago, for persistently valuable advise; Henry Oakley, who gave the immaculate care his normally gives to his orchids and the Royal College of Physicians' garden for his careful proofreading despite his horror of the torture scenes; Mike Williams for proofreading the revised document; Asqar Rastegar, my lifelong friend whose friendship and wise advise has always lighted my life, for reading and commenting on the final version of the document; and finally to my wonderful daughters Maryam for having the last word which corrected a major defect, and Nargess for her artistic and literary input into the cover.

I am deeply indebted to Sanam Hayati for designing the cover and apologise for the numerous changes we asked of her. I thank Karl French for detailed comments, which I followed closely, and his suggestion to turn this into a novel which I reluctantly ignored. I also thank Divya Kapur, a beacon of cultural activity in Calangute, Goa, who gave me valuable advice on publishing. And above all I thank my wife, Jaleh, who originally suggested I write the novel and without whose daily love and care I would not be able to write, and my daughters Maryam and Nargess who are a constant source of inspiration and encouragement.

Chapter 1

The strike

"All the women in my life," Ahmad suddenly blurted out as if entering a different memory, a dark shadow spreading across his brow, "I have either committed a crime (*jenayat*) against them or they have committed *a jenayat* against me," He used the word *jenayat*, turning love into a mortal crime. The thought appeared as if it was waiting all those years to emerge. Like a confession. Then slowly over several minutes I saw his hands, which had tensed into a grip, relax and he returned to the now, his eyes and mouth smiling as they often did even when he was talking about something serious, as if he was in love with all life had thrown in his path. As if defying death so many times had made it into something abstract.

We were talking in his small flat in Ilford, a left-behind suburb of London exchanging memories, as old friends do, filling gaps in our friendship.

"It was all pure chance I am here talking to you", Ahmad murmured continuing aloud a sentence in his head, his life-long thick moustache now grey, his slim body perched awkwardly on the chair, his neck immobile, clearly in pain as he nearly always was in the last years, "pure chance and being constantly alert" he added louder. "We fought, we lost, and we rose up again to fight once more" he paused, floating back into the past his eyes misting over with memory.

"Would you like me to tell you about the strike?" he suggested after a pause when we both had sunk again into our own memories. "The first strike in Melli University" he added. So began the many days we spent time reminiscing about our pasts in the land where we were both born, his narrative always detailed and cinematic, like he was living through it once again, his eyes expressing the moments of joy, of love, of pride, and of pain, like a mirror to his interior. I felt I was living it with him, every moment and every second. In those moments I was him, or as near him as my imagination allowed.

This is his story.

*

That first day of autumn Ahmad woke up with a throbbing headache having only slept two hours. He and his friends had been discussing the turbulent situation in the country in his rented room on the rooftop which he shared with Mansur, a poet, drinking pure alcohol supplied by another poet, Hossein, and Sia, two friends he had met while in secondary school down south in Khorramshahr. Every night the two would steal a large bottle of absolute alcohol from the dispensary of the military hospital they were assigned to as part of their national service, add dried sour cherry for taste and colour and would slip out with the bottle between the hospital's loose railings. Why no one noticed the missing alcohol is a mystery. The discussions on that rooftop were heated. The Shah had just escaped an attempt on his life when a guard at the gate to the Marble Palace had fired shots at him that missed their target but hit one of his aides. A number of people, mainly students, recently returned from Europe and belonging to a pro-Chinese split from the pro-Moscow Tudeh Party, were arrested, accused of masterminding the plot and were on trial for their life. This morning's headache was an echo of the sour-cherry-coloured pure alcohol of the night before.

Those were years when Iran was undergoing a huge transformation after the Shah, under US and World Bank pressure, had initiated reforms that undercut the power of landed aristocracy and launched him on the road to consolidating his absolute dictatorship over every sector of society. Four years earlier, Sia, while still a medical student, had set fire to the Tehran University's new Chancellor's car in protest against openly rigged elections to Iran's 20th Majles (parliament) that were meant to signal a new, freer, era. Chancellor Dr Eqbal, was a close associate of the Shah and prime minister until his dismissal after the election fiasco. The University was shut down and Sia sent off to do military service. He was lucky his punishment was light. We will meet *Hossein-the-poet* later in our story.

That autumn morning Ahmad walked out into the street unaware that it would be a turning point in his life. The plane trees on the sidewalk of the broad avenue that led northwards from the railway station to the foothills of the Alborz mountains were once again slowly and punctually disrobing, revealing a glistening white bark with patches of dark blue – like wounds healing. The sidewalk was still wet from the previous night's rain browning the ochre-orange of the fallen leaves. A hammer was banging inside his skull as he boarded the bus. As he walked over to the Faculty of Arts and Architecture, he stopped to look up at the Alborz mountain range, white with fresh snow. Below, the tangle of brick and concrete buildings of Tehran spreading southwards into the desert was once again clearly visible. Rain had washed clean the grime that normally hovered over the city like a dark, black, gaseous blanket obscuring it. Strange how nausea comes in waves as if someone is stirring. It was the first day of his year two in Iran's first private university, the National University (*Daneshgah-e Melli*). A last look at the snow caps. He felt young. He was. It was 1965.

He trotted into the classroom a little late. The hammer was still banging rhythmically in synchrony with his heartbeat. That summer of 1965 he had rented a room in *Goad-e Araboon*, one of the most deprived slums in South Tehran to study the life of the poor at close hand. It was the beginning of what would turn out to be a lifelong project of understanding how various sections of his countrymen and women lived. Understanding and recording those lives was to become his passion. He was not to know that virtually all his work would be snatched away into oblivion one day. Now he was ready for his second year of architecture at the Faculty.

The class looked gloomy. Nine classmates had been expelled because they had failed on one or more subjects. The College rulebook was explicit. If you failed to get 13 out of 20 in any subject after a re-sit at the end of summer, you were out even if you were in your final year. As a class spokesman he knew he had to act, and with that thought his eyes glinted and the blacksmith inside his head slipped away, unnoticed. He called a class meeting in the lobby. Even as a boy he had loved to have an audience, to take them into an imagined flight, to conjure up images. It was always visual even when he was being analytical. He should have tried his hand at drama.

"Are we going to take this insult lying down," he began, carefully spacing his words? "Us, I mean the survivors, might have got away with it for now, but what about next year? How many more of us will be thrown out? Think of it!" he paused, "and the year after?", he talked in a calm but slightly theatrical voice and again paused. "Four years of your life and you are thrown out like rotten fruit." As he spoke images of reproductions of paintings he had seen, heroic images, flashed and curiously settled on the image of the bare-chested woman, one hand holding up the flag and another a bayonetted musket, walking over the fallen and looking back, encouraging the crowd she was leading. Delacroix's *Liberty Leading the People* spoke to his youth, his drive and perhaps his vanity. She was addressing the future and he felt the same. He warmed. He found he could project not just his anxiety, or anger but his conviction. One more push. He smiled as he took the next step and a dimple appeared on the corner of his mouth. Only on the right, an architectural asymmetry.

"I am going to be number 10", and he lowered his voice a fraction, looked at the boy in the back of the hall straight in the eye, who dropped his gaze. "I am expelling myself before they do", he continued with a transient smile, then changed the tone of his voice, "no one could live with a sword hanging over their heads," he said with a finality. His thick black moustache made him look more determined. His eyes moved left and was now looking into that of the next person, a girl who looked straight back, unblinking. There was a pause when no one moved. There are moments of decision that could totally change the direction of your life.

"I am going to be number 11" came a voice from somewhere in the middle. He had a deep voice, the sort that resonates off the walls. It was a tall thin young man, also with a thick black moustache. He was wearing a blue shirt,

4

ironed carefully for the first day back, hair Alain Delon style, looping across to the right, then gently curving downwards giving a shadow on his brow, burnt brown by the summer sun. He must have been to the Caspian, or even abroad. These were affluent students. Within a short time, the entire class self-expelled.

Ahmad's voice rose again, now confident that he was unleashing a calming sense of group solidarity. That sense that you belong to something greater and that nothing can stop you getting what you want.

"*bacheha*, listen," he addressed them as 'children' in the way you do when you are talking to friends. "We need to convince the other years otherwise we will all be out." Three representatives were quickly elected and within an hour the entire architecture college self-expelled. About 600 boys and girls, mostly boys, gathered in the main hall. Everyone. Even those who were not in the least interested in politics. They elected a strike committee and wrote down their demands: restore the nine and remove the two articles in the Constitution dealing with expulsions.

They needed to mobilise the other colleges. Two others joined him, one the brother of a man who was currently being tried for his life in a military court accused of plotting to assassinate the Shah. That raised the stakes. They walked across to the college of languages and literature. The sun was now creeping up to its mid-day haughtiness.

"Don't let them girls distract you," somebody shouted as they were about to leave and burst into an embarrassed giggle. The running joke was that the nearly all male college of architecture and the nearly all-female literature would make a perfect match, with the added bonus of a foreign language opening the door to Europe or America. By early afternoon the faculties of economics and medicine had joined in. The thought that you could be out for a trivial failing, even after your fourth year, was persuasive. The private university, where the children of the elite enrolled, was out on strike in its totality.

"Why don't you join the strike committee?" someone asked Vida. Why not? She felt untouchable. Parvaneh needed a bit more persuasion. It was a wise move. Parvaneh, was the daughter of the capital's chief of police and the

5

Shah's younger brother was madly in love with Vida. Times were dangerous. The Shah was in total control and the dreaded SAVAK,[1] his not-too-secret secret service in charge of arresting, torturing and interrogating opponents had no leash.

Young and seemingly invincible, the entire University sat all day in the basketball grounds, feeling secure by its high fences, debating, chatting, ratifying resolution after resolution. It was exhilarating. When night came everyone went home, like a normal day. Clearly, they did not feel threatened. Ahmad prudently stayed over with a friend. The experience of an earlier arrest and beating at the hands of the political police when he was a schoolboy down south in Khorramshahr had matured him.

Eight days went by. For some days they had moved away from resolution-making to speeches and debates over the political situation in the country and the atmosphere in that crowded ground was slowly turning more radical. It was another clear autumn day and the sun beamed down; a warm, pleasant autumn sun now bearable unlike those of a month ago. Suddenly there was a commotion. Sheikholeslam, the Chancellor, walked in surrounded by a few men no one recognised. Balding as so many in their early middle age, he walked fully erect like someone who owned the earth with a paunch that made his walk look even haughtier.

Sheikholeslam had earlier bought the huge tract of land for Iran's first private university on orders of the Shah, ironically near the notorious high security Evin prison which held many political prisoners. Private money had come from that very elite who were expected to enrol, as well as from the government. It was the Shah's posthumous attempt to outdo his dead father who had erected Tehran University, Iran's first, and whose ghost hung over the son like a permanent challenge. The National University, modelled on Stanford, was to be the envy of the Middle East. He now walked past the sitting multitude of students in the court and climbed the platform they had erected for speeches.

"My children," he began in his deep voice in a tone that combined contempt with a paternal concern, "go back to your classes". He used that special tone he would use to address actual children. Or his tenant farmers. "It is beneath the dignity of people like you to squat on the floor like orange vendors and shout like thugs. Go back to your classes and we will forget this idiocy." Then silence.

Ahmad stood up, slowly, theatrically, walked over to the platform and ignoring the Chancellor, turned and addressed the sitting crowd.

"See," he began with a mischievous smile, "here is a university whose Chancellor thinks being an orange seller is an insult and uses it to rebuke his students. Is it any wonder that we are striking? Our university deserves a better head than this. We'll just have to add his removal to our list of demands!" At this the audience roared. He should have done drama.

The next day SAVAK started phoning the homes of students. The strike committee began to shrivel. Vida's father, an army general, ordered her to stay home. Parvaneh's father went a step further and had a policeman patrolling outside their house. Some others too failed to come back. On day thirteen of the strike Ahmad and Rasul, the boy with a brother being tried for his life, took the resolution requiring the deleting of the two clauses that expelled students and calling for the resignation of the Chancellor and walked the hundred metres from the basketball ground to the University main office. Behind the perimeter fence they could see troops, wearing masks and armed with machine guns around the periphery of the University. It was the first cloudy day of the term. Maybe it would rain later. There was no escape.

[1] *Sazman-e Amniayat va Ettela'at-e Keshvar* (SAVAK) literally Organization of National Intelligence and Security of the Country, was the main surveillance and intelligence arm of the regime, set up with the help of CIA and the Israeli Mossad after the CIA-led coup which overthrew the popular prime minister Mosaddeq in 1953. SAVAK was in charge of the interrogation centres across the country.

Chapter 2

The Chancellor

Ahmad

They climbed the faux-marble stairs, and walked up to the first floor, the Chancellor's office. It was a large room at the far end of which his secretary Mrs Jalali, sat behind a desk. She smiled, as if expecting them. She was stunningly beautiful Ahmad would recall later. A few chairs lined the wall. In the centre was a fine-looking Kashan rug, emphasising the emptiness. On the left through an open door into the Chancellor's office they could hear men talking. The two young men walked over, and Ahmad handed Mrs Jalali the paper containing the demands and stepped back in unison. She glanced at the paper, a faint smile, got up, and walked into the Chancellor's room. She was wearing a black dress that stopped just above her knee. His eyes momentarily moved downwards. Then he looked up, guilt conquering biology and flushed. She sensed the eyes, as women often do.

She had barely crossed the threshold when a deep voice boomed out.

"Welcome, welcome!" It was Sheikholeslam in his unmistakeable Isfahani accent with its musical intonation, lilting upwards the end of the last words. Like French. "Bah-bah. Bah, bah. They have honoured us with their presence." He articulated the words distinctly, kneading them into the sarcasm. Ahmad walked over and stopped just inside the room. Another large room and another Kashan carpet, someone in authority must have had a link to a carpet merchant, he thought. The Chancellor was sitting at the far end facing the door behind a desk of dark oak, empty except for the national flag on a pole and a sheet of clean blotting paper. On the wall behind him hung the obligatory image of the Shah. On his right stood two colonels in full uniform. On the other side a man in dark blue suit, neat and erect. Around the room six or seven men were sitting, all in civvies, like a circus.

Ahmad walked over, with Rasul half a step behind, and laid the document on the spotless blotting pad in front of the Chancellor. He doesn't write much Ahmad thought.

"To what do we owe the honour of your presence?" Sheikholeslam said with an ironic twist, looking from one to the other, eyes smiling with a hint of menace.

"We have come to get a reply to our demands," Ahmad replied pausing a beat before adding "... our perfectly just demands." this was said with a decisiveness that all but expected assent.

The Chancellor stared back into his eyes still holding his ironic smile like a mask. He took a breath as if about to say something when one of the colonels stepped forward.

"Please allow me, your Excellency, to deal with this as it falls within my responsibilities," he addressed the Chancellor without taking his eyes off Ahmad. He was tall with an athletic figure. Imposing. He put a hand behind Ahmad's shoulder and gently guided him back through the door, across the secretary's room into another room opposite and closed the door behind him. On his way he looked over to Rasul and gave him a small nod, as if to say your turn will come.

"I am colonel Molavi, head of Tehran SAVAK." He was good looking. Ahmad introduced himself in the same formal voice. "I know who you are," Molavi said and took a number of photopraphs of Ahmad in various poses out of his breast pocket. "Why have you provoked the students?" he added casually pointing to the photos. His voice was warm and soft, informal, fatherly somehow clashing with his immaculately ironed uniform.

"It wasn't me who provoked the students" Ahmad said in a slightly indignant voice. "It was the University. There are one hundred of us and nine have been expelled. Not just asked to repeat a year but expelled. That is what the University Constitution says. Even if we are in the final year if we don't score the right marks, we are out." Ahmad spoke calmly, with a tinge of exasperation, as if explaining the obvious to a dim colleague. "I don't know if you have a daughter or a son in a similar situation. Just think if that child of yours, for whatever reason, maybe they've fallen ill or in love or something, fails by just one point. They are out," he paused, "simply thrown out. This is playing with people's lives. What we are asking is nothing outrageous. Only that they are allowed back to class and all this nonsense stopped for good." He had spoken looking ahead as if addressing an invisible audience. He then looked the colonel straight in the eye, a tiny smile glinting his eyes. The colonel had allowed him to make his speech, even looking as if he was interested, ignoring the sarcasm, the paternal smile sitting still on his lips. Rather thin lips for that face, Ahmad observed. Detracts from the elegance of his face.

"Of course, we have another request too," Ahmad added, like an afterthought. "That person does not have the basic qualities to be Chancellor," he continued, nodding slightly towards the closed door. The tall man interrupted, shedding his mask.

"You are way out of your depth boy. Have you any idea of what you are saying?" He now talked like an army officer addressing an errant private. He had not yet donned his SAVAK face. Ahmad knew that Sheikholeslam was close to the royal court and had been given almost unlimited powers to set up the American model of a university. "Look my son. Go back to class and I will see what I can do to sort things out." Back to the soft smile.

"I can't go back to class."

"Why not?"

"They won't believe me. Who, after 13 days, can believe a promise? It is quite simple. All you need to do is announce that the nine expellees will go back to class and make a decision about the Constitution. That would end the strike."

"I am telling you, go back and do as I say," the colonel was finding it difficult to control his anger. Eyes speak.

Another much shorter man in a dark suit, the one standing on the other side of the Chancellor's desk came through the door and turning to Molavi said softly "just give me a minute please." He must have been listening in. Turning to Ahmad he said,

"I am Dr Foruzanfar, head of the faculty of literature in Tehran University. The prime minister has sent me as his representative. I am one of you, my son, but let me tell you that there was a special meeting of the cabinet. His Majesty's office had informed us that the National University strike is related to the trial of Parviz Nikkhah and the others behind the wicked assassination attempt on his Majesty's life.[1] His Majesty has ordered an immediate end to this business. Following his Majesty's orders, the cabinet has decided to give you until two pm to quit. Anyone staying behind after that is a free target. Do you understand? You saw the troops lined up? That colonel there is the direct representative of General Oveisi, head of the gendarmerie. He has orders to shoot. My advice to you, my son, is to give up. It is absolutely clear to me you provoked a strike. If anything happens it will cost you personally. Dearly."

Ahmad noticed that when he spoke of the Shah, Foruzanfar's eyes had changed contour, was it reverence or fear? Ahmad just repeated his sermon ending by saying that anyway Mr Sheikholeslam is not fit to run a university.

"He doesn't even know how to talk properly and compares us to orange sellers, not that that's an insult – but that is what he has in his narrow mind. He respects neither words, nor culture, neither the Farsi language nor even hard-working orange sellers. As a professor of literature, you understand, don't you?" He was having fun.

"Yes, I fully understand what you are saying. We shouldn't be talking to the young like that these days. I understand. They don't understand the young. But believe me the military are dangerous and serious." Foruzanfar's conciliatory reply to his theatrical performance surprised him.

As he was speaking the other man in uniform walked in. It was becoming a farce. Were they queuing up outside the door?

"Allow me to have few words," he said to Foruzanfar, gently pushing him aside, and turning toward Ahmad said, "I am Colonel Ansari head of the Shemiran district SAVAK. You should know that from two o'clock onward anything that happens the responsibility lies on your shoulders. Your personal shoulders." There was menace in his voice.

"Actually, whatever happens from now the responsibility unquestionably lies on the head of the University and the Constitution of the University," Ahmad shot back, the small dimple reappearing on the right. If they were playing carrot and stick, he was happy to play along.

"You are truly arrogant for your age," Ansari said, reddening, clearly unbalanced by such disregard of his authority. A small bead set on his forehead. Unlike Molavi he had a moustache. I wonder if that makes you more brittle, the thought flitted through Ahmad's mind.

"Forgive him. They are young and …" Foruzanfar interceded but was cut short by the Tehran SAVAK chief Molavi.

"Have you made a decision?" His voice was warm, even concerning. What an intriguing personality, Ahmad thought, most out of character for a security chief.

"I have a suggestion," Ahmad replied looking straight into Molavi's eyes. The other two had stepped back. Was it deference? "I will go with you, Mr Foruzanfar and colonel Ansari to meet the students. There you can tell them about accepting the demands of the student body. If they collectively agree, we will return to the classes." It took some more discussion but, in the end, they accepted the proposition.

The students were seated outside the medical school where they were more compact than the basketball court. It felt more secure and easier to escape. And it might rain. They had become a little anxious. Easier to be reckless in the open under the sun. It had taken so long that morning, and their two emissaries were returning as a group, some in uniform. Ahmad introduced them one by one: chief of Tehran SAVAK, representative of the prime minister, head of Shemiran SAVAK.

"These gentlemen have asked me to tell you to go back to work and that our demands are accepted. They will tell you themselves," he said. Molavi stepped forward.

"My children, what you ask for is quite logical. I understand you. I swear on my military honour to realise what you have asked. The University rulebook will be changed. What you ask regarding the head of the University is absurd, but we accept the change in the Constitution and that the expelled students will be free to come back."

There was an explosion of joy. The entire student body moved to the college of architecture, opened up the partitions and set up a party. Music, dancing and soft drinks, with something a little stronger, perhaps smuggled in by medical students. Ahmad stood alone in the corner. They had survived the difficult times. Now, once again, he was a stranger to the University. He slipped out and left the University grounds to walk to Pahlavi Avenue to catch the bus home. He had barely walked a few hundred metres when a military Jeep stopped next to him. It was colonel Ansari, the local SAVAK chief.

"Climb up please," he said, curt, firm and polite. It was not a request.

Ahmad was a guest of Shemiran SAVAK for 48 hours. Interrogated. Rough but not savage. Slaps and kicks and torrents of abuse. The questions were fairly standard: who provoked you, who do you know, who are your friends, where did you go to school, what do your father, mother, uncle, do, why did you provoke the strike... fairly innocuous. His roommate had found his door open and his room in disarray but searching his house did not yield much as he had already anticipated the raid.

There was the predictable uproar in the University at news of his arrest. The student council reconvened and announced a resumption of the strike, and a few started a hunger strike. The security forces quickly backed down – from a minor event it was fast turning into a political movement – the first such movement since the nationwide crackdowns after the uprising of 1963 and it was best to let things simmer down.

Ahmad had led the first strike in the National University. When he was rearrested two years later in 1967, he was the first Melli student to go to prison.

[1] UK-educated Parviz Nikkhah was one of the leaders of the Confederation of Iranian Students abroad. After returning to Iran, he was arrested alongside several others accused of plotting to assassinate the Shah. He was tried and condemned to death, later reduced to life imprisonment after pressure from, among others Amnesty International.

Chapter 3

The deception

Ahmad

That morning Ahmad walked into *Café Naderi*, the meeting place of Tehran's intellectuals, haunt of poets, writers, artists, anyone with real or hoped-for talent. As he scanned the tables, he saw his uncle sitting in the far-right corner on one of those fragile-looking brown wooden chairs with two wooden loops, one inside the other as back, and a circular seat, perhaps in imitation of a Paris bistro. Chic but uncomfortable. His eyes lit up, in that unique way eyes do when you meet someone you love deeply, as they met his favourite uncle's. He noticed the worried look on his uncle's face, which vanished transiently as he stood up and smiled and then returned. Something was bothering his favourite uncle. They did look alike, moustache and all, except that uncle Fakhri smiled more, and had lighter hair and eyes.

"*Salam, salam*" both spoke simultaneously their eyes glinting as they looked at each as if they had not seen each other for ages. Three kisses on cheeks. Right, left, right followed by a warm handshake and the interminable asking after wife, children, mother, father, brother and sister's health. Almost like flicking the prayer beads between the thumb and index finger most men did those days, irrespective of whether they were religious or not, before the beads returned to being a signal of religiosity. You just went through this motion every time. Not really registering the *khooban*[1] answer, assuring the interrogator of their health. One by one each family member was mentioned by name. It was part of the *ta'arof* ritual that foreigners found incomprehensible. There was no point shortcutting the ritual, it would only find its way back to the same trajectory, just like trying to dam a stream with stones. The flowing water will find its way round.

"I need you to do something for me," the uncle said after they had ordered some *chai* and drunk a glass or two of tea. Uncle Fakhri liked his with a lot of sugar. Ahmad was more frugal. Then a sheepish smile that Ahmad took to mean he was about to ask for something that might embarrass him, though he must have known of the deep love he had for his favourite uncle.

"One of my wife's relatives needs to have some things done at their house and I have recommended you," he said, and his voice fell almost imperceptivity at the last word. It was then that Ahmad noticed uncle Fakhri's large black pupils, dilated within his light brown iris. Why is he not using his wife's name, Ra'na? Perhaps he was embarrassed to burden him with trivial work. Uncle Fakhri knew how busy Ahmad was in his Tehran architect's office with so many projects on the go. Besides being a mere student of architecture at the College of Fine Arts, Ahmad held a high position in a very reputable office of architects.

"Of course, *dai'jan* uncle dear. That's nothing. Anything for you. Anything. Ask for my life," he added smiling (another *ta'arof*) and his dark brown eyes looked lovingly into his favourite uncle's. The pupils were now smaller. That is how the little deception began, one that could only happen in a society where much remains unsaid, to be taken on trust. What uncle Fakhri left out was that the little alterations in the home were to be a one-sided blind date.

*

"Oh, I have the just the perfect husband for Sarajoon," aunt Ra'na said without thinking, adding 'dear' at the end of Sara's name to emphasise the closeness of the two women. A smile came involuntarily, and she swallowed it. "Just perfect," she repeated.

Aunt Ra'na, uncle Fakhri's wife, was having tea with a close relative, who had married into a well-known and prosperous haulage and travel firm. Like many middle-aged women of a certain class, she had her hair dyed blonde, which clashed hideously with her dark eyes.

15

"I need to find a husband for my daughter Sara," the relative had suddenly blurted out and tears welled in her big eyes, spilling wet over her plump cheeks, now mascara-grey.

"Is she pregnant?" Aunt Ra'na asked startled, and sat up straight.

"No, no, of course not, good lord no. That would be awful. No. No," the relative said, a smile intruding on her tears. "Someone has come asking for Sara's hand." She took a tissue from the table to mop her eyes, and some of the smudgy stream halfway down her cheek.

"But that's wonderful," aunt Ra'na said grinning, wondering why she is crying, exposing her front teeth with a tinge of yellow. Was it tobacco, or just bad brushing technique? "Now that she has finished school ..."

"No, no you don't understand," the relative interrupted her voice rising in volume and pitch, then a pause as if searching for words. Eyes rewetting. "*Chejoori begam*, how do I phrase it?" the relative went in a voice that you use when about to say something truly awful. I loathe the man's family, is what she was thinking. "I just don't want it," is what she said. "He is from my husband's family, and I absolutely can't allow anyone from his side to marry my darling Sara. On no account. Over my dead body." She went on repeating, like an echo that kept getting louder every time it bounced. Sara was her only daughter. She did not give any reason, but whatever it was, it was serious aunt Ra'na thought and took out a handkerchief to wipe the remaining mascara smudges off her friend's cheeks.

"But I can't tell my husband. I can't," and she spilt her tea on the white lace tablecloth. More tears. More dabbing.

"Why don't you marry her to someone else then?" aunt Ra'na suggested hopefully. That's what I would do, she thought, and bent forward to help mop up the tea on the lace with the same handkerchief. And then the dried streams of mascara Sara's mother had missed, or were they new ones?

"Who. Who can I get that is suitable in such short notice?" Between sobs she sounded vanquished.

"Oh, I have the perfect match for your Sara," aunt Ra'na said, "perfect." She was looking behind her eyes at the serious young architect, with a thick black moustache. "This man, an architect, a close relative of my husband, is just perfect, an excellent, well-known architect, totally honest. He is simply perfect." And she went on to paint a picture of a successful saint, as fitted a perfect prospective bridegroom for Sarajoon. Smiles. More tea.

"Have another *shirinee,* a cookie. We shall bring him over to see if you like him. Leave the rest to us. Yes, leave the rest to us. Once he sees Sara he won't need much persuading, he will just melt. Fall head over heels for her. It's just inevitable…" Aunt Ra'na had a way of repeating the obvious. What she meant was once he sees Sara's wealth and family he won't resist. "A match made in the skies," and they both grinned. Both women's teeth needed Colgate.

That was a week ago.

[1] See appendix 1 for a glossary of Farsi words.

Chapter 4

The house

Ahmad

Uncle Fakhri came out of his front door followed by aunt Ra'na, he in a dark suit and tie and she in a pink dress, the sort of dress you wear for an evening party. The dress somehow accentuated her plump arms. You look nice Ahmad said and felt undressed in his work jacket. Tieless. At least I am neat, he thought. He was always neat. They drove in his car. Aunt Ra'na always felt scared when Ahmad drove, but she swallowed her fears for today. They were going to a wedding, *enshallah,* God willing. They were welcomed at the large grey metal gate by a manservant dressed in a black suit and tie. More a mansion than house. Large swimming pool. Big, expansive, lavish, sumptuous, Ahmad thought, thinking, and speaking like a thesaurus, and a little presumptuous. The mother greeted them at the door opening onto a veranda wearing a very stylish blue dress. She too seemed to be ready for a party. Pearl necklace, large diamond ring, the dyed-blonde hair. Clearly been to hairdresser early that same morning. Suddenly he felt a little uncomfortable. It was mid-morning.

They were led into the reception room. Crystal chandeliers, lace curtains, silk carpet the standard trappings of north Tehran luxury. I know where you bought the chandeliers, Ahmad thought to himself. He remembered the bet he had with Rubin, a friend and owner of a large crystal shop in *Takht-e Jamshid Avenue*, which catered for the rich. Italian imports mainly. People go for price, not quality, Rubin had once told Ahmad. The higher the better. It's a way of showing your wealth. Your worth. You take people as being dumb, Ahmad had chided him, angry at his friend's arrogance. Well, let's test it, the friend had said and winked. Rubin then took twelve identical crystal glasses and had put a price of 200 *tomans*[1] on half and 1,200 on the other half. By the end of the month all the higher-priced had gone. None of their poor siblings. You must have paid a sack of gold for these chandeliers Ahmad thought and chuckled somewhere deep.

After a while a young girl came in. Very young. Seventeen, eighteen. No more. She was dressed in a dark green dress, tight waist, splaying outwards below, cut just above the knee. The neck was low enough to hint at the top of her young breasts. Below these, there was a band of elaborately sequined small shiny white and cherry-red sequins, fashionable but old-fashioned. She wore an evening make-up in mid-morning, rather superfluous to her young skin. She had dressed with care. My daughter Sara, the mother said with a gesture of someone introducing a star on stage. Sara came over shook hands with all three, a little shy. Sat uncomfortably opposite the guests, pulling her skirt down as far as it would go, not looking at anyone. Ahmad fidgeted on his chair.

Aunt Ra'na and the mother were discussing the new George Cinque furniture in the guest room, and what is fashionable these days. Ahmad was only half listening, sunk deep in his thought when he suddenly realised the mother was talking to him. She was in the middle of saying something about Sara, about how good her daughter is, how well she has done at school, how everyone is amazed at her taste in clothes, how all the teachers were so sorry that she has finished school and won't be returning, how the headmistress loves her, all the time looking into Ahmad's eyes. It was a long monologue as if rehearsed. When are they going to get to the building and the changes they want, Ahmad was getting impatient? A pause as if for applause. Not bad looking, Sara thought, but so glum. Not a smile. She came over and asked what music he would like. What a curious question, Ahmad thought, with just me, my uncle and the three women here. Anything you like, he replied, unsure. Awkward. Perhaps too abrupt. A serious young man, the mother thought. Thick moustache, unsmiling, looks like an intellectual, I like him, Sara mused.

Then came an elaborate meal which appeared from a door on the far side, covering the table from end to end, two types of *khoresht* (casserole), plain rice with a fine saffron covering, variety of *torshi* (pickles), yogurt and cucumber, delicacies like the aubergine dishes *kashk bademjoon*, *mirza qasemi*, and right in the middle a huge dish of *shirin polo* with a sprinkling of finely sliced pistachios and almond. Could have fed my entire class, he thought, feeling even more uncomfortable. The *shirin polo* was a little odd as it is usually served at weddings and such occasions. He took small portions from most of the dishes onto his plate but spent the next hour playing around with it. They looked delicious but he was barely able to taste anything. At the end of the meal parts of his large plate looked like a winter battlefield. The conversation meandered over all sorts of places. Always directed at him with an occasional glance at aunt Ra'na who nodded smiling in agreement with everything. Uncle Fakhri rubbed his moustache downwards with his left thumb and index, in confirmation. Somewhere along the line the mother said that she has decided to send her daughter to finish her studies in Germany.

"We have been told you are such an exceptional person, why aren't you going abroad to continue your education?" She was addressing Ahmad.

And still no word of the changes in the house. Perhaps because they are so close to uncle Fakhri's wife they are interested in family matters and see me as an insider, as family, Ahmad thought. As they said goodbye Ahmad apologised that an opportunity had not risen to discuss the changes they wanted. They listed a few minor alterations and he agreed to send them drafts.

"What did you think?" Sara's mother asked when they had left, looking Sara straight in the eye.

"Ok," Sara replied trying to sound normal. It came out more abrupt than she intended and blushed.

"Maybe he was shy," her mother said reassuringly, "that's nice in a man" and left it at that.

On the way home uncle Fakhri asked what he thought of them.

"They are nice people, seem to be an honourable family," Ahmad replied.

"What do you think of their daughter?" uncle Fakhri asked.

"Ordinary" Ahmad answered almost absent, "immature' he added.

Uncle Fakhri went on to talk about the wealth of the family. What a large and reputable family they are. At length. This is a very good opportunity. We can ask for her hand for you. She already has one suitor.

"Are you joking *dai'jan*, uncle dear?" Ahmad interrupted, taken totally by surprise. "Don't even think about it," he went on, really angry. "I am surprised at you *dai'jan*. Really surprised. You know the type of life I lead. Anything could happen to me at any time. I have no fixed future. I was already imprisoned once. It could happen again at any time." He reminded uncle Fakhri how he had led the university strike, that he was bringing out the university paper. "I have no intention of marrying," he continued, "and even if I had, such an ignorant innocent girl would be totally unsuitable. What does she know about life? About hardship? She knows nothing about anything. Just look at the music she chose – some rubbish. Look at her clothes. She is not the sort of girl that would attract me. Don't even think about it," he added abruptly, ending the conversation.

What hurt was that this uncle, someone so close to him, was so clueless about him. Neither he nor his friends, his generation, believed in marriage or in any family commitment. It was a time for battle not domesticity. He noticed the annoyance coming over uncle Fakhri's face. In the rear mirror he saw aunt Ra'na unsmiling in the back. He had hurt them, and he hated himself. He did not see the determination.

That passed.

[1] One *toman* = 10 rials the basic unit of Iran's currency. At $7 to a *toman*, 200 *tomans* would have been about $30 at the time.

Chapter 5

Qezel Qal'eh

Ahmad

"Bijan has gone over to Japan," a gruff voice at the other end of the phone said, trying to sound calm "along with one of his friends Abbas" he added, having omitted the usual greeting. Ahmad immediately recognised an old friend. It was more like a telegram than a phone call.

"Salam, Hooshang jan. *Khoobi?*" are you well, Ahmad asked trying to normalise the call, "why did they go to Japan?" and why on earth is he telling me this, he thought. Hooshang was talking about Bijan Jazani who Ahmad knew without having met him because of his activities in the student and opposition movement ever since the CIA-engineered coup that toppled premier Mossaddeq in the summer of 1953 and sat the Shah back on his throne. In fact, Bijan had been in and out of prison multiple times since and on each occasion had managed to hoodwink the SAVAK interrogators into accepting that he had only a minor role as a university dissident and had got off relatively lightly. Hooshang was probably trying to tell him Bijan has been arrested again. He was about to ask that very question when his friend said, "why don't you come over for a cup of *chai* to my shop" and abruptly broke off.

Something was up this early morning which his friend did not want to discuss on the phone. You never knew who might be listening. There was an old saying, the wall has mice and mice have ears (*divar moosh dareh va moosh ham goosh dareh*). A trip to Kuwait used to be the pseudonym for the place with bars on doors and windows, but maybe SAVAK had decoded that usage. But if that proverbial mouse-in-the-wall was listening in to today's conversation, he or she would surely have laughed at the amateurish subterfuge.

"What's this story of yours about Bijan and Japan?" Ahmad asked as soon as they had gone through the lengthy ritual of greetings and sat down in a room at the back of the shop around an Aladdin paraffin oil heater, "I take it you meant he and his friend have been arrested, in your weird way?" Ahmad's eyes were dancing with mischief. "How on earth did you come to pick such an unlikely place as Japan to exile poor Bijan and his friend?"

"Oh, this is a long story," the friend began having first poured a glass of freshly brewed black *chai* for both, offered the bowl of *qand* sugar-lump to his guest and sat back and taken a mouthful of *chai*. "Some years ago, a childhood friend of mine was arrested. When friends and family asked his parents about him, they pretended he had gone to Japan to study, just to keep them from questioning further. Maybe they were ashamed. Maybe they just didn't want to get into a political discussion. You know how it is. Who could be sure he had not gone to prison for stealing or for thinking? Once out after a couple of years or so, for months afterwards the poor boy had to invent an entire life in Japan, from his courses, his tiny flat, their food and their habits, the girl friend he had found there. Everyone was curious. They wanted to know about his girl. What did she look like? Was it true their body is different? Not many people go to Japan. It sounds so exotic, doesn't it. They and their boy could make anything up and no one would be the wiser. It is such an odd place to go I thought you are bright enough to pick that up immediately. I didn't for the life of me think you..." and he let the rest of the sentence float away in silence of mutual understanding, and a twinkle. "Do you want to hear what happened to that poor boy afterwards?" he added to soften the blow to Ahmad's ego.

"Maybe we should try to concentrate on the present. Your news about Bijan sounds bad, we should perhaps expect more arrests. Do you have any more details on how they were arrested?" he asked, ignoring the question with his own. He had listened to his friend's 'long story' with a self-depreciating wry smile throughout. He had known from the beginning what Japan had meant.

"They were betrayed by someone who knew they were having a rendezvous and fell into a trap" his friend said in a voice suddenly rippling with emotion. Ahmad later discovered that one of Abbas's extensive and rather poorly disciplined underground revolutionary network had been recruited by SAVAK and had lured Bijan and Abbas to a meeting place, ostensibly to buy a handgun from his old Tudeh colleagues, unaware that SAVAK had penetrated not just Abbas's group but the Tehran Organisation of Tudeh. SAVAK were waiting for them and arrested them after the handgun had been handed over. This time it was not going to be easy going for Bijan. "They won't crack", the friend said in an unsure voice. He meant they wouldn't betray anyone under torture. How savage that torture was Ahmad was to discover. Neither man betrayed anyone.

They spent the next few hours talking at the back of the shop. They spoke about their frustration at the feebleness of the remains of Mosaddeq's National Front, the only opposition allowed to operate semi-clandestinely for now, and that there was little to stop the Shah's rapid march towards re-establishing his absolute control over the country. Everything looked bleak. Since the brief modest easing of the political atmosphere a few years previously under pressure from the new Kennedy administration, the silence of the graveyard was rapidly descending on their land and they, like so many restless young men and women were looking for ways to break that silence. It was becoming difficult to breathe again.

"We've just got to do something. We can't just crawl under our warm cosy *korsi* (quilt-covered brazier-heater) and wait the winter out," was Hooshang's reply, and Ahmad left it at that. During a long pause, both men sipped two glasses of hot *chai* straight off the kettle that was brewing over a light-blue Aladdin paraffin stove, each sunk in their own thoughts.

*

"Ahmadjoon. Warm the car up and I'll get her ready," his father called from the kitchen. They were taking Ahmad's mother to the doctors, yet again, though this headache was unlikely to be her last.

He walked downstairs and out through the front door. A chilly early morning winter wind blowing from the east made his thick black moustache quiver. He drew a sharp breath in. Overnight rain had washed the soot and grime into puddles. As he walked towards the Chevrolet, Iran's only locally assembled luxury car, he looked up and saw the fresh snow on the lower slopes of the Alborz mountains. Clouds obscured the peak and much of the sky. Bits of the luminous blue sky were washed by rain. For a moment he felt he could reach out and touch the snow, its whiteness briefly exposed.

He was about to turn on the switch when in the rear mirror he saw a white car, the common Peikan, backing towards him. It braked, bumper to bumper. Seconds later another, equally white Peikan blocked his exit. Like in films. He smiled. He felt incongruously calm as if he knew the ending. Seconds later a man in a suite held a gun to his temple.

The events of his last arrest flickered like a projector on boil. The jeep that had drawn up, the SAVAK Colonel Ansary politely asking him to step in, the less politely delivered slaps and kicks at the station, few days in jail and then release after the student hunger strike. Then, the government had more important matters to attend to. Amazing how much memory you can squeeze into a couple of seconds.

"Please get out of the car, the officer said," his polite tone totally out of step with the gun he continued to hold to Ahmad's temple. His suite was crisp as if he had dressed up for the arrest, a contrast with the unwashed car he drove in. Somewhere crows screeched, though he did not hear them.

He walked out of his car slowly. Other thoughts flashed around his head like a newsreel. Incongruous thoughts. A world in turmoil. Guerrilla movements across Latin America. Che's corpse still warm on a slab in Bolivia. Vietnam, where the Tet offensive had begun days earlier and it rained napalm and Agent Orange.[1] Hundreds must have been experiencing the same fate as him at that very moment. That too was calming. Indeed, he had vaguely expected the visit. A wave of arrests had followed since Bijan Jazani's arrest a few of weeks ago, along with almost the entire leadership of what later became the Fadai' organisation.[2] Ahmad did have a theatrical thought process. Anyway, he hadn't done anything. Exchanging books, discussions, winning someone or other over to his way of thinking. That was all. It wasn't as if he was preparing for armed rebellion. Nor had he left any incriminating marks. He had been ultra-careful. Calmly he turned to the officer.

"My mother lies ill upstairs, and I was about to take her to the doctors. Can you make sure she is all right please," he said, slowly, like talking to a child. He later found they did. Weird times.

The larger, the broader, the bloodier the field of battle in his head the calmer he felt outside it. He was calm as they put a hood over his head. He was calm as they took down his details in Tehran SAVAK headquarters. He was calm as they put the hood on again. What did they have on him though? Beneath that hood he had to think fast. They can't have much on me.

Not much, it turned out. They unhooded him after a long ride and he saw himself facing a long rectangular building surrounded on four sides by a bare earthen area like a dry moat with a few smaller buildings dotted about. Behind him an outer wall fenced it all in. A big, tall metal gate, painted brown, with a small window cut into it was the only visible opening into the long rectangular building. With architectural eyes he surveyed it all. This must be the old fort of *Qezel Qal'eh*. The red fort. One of SAVAK's two interrogation centres at the time. The outer perimeter walls were high, like an old fort built in previous centuries, made of baked mud bricks. The longevity of the building was curiously reassuring.

He was taken to a stand-alone building outside the main fort, the interrogation centre he later found out, and handed over to a sergeant wearing a well-worn khaki uniform, who introduced himself as Ostovar Saqi in a way that implied you know what that name means. Tall, with thick black eyebrows and thicker Azari accent, he had a ferocious reputation. Ostovar Saqi had been around since the coup against Mosaddeq, when Tudeh members were rounded up and tortured in their hundreds.[3] Beside him was Taymuri, another sergeant with a reputation. Ostovar Ayub Saqi was now in charge of the prison-fort.

"*Fekr nakon inja hoteleh*," Saqi sneered in his thick Azeri accent making his j's ring in the air with a twang. Don't think this is a hotel! "This is *Gezel Gale'h*" using a soft 'g', unable to pronounce the more guttural deep 'q' sound of Farsi. "Here we wrench tears out of bricks. Bigger fish than you have crumbled. You best just give us the information we want." He had a strange voice. Like an echo. Ahmad, like many, could recite Shamlu's poem *Vartan sokhan nagoft*,[4] an ode to unbreakable Vartan as he was tortured to death with an electric drill, silent to the end, never speaking. Was it Saqi who had pushed that final electric drill into the skull of the obstinately, heroically, unyielding Vartan? They say Saqi had a soft spot for whoever survived torture without cracking. Would I crack? the thoughts flitted through him like a shudder. But I haven't done anything, he thought. Saqi's sweat had a sweet smell.

But there was no interrogation that day.

They searched him and took way his belt. No prison clothes. Lucky his protruding iliac crest could hold up his trousers, one advantage of being thin and fit. He was led to the big metal gate with the peephole. No hood. No blindfold. The gate opened with a non-musical creak and another sergeant took over and led him through a short corridor which opened into a long rectangular inner courtyard. In the middle was a pond, also rectangular lined with cracked blue tiles, empty. In front was a small garden with an evergreen bush. He smelt food. That must be the kitchen on the right. He suddenly felt hungry. The central yard, paved in brick, was surrounded by the brick building with a flat roof from the middle of which projected domes running all the way to the end. It looked exotic. A few armed men were patrolling on top. At the far end were three doors. Then he saw a willow tree floating sinuously, leafless, nostalgic, a real incongruity in a prison. The ground was peppered with orange-brown curly leaves. On either side were little windows going all the way down to the end. Prison blocks one and two. He surveyed all this in a strangely detached way, as an architect rather than a prisoner.

He glanced at the sky which had totally clouded over now, submerging the blue bits. May not see that blue sky again for some time, he thought. Then he was taken to the left-hand building through a wooden door halfway down the courtyard and handed over to sergeant Baqeri, in charge of prison block two. A guard in khaki, sitting smoking on one of the two raised platforms on either side of the entrance, glanced up without seeing. He later found that was where the guards slept. His new home was a corridor on both sides of which were cells with long wooden doors with a barred window on top, and a small aperture for peeping. There was probably an identical block on the other side of the courtyard. All this was surprisingly unthreatening.

An ageing prison absurdly inconsistent with the Shah's modernist dreams, Ahmad thought as he surveyed the building with an architect's eye. Perhaps it was an old *caravanserai*,[5] later turned into a storage depot, and now converted into a prison. He felt even calmer. As they led him down the corridor to the end, he heard voices from right and left. All the cells seem to be occupied. A few prisoners pulled themselves up to the top of the door and peeped over the barred window above the door.

"*Khosh amadi*," welcome, they greeted him as he was walked past each cell.

His was the last cell, number 35, on the right that would have had a window opening to the inner courtyard had it not been blocked by the wall separating their cellblock from the three rooms on the far end of the courtyard, the open wards for prisoners who had finished their interrogation. Post torture convalescence, so to speak. His cell was windowless with only a barred opening above the wooden door, letting in a dim light from the electric bulb in the corridor. This would be home for the next nine months. He was pushed in, and the door shut.

[1] Ahmad was arrested in February 1968.

[2] Organisation of Iranian Peoples Fadai' Guerrillas - OIPFG (Sāzmāne Cherikhāye Fadāi' Khalq-e Iran - OI), the name it finally adopted. For a brief outline of the guerrilla movement see Fred Halliday, Iran: Dictatorship and development, Penguin books Ltd, London 1979. For a more detailed account see Maziar Behrooz, Rebels with a cause. IB Tauris London 1999; Peyman Vahabzadeh. A Guerrilla Odyssey, Syracuse University Press 2010.

[3] See Ervand Abrahamian, *Iran between Revolutions,* Princeton 1982.

[4] *Vartan did not talk* by one of Iran's greatest modern poets, Ahmad Shamlu. See http://www.parsagon.com/vartan-a-poem-by-ahmad-shaml ou/. Vartan was a member of the Tudeh Party.

[5] The equivalent of inns originally built along roads to cater for passing caravans – hence the name caravanserai, home of caravans.

Chapter 6

The Doctor

Ahmad

Alone, he looked round. There was a raised platform at the back, covered by crooked, cracked square bricks. Two grey army blankets were crumpled in the corner as if discarded in a hurry. There is going to be some rough sleeping on those cobblestones especially against his bony body. There was a small area behind the door, about half a metre wide, where he could walk. The ceiling was high. Must be a second ceiling put up when they converted the old caravanserai. The walls were grimy brown. He imagined that the darkish red smears were dried blood, but then dismissed the thought. There was a putrid smell of urine and more hanging over the cell telling him the toilets were not far. Over the door, someone had scratched *khosh amadi*, the same words he had heard walking down the corridor. He heard someone calling from the corridor. He pulled himself up out to the window on the door. In the cell opposite a young man was waving at him.

"What is your name?" Ahmad asked, not expecting a real name.

"Aziz," came back the real name. Aziz was standing on his platform looking through both windows. Ahmad introduced himself with his real name. He was soon to get to know Aziz Sarmadi who had been captured the day after Bijan Jazani and charged with preparing for an armed struggle.

That first lunch, delivered to each cell, was a rather tasteless green rice dish with cooked herbs and a peculiar odour, served on an aluminium plate and an aluminium spoon, a spoon with a crooked handle, a spoon with a history. That night he found he could easily prise the door open, held closed only by a latch outside, by sliding up the spoon's crooked handle. The idiocy of a keyless prison was symbolic. In a country that was a bigger prison, maybe you don't need keys to its cells.

They would communicate, *sotto voce* whisper, when the guard was at the other end of the long corridor, with Aziz signalling when to start and stop. Two or three guards paced up and down in slow motion, but they often stopped halfway to have a rest on the platforms. Or a smoke. And their army boots echoed on the brick floor, a metronomic siren. A fellowship slowly developed between the two men that ran deep until the day Aziz was shot.

Here, in the silence of the night and in the solitude of the cell, with its stained walls covered with scratch marks that echoed a history of hope and pain, its darkness and stillness and even the soiled blankets and the stench, a place where even perception of colour changes and all of one's senses experience a rebirth, a new and powerful feeling of love and compassion for his fellow inmates began to envelop Ahmad. What started as simple friendships morphed into profound understanding, an understanding that is closer to the way we read poetry than a novel, chewing the words, seeking its inner meanings, and across the narrow corridor that could not be crossed, interacting through whispers that penetrated the core of the other.

The whispers were how Ahmad heard how Zia, a close comrade of Bijan, was pushed down onto a red-hot bed of criss-crossed wires mimicking an electric heater and as the whispered words crossed the corridor Ahmad saw and even smelt the burning flesh, and as Aziz told his story, his voice quivered, and his eyes shrank back into the memory of what he had seen and felt. And it was through the whispered words that Ahmad learnt how Abbas, despite being whipped day after day till he was unconscious, and then his battered body dragged to a mock execution refused to admit that the handgun found in his car belonged to Bijan, and Ahmad felt his pains as the words floated across. And after they both travelled on whispered words alongside Bijan through 39 consecutive days of lashes on his back, his legs, the soles of his feet, and when they ran out of skin, on his belly, and when that failed to break him, threating to torture his father, and the ultimate weapon of threatening to whip the young Babak, his son, in front of him, and yet he still did not break, and Ahmad could listen no more and sunk back into his dark cell living the pains that were no different when transmitted in whispers. Aziz had said nothing of his own journey.

The next day it was difficult to talk. They had both been to the depth of hell, one for the second time. Slowly, over the next two or three days their conversation turned to the future. Aziz, who alongside Bijan, Zia and others had been attracted by guerrillas in Latin America, and closer to home, the Algerians fighting the French had formed a circle and their small group had gathered around them an underground network of groups of men and women, mainly students. They were slowly being drawn to the idea of creating an urban and rural guerrilla movement. Before any of their ideas could be translated to action, SAVAK had destroyed the initial group and many of its network through their informers. Many now occupied the cells in *Qezel Qal'eh*.

Three years later, almost to the day, the regrouped and restructured Fadai' attacked the Siahkal police station in Gilan province announcing the beginning of an armed guerrilla movement across Iran. Though SAVAK was able to finally deliver a near-fatal blow about 18 months after Siahkal on the Fadai' and the other movements that had mushroomed across Iran,[1] savagely crushing even the tiniest spark of protest in the country, the silence of the grave did not last long. Within two years the selfless dedication of these young men and women inspired an entire generation to rise up and overthrow the Shah's dictatorship.

*

It must have been early morning. He had no way of knowing in the windowless skyless cell. Two guards yanked him out of his new home with rough, purposeful jerks, a theatrical gesture heralding what lay ahead. He was not blindfolded. Odd, he thought, but remembered that they had let him see the entire layout of the prison when he arrived. Like someone showing a property for development.

He was pushed into a room and two men grabbed either side of his arm and pushed him forwards and kicked him onto a metal bed in the middle of the room. One man took him by the wrist, yanked it over the left shoulder, pushed it down and tied his two wrists behind his back one arm over the shoulder in what they called a *qapan*, a stilyard, locked them with a chain and hung a heavy weight on it. He sat waiting for the pain which began first in one shoulder and then spread to the other and as he arched his back to reduce the distance across his whole spine in a pain that went beyond language. He felt as if his shoulders were being sucked through his bones into the core of the earth. In desperate attempts to find positions that eased the pain he lost track of time. They then forced him face-down on the bench and someone he had not previously seen whipped him all the while raining filthy insults. The cable did not just tear into his back, but with arms and shoulder pulled back in a forced embrace, the blows jerked a lightening barb across his sternum. And still no one asked him any questions. This must be the softening up, he thought, they must stop soon. Time is elastic when you are desperately trying not to dislocate your shoulder, and not scream. He tried to concentrate on the sound of the whip, to predict the moment of landing, through the cloud of pain he saw whips tearing into Bijan's back, that swishing noise cables make as they tear the air, then they land, thud, thud, thud, I mustn't scream, mustn't let them see my pain and he pushed himself to the whispers and the criss-crossing burnt flesh on Zia's back, or was it his own now, they must stop soon, back to the talking whispers which helped distance him from the piercing pain, the cooker returned and remained suspended, alongside the sound of the whip flying through the air, and now became his. His very own.

All of a sudden it all ceased. They yanked him up and sat him up on a stool. The guard who had whipped him unlocked the weight and released his wrists. Write everything you know, all your friends, everyone you know, everyone you see, everything, he said and pushed a blank sheet of paper in front of him. The voice was curiously neutral, as if he was being asked to fill a form. His thumb was numb and no matter how hard he tried the fingers appeared to belong to another body.

It had been a fairly routine torture session without much passion. Then a man in a grey suit entered the room.

"We know everything about you, you son of a whore. We know everything. No point dodging. We can see through the likes of you *madar qahbeha*, (sons of whores), like the *dayyus* pimp that you are," the interrogator said having barely glanced at his written page. Farsi is such a rich language in swearing. Impossible to echo its expletives in English. "I can squash you like a cockroach". It was 'doctor' Javan speaking. For some reason they had brought him over from his usual haunt, Evin prison. A more terrifying interrogation centre, everyone said. He was probably there to interrogate the Bijan Jazani group.

"What did you mean by the *leaden atmosphere*? What is this lead you...?" another obscenity as the cable tore into his back and his sternum yanked backwards and sideways in a curiously creative way. He was back on the bench, lying prone, this time without the stilyard.

"What leaden atmosphere?" he managed to blurt out between the blows. The doctor seemed uninterested in the answer. Must be enjoying himself watching. Now it was sergeant Teymouri performing, aptly named after Teymour the Lame, or Tamerlane, the Mogul conqueror of Iran who was famous for his cruelty. Was he more savage than the other guy or was it just raw skin responding differently?

"The letter," Dr Javan finally said in a strange voice. "The letter," the 'doctor' repeated. They all called themselves doctor in that unreal hole, as if they had a higher degree in extracting information. Tall, with closely machine-cropped head, Javan always managed to look fierce but calm with eyes that mirrored back other people's pain. He even swore without raising his pitch or volume. Clinical but severe. Bright. An intriguing, warped personality. He was an experienced interrogator.[2]

"What letter?" Ahmad said between two cable strikes.

"The one you wrote to your comrade, you *naneh jendehe dayyus* (son-of–a–whore pimp). Mansureh. She has confessed to everything. She has told us how you are a pathetic leftie so-called intellectual. How you have corrupted her with your Marxist drivel. Better tell us all. We have the letter, and we have Mansureh's confession. There is no escaping now, you *madar qahbeh* (son-of-a-whore)." So many names for the same profession. "Here all your high and mighty connections outside don't mean nothing! Nothing!" he said that last word with particular venom, his voice uncharacteristically rising a decibel or so, like envy. What connections is he talking about? Ahmad thought and blanked. "Just tell us how you had started yet another university strike in Shiraz. Who are your links?" the 'doctor' said followed by the whoring of mothers and sisters in one sentence. Most unmedical for a doctor.

So, they know about his role in the strike in Melli University.

But they had nothing on him, he realised. Slowly he gathered that a strike had taken place in Pahlavi University down south in Shiraz. They had arrested a group of students. On one they found a letter from Ahmad. A pretty ordinary letter written in the sort of poetic language you used to disguise political criticism. Nothing more.

"What did you mean by leaden air?" Javan repeated and nodded to Teymouri. The whip was particularly painful as it landed on an already raked skin. His chest burst its banks. He let out a loud cry and felt immediately ashamed at having shown weakness. An animal cry from somewhere in the ur-forest.

"It was just some poetic metaphoric nonsense," he managed once the animal in him had crawled back into its cave.

Over the next days, in between more pain, he was able to convince the 'doctor' that Mansureh was a childhood family friend and neighbour from the port of Khorramshahr. I have never been to Shiraz and neither has she been to Tehran, he argued. We met again in Khorramshahr when I went there for the summer. She's a family friend. I am into literature not politics. All almost true.

"She must have made it up about me being a leftie to stop you doing to her what you are doing to me," he said and waited for the sound of the whip, but it never came. The 'doctor' had given up.

They kept him in solitary, but no one bothered him anymore. As if they didn't know what to do with him. He later found that there was a lot of activity outside to release him. His torture had been relatively mild by the standards of others. And as the new year Spring festival of *Eid* approached the whole cellblock became more relaxed. They found themselves able to speak more easily and, via prisoners in the open cells walking past their windows during their airings in the courtyard, send messages to other solitary prisoners.

[1] Over 230 Fadai' members and supporters were killed alongside many in the Mojahedin and other groups, and thousands imprisoned and tortured. [2]Parviz Bahman Farnejad, alias "doctor" Javan, was one of over 40 regular torturer-interrogators working for the Third Bureau of SAVAK – the *Komiteh Moshtarek* - there since its inception.

Chapter 7

The void

Ahmad

Over the next few weeks, he deepened his friendship with Aziz and over the next months, now moved to a different cell, with Zia and Abbas.[1] All three, as well as Bijan had moved from the increasingly sclerotic Tudeh party,[2] through the left wing of the coalition that was the National Front[3] to the radicalism of today entering an uncharted jungle, drawing the maps as they went along.

Those were years of global reawakening. Campuses and neighbourhoods in the US were rejecting the slaughter in Vietnam. Students in Paris and other capitals were challenging the prevailing values of society in the most open revolt the industrial west had seen since the war. Cubans, who earlier had inspired a generation in Latin America and beyond, were trying to erect a new society. The Algerian war of independence, soaked in blood and hope, proved a quagmire for the French army and ripped French intellectuals apart. In Palestine the young poet Mahmoud Darwish had shaken Arab youth with his poem *Identity Card*, read to a crowd in a movie theatre, and the secular Popular Front for the Liberation of Palestine (PFLP) challenged the Goliath of the Israeli state. Whilst in Biafra a whole people were being starved to death and kids walked with pot bellies and brown hair and skin wrinkled like tissue in what looked like deliberate genocide. You felt you belonged to a larger world and their struggles to achieve their vision were both a comfort and a challenge. With immense courage many walked out into the unequal battle. Almost unprepared.

It felt strange whispering about life outside in a place so devoid of life, light, or sound of nature other than rats and cockroaches. Yet their whispers, as it rose into voicespace, joined hundreds of other voices, whispering, talking, thinking across the cities in that vast country. Iran had become a buzzing sea of discourse and exploration, like the chorus of birds at dawn, behind closed doors. A time of turmoil. Students, young men, young women, finding friends, reading, exchanging, discussing, dreaming, learning, doubting. Groups and circles would coalesce spontaneously. When they read something or found something new, they would pass it on. Hand-written or stencilled pamphlets passed from hand-to-hand in secret. They would recruit from among friends and close acquaintances. The passionate quest for answers and solutions that later came to be known as the new left was being born. Like seeds scattered across the country, some would germinate, and others wither or merge, some dying and some weeds. Some quit to avoid the heavy price. Many went beyond talking, beyond mere understanding, to doing. Some groups morphed from discussion groups into cells. A frustrated generation of the young was exploding into action. Scattered. Impatient. Maybe gems. Maybe dross. Then the smaller groups coalescing together like drops of oil on a river that was history. Some chose arms, others tried to melt into the working class. Prisons like *Qezel Qale'h, Qasr* and Evin were being filled with men and women torn from dozens of such groups. For Aziz, Bijan and Zia this was to be their last.[4]

Ahmad's own journey began with reading Jack London's *The Iron Heel* and Gorki's *Mother*, moving on to Brazilian and French poetry, and the angry voices of modern Iranian poets muffled in metaphor to hoodwink the censor, then on to whatever political books came to hand. The written word was both soft and hard, like carbon. Literature as a form of action. The magical transformation of poetry into rugged resolve. In secondary school back in Khorramshahr a circle of schoolboys read Lenin's *What is to be Done* without really understanding it, then went on to Stalin's easier *Dialectic and Historical Materialism*, the oversimplified *Elementary and Fundamental*

Principles of Philosophy taught by Georges Politzer at the Workers' University in Paris, and on to Regis Debre's *Revolution in Revolution* that painted the Cuban experience as the way to the future. Anything they could lay their hands on. Ahmad belonged to a generation hungry for forbidden knowledge, hungry for answers, searching for the right questions, trying to understand where they are, so that they can move to where they want to be, in a country where the price you paid for learning was savage. Reading became a crime and thought was lethal. Most had only a narrow view of their country. Knowledge gained from scraps foraged here and there was inadequate for the herculean task they had set themselves.

The summer after that first year at university Ahmad had taken a room in the poorest part of town near *Meidane E'dam*, where in days past public executions turned into public spectacle, and close to the depression which housed the poorest of the poor – *Goad-e Araboon*, the 'Arab hollow'. The house belonged to two young acquaintances who worked in the nearby slaughterhouse and was flanked on either side by a *chai khooneh* (tea house). There you could sit and chat to labourers and bit-workers who would drop in for a smoke and piping hot tea served by the *qahvehchi* boy in a curvaceous, waisted *estekan* (small glass) sitting on a glass *nalbeki* (saucer) and taken round the customers on a metal tray. Before any words the scorching tea was poured into the saucer, tolerably cooled by blowing on it, before being sucked through air-dried lips with an audible '*hort*', the chin raised a tiny bit to prevent spilling the valuable liquid, sweetened on its way down with a lump of sugar, pre-dipped in the piping-hot tea and waiting impatiently, as yet unmelted, between gum and cheek, before sliding over the tongue and down the pharynx, warming the gullet all the way. A theatrical ritual enacted endlessly every time tea was taken, in exactly the same sequence, between each burst of chat.

Then in the depth of the night, he would record what he had heard and seen into a detailed monograph, written in black ink in his neat handwriting one tightly written sheet on another, not stapled, neatly stacked in brown cardboard folders, his first foray into understanding a particular neighbourhood. It was the beginning of a long journey into knowing your land and its people, places to witness and explore, and filling the gap in knowledge. The 'Arab Hollow' was the beginning of what was to be a life-time project.

Later he enrolled in the nearby Karaj city's urbanisation project, to work in places like Akbarabad where rounded-up street children were now confined in the derelict steel works. His team of architects had gone on to win the bid for the Tehran municipality's 25-year project for the capital where he engaged with a wide range of people. Now known for his efficiency, he was hired for other urbanisation projects. He kept copies of the monographs he submitted, while reading all the workings of the Iranian state, closely following and archiving all news, all official publications, the *Majles* (Parliament), the central bank, the Council of the Economy chaired by the Shah in person. Writing, archiving, in detail, filing away out of SAVAK's clutches. Obsessive. All that summer he was transmuting urges into anger, suppressing those that normally metamorphose boys into men, bypassing biology. There was no time for love. Knowledge, thought and biology were being weaponised.

A land was suffused with dark shadows of lies and terror and the young were afraid, and then they stopped being afraid.

[1] Hassan Zia-Zarifi together with Bijan Jazani created the ideological foundation of the guerrilla movement in Iran. The Jazani group joined up with Abbas Surki's *Razmavaran* group to create the Fadai' Organisation. After the revolution the Fadai' grew into the largest left-wing organisation in the country with thousands of activists and hundreds of thousands of supporters.
[2] Tudeh Party of Iran was formed in 1941 and grew into a mass party with deep influence in the trade unions, intelligentsia and even the army until it was crushed following the CIA-coup of 1953. See Ervand Abrahamian, *Iran Between Two Revolutions*, 1982.
[3] For a history of the National Front, *Jebh-e Melli*, see Christopher Bellaigue: *Patriot of Persia: Muhammad Mossadegh and a Tragic Anglo-American Coup*, Bodley Head, 2012.
[4] Bijan Jazani, Hassan Zia-Zarifi, Abbas Sourki and Aziz Sarmadi were shot by SAVAK agents alongside five others in the hills above Evin prison in

October 1975. Officially they were shot trying to escape.

Chapter 8

Zia and Bijan

Ahmad

Over the next months, Zia replaced Aziz in the cell opposite but at the other end of the long corridor. They looked so alike, even physically. Moustache, glasses, thick black hair, thin muscular body, fit. Taller, though. It was like looking in an old mirror with bits of backing missing. Zia had been a student of law, but after his first arrest had been conscripted into the army. On his discharge he had found a job in a factory in Mazandaran province. Badly, savagely, tortured on an electric cooker, Zia remained unbroken. The two talked in whispers through the pain which would not leave Zia.

For both the question was clear: How do you find a solution to the stultifying stasis of the people at a time of spiralling inequality, when workers living in makeshift hovels in shanty towns and dreadful working conditions had apparently accepted their wretched fate and were oblivious of their own power to change it? The two argued night after night in subdued tones. And as their voices floated across the silent corridor, Zia would insist on his vision in short, clear succinct bursts of words, like water spurting out of a hand pump, or perhaps, like bullets coming out of the barrel of a machine gun while Ahmad would reply in his customary long, detailed and precise prose, as if he was talking to an audience, or arguing inwardly to himself.

It was a dialogue between deep conviction and a questioning doubt. Zia, hoped to break through what he called a *muzhik-like*[1] mentality **of** the

41

peasant in the newly arrived urban worker, still stubborn as a mule but deferent, or indeed fearful of authority. Yesterday in the village they fought their neighbour for a few drops of *qanat* water[2] to irrigate a tiny strip of land. Today that same peasant, now working in the city, would fight their shanty town *halabiabad* neighbour for one or other amenity stolen from the neighbouring municipality. Yet that same old peasant and today's worker is cowed when confronted by a figure of authority, be that the landlord's foreman or the puny gendarme in the village or the Shah and his savage SAVAK in the city. To break down the passivity of our urban *muzhik*, Zia argued, you needed an army of dedicated men and women who had the courage to take on this colossus and, as he put it "crack the wall of fear and the silence of a graveyard and show that the Shah's 'Island of Stability' is a mere balloon that can be burst." Zia's was the voice of a determined young generation with immense courage and confidence.

Ahmad was more sceptical of possibilities. He understood the deep historic roots of the monarch as protector of the peasant against the landlord, roots as deep as the roots of the large oak tree in so many village centres where men and women hang bits of cloth voicing their wishes, their messenger of hope. "The Shah is that tree," Ahmad said one dark night. "And now those villagers have a job in a factory, poorly paid, yes, but a job all the same, and a land reform that handed them a morsel of land. At a price, yes, but their land to do as they please. It confirms their faith in the Shah." The peasant holds on to things and holds on hard, he once said. He had seen the same stubbornness, the same faith, and the same fatalism in the hovels ringing Tehran.

"So long as some have a job, any job, others in the tin-town *halabiabad* have hope," Ahmad whispered aloud. "You underestimate the deep faith of a people who believe in the coming of Mehdi,[3] who believe a saviour who will come to their aid, pull them up from their miserable life, a living hero, a father figure in authority. Such a people readily clutch at any outside force that can promise them an earthly paradise. It is not repression that feeds their delusion. It is history," Ahmad's voice rose a little, he was talking to the crowd again. It would take a lot of work to shake them into seeing reality. And even more in working together to change it. Ahmad wondered what a group of armed men and women, no matter how courageous and how experienced, could achieve under such imbalance of power. And he pointed out the terrible fate of Ché Guevara,[4] in the Bolivian jungles. You cannot explain everything by repression and fear, he had concluded. The state, any state, has much wider powers than mere repression. His was the voice of the committed intellectual seeking to understand their country.

"Look!" Zia finally finished on one silent night. "You want to use historic religious figures? Then look at their Imam Hossein.[5] Here is a national symbol of heroic resistance against tyranny if there ever was one. But today Hossein is portrayed not as a hero but as a victim to be pitied and wept over in the *rowzweh khooni*.[6] What else but repression could have turned heroic resistance into a mere death to be mourned and wept over?" Zia felt that he had made his point.

And so, over the next few weeks, as a dialogue in whispers of determination and heroism and of questions and doubts floated across space and hung in the heavy air over the corridor, mixed with the noxious smell of the toilets, the two slowly became one. And by reliving their lives backward into time they united as if they were childhood friends.

*

At night he would lie back on the uneven platform of square bricks and think over what was said and how he could respond. He was enthralled by Zia's enthusiasm. There was something utterly mesmerising in this display of selfless heroism. He felt humbled, but deep inside he was unhappy with abstract action plans. Unhappy with a vision of a world where words, or sacrifice, no matter how heroic, would wake a sleeping people from their deluded sleep. Where heroism became a substitute for knowledge. Knowledge of the people they were preparing to die for. He knew the edges of the city well, sprouting in *ad hoc* shanty towns that slowly transformed into permanent neighbourhoods, housing millions of newly urbanised masses with their own community often coming from the same provinces, with their own shops and their own bakeries, alleyways, electricity, and water, at first stolen, and later squeezed out of the municipality. The city, bright and light, was their hope for a better future. And the Shah fed those hopes with promises. Cities were spreading outwards like cancer and one day they would explode.

But not yet.

He did not have an alternative though, he admitted to himself. A spirit had caught a generation, who had to act but were unsure how. He resolved that when he was out, he would explore his country further and document its problems. And he realised he did not know the problem. Not really. Concretely. Objectively. You need the right questions before looking for an answer and he had more questions than answers.

His thoughts sometimes drifted elsewhere. He saw his favourite uncle and remembered how even he, uncle Fakhri who had always been so sensible, with feet firmly planted in reality, had misunderstood what life meant for Ahmad. How could he even for a second think that he would agree to such a shallow wedding. Did that not say something about how society had become rotten at its core since the fall of Mossaddeq and the crumbling of the hopes of those times.

Above him in the false ceiling, rats scurried about. You could almost feel their feet shuffling here and here, foraging for who knows what up there? Maybe they thrive in the mephitic air that hung immobile like a curse in their corner of corridor, next to the toilets. These rats knew what they wanted he was thinking, and he imagined them running from one end of the roof to another, stopping, sniffing, looking around before scurrying off and he drifted off into a dream where rats were running the nation. A rat was sitting on a throne made of bits of wood, dangling a whip when he woke with a start, sweating. Suddenly he felt something crawling up his leg. It was a cockroach and he swiped it away in disgust. I live in a country where rats and cockroaches rule, it was not a random thought. It was a challenge.

His back was hurting from the uneven bricks grinding against healing strips of skin. He tried to get comfortable by moving up a brick and wordless images of the past began to swim in his head like leaves caught in a river rushing towards rapids, then he was flying over the hills above Khorramabad looking down into the valley, the ochre wheat fields with a line of green meandering across, willow trees marking the border of the *nahr* (stream), their non-weeping branches reaching up to the clear blue sky, that water so precious, lives were sacrificed for it, flowing to the dry wheat in fields on either side of the stream, then suddenly he was hovering like a kestrel over the brown of the dried mud roofs just like the colour of the wheat. Here and there blotches of dark red, the alizarin crimson red of sun-drying plums, readying for winter. He remembered as if he was looking at it through the vacuum-clear air that made the detail stand out even from the distance. Was he awake or was this a dream? They merge.

And as he dreamed, he heard a voice singing from the other end of the corridor. High falsetto, in Azeri Turkish, mournful, beautiful, an Azari *ashiq* folk poet-singer-storyteller singing. The words meant nothing to him, but the voice squeezed his heart.

A month or so later he was moved to the open cells in Block 3.

*

Salam he said, and saw the many eyes looking at him, smiling. One by one they introduce themselves. They know about him already through messaging. There was Bijan and other members of his circle. There were a few radical Muslims from the *Hezbe Melale Eslami*.[7] There were a number of students arrested in relation to the funeral of the wrestling world champion Takhti, adored by both the left and nationalists. Their paths would cross again.

And there was Bijan, having survived weeks of torture, now in the communal cellblock 3. Although Ahmad had not met Bijan before he was arrested, over the next couple of weeks, they walked in the central courtyard from one end to the other talking in a low voice, open air whispering. What did they talk about? They discussed the preoccupation of their generation: revolutionary transformation of the Shah's 'island of tranquillity', with its tranquillity of a graveyard. Ahmad had already rehearsed his arguments, even though he was not entirely sure of their validity.

It was early spring. The sky was that pure blue that only spring can bring. Gone the melancholy light of winter, the orange-tinged sun. The blue of hope. The willow tree by the tiled pond, still empty of water, had grown bold, its light green leaves curving in all directions as in a frenetic dance, its green yielding a little towards blue on one side shining through a film of white. Even deep in conversation Ahmad could not ignore its beauty. The familiar pungent smell of the toilets at one end of the yard did not dim the peculiar sensation spring evokes, that vague yearning-longing, so particular to spring. That biological longing that Ahmad had suppressed but could not kill.

Their discussion showed how you can come to a different answer to the same question depending on the angle of approach. In answer to the question: 'which way?' the two approached it through the different images of the country they carried inside. Bijan, having founded a highly successful advertising agency, had developed a deep knowledge of the new bourgeoisie fast-growing under the shadow of the autocrat, a bourgeoisie whose wealth came from oil money. Ahmad had travelled widely, studying the country close-up, from below, so to speak. He also had close ties with the literary and artistic community. Both thought they knew their country well.

"I've been everywhere," Ahmad said in a way that made Bijan uncomfortable, as if he had a monopoly of the country. He saw the change in Bijan's pupils and quickly corrected himself. "It's my job, with projects everywhere, all across this country, he continued. I get to know people intimately, at close quarters…." he stopped in mid-sentence. Bijan was looking at the willow tree as if he had seen it for the first time.

Ahmad wanted to take Bijan's hand and fly with him to the fertile valley below Borujerd where fields of wheat spread golden. Or the barren hills outside Chah Bahar next to the Pakistan border where a gigantic multibillion dollar project was creating jobs, to Firuzabad where the Qashqai' tribal girls would put layer upon layer of skirt, each in a garish colour, ending up as a spectacular display of harmony. Wasn't that where Bahman Qashqai', son of a khan, had been surrounded and betrayed?[8] This was the country with its unimaginable variety. How could a handful of impatient young dreamers, hope to understand it, let alone change it? Ahmad's scepticism had a logic. Bijan's deep understanding of certain parts of his society was tinged with a romanticism. Maybe he too was having his doubts.

And then in that communal cell there was Abbas. Abbas Sourki, *amu palang*, 'uncle leopard' to the boys, because of his speed and daring. And, in his early forties, he was somewhat older than most of the rest. A quasi father figure. Or an older uncle. The story went round that one day, being escorted back to his cell by Javan, the 'doctor', the chief interrogator had sneeringly asked him.

"Why don't you run away then?"

"Escape? When?" Abbas replied unblinking, grinning.

"Why not now?" the 'doctor' had said in his peculiar voice. And before the sound vibrations had reached the outer wall Abbas was clambering over the barbed wire, which tore into his already torn skin. He had to be taken to the infirmary for stitching. All the time smiling. He had a great sense of humour.

"But there is no possibility for open political struggle in Iran," Bijan said one day in one of their walks. "You just wouldn't survive for a second."

Ahmad did not reply. He had no alternative.

[1] Russian peasant-serf
[2] Underground aqueduct conveying water across often large distances.
[3] The twelfth Imam in the *Shia'* pantheon, who was occulted in the eighth century and who the *Shia'* believe will one day come back to save the world.
[4] Ernesto (Ché) Guevara, revolutionary and close associate of Fidel Castro. He was captured by a special military force trained and led by the CIA while fighting and leading a guerrilla army in the Bolivian jungle in October 1967, and murdered the following day.
[5] Hossein was the Prophet Mohammad's grandson and in Shia' Islam his rightful heir. On his way to the city of Kufeh to claim his rightful heirdom,e and his followers were intercepted in the desert of Karbala, on the banks of the Euphrates by the Umayyad Caliph's troops in 680 CE and his entire family massacred. The legend of Hossein's martyrdom is commemorated every year in the month of Ashura across the Shia' world.

[6] *Rowzeh Khani* (colloquial: *khooni*) is the ceremony when a preacher (*rowzeh khan*) describes the martyrdom of Hossein and members of his family in graphic, and at times gruesome, detail to evoke tears and wailing in his audience. The more tears he evoked, the better his pay.

[7] *Hezb-e Melal-e Eslāmi* (Islamic Nations Party) was a small clandestine group of radical Muslims, mostly high school teachers and university students. Many of its members and its founder, were arrested in 1965 and four executed. See Peyman Vahabzadeh, *A Guerrilla Odyssey*, 2010.

[8] Bahman Qashqāi', son of a Qashqāi' chief Sohrab Khan and niece of the head of the Qashqāi' tribe, one of the largest tribes in Iran, had studied medicine in the UK and later joined the pro-Mao breakaway group from Tudeh, *Sāzman Enqelābi*. On returning to Iran, Bahman was arrested by SAVAK, but later released. He secretly slipped into Fars Province, rallied some of the Qashqāi' tribes, and tried to get a coalition of other tribes. A year later, abandoned by most of his followers, and with his mother and sister arrested, he gave himself up after Alam, the Shah's closest adviser, promised him immunity. It proved worthless. Bahman Qashqāi' was executed on November 8, 1965.

Chapter 9

The Little Red Book

Ahmad

Two weeks later, they came for him. It was the same Sergeant Saghi who had received him, today looking particularly grimfierce.

"Don't delude yourself that you can get away with it as easily as last time. Them days of lounging around in the hotel are over" he sneered in his deep, deep Azeri accent as he pushed him forward so roughly that Ahmad staggered and almost lost his balance. For a brief flash, he imagesaw the drill holes in Vartan's head.

Some weeks earlier, while still in his new solitary cell, he had heard that a group of childhood friends from the port city of Khorramshahr had been arrested and that one of them Qoreisi was in one of the solitary cells in block 2, across the courtyard. 'We don't know one another' Ahmad wrote on a piece of paper, wrapped it around a comb, passed it through the window to *uncle leopard* Abbas who was walktalking with a fellow prisoner in the central courtyard, whispered something to him. *Uncle leopard* suddenly got the urge to use the toilet, persuaded the guard to let him into the opposite block and on his way to the toilet glanced into Qoreisi's cell where a young man aged 25 or so, his unwashed jet-black hair pushed back showing a somewhat greasy forehead, was sitting on the platform of his cell his legs dangling. He was beginning to go thin up front.

"Read and destroy," Abbas whispered rapidly as he passed the door to his cell and threw in the messenger-comb.

On his way back he looked in and saw the young man, squatting at the back of the platform, same place as pre-toilet visit, legs pulled up now, knees touching his lips, still staring at the note as if it was a scorpion. Thinking fast Abbas, looked up and down the corridor, unlatched the door to the cell, grabbed the paper-comb and swallowed the paper. You stupid ass, he muttered softly, cowardly ass, he repeated louder.

Uncle leopard recounted this story with a twinkle in his eye when a week or two later Ahmad was transferred to the communal Block 3. Good thing the cell doors were only on a latch, Abbas added and grinned showing his perfect teeth unperfected with gaps by 'Dr' Javan's team. They later heard that Qoreisi was released, though in fact he had been transferred to Ahwaz prison.

Now back in solitary cell 35, as if they had reserved the old cell for him, Ahmad knew the transfer must be somehow related to Qoreisi.

This time the interrogation was serious. 'Dr' Javan had withdrawn and another interrogator, Mostafavi, had come over from Ahwaz, the administrative centre of Khuzestan province, to tie up the Tehran end of the arrests. Those arrested had all been Ahmad's school friends from childhood. They used to meet every afternoon after school to talk, pass on books and whatever else had been available in Farsi. They were his circle, crossing together the torrents of adolescent years. After Ahmad left for university in Tehran, the loose network had moved on to writing, holding poetry readings and publishing. Nothing more. But subversive enough in this land where independent thinking was perilous.

Interrogator Mostafavi's accusations came in dribs and drabs with the whipping and the steelyard embrace as an entr'acte. Like a play, but more challenging than the previous one. He found out that under torture Qoreisi had confessed to being part of an existentialist circle, but that Ahmad had tried to win them over to Marxism, that Mansur,[1] another childhood friend from the circle and the same Mansur who had shared his rooftop room when

50

Ahmad had organised the university strike, would receive copies of Mao's Little Red Book from a Chinese ship in the docks where he worked, and passed it to Ahmad for distribution in Tehran.

After a few hours of being on a modern version of the rack, his bones and joints in a grossly unequal battle with a gravity that seemed to enjoy tearing him apart, he was returned to his cell. Pain that is so general it can't be localised is not human. Pain was something nature invented to put your bad bits to rest, he thought. A useful evolutionary tool his medical student friend, Sia, the bringer of sourcherry-tinted absolute alcohol to the rooftop feasts, had explained. But if all your bits declare themselves bad bits, pain is counter evolutionary. It took over a month before he could walk properly. His shoulder remained out of joint for much longer. Torture has a long tail. Mostafavi, dreamy eyes belying what lay behind them, was even cruder than 'Dr' Javan, less refined.

"Listen you son of a ***," an expletive which in repetition showed a variety worthy of a poet, "those powerful connections of yours in the world outside just don't count for nothing in these rooms. In my hands even stones will cry," he boasted through his thick lips. "Stones." Then more mother-sister expletives.

Ultimately, he convinced interrogator Mostafavi that Qoreisi had a child-hood grudge against him since school and that he had made it all up as revenge for some insult or other he had received earlier. In the end they left him alone. No one else had implicated him and his defence seemed plausible. The powerful outside connections he was vaguely aware of had prevailed. But they kept him incarcerated till the end of summer. The same old cell. Windowless. Opposite, once again Zia, and their friendship deepened.

It was in those months that the two hatched a plot to pounce on the vehicle carrying the Jazani group to the courthouse attendance that was due in autumn. The plan was that on his release Ahmad was to liaise with Abbas's brother who had a small booth in the bazaar and Zia's brother who ran a laboratory in north Tehran. They would know the timing of the court from prison visits and could also help in setting up the ambush. Everything was being prepared for the ambush, but at the last minute the date of the court appearance was suddenly put forward. As if someone knew. Leaking?

Zia, Abbas, Aziz and Bijan, alongside five others were murdered some years later on the hills behind Evin Prison. The regime announced they had been shot while trying to escape.

Then one sunny summer day the prisoners in their courtyard saw a black Cadillac drive through the outer gate into the outer courtyard.

One love and one deception had got Ahmad out of prison.

[1] Mansur Khaksar, poet and revolutionary killed himself in exile many years later.

Chapter 10

Release

Ahmad

He didn't recognise the big black car, nor the driver, a middle-aged man in a grey suit, tieless, with the suppressed bored look of someone who is used to hours of waiting, to time gluing. They had come for him, and he didn't ask. It felt good to be out. It was not the usual way prisoners left *Qezel Qale'h*. But you don't count the teeth of a gift horse.

This was the coda to a series of strings and pulleys that ended with Ahmad inside the big black car in the courtyard. The big black car drove Ahmad home, but no one was home. They must have not known of his release. As they were about to drive to another relative a neighbour came out, hugged and kissed Ahmad till he felt like an *ablamboo* squeezed pomegranate. I know where they are. They are expecting your release any day and have kept me informed of their whereabouts in case you came when they were out. She took over five minutes to say this, swerving and weaving, while Ahmad listened shuffling. The big black car again.

There they sat, mother, father, sister Tal'at, aunt, uncle Fakhri, his wife Ra'na, the entire immediate family having lunch. Tal'at quickly ran into the kitchen and brought back an extra plate. It was his favourite dish *khoresht bademjoon*, aubergines and chicken. The rice so white. So clean. Dancing taste buds.

In fits and starts the absent time was painted in, like a colouring-in-book by numbers. The sort they gave you as a present when you were little. Since you disappeared, I have drawn close to Sara, Tal'at said. We often went out together. She is so lovely. So kind, Tal'at said. And after you were arrested wheels began to move, mother said. You were so well known. Such a good architect. Everyone wanted to help, Tal'at said. Strings were being pulled here and there, everywhere, mother said. You remember cousin W who works in SAVAK, uncle Fakhri added. Well, he holds a high post. He got Colonel Ali Zibai', you know, the one they say is an interrogator, Tal'at said. Well, he pushed for your release, uncle Fakhri interjected. Your immediate release and for your file to be closed, mother said. That was before those friends of yours got arrested in Khorramshahr, father added. They told us something about a little red book, but couldn't tell us more, Tal'at, who had her own sources corrected. He assured us your file was lightweight, she added and grinned. And you cannot imagine what that family did for you, mother said. Sara's family, uncle clarified. Through their own links with the security services, auntie Ra'na said in a finite way.

He just listened trying to grasp the tail of the lizard as it flitted round the room. They talked as if the two of them were engaged to be married. Talked as actual in-laws. No one had asked him about the prison.

"You don't know how much that family fought for your release," mother said in an excited voice, talking as if she were discussing a lifelong friend or family. Others interjected from all directions. Amazing, generous, loving, honourable, one adjective after another. Tal'at spoke in praise of Sara's devotion. Uncle Fakhri cut in with more praise. Poetic praise. They have invited us to dinner tomorrow to celebrate your release and announce your engagement.

A waterfall of synonyms cascaded as he listened. His mouth dried. She had fallen in love with an image. A memory. An imagined being that must have been embellished and painted and repainted by mother, sister, uncle, different members of his family, her family. She had only seen him one afternoon. Love at single sight. Imaginary. Poetic. Chimera. Distorted. A dream. Lovedream.

He restrained himself, listening, but finally lost his temper. First day back. How could you misread me? I thought she was the best match. You didn't seem to object. How could you misread my feelings? I had made it absolutely clear when you suggested an engagement uncle, hadn't I? But they are such a good family Ahmad, dear Ahmad. And they helped get you out. It was their influence that got you out. Without their help you would still be rotting in there. It was heating up.

"How could you misunderstand me so much?" he said again and again.

Years later his eyes would fill with sadness and moisture when he talked of this episode. At his deep disappointment at his closest uncle, the uncle he loved above all others. And for the girl, pulled and pushed along the path of her dreams.

Yet it was he, Ahmad, so observant of the world, yet so ignorant of those close to him. He had seen the sky and missed the cracked window.

*

The phone rang. It was Tal'at.

"Ahmad has asked to meet us," Tal'at said after the lengthy "how is this person and that person?" preamble. Sara's heart began its sprint. "Somewhere in town," neutral territory, she could have added, "in a café." Sara's sprinting heart slowed just enough to last the marathon of the overnight wait.

"I'll pick you up," Tal'at said and quickly rang off before she could betray the future. Tears were rolling down Tal'at's cheeks. Phones disguise emotions. Sometimes. Sara and Tal'at got there first. Why is she so sombre? Sara thought. Why are you so glum? Sara said. Oh! Nothing in particular, Tal'at said, it's that time of the month.

Ahmad walked in, found the two sitting in a corner table, walked over, and shook hands. Firm. The café was not full. The girls ordered café glacé, coffee with vanilla ice cream topped with whipped cream. He ordered tea. An awkward silence. She looked at him straight, no longer bashful. She had grown up far more than the year she had had to grow up. How were your days inside? she thought of asking. Glad you are out, is what she managed to say. Awkward pleasantries. The young waiter brought the café glacé and tea. He still looks angry, she thought, but it suits his soft eyes. Kind eyes. My kind of kind eyes.

Slowly, in the way the clergy gradually build up a sermon, sitting round a circular metal table on wooden chairs, he let out a long monologue of how they had all misunderstood his motives, the reasons he had come to their house on that day, how unsuitable he was as a husband.

I am a man with no future, you saw me imprisoned for nine months, any moment now I could be rearrested, even killed, I am not a man for marriage, I have no life, you won't have any life, any future, you are young, you'll forget me, one day you'll thank me for what I am saying. It was a long, repetitive sermon. Priestlike, in long sentences with multiple verbs. All the time he looked just below Sara's eyes, avoiding pupillary contact. As he was talking, he felt more and more sorry for the girl and for himself. He was seeing himself talk in a play. A spectator to himself as the actor and his words became more poignant to his own ears. Then he noticed for the first time how pretty she looked in her summery dress, an image of youthful energy in mid-autumn.

He spoke and failed to notice the new lines on her smooth young face. The torrents of soft words, mostly incomprehensible, were pounding her head like under a tumbling waterfall that blurred words. The terror of hearing something that she had not even imagined was possible. Her dreams, the house they would build themselves, her own personal architect, the yellow and light blue walls of the bedroom, waking up before him and checking on the *samavar* just like she had seen her mother do when she was a child, that is before they got all these servants, mother doing her eyeliner and face cream so baba never saw her unmade-up-face, and tears rolled down her cheeks. She cried and cried until she looked like an old woman.

What does he know about love? What does he know about anything? What does he know, droning on and on? I hate you. I love you. I hate that waggling moustache. Those eyes that look at me like at a child. Beautiful. Brown. I detest you and what you are doing to me. Those wasted days. She looked at him all absence. Sobs welled like the waves in the ocean, sinking inwards, more at herself. Then longing. For a moment she became the ocean without having ever seen one. And the moustache which on that day, so long ago it could have been an entire childhood, seemed so magnificent that she had dreamt of kissing it and the lip below it now looked hideously brush-like. She hated everyone. She hated the world. Hated life itself. In those minutes a sensation was turned inside out like a soiled shirt being taken off. Why is there a cloud surrounding our table?

Tal'at cried too, tears that she could not stop, tears of compassion for a friend, but also tears of shame for being part of this deception that had shattered a young dream.

Ahmad too felt sadness, and guilt. Guilt. A religious guilt. Sara said nothing.

When they shook hands they were wet and unclear where the wetness came. He had never cried for a woman. He was also crying for a betrayal of trust.

The café glacé was half consumed, the vanilla ice cream melted into milk. His tea was cold. That day Sara aged. He too.

As Ahmad recounted some of this, years later at the other end of the phone, I saw the faint blush on his cheeks and heard the quivering in his voice. He was reliving a tragedy. After a long pause when all I heard was breathing, he said. Slowly.

"All the women in my life, I have either committed a crime (*jenayat*) against them or they have committed *a jenayat* against me." He had used the word *jenayat*, turning love into a mortal crime.

There was no need to talk anymore.

When I disconnected, I leant back and wondered how a whole generation had taken themselves so seriously.

Chapter 11

The Play

Jina

Someone covered Ahmad's eyes from behind.

"Do you know who I am?" came the question for which there never is an answer, then a grinning face. "Don't you remember me?" No, he thought, but smiled politely. The other understood. A young man with grey blue eyes and a remarkably pale complexion was speaking as Ahmad was desperately searching the depths for a recognition card, but it was locked tight in his memory strongbox. It's me. Philip.

"Oh. Faramarz," Ahmad blurted out using his Farsi name, smiling that deep relief now that his strongbox had been decoded. It was his old school mate from Khorramshahr. Secondary school, mathematics stream. Philip-Faramarz was a couple of years below him but because they lived close by, they had got to know each other, and each other's family. Slowly the past unravelled. There were three children, Philip, and two girls.

"You remember Jina, don't you? She is in your year here," he added. Ahmad hadn't noticed. He vaguely remembered a young girl who once came to sit the mathematics exam with the boys at school, as they did not have a mathematics stream in the girls' secondary school in the port city. She had studied maths at home but sat the year-four final examination with the boys. She had left no marks in particular, but that was the time the boys had shut off their hormones. Almost. They were serious. Almost.

"We went to Rezai'eh[1] and lost touch," Philip said. "We're now in Tehran. I have switched to architecture too. I didn't like the decorative arts section."

Ahmad was fairly well known round the college now. He had organised the strike and he had served time in *Qezel Qale'h*. And he was co-editor of the university paper with Mousavi[2] where he wrote critical articles on all aspects of art and culture. These days he spent little time in the college. He was working in a few offices in Tehran and in addition had opened his own architectural office with another classmate.

A few weeks later, he was standing in the middle of the bus on his way home south on Pahlavi Avenue. The plane trees on both sides were beginning to strip to their winter look. You could see the bits of dry wasteland on either side interspersed by new buildings, homes, shops and flats. They had just passed Meydane Vanak and a few people got off. He found himself facing a girl. He immediately recognised Jina. She had just walked on.

They exchanged greetings followed by the usual asking after family. Jina had blushed on seeing him, but he did not notice, which was nothing unusual. The blush was not for him, anyway. She flushed with the memory of that first day of autumn a couple of years ago, when standing on that back row he had looked her straight in the eye, with no recognition. She didn't know that he was looking inwards for strength.

Later that year Jina joined their team of three for a year-four project; a project for the Udlajan district of south Tehran, which the college specified had to be done in groups. It was another one of the regime's grandiose schemes to transform the traditional neighbourhoods around the Tehran Bazaar and weaken the *bazaary* merchant's hold, *á la* Baron Haussman's Paris renovation. Initially, Ahmad, at heart a loner, had carefully selected two close friends and closed the list.

"And oh," the shorter classmate in the group had interrupted during a brief pause in the conversation about the project. His deep booming voice vibrated like a cross between a trombone and a bassoon. Of the three, he was the only one without a moustache which made him look even younger than he was. "We need to take a girl," he said looking distinctly sheepish. They were sitting in Ahmad's office in fashionable Boulevard Elizabeth, planning for the project.

"We don't need anyone else," Ahmad shot back in a way that said there is no further argument to be made. "And anyway, we closed the list." He definitely did not want anyone that was outside his small circle. "We don't need anyone else, most of all a *susul* girl," he continued visualising a classmate with long painted nails and a miniskirt.

"Don't be such a prude Ahmad," the taller classmate said, interested. "Who do you have in mind?" he addressed his shorter colleague with a glint in the eye.

"It's the Assyrian girl," the young man without a moustache said and his ever-moist eyes smiled, "Jina. She was out of the country when all the lists were closed and she asked me if she could join our group," he talked fast and deep. "Seeing we are only three and everyone else has five or six in their group, I'm afraid I agreed. Anyway, she said you know her from the south." Ahmad looked unhappy.

"We'll do our reports separately," he said after what seemed like a long pause when both were looking at him. "That way we can distil the best ideas. And she should not interfere." Ahmad's had barely finished the sentence before the office was flooded by the usual crowd of writers, students, artists and intellectuals; *araq* vodka and laughter.

Later Jina acknowledged that Ahmad's report was on a different level to the other three. They had hardly spoken other than the minimal. A stretch of dry land separated the two.

*

Jina was still wearing the simple grey dress she wore to college, with a short cardigan on her shoulders, the one with two buttons missing, as she walked across the light brown Travertine flooring towards the group gathered round a long table at the other side of a large room. It was the usual meeting place of the new theatre group Sai'd, writer, poet and theatre director, had set up some months ago under the name of *Anjoman Melli Ta'atr-e Iran (National Society of Iranian Theatre)*.[3] She was a little late as she had to juggle university, parents and her passion for the theatre.

Men and women, actors, friends, were standing or sitting around in a jumble around a long table. Some came over and kissed her. Left, right, left. Others stood up but waited for her to come to them. Greet. Kiss. *Khoobi?* Yes, I am well, *merci*, using the French as was usual among some sections of society. We are waiting for Sa'id, a young man said, having greetkissed her without making eye contact. He wasn't normally shy and maybe that was his way of avoiding the exchange of some deeply hidden emotions. A few minutes later Sa'id walked in, hopping toward the group like an excited child.

"We have a new play," he blurted out even before the door closed, letting the news get to them, before he did. "Yashar has written his play and we are going to work on it." He sounded almost breathless, his large black eyes sparkling beneath a large canopy of thick black hair, walrus moustache, equally deep black, oddly tremulous.

"I do hope it won't meet the same fate as *An Enemy of the People*," Jina quipped, "I mean *Dr Stockholm*" and giggled almost to herself.

"Don't be silly it won't," Sa'id said turning to her with a mock-serious face, his eyes glistening with joy. A few months ago SAVAK had closed down Ibsen's *An Enemy of the People* and arrested some of the artistic team, including Sai'd, despite the play's disguise under the name of *Dr Stockholm*. They probably would do the same, is what he decided not to say. "But what of it?" is what he actually said. "If they let it play out, it's propaganda, and if they ban it, it's propaganda. Didn't they stop our *Hamlet* because it dealt with regicide? We have a powerful tool here, our theatre group," he opened his arms in a theatrical gesture and grinned mischievously.

Rahim, a young man, arrived with a strange bouncing gait.

"*Salam*," he half shouted across the room. "Did you know that Sa'id has agreed to do Yashar's new play," he was talking to the room, and then saw Sa'id and cut. "You got here first. You always manage to be there first. I was going to give them the good news, the *mojdeh*. Anyway, who will buy the *shirini* (cookies)?" He looked round as if expecting everyone to jump forward. "Never mind," he said after a suitable pause, and pulled out a box of *nan berenji* rice cake, from his battered leather case. That case must have belonged to his father and was the joke of the group.

"What on earth is this you brought? These are all crumbled Rahim-jan,"

Sa'id said using jan to express the intimacy between the two friends, and reached into the standard patisserie issue white cardboard box, thin walled and rectangular, and took out a fistful of once-whole-white *shirini*. "These simply don't count," Sa'id added talking through a mouthful of *nan berenji* with bits of white crumb all down the front of his black sweatshirt. "You will just have to buy us a fresh box," his muffled words fighting their way through the crumbs and he passed the box over to a young man with a black polo-neck shirt and blue-green eyes standing beside him. Jina had crossed over for her share of *shirini* when the playwrite, Yashar, walked through the door followed by Ahmad, still chatting. The theatre group that day was becoming like a French farce with a rotating door.

"Salam. Salam. What's the celebration about?" Yashar said, eyeing the square thin-walled white cardboard box being passed round. "Anyone getting married? Anyone died?" and almost ran across the hall salivating.

"Stop pretending," a young girl in dark maroon sweater and navy-blue skirt said. "You know perfectly well what we are celebrating," and Jina saw a flash of red lipstick on her perfect white teeth surrounded by bright red lips.

"*Be vallahe na*" (swear to God, no!), Yashar said genuinely. "What's going on?"

Why do we keep using God's name when we don't believe Jina thought and for the first time she saw his succulent lips giving his black hairbrush moustaches piggybacking lips almost like that of the girl in dark maroon sweater and navy-blue skirt.

"We're celebrating your new play, *The Teachers* of course Yashar-jan" the girl in maroon sweater and skirt said, somewhat perplexed.

"But I haven't finished it," he said. Yashar was now genuinely surprised.

"Don't worry about that, Sa'id will almost certainly change it during rehearsal," Ahmad said and stopped himself from reaching into the box. "Saves you from taking the blame if it's a disaster," he added with a mischievous grin, still addressing the playwright. As Ahmad was talking Jina was thinking, here is this guy, so obsessive about his own work he wouldn't let a single soul touch it, telling Yashar to let go of his creation. But she said nothing.

"No, he won't. It wouldn't be my creation any more, would it? But then I guess if he can change Ibsen, who am I to object?" Yashar was almost speaking to himself.

"What is it about anyway?" a young woman with dyed-blonde hair in a pigtail asked of no one in particular.

"Don't tell her," Elie, another actress, interrupted, and Yashar had to pause his reply on his succulent lips. "Shouldn't we read it before Sai'd-joon entirely garbles it," Elie added smiling.

"No, Ellie-joon, it would be better to start by ad-libbing round the overall plot without preconceptions, the way Sa'id likes. That's much more creative," the girl with dyed-blonde hair said twinkling, and almost danced across the table, took the square white cardboard box and emptied the remaining crumbs into her mouth, lungs and down her blood-red sweater followed by a fit of spluttering cough. The dyed-blonde pigtail coughed in unison. A few people laughed.

"Yes, that would make it more Brechtian," Jina said as she banged the dyed-blonde girl's back to direct the crumbs to their rightful orifice. Why did I say that she thought? Ahmad looked at her and saw her for the first time.

Rahim listened with increasing frustration. "No!" he said emphatically before anyone else could have a chance to speak. The group had drawn closer with everyone standing in a circle, "No, we must read the whole thing aloud first. How on earth am I expected to act if I don't know what it is I am acting out?" Rahim said in a frustrated voice. He was after all their lead actor.

"It's only half done," Yashar objected, but pulled the typed sheets half out of his dark blue rucksack. On second thought he let it slide back.

"Ok, just give it to us in your own words. You all know how Sa'id likes to go into something with an open mind." It was the girl with the dyed-blonde hair speaking and went into another prolonged fit of coughing. Sa'id smiled at her. Her dark black eyes really do clash with that dyed-blonde hair, Jina thought. I won't dye, ever. She must be modelling herself on Bardot.

"How can you prepare if you don't know what you are preparing for?" Rahim the lead actor said looking over to Sa'id, but his look was of half-resignation.

"For God's sake say something Sa'id-jan, shall I read it or not?" Yashar asked. "You always have the last word anyway."

"It's our poet-director's prerogative of course," Elie said and saw the girl with dyed-blonde hair who had stopped coughing, all the bits of rice-cake safely tucked away in the right compartments looking at Sa'id with her mouth pinched. She is in love, Elie thought and laughed to herself, only a faint smile peeping through. They were all in love with Sai'd one way or another and she looked over to the playwright. "Tell us at least what it is about," she asked. Yashar began to give an outline of the play he was writing, but after a few minutes, with Sa'id constantly interrupting, he suddenly stopped in mid sentence.

"What the hell," he said in an irritable voice " this is hopeless," and re-retrieved the typed manuscript from the rucksack. "I'm going to read it as far as it goes." As he started reading a hush settled on the room, everyone had gathered around the long table creating a mini theatre. Sa'id occasionally interrupted but in a quite, subdued voice, so as not to break the flow. It would be a success almost all of them thought.

They would start rehearsals next week. They weren't to know that SAVAK would break up the show after 10 days and imprison Sa'id and Yashar for three months in *Qezel Qale'h*.

*

I am going to Damavand this weekend, Ahmad said having walked over to Jina as she stood by the table. Why don't you and Philip come? He had added her brother Philip as he was about to let the words out. Makes it less provocative. Have you ever been there? it is a spectacularly beautiful village, he added superfluously as everyone in Tehran knew about the sprawling village, nearly a town, on the foothills of the tall silent volcano overseeing the capital. We might get inspired. I will ask him, she said looking into his eyes and then dropping a centimetre or two to his mid cheek. The invitation had taken her by surprise. Ahmad hadn't exactly shown an interest in anything she or her brother did, Jina had commented one late night after their father had gone to bed. She too had not really thought of him as anything but the successful architect everyone at college looked up to. Yes, please do, he said, lacking words. It was unusual for him.

[1] A city in North-West Iran, now called Urumieh.

[2] Mir-Hossein Mousavi who later became prime minister in the Islamic Republic.

[3] Sa'id Soltanpour was arrested by the Islamic regime in 1981 at his wedding and executed a few days later.

Chapter 12

Damavand

Ahmad and Jina

The road to Damavand was dull she thought until they drove between two barren hills round a corner and a lush green valley appeared on the left with its rows of *tabrizi* trees, the unique poplar trees with their straight white trunks and an inverted pear-shaped canopy, the blueness of the sky dancing eyewards through the darker green late summer leaves, tickling the eye, defining fields of cucumbers interspersed with wheat. It was Roodehen. Philip had politely excused himself.

They came to a fork on the road. The left-hand fork would take them on a spectacular journey to Mazandaran province over the Alborz mountains that Jina knew so well. The road would climb up to Abe-Ali where the Shah's father had built a luxury hotel for the Tehrani elite;[1] then through Mosha', Polour and Abe-Ask where many well to do Tehranis had a family orchard and where they had either built a mud cottage or camped during the dry hot Tehrani summer months; then skirting the mother mountain, mount Damavand, sitting majestically with its permanent white summit like an old-fashioned night cap, a silent volcano, maybe waiting to spew molten rock and ash on the capital one day; then along the valley of the River Haraz, giving the road its name, with its brown-black-purple rock formations rising steep on either side; on to a the lush green mountain forest later named after a national hero, Mirza Kuchek Khan[2] through the small village of Razekeh,

66

and beyond; descending down to the rice paddies circling the city of Amol with their emerald-green shoots dotted in the Spring with women and girls in multicoloured dresses tucked above their knees bending, planting, knee deep in water. Where were the men? Jina had thought every time she had seen them. And down to the small town of Mahmud Abad turning right along the coastal road to Babolsar, where the late Reza Shah had built another hotel for the elite on land he had seized by force, passing *en route* hundreds of holiday villas built by the Tehrani old and nouveau rich. The Haraz road was, above all, a road for a class of people with time on their hands.

But Ahmad took the longer Firuzkuh road towards Mazandaran, the road of lorries and buses. Longer and duller. Do you want a cup of tea, he asked as they approached a roadside *qahveh-khaneh*, the first word that had passed between them? Why do they call them coffee houses when the only hot drink they serve is tea? *chai*. She nodded. They sat on a wooden bed covered by a *kilim* that was once red, beside a running stream. Jina asked for a couple of eggs fried in butter remembering how they tasted totally different from those made at home. Somehow the air, the clear mountain stream, the willow trees and the row of *tabrizis* (poplars) on the horizon changed the taste. He had the same. And *chai*. Silent but for the song of gurgling water.

They turned left after another half an hour, on to the road that ended in Damavand. Serpentine, skirting the barren hills on the left with their dry thorny bushes waiting for a wind to blow them around, and on the right, willow trees lining a brook, the *nahr*, marking the boundary of the green valley below. In between the trees they could see, sliding down the valley, orchards once emerald-green in the spring and darker now in late summer, more viridian than emerald, interspersed with yellow ochre wheat fields waiting for the scythe, and fields of tomato or cucumber. After one particularly sharp bend Ahmad stopped the car in a natural lay-by by the brook.

"The water comes from the river further upstream," Ahmad explained, as he got out, maybe to break the silence. They had not said anything since Rudehen, as if still mesmerised by the sound of the river rippling over the stones and the fried eggs. Or just silent for lost words. There is a *baq* down there, an orchard belonging to a dear friend. He calls everyone a dear friend,

Jina thought. He did that.

The *baq*, had a story. It had been split in three by the three sisters who inherited it from their father, a prominent *Shia'* cleric who gave some land in the deserts of north Tehran to his sons and the fertile orchard to his daughters thinking he was doing the girls a favour. The old *mullah* could not imagine how Tehran would balloon mountainward through the desert land that today includes the classy boulevard of Ahmad's office.

They walked downhill on the rough stony path along the side of the wheat field, seemingly ripe for harvesting, crossed another brook and entered the *baq*. Ahead were two mud-brick huts. Two rooms each. Whitewashed. A veranda circling three sides. Huts very close together. A small crudely dug pond in front of each, fed once a day from the stream by the water man, the *mirab*. Precious water. The one they had just jumped over. Both huts looked like no one had lived in them for years, the walls were peeling and one of them had a crack in the back. Two huge walnut trees stood erect spreading their benevolence through a large, shaded area, but the sour cherry trees looked abandoned and sad. The entire baq looked neglected, as if the owners had ceased caring.

At the bottom of the *baq* they could hear the Damavand River rolling over, almost caressing the stones, life-giving water. They walked across, trying to step on stones. Slippery. Shoes wet. She had come unprepared for a river crossing. So, clearly, was he. Carried away. They climbed the steep slope on the far side of the river into Veleroon. A small mud village surrounded by a mud wall, a feeble protection against the hostile world. Mud huts around a central plaza, once housing 10 or 12 families, now almost empty, another sad relic of a changing world.

They sat by a wheat field that had been harvested recently; you could still see the odd grain on the ground, yet to be scavenged by the birds or ants. She spread her cardigan on the dry, bristly earth, laid her head and looked up to the blue. He followed. It was coming up to late morning and the sun was warming up. Never intolerably hot at over 2,000 metres on the slopes of the silent volcano. She closed her eyes in the silence that was earth. Suddenly she heard a sound that grew louder and louder, like an orchestral tutti of buzzing. She felt as if she was being attacked by a swarm of insects but when she opened her eyes the sound ceased. Abruptly. Just the blue sky with a dash of grey-white here and there, and the cut wheat and the rustling trees towards her feet. She closed her eyes again, this time listening to the crescendo of nature. She felt a warmth that was more than that of a mid-morning sun. She was nature and nature was lying beside her.

She opened her eyes. He was on his back eyes closed. She turned. Hands touch, linger, untouch. Maybe they kissed. They should have. You don't discuss such details.

Kabab lunch in Damavand, the long walk to *Chesmeh-Ala'* where they drank the cold clean water of the mountain spring. The walk and drive back were different.

*

A few days later he rang her to say that he was going to Rasht for a large project he had agreed to lead, an undertaking to build the new seaside village of Qazian, on the shores of the Caspian Sea. In Rasht his old drinking friend, *Hossein-the-Poet,* a local, tall with a deep bass voice and a laugh that came from below the diaphragm, took charge of the office they set up and promptly hired two of the most beautiful girls in town as secretaries. Ahmad rented a large flat in nearby Bandar Pahlavi (now Anzeli), that he shared with a number of people engaged in the project. Later he rented another, smaller, flat in Rasht for when he was working in the office.

Jina travelled north to Rezaieh (now Urumieh), a city bordering the large salt lake bearing the same name, to be with her relatives.

[1] The first concrete building in Iran built by Soviet architect Megnov and his two German assistants in 1935-37 close to the Ab-Ali ski resort, Iran's oldest ski resort. It belonged to Reza Shah and was part of the vast Pahlavi Foundation.
[2] Mirza Kuchek Khan Forest named after the revolutionary leader who in what is known as the Jangal Movement, briefly helped by Bolshevik troops,

set up the Socialist Republic of Gilan in the early 1920's. He died through frost bite while fleeing troops sent by Reza Khan, the later Reza Shah, the father of the last Shah. See Cosroe Chaqueri *The Soviet Socialist Republic of Iran, 1920-21: Birth of the Trauma*. University of Pittsburg Press 1994.

Chapter 13

Rasht

Ahmad and Jina

Deep emotions sometimes appear almost out of the blue, unexpected. Jina was walking on the shores of Urumieh lake, this remnant of that ur-ocean that had once covered the entire land. Not quite a déjà vu, she felt united with that ocean of old. Maybe the remnant of fish in me, she thought, and then an intense feeling of longing spread outwards from somewhere inside her to touch her breasts, tingle, then her neck and down her arms to her fingertips. Longing for the warmth of flesh. Not any flesh. Specific. With its own markings, the odd freckle peeping through the dark hair lying synchronously on his arm, bending away from his body as if blown by an invisible wind, like the undulating wheat she had seen walking down from the stream on the day of the buzzing orchestra.

Distance nurtures closeness.

For him it happened a day in early spring. The Udlajan project group had finished working. Jina was the last to leave his flat on the upper floor of a house at the end of a cul-de-sac. He watched her walking down the stairs, watched her through the vertical glass frontage walking along the alleyway, watched the girl wearing a white raincoat, beneath it the hem of the black skirt she always wore underlining it like a line at the end of a chapter, watched her disappear round the corner into the street, and felt an alien sensation he could not name. Maybe that was his moment, and he instantly brushed it inward. He never told her.

Slowly they sank into open love. Her memory of buzzing insects and his trapezoid image of her disappearing round the alleybend tied the two into a union. Slowly, as befitted his reserve and her principles. But that's not how it actually was. It was not a slow metamorphosis of friendship to love. Love was like opening a bottle of *doogh abe-ali.*[1] You desperately try to stop its white creamy content spilling out, but escape it does, yogurty, foamingly, explosively. Love comes into consciousness in an instant. One minute you are not, the next you are. A sort of dialectic evolution of quantity into quality, exploding, she thought as she walked by the water, having read about dialectics in one of those clandestine books with plain white cover that was no longer as white from all the hands that had rubbed off something. Something must have built up to suddenly explode as love. She had felt hers by the salty lake and he had denied his by an effort of will. Neither had wanted to fall in love. There was so much to do.

Yes. Distance was fire beneath the kettle. It just warmed up the absence into sudden presence-in-absence. That's what love is, she concluded one day. Absence being transformed into longing. Togetherness even when distanced. The distance between this smaller salty lake and the other, much larger salty lake, the Caspian, large enough to be elevated to a sea, now joined by invisible strands pulling the two together.

They never spoke about it. Open love was never expressed in words.

*

We have to get married, she blurted out, without any run up. He looked startled. Commitment. Not for a fighter, he had said, thought, and believed deep. They were at war.

'It is becoming more difficult with father" she said. Ahmad used to go into their home back in the capital to drink wine with him, on the days he walked her to her home which was close to his office. "You know father was training to be a priest when younger. Me staying over in Rasht is too much for him," she added. She was a little afraid of her father, he thought. And he was nominally a Muslim and she a Christian. Equally nominal. Mother had had an Assyrian boy in sight for her. For appearance's sake, is what they finally agreed, knowing different. Neither of them had used the taboo word love.

Next time he was in Tehran he called her. Let's do it today. Two friends from the college. A notary office. Eisenhower Street. Just the four of them. A civil marriage Muslim style. She took the name Jina that she had used at school. No parents present. No presents. Signed. Certified. Illegal as there was no paternal agreement. A glass of *araq* downstairs in an *araq* store. Then all four went back to work or to college. Next day they hired a car to take them to Rasht as man and wife. In name. Formal, they said. She would divide her time between flats, his new flat in Tehran and Rasht. It took another seven months before either parent found out. Sulking. Anger on both sides.

Jina took charge of the Rasht office.

Then one day that winter the gendarmerie post near Siahkal, a village 40 km southeast of their office in Rasht was overrun by a group of guerrillas. Most of the assailants were either killed or captured. The Shah, taking no chances, dispatched a huge army and helicopters. The radio announcer on that February day in 1971 reported that security forces had killed or captured 16 '*kharabkars*' in Siahkal, and went on to report on a 'cowardly' attack on the gendarmerie station near the village of Siahkal in Gilan province.

This was the first attack by what came to be known later as the Fadai' Organisation. It was their first guerrilla attack in the depth of winter.[2] The guerrilla war had begun in earnest, despite many of its founding members being in prison.

That night Jina, Ahmad and the boys trebled their *araq* drinking.

"It is not a defeat, it's a symbolic victory" Ahmad said. They will get new recruits. But he remembered how he had argued with Bijan, warning of the futility of unequal battles.

*

There is a man here looking for a job, his foreman said one day. He says he is a carpenter. He has been turned down wherever he goes.

"Why is that?" Ahmad asked and guessed the answer.

"His brother is a *kharabkar*" the foreman said using the word saboteur, or wrecker, the term used by the press and radio for the guerrillas who had recently overrun the police station. "No one dares to employ him," the foreman added in a neutral voice.

A young man walked into the hut they used as a site office, tall in a white shirt, grey somewhat worn trousers, carrying a small battered brown suitcase. He hung a blue jacket on the other arm. It was an unusually warm spring day, hot and sticky as only Bandar Pahlavi could be. You could see the ring of sweat, fresh and dried, conquering outwards from the armpit. He looked like he had not eaten for days with a face of hopeless resignation.

"I am a carpenter," Zeibaram replied to the question. "Good at my job," he added and looked straight into Ahmad's eyes. Black on black. He would not be defeated.

"You can start today," Ahmad said turning to Jina who was now in charge of the Rasht office and had come down to the village they were constructing to survey progress.

Early next morning as Ahmad was driving north into the construction site from Rasht he saw a man in white shirt, with a blue jacket thrown over the left shoulder and brown suitcase that had seen happier days in the right hand climbing the hill that bounded the site. He ran up to him.

"Your boss threw me out," Zeibaram said, calm as if expecting nothing else. There was a sarcastic smile on his lips and eyes saying I can survive whatever you throw at me. A determination that seemed to light his eyes that the dilated pupils had blackened further. A defiant light.

"Just wait here. Wait here a second" Ahmad said, looking flushed, sweat of rage appearing on his forehead and round his moustache. He walked over to the office. The owner was there.

"Is it true that you sacked Zeibaram?" He demanded his voice shaking with anger.

"Of course. Didn't you know his brother is a *kharabkar*," a terrorist.

Ahmad flushed scarlet, turned round, walked out wordlessly, drove to Rasht office with Zeibaram, told *Hossein-the-Poet* who was still the day-to-day office manager to pay a month's wages to all the staff including the new recruit, pay their debts and then close the office. Jina watched him. The moment she heard the boss had come she had anticipated it all and had already packed her bags. Love is better than a telegram.

They drove to Tehran. No words. He went home and for six months did nothing but read Marx's *Das Kapital* and drift into dreams.

Love is like papyrus. Even if the edges are frail or the writing fades you can still see the love that went into its creation. Jina survived on that love.

[1] A special fizzy drink made of yogurt and served cold. On opening the contents fly out, not unlike champagne.

[2] They had chosen Siahkal as they felt that the forested mountain would give them cover, while the fertile land and existing disputes between tea growers and the central government would sustain them in what they saw as a long battle – *à la* Cuban revolution – in town and country.

Chapter 14

The guest

Ahmad and Jina

A grey-black carpet of smoke that normally lay on the capital, had been washed away by the recent rain. Ahmad arrived home to find her sipping tea with someone he did not know. This is my friend, Jina said with a smile, introducing Azadeh. She was always careful not to show her teeth with their faint tobacco stains. She had tried to give up so many times but everyone she knew smoked. Cigarette-smoke was only second to car fumes and just as reluctant to shift away in the plate-shaped city. Here everyone smoked, all except him. He hated smoke, just as he hated clutter.

"She works with Sai'd in the theatre group; you may have seen her," Jina said. He hadn't, but said nothing, though she had noticed him. The two women were sitting side by side, the light coming from behind made both their hairs look lighter than real. He glimpsed the mountain behind their silhouettes. The snow line had come down since he last looked. The late autumn rain had descended as snow up the slopes, now brilliant white in the sun. Down here it had washed down yesterday's soot and was already running down the gutters towards where ordinary people lived in the south of the city. Real people, as Jina called them. The mountains seemed closer in the clear afternoon air. As if a gigantic magnifying glass was hanging outside the window.

They shook hands firmly, out of keeping with her shy smile, he thought. And as their hands parted her eyes turned downwards, as if to indicate that her smile was not too provocative. She wore a simple black dress, somewhat old fashioned, knee length, with a black collar that reminded him of schoolgirls, narrow and circular coming to a round edge at the front. Not white like a schoolgirl but hinting at a uniform. His daughter Nina has a long way to go before school, he thought. So much could happen in this country by then. Then his mind wandered ahead. He said a few words of welcome and walked over across the hall into the corridor to the bathroom at the end to wash his hands. He always washed them when he got home, washing away not just the city grime but also the grime of all that he hated, and loved, about it. Wash.

He disliked the aggressive mendacity that stamped itself on all capital cities. In Khorramshahr, where he had spent his childhood there was more laughter, more honesty and not so much calculation. It must have been the extreme summer heat that drew people together. Or perhaps because it was a port. Whatever the reason, and perhaps there were many, the people of that southern province were more friendly, more open. That is how he remembered it. Though memory filters.

He too thought of himself as open. For someone so meticulous in his thinking he was remarkably ignorant of himself. He occupied a number of worlds, each carefully concealed from the other. His outward consideration for others and his near-incapacitating politeness hid a turbulent world of passion. Somewhere too he had to accommodate immense self-confidence, quick intellect, analytical mind and deeply held beliefs with his reticence, with his respect for opinion of others, with his politeness, and with an explosive anger. Complex being. Perhaps we are all complex. He yearned for the simplicity of his father and the purity of his mother. He yearned for Yazd where he was born, the city of honesty where the legacy of Zoroaster still floated over the light brown earth buildings with their peculiar air vents directing the desert wind into the house. The place where the desert acted as a cooler. Maybe that explained his ability to accommodate heat and cold in the same body.

He did not return to the sitting room immediately. It was usual to have people coming into his home at all times. They held an open house like many. Friends, semi-friends, friends of friends, would drop in, often unannounced.

It was a perfect cover. That and the fact that he was now a highly successful architect with multiple contracts from private and state funding.

Their apartment was in a fashionable northern suburb, on the slopes of the mountain where large houses were hidden by expanses of trees, plane, pear, persimmon, pomegranate, apple, and sour cherries in huge orchards, surrounding the owner in green seclusion. Old gardens with hundred-year-old plane trees, the ones planted close to one another reaching high into the sky, reaching for light, concealing buildings with thick walls and small windows that protect the inhabitants from heat and cold, thieves and strangers. His apartment block was one of the new ones springing up in the spaces between the large gardens paid mostly by the money that that had come from oil – one he had designed himself – competing with the plane trees in its upward reach. A competition the concrete won. Concrete always wins these days, he had once said to someone. The apartment was spacious with the statutory L-shaped sitting room. And large windows that transformed air-conditioning from a luxury to a necessity. The new ignored the wisdom of the old vernacular. Deliberately rejected it, discarded like a faded rose. But then the new rich looked to the west, not to history, for inspiration. He was steeped in history but had to work with new expectations. Here was another irreconcilable layer added to his complexity. But a more useful cover. Who would suspect of disloyalty a rich, successful ultra-modern architect? The wide clean windows looking outwards over the spreading city spoke of openness, concealing his opaque unadjusted interior.

Back in the room, the two women were deep into conversation. As he arrived the young woman stood up in mid-sentence, turned to him and stretched out her hand.

"I must be off," she looked just below his eyes. They smiled, the eyes just missing one another. "I'm meeting someone," she used an expression that could be an amorous meeting or a political one or business. The handshake was firm. Then she looked him straight in the eye, with a look lasting just that split-second longer. His wife smiled, unsure, then looked over to him and beamed as if he had just come in.

*

That same week a young man was walking down Molavi Street in Tehran. You could pick him out in a large crowd, especially a moving crowd, what with his peculiar bobbing walk, up on his toes and down again like an undulating seesaw, or ocean wave, his brown hair with a tinge of jujube, almost as if he had used henna and scrubbed the colour into the brown, and his brown eyebrows separated by an always-pink-tinged brow, now expanded by a bald patch, poking, rising and falling tall above the crowd. Yes. You could pick him out even if you left your glasses home.

We have not met Changiz, a young man in his early thirties from the lands bordering the old Soviet Union, though we have heard his evocative voice singing an Azari *ashiq* song which echoing down the corridor *Qezel Qal'eh* to move Ahmad lying on his uneven stony bed in his cell. A year ago, he had been instrumental in forming an urban armed group[1] with some friends and had disappeared into the urban jungle.

Today it was early spring and the mature plane trees in that old part of town were being reborn. Suddenly, descending like a pack of wolves, he found himself surrounded by armed police. Seeing them, he ran into a group of bystanders shouting, 'Death to the traitor Shah' and 'Death to America', swallowed a cyanide capsule, lost consciousness, was rushed to a police hospital where he was rescued from death and handed over to the 'doctor-interrogator-torturers' of SAVAK. Another romantic revolutionary caught in the web.

---

[1] The group's name, *Raziliq*, was given to it much later by SAVAK who found the name of a village called *Raziliq* in a document (actually just a field study about the Shah's Land Reform) in the house of one of the group. It stuck. Changiz's group, founded in 1973, were close to another founded by Siamak Sotudeh that believed more in working among the masses, though there was not much contact between them before most their members were arrested. Changiz was arrested in April 1974 and released on the eve of the Revolution of 1979.

Chapter 15

Komiteh Moshtarek

Changiz

How do you write about pain? Beyond words when present and lost to words when past. An experience you try to send to the forget box even before it fades. The loss of descriptive memory is your survival kit, Darwin's selection. The deeply encoded urge to obliterate that sharp scream inside your bones, your skin, your very being, the you that is being assaulted. Then the afterburn. But wire-whip-pain is in a different language. There is the slash and there is the echo. But not like a normal echo. It echoes locally, then travels inwards, echoing deep somewhere in the brain, ricocheting off the thalamus, as if it has walls. Each echo is like shriek. Screeching pain, beyond description, crying out for a language, some as yet uninvented, unuttered words to identify with the skin, the bone, the living meat, the girl or boy, man or woman being whipped. To become that pain. That person being pained. Rotating, agonisingly pained. I can't take more. Then the next blow and the spiral of pain on another plane.

Stop. Pain. Just for a second.

Stop.

When will this damn pain stop?

Another blow tore the soles of his feet. Time stood still like a spectator as if it too enjoys watching pain, this pain unlike anything human. Changiz tried to think away the pain. Another blow shooting like an electric current through his prostrate body. Is the bastard hitting harder or is it just raw skin? Oh God, when is he going to stop. Did I say God? Each blow was a crescendo of tearing, squashing, imploding of cells, leaving a distortion ready to putrefy. Bring back the good pain he begged to himself. Yes, there are good pains, like when he, a boy, fell off the tree and broke his arm. Anything but this. Anything. Hope I can last out. I can. I must. Wasn't it Stalin who said beat them and then beat them again. Everyone cracks, he had said. But I will not crack. I will prove him wrong. I'll make it. A blow at a time. A blow at a time. A blow…This bastard doesn't tire. If only I could see his face. It would help cope with pain. I have lost count. Give me the good pain, the good pain. Just bear it blow by blow, a group at a time, that's how you should do it. Stop that pain. Maybe if I count them, in groups, five cable beats at a time. Then he lost count. He felt like bits of him were flying away every time that whip came down, screeching through the air like a child screaming. Stop. Damn it, stop. Time had stood still. Time had become eternal, as was the pain.

"Are you ready to confess you piece of worthless shit?" The *doctor* said in his high voice, young for his age. For the third time, maybe. Or fourth. You filthy whore-of-a-mother-fucker-sister bastard. He was lying face-down on a bed, his hands and feet fastened by some straps. As they were laying him down his blindfold had momentarily slipped, and he had a glimpse of the grey walls, filthy with grime and dried blood and bits of something.

"I haven't done anything to confess, I really havn't" Changiz replied in a croaky voice trying to sound strong. He managed a smile. He always managed to smile. It strengthened him. Somewhere there was a huge store of smiles, all ready to emerge. Like the five toman notes he used to save for a rainy day. Should I pretend I am not hurting? Is it better to scream? Another blow and his feet caught fire.

"Stop," he shouted after a particularly painful blow that had made him scream as if someone else had taken control. His body felt like molten flesh.

"Hold it," the high-pitched *doctor*, they were all called doctor, said from somewhere remote. Are you ready to confess you… and he followed it by soiling his mother and sister in filth. Never father or brother.

81

"I'll confess. I'll talk." The cable lashing stopped. "Except I haven't done anything," he added, his Azeri accent even more pronounced.

"Hit this filthy cunt of a Turk. Tear him to bits," barked the *doctor*, his voice an octave higher.

Make it. Must make it. He remembered a comrade's advice on how to bear torture. Yes. I will imagine a peasant. In between the blows of the wire-lash he summoned every ounce of the piled-up anger at the injustices that had been the motor to his struggle, all the piled-up reserves of energy only the young have, into a huge effort of imagination. There he is. My very own peasant. An old man with his felt hat and sun-furrowed, sunburnt face. Furiously digging the earth. Dry earth. Stony earth. Lots of rocks. Concentrate now. That's who you are fighting for and ready to die for. All your pain now is nothing to his lifelong pain. Concentrate. He concentrated all the energy that had not yet been subdued and fixed the image in all its intricate detail. The detail that spoke of the life-pains that old man has had to endure to become his image. It was right there in front of him, the old peasant, they age so quickly, with his light brown felt hat and sun-furrowed, burnt face furiously digging the earth, just like the earth in his own village in *Qareh-Daq*, the summers he would visit, his childhood home. Dig that stony earth *amu-jan*, (uncle dear) he thought aloud and furiously concentrated on the old-man's face. He focused on the furrows. Furrowed eyes. Furrowed forehead. Furrowed face. Course leathery skin. Suddenly the head was gone. Just vanished. There no more. No matter how hard he tried, he, the old peasant, stood headless, digging the stony earth without a head. The head obstinately refused to come back. Headless peasant, digging away at the stony earth. Another wire-lash tore into both his calves. Must focus on the hands, hands of a toiling peasant, calloused, rugged, brown, nails broken, dirt, lots of dirt and rough, spade. Digging. Dig! Digging. Then one hand and its arm vanished. Simply flipped out of the image. The shovel was still there. The pain. Pain. It isn't going to stop. Can't lose that other hand. Really can't lose that hand. Must have that hand. He lost. Both hands vanished and took the shovel with it. Body, all that was left was the body, firmly planted on the stony earth, no arms, no shovel, headless, *amu-jan* still has his body, and his feet, firm on dry stony earth, brown earth. But no shovel. The pain, pain. I still have my feet. Such pain. Why can't I be dead? Or non-human. Snails don't feel pain. Concentrate. Bring *amu's* bits back. But no matter how hard he tried, the head, the arms, the hands, the shovel obstinately refused. They had been rubbed out.

And then the torso slowly began to fade, not vanish. Just fade away like a dream. Somewhere came the high-pitched voice of the *doctor*, from afar. Far. Ready? Ready? A voice from over the hill as the stony earth too faded upwards towards the sky. He woke up with a jolt. He was being marched round the room by two guards to bring back sensation to his legs. The bottom half of his body was wet. Water reddened by blood. Blood stays red no matter how dilute. How odd, he thought, not pink. Why not pink?

They dragged him to the cell and dumped him by the door. Everyone woke up. He crawled into the cell. Walking was excruciatingly painful. They had made him walk. Someone helped him pull off his blindfold. Somewhere down there his bladder was about to explode. How had he kept it locked in? He had not drunk anything. He couldn't remember for how long. Time lost in time. The cellmates were sleeping when he came in, so it must be night. Slowly, very slowly, his eyes adjusted to seeing. Familiar faces. A few new ones. Anyone from his group? Had they been captured? Had anyone cracked? I need to piss. A fire is burning my feet. Must pull away from the fire but something was restraining him. Someone silhouetted against the yellow light coming into the cell through the metal bars was doing something to his fire. Then slowly, as if emerging out of smoke he saw an unsmiling young man cleaning up his bloody, swollen feet. Changiz smiled through the fog of pain and recognition and asked him to call the guard for the toilet. He could smile. He could always smile. That was encouraging. He hadn't cracked.

In the Combined Committee, *Komiteh Moshtarek*,[1] prisoners were let out twice a day. It worked out two or three minutes for each prisoner. You learnt to shit, piss and wash overlapping. At any other time, you needed the guard to agree to let you out. It didn't need too much pleading tonight. The less bad guard was on. An Azari Turk. *Hamvelayati* (someone from the same province). *Hamvelayati* allowed Changiz to crawl to the toilet on his knees at the end

83

of their corridor on the second floor and allowed him to stay there that bit longer. Drip, drip, the urine came out of a full bladder. It must be that kicking I got, he thought. My kidneys aren't packing up. That's good. Drip, drip, it stings like hell, like pissing razor blades. That was how his uncle Ali described it after catching the clap in Tabriz. A slow crawl back and *hamvelayati*, who was less bad, only kicked him once on the way. Funny creatures we are, adaptable, pliable. Maybe if I get beaten long enough without cracking, I would even get used to pain. Cracking like a mirror, one minute you reflect light, one minute not, a fractured human being. How could I face my friends in little pieces were I to crack? Just one week and this cell would be like home.

When he got back to the cell a cellmate put a plate with some foul-smelling green rice in front of him. Courtesy of the less-bad guard. And a metallic mug of water. Looked unclean and a bit battered. He took a sip and pushed back the plate. Mamaqan, that was the name of the serious young man, started to clean his feet again. Already a veteran, he had been arrested two years ago, a Fadai'. Changiz looked down at his feet. They did not look human. His blood sank unto the matting which had grown even stiffer from the blood of all those bleeding, ripped-up feet that had come before. This mat and all the pus and dead skin now embedded in it was a sculptured witness to this hell. They used to whip prisoners on the thigh, legs and stomach but that just knocked out their kidneys. Feet are more resilient, and they can just go on and on and on beating the same bit of anatomy. And the feet bear weight which transforms them into a kind of permanent lashing. Very effective, it was.

He was called again the next night, and the next for three weeks with only two short breaks. That mirror didn't crack. The mirror smiled.

[1] *Komiteh Moshtarek Zedd-e Kharabkari*, to give it its full name [the Anti-Sabotage Combined Committee] was established in late January 1972 by combining the interrogation centres of the municipal police with those of SAVAK. The interrogation and torture of most political prisoners initially took place in the *Komiteh*.

Chapter 16

Conquest of the garden

Ahmad, Jina and Azadeh

Foruq writes so beautifully, Jina said as she entered the kitchen holding her anthology of Foruq Farrokhzad's poems. Listen to her magical poem, *fath-e baq* (conquest of the garden),[1] she said in a hushed voice.

Everyone knows,
everyone knows
that you and I have seen the garden
from that cold sullen window
and that we plucked the apple
from that playful, distant branch.

A film of water coated her eyes, dissolving him into a mist. She went on and he listened.

Everyone's afraid,
everyone's afraid, but you and I,
joined with the lamp
and water and mirror and we were not afraid.

He sat on the edge of the sofa and continued, reading from his inner book:

Everyone knows
everyone knows

we found our way
into the cold, quite dream of the phoenixes:
We found truth in the garden
in the embarrassed look of a nameless flower
and we found permanence
in an endless moment
when two suns stared at each other.

You skipped the erotic bits, she said and grinned wide. Don't tell me you had not memorised that bit. And she filled out the missing words from the written page:
I am talking about my fortunate tresses
with the burnt anemone of your kiss
and the intimacy of our bodies,
and the glow of our nakedness
like fish scales in water.

"I couldn't speak for you could I, in your voice, the voice of a woman", Ahmad said his voice trailing downwards and a faint warmth rose upwards on his neck. You are not being truthful the rising warmth was whispering. He could not talk about nakedness with a woman, even one whose body had touched his. Naked. Tresses? Whose tresses? That was a woman speaking in the *baq*. Openly. Courageously. Uniquely. No one has had her courage.

He stopped himself.

We have a long way ahead she wanted to say and said it in a faint melancholy smile. She had felt the warmth of their naked embrace as she was reciting the poem. Foruq's *fath-e baq* was wild honesty by our most honest female poet and honesty had to be heard loud to be honest she said to herself, still looking inwards. He understood her unsaid words, but reserve is like curare, it paralyses the tongue. He bent over and kissed her. On the forehead off centre, a little to the left. He had never before talked of love.

*

That evening Ahmad warmed up last night's supper, placed it in an old

86

China dish that his mother had given them, telling them that it was from Russia, and carried it to the table.

"*Khoresht* casseroles always taste better the day after", Jina said as she reached over with her spoon. Before he could reply there was ring at the door. Someone must have let them in at the front gate. He looked through the peephole. He always did. A sensible precaution these days. It gave you a few seconds to prepare your face and your thoughts. Salam he said in his friendly face and voice. Salam Azadeh said. Come and sit down and have a bite to eat, he said in his neutral polite voice coming from a neutral polite face.

"Sorry, I have come at a bad time", she said as she and Jina kissed, left, right, left cheek. "I didn't know if you knew, but SAVAK raided the theatre during the night and broke up the show. Sa'id and Yashar and some of the cast have been arrested".

"I am not surprised", Ahmad said in his surprised voice. "This is Sa'id's second time, and it won't be easy for him. I must go to his mother", he added, and his face and voice betrayed his anxiety.

"I'll look after Nina if you want to go too", Azadeh said looking at Jina. She did. They didn't bother to change. Jina showed her Nina's room where the little girl was sleeping, walked around the flat, pointing out the bits Azadeh needed to know while he stood with his agitated face by the half-open door.

Sa'id's mother already knew from one of the crew and had gone by herself to Evin, *Qezel Qal'eh* and *Komiteh Moshtarek* in a vain search for her son. It took another two days and enquiries using Ahmad's influential contacts in the military and security services to find out that he was held in the *Komiteh*. Sa'id was released after 45 days. The usual beating and torture for a short stay. There is a Persian saying *ta seh nasheh, bazi nasheh* (there's no game till it gets to three). Sai'd's next time would be longer and harder.

Thereafter Azadeh would volunteer to baby sit for Nina. Regularly. Sometimes she would come earlier and cook them supper too. Then even earlier to chat. Always there to help out, not intrusively, at least not noticeably so, but helpful and dependable. Part of the apartment, though not quite family.

[1] *Fath-e baq* was written by Foruq Farrokhzad one Iran's greatest modern poets. Foruq was born in Tehran in 1934 and died in a car crash in 1967. She was the first female poet writing in Farsi to address the intimate details of female desire. Excerpts of *fath-e baq*: Michael C Hillmann, *Forugh Farrokhzad and her poetry*, Mage Publications and Three Continents Press 1987.

Chapter 17

Mamaqan

Changiz

The boys were sitting around on the battered mat, all young, all belonging to one or other group on the left. The thick crisscrossing metal bars in the single small window that opened to a view of the Alborz mountains formed more than a metal barrier between those inside and the outside world somehow alienating them even from so magnificent a view as the snow-capped mountain range stretching east to west across the north of the capital. Even the boys who occupied the top bunk of the two-tiered metal beds lined up against the walls rarely looked out. They had their own community inside and it was easier not to think of the outside world in concrete terms except on visitors' day. Here in the former Qajar palace turned into the Qasr Prison, the cell doors were often left open, and inmates could wander along the central corridor at will visiting each other's cells, a world away from the claustrophobic horrors of *Komiteh Moshtarek*. Today was visitors day.

Five fellow prisoners shared this cell, among them a young man Changiz knew from his Tabriz schooldays, Mamaqan, who got his name from his tiny village in Azerbaijan where he lived with his widowed mother. Somewhere along the journey through numerous prisons and prison cells his real name, Abdollah, had been left behind.[1]

It was late-morning when Changiz jumped into the cell as if he was about to say something comical and then changed his mind. His normal blush crawled up slowly from his neck. He looked awkward.

"Who was your visitor?" Mamaqan asked, guessing it was the father with or without his mother. It was Changiz's first outside visit since he was transferred from the *Komiteh*. He spoke in Azari. A sheepish smile appeared, unlike Changiz's usual grinsmile. Even his eyes were sheepish.

"No one", he replied after a pause, and flushed more at the stupidity of the words. "No one in particular", he quickly corrected, "a family member", and he would have flushed more if his capillaries had expansion room.

"Come off it", Mamaqan said. "Here's you without a single visitor for over three months and suddenly a nobody-in-particular comes for your first visit? You, a son of a khan, a *bacheh khan*,[2] and nobody-in-particular comes to visit you? Do you take us for a Turkish ass, *tork-e-khar*", Mamaqan went on in his deep, deep bass voice and thick Azari accent that reverberated round the cell, and he gave baby-face Mamali a wink as apology for the unintended insult? He had switched to Farsi to avoid others around the mat asking the same question. There were a few other Azari speaking cellmates with a majority Farsi speakers, though some of them could understand Azari. There was an unspoken agreement to speak Farsi in the cell to be inclusive. Everyone called him by his nickname, Mamaqan. Changiz was definitely the son of a *khan*. A destitute *khan* but nonetheless a son-of-a-khan, a *bacheh khan*. No mistaking that, the way he stood erect. And his reserved confidence, not totally concealed by his natural modesty.

"Alright. Alright. Stop pestering me", Changiz said, and his shy smile slipped back and expanded into a grin, looking comical sitting beneath the bristly thick dark brown moustache harmonising well with the now crimson background. "You won't believe what happened". He fidgeted. Then a bigger grin pushed his moustache up against that dominant nose of his, followed by an even deeper flush. "It was my father the old *khan*. He had come up from the province, the *velayat*,[3] and came straight from the bus station here, to Qasr. As soon as the old man saw me, without as much as a how-do-you-do-how-has-it-been, just blurted out, '*pesar-jan*, son dear, just go ahead and do whatever they are asking you to do and I'll take you back with me to the *valayat* this very afternoon', and then dug up two bus tickets to Tabriz he had already bought from his pocket." Changiz chuckled, the brown bristles tickling his nose as it rode up and down the upper lip.

"What on earth are you talking about?" baby-faced Mamali said in his soft, almost feminine voice totally congruent with his baby-face and twittered as was usual after he said anything. "Sit down man, and tell us exactly what happened," baby-faced Mamali went on twittering high-pitched. Changiz sat.

"You know my father, don't you?" knowing full well they did. He had talked about his father enough times. He took a swig of water from a half-full mug to calm his laughter. "Well, there he was, the old *khan*, still a *khan*, albeit a little lost for wear, on the other side of the glass partition, there he was, my father, traveling all the way up from the *velayat* today, his first time in the capital, and he drove straight here from the bus station, not even stopping for lunch. We hadn't seen each other for months, not since my arrest, a hundred and nine days to be exact, and without any preface just blurted out: why don't you just give them what they want, and I'll take you back home with me this afternoon? It wasn't a question. It was an order, a command. To be obeyed." Changiz took another swig of water. His eyes were dancing between the listeners, one or two grinning as they pictured the dialogue of the old man and the dutiful elder son. "This is what I managed to get out of him," Changiz went on putting the mug down. "When news of my arrest reached the village, the villagers had gone up to him and had said: 'Khan, why don't you go up to town and fetch your son back?' they had said. To them Tehran was just like Tabriz, another large town without door or form, *bi dar-o-peikar* as you say over here. If he is a *khan* here in the village, he must be a *khan* there too, in the city. A *khan* here is a *khan* everywhere. And a *khan* has to do what *khans* do. And that's what the old *khan*, did. He took himself off to the capital to fetch me, his oldest son, back. It took me the entire ten minutes visiting time trying to convince him that it was not up to me. But it was utterly useless; he simply didn't get what I was talking about. I can't go back empty handed, he kept repeating. My entire honour, *aberu*, depends on you. Just get down from the devil's ass[4] and do as I say. You all know I have never refused my father anything." They knew and they knew his father too. You don't do that to your father. Not up there. Not to a *khan* no matter how down and out. "Don't you understand, you stupid mule, he kept saying to me, I can't go back to them empty handed." When he spoke the words of the old *khan* he switched to his father's Qareh Daqi Azari. Another burst of laughter. Baby-faced Mamali twittered.. Everyone sat around silent, each creating their own image of eh old man pleading with his obstinate son. Mamaqan too was seriously deep in thought, but then he nearly always looked serious, then after a pause, a mysterious smile appeared.

"Didn't I tell you about my aunt?" Since no one said anything Mamaqan stood up. "One night they, the villagers in Mamaqan heard someone howling in our village graveyard," Mamaqan said, his deep bass voice resonating again. It was the middle of the night. Everyone, young and old, men, women and children rushed over to the graveyard. And there she was, my old aunt, looking up to the sky howling like a wolf, howling at the full moon. She was talking to God. In Mamaqan that howling means I've stopped believing in you, God! I don't believe in you anymore! That was soon after they had arrested me, you know. She was cursing God because he hadn't stopped them arresting his favourite nephew. When she saw a crowd gathered around her, when she saw that she had an audience, she became even bolder and started hollering, cursing God, real crude curses. Cursing God's mother, sister. Curses with words like whore, and more. No one dared go closer. Everyone was afraid they would get caught up in her curse." And Mamaqan looked up to the concrete sky and repeated the aunt's curses.

"Oh, God doesn't mind. He loves being cursed." It was Mehdi, another Azari friend visiting from another cell, who had sat quietly in the corner. "God is pretty used to curses. He's been so busy unleashing evil on us humans that he's got used to being cursed," and he gave out a big guffaw, then suddenly felt guilty. As a relapsed Mujahedin member, Mehdi had been close to that God not that long ago.[5] He was in the process of rejecting one path and not quite sure what to put in its place.

"You should know. You were carrying his gun!"[6] Mamaqan said with a mischievous grin.

"Well Mehdi's God got his own back on Mamaqan, didn't he?" Mamali quipped and took a deep breath and twittered. "God couldn't touch his auntie but his henchmen here on earth sure gave him a good hiding, didn't they," he added almost as if he was jealous.

"True but this *hamvelayati* of ours, Mamaqan, sure paid them torturers back good," Changiz quickly interceded, long sensing the imperceptible friction slowly developing between the frustrated artist Mamali, and the tall burly village boy. He looked over to Mamaqan who was still standing, still in his village graveyard. "Remember that time when you were being carried up the stairs to the infirmary on the back of that policeman, when you were sort of semi-conscious, didn't you give that poor policeman following close behind a god-awful kick. Like the *turk-e-khar* donkey that you are. Just like that. Knocked him down the stairs. You may not remember, you were too far gone, but that must have cost you a nice thrashing afterwards! Isn't that the case?"

Mamaqan just smiled. He was too humble to agree. A long deep smile of satisfaction and memory spread over his face with its month-old-growth of hair. He had survived the torture, the Apollo,[7] and whatever they threw at him, and kept his mouth shut and his inner dignity.

The old *khan* spent another four months in Tehran. He could not face the villagers back home. When the *khan* finally plucked enough courage to return to the village, his mother, Changiz's grandmother, became convinced that her beloved Changiz must be dead. No amount of reassurance would convince her otherwise.

"He would have come back with the *khan* if he were alive," the grandmother kept repeating. "They killed my boy," and she would just sit in a corner and sob.

"But why would anyone kill our Changiz?" everyone would say to her. Even though he had been to Tehran and gone to university, the only one from their village, Changiz was still one of them. There was simply no one like him. No one would kill such a good man, they thought.

"No one would kill such a good man *ammeh-jan*," a cousin told his aunt. The grandmother gave him a strange almost angry look with her tear-red eyes disbelieving every word.

"No, she said, he is dead otherwise he would be sitting here in front of me.

If you are so sure he is alive, then curse him. Curse him real good. Go on, curse him if you dare!"

You never cursed a dead person if you didn't want the dead to come back and haunt you. And that is what the young cousin did. Real heavy curses, mother, sister, father, not a soul spared. The old woman smiled and smiled, and her eyes became young.

*

Later that year Mamaqan's mother sold a goat, her only possession, bought a bus ticket to Tehran and visited her son. Just that once. It was the only visit Mamaqan had in the seven years he spent behind bars. He was released five years later, just before the Revolution, took part in it, in a newly created revolutionary left wing group alongside Changiz, baby-faced Mamali and Mehdi;[8] opposed the newly formed Islamic regime, went back to his beloved Mamaqan, set up a children's library there, then moved to Tabriz and shaped the organisational network for their group, was arrested by the Islamic regime but managed to hide his true identity and was released after a month or so, returned to Tehran and took a house in one of the villages around the capital, was recaptured, endured once more terrible torture without cracking and was executed in 1983. At his death he was 31.

[1] Abdollah Afsari, nicknamed Mamaqan, the name of his birth village in Azerbaijan. He too joined the new organisation Rahe Kargar, after his release on the eve of the revolution, after 7 years in captivity. He was arrested by the Islamic regime in spring 1983, tortured and shot in autumn of 1984.
[2] Khan is a tribal chief or a large landowner. Changiz's father was a landowner without much land.
[3] *Velayat* here refers to the province, in Changiz's case a village in *Qareh Daq* in East Azarbeijan.
[4] *Az khar-e sheitoon biya pai'n*, a popular saying in Farsi.
[5] Mehdi Khosrowshahi Baradaran was born in Tabriz, but studied in Tehran Polytechnic. He was involved in the formation of what later became the

Mojahedin Oganisation. He was arrested by SAVAK in 1971 and endured severe tortures. In the Shah's prison on a life sentence, he became attracted to Marxism and helped form the communist organisation Rahe Kargar. After the revolution he helped direct the heroic resistance to the so-called cultural revolution in Tehran University. Later he took charge of the Khuzestan province in the south at the onset of the Iran-Iraq war. He was arrested alongside his wife and sister by the Islamic regime, stood up to the torturers and was executed in autumn 1981. We will meet his sister Nayyer later in our story.

[6] The Mojahedin were a radical Islamic organisation greatly influenced by the teachings of the Islamist thinker, Ali Shariati, but also attracted by aspects of Maoism. They were discussing tactics when the Fadai' attacked the gendarmerie outpost in Siahkal. After that they too resorted to the armed struggle.

[7] For a description of the famous Apollo see chapter: Third Time Less Lucky.

[8] Abdollah Afsari (Mamaqan) helped create Rahe Kargar, a Marxist group formed inside the Shah's prisons from the amalgamation of many experienced cadres from a range of revolutionary groups, Marxist and non-Marxist. They rejected the armed struggle, and also subservience to either the Soviet Union or China. The organisation grew and was to play an important role in the early years after the revolution. He was executed by the Islamic Republic in May 1983.

Chapter 18

Iran-shenasi

Ahmad

I need to understand my country, Ahmad was explaining to Jina. It was not clear, not even to himself, if he was explaining his mission or seeking approval. *Iran-shenasi*, he called it, Iranology, on par with sociology or biology, the '-ogy' flicking it up the ladder of worth. And he plunged into it in his usual obsessive way, traveling to all parts of that squatting cat that looked back at you from the map of the country, with its head in Azerbaijan, its front paws resting on the oil rigs of Khuzestan, and its back legs stretching back into Pakistan. A cat carrying the huge salty Caspian on its back and seemingly floating on the Persian Gulf. Before his travels there was an interlude.

After coming out of *Qezel Qal'eh*, the idea of forming an armed group and going to Palestine for training with some of Zia Zarifi's comrades had briefly preoccupied him. Zia had not cracked under torture and his former contacts were still active outside. Their revolutionary fervour, that excitement, the sense of self-sacrifice for something greater echoed his own. Like two vibrating strings, one passion jumped across to vibrate the others. But he could not entirely convince himself. The whole project seemed too schematic and not really thought through. Maybe it's my obsession for perfection, he thought. Maybe I read too much. Maybe I sink into detail. But in the end his doubts over tactics remained. Maybe I am right to doubt. Had not the world's greatest, most experienced guerrilla commander failed in the Bolivian hinterland?

I don't think we know enough about our people, he argued with his new friends, as he had with Bijan. Jina stayed behind with her little Nina and worked in the office.

He travelled the lengths and breadth of the country, from Bonab in Azarbaijan in the north, to Marivan in Kurdistan, Ilam on the borders of Iraq, down south to Bandar Lengeh a port half hidden from the rest of the country behind mountains, with its women wearing the eagle-like *neqab*,[1] a particularly dehumanising form, its Arabic-speaking people forgotten by the Farsi-speaking Tehrani elite. In central Iran on the borders of the Kavir desert he visited Shahr-Babak close to his birthplace Yazd, and breathed the hot desert wind.

He would accept any assignment that gave cover to his project. Picking up any hikers, staying in remote villages, *caravanserais*, tea houses, anywhere that put him in touch. What did they cultivate? Who bought it? How did they deal with extortions from the local gendarmes, landlords, *khans*? Trust had to be gained. His warm, sincere smile that danced around his eyes even when his mouth was busy asking. People know, no, instinctively feel, honesty when they see it. He would stalk the poorer quarters of the towns. He would note down the different districts, their economy, what people did for work. And he wrote monographs. Monograph on Bandar Abbas, its poorer districts, its migrant inhabitants. Monographs on the smuggling trade in the Gulf ports. Monographs on Chabahar, the tail of the cat that floated on the mat of the Persian Gulf, where the Shah was about to erect a huge project for a deep-sea port, outside the Hormuz Straights, that was open to the Indian ocean and hard to blockade. Ahmad himself later became part of that multi-billion-dollar project. He was particularly interested in the Arab tribes, the villagers, in the area close to his childhood Khorramshahr. How did they relate to the *sheikhs*? And to the security services who were particularly active in those oil-rich provinces, the cat's front paws.

He was writing, and his soul, his mind, his hopes, and his intellect crystalised into the clean, neat handwriting, where the slope ending some letters glide into his optimism and the precision, and chain of adjectives try to define his world as precisely as language allows, and where the structure of the document speaks of his determination to help transform his world for the better. This was script as an intimate mirror into a life in the making.

One memory, however, stayed with him till old age. A friend took him to see a derelict mansion in West of Bushehr, that had once belonged to a tribal *khan* or a smuggler. He wanted Ahmad to convert it into a modern hotel. They walked into a huge almost derelict rectangular mansion, once white and commanding, sitting once proud on the banks of the azure Gulf and he emerged into the sea air weeping. He had entered the static world of the forgotten, walked past family after family cramped from wall to wall in rooms on either side of the long, corridor spanning the rectangle's length, the look of timeless hopelessness of the children as they gazed out from their rooms, on either side of that interminable central corridor sharing dust, dirt and hunger in that old white building whose better days are buried in memory, age-unfathomable children looking up at the two alien men walking by, eyes too large for their emaciated faces, glaring and not seeing those two strange beings from the world of the living, haunted him, haunts him, haunts me as he narrates it.

Jina bore it all but gradually the passion oozed out of their relationship. He was too preoccupied with his passion to know his country, to nurture the love between them, and love needs to be nurtured like a garden. And the nature of their relationship changed, rather like the yogurt the peasants hung up in a cotton sack allowing it to drain away and concentrate, becoming more compact but without the runny ease of its more fluid former self. She bore his preoccupations with less and less runny ease. Love got left outside. But at their core was still a deep love.

They did share the theatre together. He had originally met Sa'id Soltanpour in a bookshop opposite the gates of Tehran University. Said's book of poetry *Sedaye Namira* had just been published and they ended up discussing it in that shop, standing up. It was the beginning a lifelong friendship. Ahmad contributed to the design of Yashar's *Teachers* that Said directed. It had a brief life in the Iran-America Cultural Society before being raided out. SAVAK objected to a scene where one actor gave a red book to another. Everyone understood what that little red book signified in that leaden atmosphere. The next play Brecht's *The Visions of Simone Machard* came on the screen in the amphitheatre of the Tehran University's School of Beaux Art with great success. No empty space, even for standing. It had become a place for the left to assemble. Ahmad had both designed the décor and made major financial contributions. SAVAK watched, noted, but did not interrupt. The play was not put on stage again.

They started collaborating on Maxim Gorky's *The Petty Bourgeois*. Ahmad hired a large house with a large hall for the rehearsals. It soon became a meeting place for anyone with a left leaning.

It was mid-autumn, a clear orangeing morning, when Ahmad knocked on the grey door of the rehearsal house.

[1] Also spelt *niqab* - a garment of clothing that covers the face leaving only the eyes exposed, worn by some Muslim women as a form of *hijab*. In the Gulf provinces the *neqab* is like a face mask covering eyes, nose and mouth.

Chapter 19

The diviner

Jina

It was an unusually warm day. Late autumn day in Tehran, warm and dry. The air was pungent, almost brittle. Stagnant fumes scratched the back of your throat. He got up later than his usual six. He had had a late night at Philip's wedding party. Philip, Jina's brother, was a gentle, quiet person. Not the same as his sister who could be quite fiery, explosive, even intolerant, but with a sharp perception of nuances. Sometimes she could feel the waves of thought as if they were wet on her nose. It is a form of empathy, Jina believed. Reading feelings and thought by tiny gestures, movements of eyes. Pupil size. Faint changes of colour imperceptible to all but the empathic. Tiny lines around the mouth and eyes. That's how soothsayers work, isn't it?

Once, midsummer, she had gone with Ahmad's old aunt to see a wise man. Deaf and dumb. Aunty couldn't read. Brought me along to read for her, she said. They had to change taxis four times. It was somewhere south of Tehran's railway station. Beyond Meidan-e Qar. How did that get its name, a name that rhymes with 'far' and describes a place that is both roundabout and cave? Probably some caves in a hill, or depression, that were turned to hovels. Long ago. Ahmad had told her how he had rented close by for his immersion in the life of the marginalised. They walked a long narrow winding alleyway that took her back to her nanny's stories. Strange how history coexists with brash modernity? Uneven development Ahmad had explained. That's the way capitalism spreads.

They entered a courtyard, sunk a few steps from the alleyway, through a low wooden door painted dark olive-green. Vomit-like, flaking, revealing cracked wood underneath. Seen the world. All round the courtyard were rooms with doors opening to a raised veranda. In the centre was a small pond filled to near brim, a raised brim with a shallow gully, the *pashur,* running all round to catch the overflow. A copper tap, on top of an upside-down L-shaped pipe rising vertically from the side, leant over the pond. Dripping, Jina noted. Never much good at plumbing here. Like a good architect she had scanned the architecture before noticing that there were people, all women, sitting round the courtyard against the wall. With gaps where there were doors opening on stairs going down into the deep. Must be the toilet or kitchen or the *ab anbar* where they stored water. Gets a bit stale down there. All sludgy that water. I do hate that slimy feel. And the smell. Most of the women were wearing a white cotton *chador*[1] with tiny flowers, like her's. She was glad she had chosen this and not the black one as *aunty-joon* had suggested. Some were wearing black though. How could she know the etiquette, or customs? Assyrian girls don't cover their heads. She was sweating even under white cotton. What was it like under *aunty-joon's* thick black silk?

Their turn came some hours later. A young girl was sitting at the door, no more than thirteen or fourteen, she guessed, her flowery white cotton *chador*, over a fading-flowery cotton scarf, perhaps a hand-me-down from her mother, the *chador* wound round her waist and tied in a knot in front, firm, freeing both her hands which she regularly used to pull the slipping *chador* back over her scarved head. The aunt pulled out her purse from under her black *chador*. You pay when you leave *khanum*, the young girl said, and adjusted her *chador*. *Aqa* only takes money if he can solve your problem. The old, white-bearded *sheikh* sitting on a *kilim* at the end of a room otherwise bare, leaning slightly forwards, his back not touching the hand-woven carpet-covered cushion. He pushed towards them an exercise book. The sort you bought for primary school. It was open on a blank page. Obviously passed many hands. The corner of the blank page bent forwards revealing a tightly written handwriting. Child-like. What is the problem? it read. Jina wrote down the aunt's problem in her neat, slightly slanted script. Her son was addicted to heroin. Nothing had worked. She was desperate. As the aunt spoke and Jina wrote she saw the old man looking straight into her eyes. He is lip reading she thought. He had remarkably large eyes for such a small face. Set deep. Deepened more by the silvery beard. The bearded *aqa* then took the aunt's hands, both hands, and looked into her eyes. For a long time. Can I blink, the aunt wondered? I can't help you, he wrote in his child-like tight script. He is beyond my control. There is little anyone can do for him, and he pushed the exercise book towards them. Tears rolled down the aunt's cheeks, like translucent pearls, as Jina read the words. Actually, they had escaped her eyes when he had begun to write. She had pre-read it with the eye-to-eye tongue. A language of many adjectives and a few emotive verbs. Read it again the aunt asked. Now she looked calm. The last door had closed, and she resigned herself to fate. She was a believer. Not I, the atheist Assyrian Jina thought and on impulse reached out and took the exercise book, turned the page and wrote on an empty page. She was married. Bilateral love. Something felt not right, she could not tell what. Could *aqa* untie the knot? He went through the same motions for an uncomfortable time. When you are in skin-to-skin contact, time follows different trajectories. Different time rules even for hand-to-hand. He was feeling his way through her reactions. Someone very close to you faces grave danger, he wrote. And there is another person, a woman. Problems. You face many years of turmoil that won't resolve until you take a long journey. A one-way journey. She shuddered slightly. Felt a blush. Then smiled inside. Nonsense. Platitudinous commonplace. She often expressed doubts in big words. Every woman has another woman in the wings. And men too. They paid for one visit to the young girl as they left the room. Who was she? It was late afternoon. The rows of chador-clad women covered the courtyard walls.

She jumped out of her daydream as Ahmad was leaving, having had his *sangak* flat stone-baked bread and white cheese. His one glass of slightly sweetened tea. The last sip left forlorn in the glass. Yes. I could have made a successful career as a soothsayer, she thought. If I was male. And old. And with a dreamy white beard. Grave danger I would say, deepening my voice.

"Why don't you get some *sangak* bread on your way back? I have lots to do in the office," were her last words.

He took the car out of the communal parking space. I will drop by the rehearsal on my way. They were working on Gorky's *Petit Bourgeois* in the big house he had rented for the purpose.

[1] *chador* - the shapeless piece of cloth, often in black, that covers everything, exposing only the face, or in the more devout, only one eye.

Chapter 20

Their Apollo

Ahmad

"I knocked on the grey door of the house," Ahmad began, and his voice took on *that nostalgic opaqueness that he used when he sank into memory, the past floating out to the present like it was being filmed it in a single take. We were talking by phone. This is his story:*

He parked his Cadillac a couple of alleyways away, a distance from the rehearsal house. That was a routine precaution and he walked over to the grey door and knocked. The door opened and immediately an arm shot out and a man in a grey suit took one arm as another grey-suited man took the other. They both wore scruffy suits looking as if they had been slept in, he noticed, as he quickly assessed the situation. Quite a contrast to his elegant navy-blue jacket, under which he wore a simple light grey pullover over light blue shirt. His trousers were well ironed. He looked like a man on his way to an important meeting. It was still late autumn.

Tashrif biyarid too, come in, one of the two men said politely in a soft feminine voice issuing out of a very forgettable face. It was as if he was being invited to a party. The entire theatre crew was lined up along the walls of the courtyard. He wasn't really surprised at the raid. SAVAK must have become suspicious of the comings and goings in that house, so close to Tehran University and the Shah's Marmar Palace. It had, after all, become a meeting

104

place for anyone on the left.

They were loaded onto a bus without any blindfolds and he felt even more reassured. Couldn't be that serious then, he thought. They took them to *Komiteh Moshtarek*, the interrogation centre shared between SAVAK and the municipal police. It was a purpose-built three-floored brick building, circular with small windows facing the street, sinister looking, perhaps by design. It was situated in a back street behind the old *Baq Melli* and the old *Sepah Avenue* leading to *Toopkooneh*,[1]

"That's the square where they hung your great-grandfather," he quipped, interrupting the flow of narration and immediately went back to his memories, without waiting for me to comment.

They were lined up along a wall in what appeared to be a large reception room. The two grey-suited men stood on one side, hands behind their back. A tall man with thick black hair entered the room. It was Azodi, one of the chief interrogators and in charge of the *Komiteh* whose reputation for savagery preceded him. He walked towards them with his thick black eyebrows in a frown, in a studied fierceness, and walked along the line looking each in the eye. He stopped in front of Ahmad.

"What is your name?" Ahmad told him his actual first name.

"Family name?" he gave the second part of his double-barrelled name.

"What do you do?" Student, he replied. I wasn't lying as technically he was at the university though by now it was 12 years since he had enrolled.

"Address?" he gave his parent's home.

"Ever been arrested?" No, he said.

"Ever been called in for questioning?" No.

Azodi frowned then passed on and asked a few of the others the same questions. An hour or two later they were back in their cells. Ahmad shared his with Reza Kianian, an actor in the theatre group. It was the poor boy's first arrest, and he looked a little scared. Ahmad immediately chatted up the guard who was a young conscript.

"If you are putting on the kettle for tea, or need any mopping or cleaning with a tee, I'm at your service. Any time." He was a veteran prisoner and was trying to reassure the poor novice.

That same evening, they took him for his first interrogation. He was taken to a bare room with two smallish metal desks and another interrogator, a young man he had not seen sitting behind one of them on a metal chair. The questions had barely begun when they brought in a young man into the room. He was deathly pale, sweating, scared, his head bowed, and he was avoiding eye contact. Ahmad recognised him from his Khorramshahr days and immediately saw the trap. His improvised alias was about to melt. He tried to ignore the new arrival.

The interrogator turned to the young man and asked him the same routine questions. Then came the question: have you ever been in prison or called in for questioning?

"Yes," the young man answered, in a whisper.

"When?"

"Because of this man," the young man answered pointing to me with his chin still avoiding eye contact. "He gave me stuff to read."

"What's his name?"…

They took him back to his cell. At six next morning they came for him. This time he was blindfolded. he immediately recognised the distinct high-pitched voice of Javan, the bogus doctor who had interrogated him in Qzel Qal'eh. Peeping from underneath the blindfold he saw a thick folder on the table. They had caught up with his subterfuge.

They took off his blindfold. The room was full of menacing-looking men in suits. There was Hosseini whose real name was Mohammad Ali Sha'bani. He too liked to be called 'doctor' even though he had only four years of schooling. With a face that others had likened to a gorilla, he looked like a thug and behaved like one. There was Hooshang Azqandi who was also called Manuchehr. There were a few others Ahmad did not recognise, all standing round like they were waiting for a wrestling match. And of course, Javan, who knew him from the *Qezel Qale'h* days. Hosseini came forward.

"What's your name?" he gave the same names he had previously given. A lightening slap hit his left cheek. Hosseini's hand was heavy.

"What do you do?" Student. Another slap. Same side. "We are not those same idiots you fooled four years ago," Hosseini shouted. That barrel chest of his was an impressive bellow. "We have your university strike file as well. We know everything about you. Are you going to talk or no, you son-of-a-whore?" he screamed in his left ear, so close he felt the warm spittle.

"I don't have anything more to say," he answered as calmly as he could. Hosseini grabbed him by the scruff of the shirt and dragged him to the door. "Let me show you something," he said as he dragged him out of the door onto the veranda, turning left there. The *Komiteh* was a circular building with rooms on each floor all round opening inside onto a veranda, no more than a metre and half wide, that encircled a central courtyard with a pond in the middle. It had three floors. The verandas were separated from the central courtyard by a fence and a metal mesh that went all the way from the first floor to the top to stop anyone jumping off. The building was purpose built.

Hosseini dragged Ahmad by the collar to another room a couple of doors down. Almost identical to the one he had before. There, crumpled by the wall that was smeared with dried blood, was one of the boys from the theatre group who had been arrested a couple of days earlier.

"Tell him what you told me," Hosseini barked, and the young man shrank into himself.

"I told them everything," he said under his breath without looking at Ahmad.

They had found a pamphlet by Pouyan, one of the founders of the Fadai', in his possession. Ahmad had given it to him, according to what he had told them under torture.

"I told them everything," he repeated barely audible, glued to the bloodied wall.

"*Goh khordi gofti,*" is what Ahmad said to him in a voice full of anger, contempt and pity. You eat shit!

The next few minutes were lost in a haze. All he remembered were the blows and kicks raining on him from all sides on the way to another room. He seemed to be flying in the air with kicks and punches keeping him airborne.

Doctor Hosseini was in charge of the torture but there were five or six of them. All working on a single body. From six thirty that morning till about 9 at night. Just before that he heard through the clouds someone say, 'looks like he is dying'. Two soldiers carried him like a sack of watermelons in a blanket and dumped him in his cell.

His jaw had been broken. His testes were swollen. His legs were a mess. His feet were bleeding. His hands unrecognisable. They had burnt him with candles. He could not open his eyes. His scalp had cracked in several places. His spine was broken though the pain in the legs masked all the other pains. He didn't know about his eyes or spine till later. No unscathed spot in his body. Nearly 400 blows of the cable he had counted before he lost count. And then came the Apollo, nicknamed after the moon mission.

That invention, a modern version of a mediaeval rack, a monstrous contraption that only sick minds could have concocted, consisted of a metal base with straps that bound your hands on its arm rests and your legs straight down on the metal base, strapped down at the ankles with the soles of your feet exposed to whipping. You sat bolt upright against a metal pole and a metal hood was lowered on your head with two metal projections poking in your ear, immobilising the head. Your screams reverberated around that hood.

The interrogation was a replay of the inquisition, the home-made metal box, our Apollo. The questions, repeated between beating were the same: who gave you the pamphlet? Ahmad had only one reply.

"It came in the post" he replied, and he stuck to the same story. "I have no idea who sent it. I put it in the dashboard of my car. I was giving that man a lift. He asked for a cigarette, and I said take one from the dashboard. He saw the pamphlet. Can I take it? Yes, if you want, I replied. I don't know what it is. I did not give it to him. He took it." That was his story, and he stuck to it. Two or three times he asked them to stop the beating. He will tell all, a chance for a breathing space, and then repeated the same story. The car, the dashboard, the cigarette, the request. He didn't give it to the man, he insisted. Persisted. Somewhere floating around he held the image of Bijan and Zia Zarifi, who too had ridden the Apollo uncracked.

"He took it himself. He took it himself. I didn't give it to him." It was his story, and in it was his dignity. His self.

Five or six people worked on him. Sometimes together, sometimes in relay. They needed a quick answer if they were to catch those who had passed on the pamphlet to me. He stuck to my story. They strung him up. At first they avoided hitting his right hand, maybe to allow him to write his confessions, but later they burnt that too. Then they broke his jaw. A hand had appeared from somewhere within reach of his teeth and crazed with pain that he was, he just sunk his teeth into that hand. Biting, biting deep into flesh, oh, it felt so good. He heard Hosseini scream, and he bit harder. There was pain and real hatred in that bite of his and they had to hit and hit and hit to make his jaw let go of the bleeding hand and only unlocked it by breaking it. That was an animal biting.

Then they dumped him in his cell, half dead.

"What happened?" Kianian asked terrified. He must have looked like a skinned prey.

"I hadn't done anything" I managed to whisper through my broken jaw. *"But even if I had I wouldn't tell it to these madar ghabeha, those motherfuckers."* I wanted to give Kianian courage to resist.

But it was hard, hard. Very hard.

His voice trailed downwards, a ribbon that flew round the world tying up all the pain in a timeless cocoon. Yesterday, today and always.

"What happened from this night onwards is another story. I'll tell you another day, he ended."

He was there in that bloodied cell. Reliving that hell. I put the phone down and wept.

[1]Now *Emam Khomeini Square.*

109

Chapter 21

Lump of meat

Ahmad

It is amazing how long it takes to rebuild what had been destroyed in a single day. They had carried him like a watermelon and now treated him like butcher's meat. Every day he would crawl to the infirmary. The cold concrete floors burnt like red-hot coal, and the twenty-centimetre climb over the iron rim to the cell door on his return was like climbing a rocky mountain on a raw stump. There they bandaged his foot, where skin had been beaten to death and meat had detached from bone.

Every day he had to make the same drawn-out short trip up the iron rim-rocks on glowing red-cold concrete. Afterwards, chained to the rails in the balcony facing the central courtyard all day, waiting to be interrogated. He had nothing to say and, in any case, would have difficulty saying much through a broken jaw. Some guards, passing him lying chained, would give him a kick as they would a dog's carcass. Once Azodi, the chief interrogator whose real name was Mohammad Hassan Naseri, with his huge bulk came, looked at him, grinned, mounted and stood on his leg. Even if he wanted to scream, there was none left to be let free. In that sealed world of Dantean inferno, humanity had been almost shut out. Scientists say humans are by nature empathic. Altruistic. In that sealed space, science had been erased leaving only the sorcery of pain.

Talking about pain is like talking about a smell, it alludes imagination, memory, words, and emotion. It is a survival tool for a species with ability to plan a future. He could not sleep for three days. Kianian also felt his pain and he too did not sleep for three days, spending moment to moment at his side. Empathy too is a survival tool. Years later when he was telling this for the first time to me, I too melted and saw the image of Christ on the cross. Not the lurid Spanish versions, but the one by Matthias Grünwald with its details of torn flesh crisscrossing the torso on the cross. A pain that was deeper than mere flesh. The pain of our history.

Empathy, however, must have found a crack and had crept into the cell. Empathy is immortal. You can always find me, empathy said through his cellmates. They gave up their one cigarette per person per day ration. Lighted one and put it in his broken mouth for a few puffs. Then extinguished it to prolong its life. Three cigarettes to last the whole day, his sole analgesic.

It was day four. They took him to an interrogation room on the second floor. Two or three people whom he knew from the rehearsals were writhing on the floor. Others were standing with their backs to the wall, like gladiators waiting their turn in the arena. Strangely, they told him to sit on a high stool, the sort you get in bars with a cushiony top. To get those on the floor to start talking, they had to see the state he was in. They weren't interested in what Ahmad had to say anymore. Ahmad was the spectacle. Ahmad was the torture.

As he struggled up and sat down the foam let out a fart-like noise.

"Ahmad is deflating," one of the interrogators quipped, meaning he has lost his pride.

"I am only just starting to puff up," he managed a reply through his broken jaw. The interrogator muttered some insult, but left it at that, not wanting to lose face in front of the occupants of the floor.

Another day, day eight or nine, while having his bandage changed in the infirmary Hosseini, the one who had his hand bitten, came in by chance.

"Is this motherfucker still alive?" He screamed and kicked him off the infirmary chair, and kicked him through the door, kicked him down the corridor, kicked him down some steps.

Every day he would crawl up his mountain path to the infirmary. One day the cell door opened and in walked a familiar face. It was the guard who Ahmad had helped with the cleaning and distributing the food those early days after his arrest. A giant Kurd, with rather an ugly face and a squat nose as if someone had inadvertently squashed it as a kid. He had been away somewhere on some duty or other. As he walked into the cell his squashed nose was hit by the stench in the air. At first, he thought someone had defecated and was about to shout an abuse when he saw Ahmad lying in the corner. A wounded wreck of a man he had got to know.

"What have they done to you?" he almost shouted in Kurdish. "Didn't you tell me you are here on a misunderstanding?" he said to Ahmad, now in Farsi in his deep Kurdish accent.

"They beat me for no reason," Ahmad replied and grimaced for a smile.

The big Kurd picked him up and carried him on his back across the iron rocks of the cell door, up the flight of stairs into the infirmary. As he entered a halo of stench preceded and followed him, like an invisible cloud. The nurse began to open the bandages and the putrid cloud thickened into a suffocating fog.

"Why have you got yourself into this state?" the nurse blurted out and started swearing at him and at God and the prophet and everything he held sacred. He was looking at the pus oozing from the green-black rotten flesh hanging outwards from the sole of his feet. Behind it the yellow of the metatarsals were discolouring in protest. Thereafter the nurse would come down to the cell every day, change the bandage there and give him an injection. An antibiotic of sorts.

"You are a mess. You either go to hospital or die here" the Kurd said one day in his beautiful Kurdish accent, and the Kurd went off. He returned that afternoon, was it afternoon, with someone. Ahmad, lying supine in his burning fever, his clouded brain barely aware of General Zandi, head of the Anti-Sabotage Joint Committee standing over him. Zandi had one look at his foot and almost vomited.

"You, with your education, with that social standing of yours, what have you done to yourself? Why have you brought this onto yourself?" Ahmad was about to correct the general but decided to keep his reply to himself. Or maybe he only half heard what the general had said, or maybe he was just too exhausted. "I will send you to hospital," Zandi almost shrieked and walked out.

The big Kurd did not wait. He got a car, lifted Ahmad on his back, took him through the corridors, through the gate and out into the street, placed him somehow on the back seat, sat next to him and drove across Tehran to the police hospital in Bahar street. That was a street Ahmad knew well and had sipped *chai* in one of its many cafeterias many times. There, the Kurd fetched a wheelchair, with the help of the driver took him up the front stairs, through the door, into a big hall where the reception was and presented the documents to the receptionist. A man in a white coat came over, had one look at the foot, grimaced at the stench that had filled the hall, and refused to take him.

"We have told you guys hundreds of times you should have brought him earlier. We won't take this mess. Take him back", the white coat said and walked away.

No white coat was going to deter our Kurd. He rang back to the *Komiteh*, haggled at both ends and finally got Ahmad accepted. With a victorious smile on his thick brown lips, he wheeled him through two corridors, crossed a dirty grey screen behind which on the right was a room with three beds. Only the middle one was empty, the other two being occupied by young men. The same day he was taken to theatre to cut out the rotting tissue and place a drain for the pus.

Years later he would remember how the squeaking wheels of the nurse's trolley approaching his bed was a messenger of impending unbearable pain and he would grip the bars on the back of the bed and squeeze the metal till his fingers hurt to stop himself screaming as she cleaned his wound. There was no skin on the sole of his feet, just raw bone. It took two months and a skin graft to begin healing. He was to endure two more months of daily torture.

A week later they wired his jaw. ·

*

Then came the long hurting and ambiguity. Taken back to *Komiteh Moshtarek,* he was at first thrown into a stony cold basement cell. In the corner a forlorn young lad was lying alone, crumbled like a rag. Ahmad smiled at him and shuffled closer to the young man who smiled back. He was a student wrapped up in a single grey army blanket, softly shivering. Soon the cold that permeated every corner of their cell sank through Ahmad's battered flesh and deep into his bones. They exchanged names and an immediate friendship developed between the miserable young lad and the physical wreck that was Ahmad, and when after an hour or more a hairy hand threw in an army blanket, a blanket which may have been grey from birth or simply dirt-grey, they shared their two blankets, wrapping themselves tight, trapping whatever air could be heated by their body. Gone was the caressing softness of a hospital bed.

They took him once a week to the hospital to change his bandages. He could not yet walk. He would not walk for many months. On one occasion they unwired and rewired his jaw. He could not eat normal food. Back in the cell, the student and later other inmates who shared that small space, fed him his daily allowance of a bottle of milk through a straw. On such a ration his body cannibalised whatever tissue was available, and he gradually shrank to a skeleton, covered by a layer of fat-free skin. His once fit healthy body, that had sent a shivering fire through Azadeh's veins that first time they met in his apartment, was now a wreck. His wounds, in competition with meagre food, were very slow to heal. And bones are utterly hopeless at retaining heat. It was cold that winter. Cold.

They moved him a floor higher, a little closer to the sun and warmth. Every time his name came up in someone else's story, he had to crawl on the floor to different parts for more interrogations. His file was thickening without gaining depth. They had one question, and he echoed the only answer he had. He stuck to his story, and no one could push him out of it. He had no visitors because he couldn't walk to the visitors' gallery. Out in the world, Nina grew fatherless, and others fought and died as he very slowly healed in that land of pain. The door to the world would open and close as bits and fragments of information came from cellmates who had visitors, like clips of old films being projected onto the wall, flickering, in segments and with important bits missing.

Four months after his arrest he heard of the murder of Bijan, Zia, Abbas, Aziz, and his other friends. The Argentinian-born Illich Ramirez Sanchez, nicknamed *Carlos the Jackal*, had taken hostage on behalf of the Palestinian group PFLP,[1] the Oil Ministers from OPEC countries who had gathered for an annual OPEC[2] meeting in Vienna. The next day SAVAK took Bijan Jazani and ten other prisoners from their cells in Evin, drove them to the hills behind Evin and shot them, presumably to pre-empt any attempt to ransom their release.

And so, for nearly two years, he gradually moved up in the building, going from single occupancy cells (though rarely alone) to ones for three or four. He met people he knew, artists, writers, students, workers, mostly people who had finished their preliminary interrogation. Some shared the space for days or weeks. Others were in transit from one circle of hell to the next. Some left for the airy prisons such as *Evin, Qasr, Qezel Qale'h* or *Gowhardasht* or prisons in the provinces, where there was more light and the sun occasionally shone, and where there were glimpses of the sky. There was no shortage of prisons in the Great Civilisation.

In those two years, the Fadai' and Mujahedin were engaged in their unequal battle against the regime across Iran. Hundreds died in street battles or police raids. Thousands were arrested and churned through the torture chambers of *Komiteh Moshtarek* and others. Ahmad never got to see Evin or *Qasr* or any other prison. He never experienced the prison communes being set up by political prisoners serving their sentence. Some would be returned to the *Komiteh* for more questioning and in a fragmentary way Ahmad became aware of the deep political debates and re-examinations that were taking place among the survivors of the armed struggle. Ahmad's own misgivings about strategy and tactics were being echoed by many others. Entirely new perspectives for struggle were being opened up. Prisons became a roving university, with many teachers coming through the revolving door that were prison cells. Right inside the Shah's prisons, there was an upward spiral of knowledge and resolve for the survivors of the generation of our story. For Ahmad it was a bit like 'reading' a book with many volumes in a random order and having to put it together in your head. It was also there that he learnt, again in broken fragments, like a stained-glass window, the bloody blows inflicted on the Fadai'.

The prison authorities didn't know what to do with him. They really had nothing on him and outside the walls of the Komiteh, wheels were turning in his favour. People of influence were working for his release. He had built the village by the Caspian that belonged to one of the Shah's brothers. A general, close to the Court, owned a haulage company and wanted a contract which needed the help of an executive who happened to be a close friend of Ahmad's father. A man high up in the SAVAK hierarchy needed the Karaj city's electricity board, who happened to be closely related to Ahmad, to connect and wire his large orchard for free. The general, close to the Court personally guaranteed Ahmad's good behaviour. Wheels turned and turned and slowly, after nearly two years, the drawbridge lifted. The country was slowly waking up from the sleep of passivity and fear.

[1] Popular Front for the Liberation of Palestine.
[2] Organisation of the Petrol Exporting Countries

Chapter 22

The phone kiosk

Fadai'

Bahman[1] usually left an indelible impression when you met him for the first time. Tall, handsome with large black eyes that spoke of depth, below a pair of thick black eyebrows poised above them like two scimitars. His moustache was carefully tended to match the curve of his eyebrows. Two scimitars up and two down giving his face a curious architectural symmetry. Definitely not a Stalin look. For some years he had lived a semi clandestine life but a few months before he had gone completely underground. Along with his sisters. The leadership had quickly realised his potential and given him the responsibility of running the Mazandaran[2] branch of the Fadai'.

Early morning that rainy day he left the regional capital, Sari, and crossed the Alborz Mountains southwards in a shared taxi. As he approached the village of Gadouk the early winter snows appeared on both sides of the road. A chilly wind through the top of the open front window of the Peikan flew passed his right cheek and slid down the back of his anorak. He tried to close the window.

"*Mibakhshid agha,*" sorry mister, the diver apologised in a squeaky voice that appeared to come out of his nose. "It's stuck," he added with a half-smile.

"Then put the heating on please," Bahman said. His voice was even warmer as it ricocheted off the driver's.

"Sorry, that's not working either, *mibakhshid,*" the driver said and sounded even stranger. A grin.

Bahman was traveling to Tehran for the day to make a few contacts and was due back in Sari, the provincial capital, that night or early the next morning. Once in the capital he took several taxis and arrived at a not-too-crowded street in Narmak, paid the taxi and walked casually to a phone booth, having surveyed the block, walked round it, approaching it from two different angles. He always took great care that he was not being followed. He fished in his pocket for a two-rial coin, the cost of a local call, fed the phone, and dialled his number. He only had four coins. You didn't carry too many 2-rial pieces, as it looked suspicious if you were stopped. He was dressed neatly with a dark blue anorak. Autumn had fallen off the trees and its rot curdled on the pavement. The cold early winter wind chilled the back of his neck in the open kiosk and slipped round to his unbuttoned shirt. He did not turn up the collar of his overcoat so as not to stand out. Then a SAVAK patrol Peikan passed by. You can only control what you can control. Death was sitting in that patrol car. Death in the form of a penitent collaborator[3] sitting in the back seat of the patrol car identifying comrades. Death saw him, pointed him out, and perhaps squirmed in inner shame. Death is often repentant but goes ahead anyway.

Bahman was deeply absorbed on finishing what he had to say in less than two minutes – that was a directive. In that way they thought they could avoid the call being traced. Momentarily he took his eyes off the road and death closed in on both sides, two carloads of armed men. No time to swallow the cyanide pill. No time to pull the pin of his grenade. He tried but they had pinned him down. He was overpowered by the wolf pack.

Death was particularly cruel to Bahman. Two or three days later, with legs gangrene-black he was transferred to military hospital number 502 only to die a few days later. Savage torture to get information rapidly before it became useless did not break his will. He held back for twenty-four hours, time enough for his comrades to vacate their lodgings. In death, the blackness of his beautiful black eyes seemed to spray pain across the watery curtain that dimmed his pupils. Silent and unseeing. He had invited death to block the pain. His moustache remained proud.[4]

They took a blue booklet from him. Some phone numbers. He knew that this was a foolish thing to carry around but what could he do. He had a terrible memory for numbers. A kind of numeric dyslexia. Like many of his comrades he took risks. Were they important numbers? Were they in code? Did they come in handy for SAVAK? No one can be sure.

Back in Mazandaran, Shamsi,[5] walked down the street and passed the meeting place casually looking around and entered a shop. It was a good place to meet, she had once said, because there is a SAVAK local headquarters nearby and where would be safer than meeting under the very nose of the devil. Shamsi was quite meticulous when it came to questions of safety. She always dressed neatly like a teacher when going to a rendezvous with a male comrade. It was not easy for a young man and woman to meet without being noticed in a provincial town like Sari even though the regime was happy for the young to get involved with issues that the young everywhere do. Only politics was out of bounds. Today there was the added safety of a light drizzle, making people less likely to be curious.

But today, this neatly dressed young woman in a light blue shirt under a blue-black hip-length coat and blue skirt over thick stockings, wearing an unremarkable cotton scarf tied up under her chin in a non-provocative way, with a rather child-like fringe of dark brown hair protruding in the front, was singly noticeable. This was not only because of her sparkling eyes, but because there was a white plaster cast poking out from the sleeves of the coat on her left arm on which she hung her otherwise unremarkable handbag.

"What happened to your hand," was the first thing Mostafa[6] said once they had met outside as she emerged from the haberdashery shop as if by chance and had shaken hands and exchanged the usual greetings usual people do when they meet outside a haberdashery shop.

"Lets walk and I'll tell you" Shamsi said through a smile. They walked up Ferdowsi street as Shamsi recounted how she was hit by a passing motorbike and broke her forearm, how she had to pretend it is not serious as the police had come over to investigate, how the bystanders had insisted that she should go to the hospital and how one of them brought her car and drove her over to the hospital, chatting in a nosey way, you don't sound Mazandarani, what will your husband say, oh not married yet? Oh dear, what a shame for someone so pretty, I have a girl like you, but I got her a really good husband and now she has two girls *mesl gol*, like a flower. She stayed with her right through the hospital visit and insisted on coming home with her and how she needed all her guile to put her off.

"I think I upset her" she ended. All this was said like machine gun fire, and they separated, having exchanged some written reports and instructions and agreed on the next meeting in two weeks.

"Ask him to meet me outside the Sepehr Cinema – that's where many boys and girls meet up and it safer" Shamsi said and they shook hands. She was referring to Bahman. Did the blue book know?

Zahra[7] also took risks. Even though she could not be sure of Bahman's safety, having not received the agreed safety signal, she decided not to vacate the apartment they shared in Sari as man and wife. After all they had an important meeting that was difficult to rearrange. The day after Bahman was arrested by that chance encounter on the phone booth, all the heads of the various teams in Mazandaran province were to meet in their house. Early that morning Zahra went out to meet Mostafa in the street.

"Bahman hasn't given the safety signal," she said, and a smile spread across her full lips. She was wearing a simple grey dress with thick stockings that hid her legs. Her black hair was cut to the chin and had been straightened to cover up their natural curls. Unmistakably a housewife her demeanour said.

"You can't go home then" Mostafa replied curtly looking her straight in the eye.

"Don't be silly," she said her smile confirmed by the glint in her brown eyes. You could see the passion in those eyes. A determination. Courage and a dash of recklessness. Undiminished, even boosted, by the killing of her partner a couple of years ago. Bahman often forgets to send safety signals, she thought. "He often forgets to send it," she said and was less sure.

But Mostafa was more cautious.

"If you are worried, I will go ahead and let you know if the house is safe," she said and walked away, doing a detour to make sure she was not being followed. Only she and Bahman had the keys to the house. As she unlocked the front gate two large men in almost identical crumbled brown suites pounced on her. Her grenade remained untouched in her bag. She would be the first Fadai' women to be executed eleven months later, having survived interrogator Azodi's treatment.

Mostafa walked round the city and casually passed by the house. Not seeing a safety-sign, he walked to the bus station and took the next bus to Gorgan in the North-East where he shared an apartment with two men. As he approached his apartment, he met a neighbour by chance.

"The police were there in your house," the neighbour said, after the customary salam, *khasteh nabashid*, and how is the family, good, thanks to your kindness, and yours, good, thanks to your kindness, "maybe they were looking for some smugglers," he added almost as an aside.

Mostafa walked over to another safehouse nearby. Crowds had gathered outside. Then he saw smoke rising up from that house and as he turned to go, he overheard a woman in a *chador* excitedly telling another that the house had been surrounded, and a grenade was thrown from somewhere, she couldn't be sure from the house or by the police, and a man and a women had emerged from the front door, and there were some shooting, and a policeman was shot, she didn't know if he was dead or not, and the two had got clean away through the back alleyway. She described the scene with such breathless agitation it was like listening to a child.

He realised that something huge was underway and retraced his steps back west to Amol. The young Amol taxi driver from the bus station was chatty.

"There has been a battle with the guerrillas," he said excitedly like he was describing a cowboy film. "This tall girl was so, so brave. Yes, she was so brave. She had this machine gun and fought a whole bunch of police and then blew herself up. I guess she had run out of ammunition." Mostafa saw the driver's eye mist over. His own eye also misted, and he had to use all his willpower not to burst into tears. It was his sister, Fatemeh, the young man was talking of.[8] He spent the night in a relative's home, returned to Sari because he was due to meet Shamsi[9] again but she did not turn up at the rendezvous site. He walked into a grocer shop to make time, wondering if she had been delayed. As before, Shamsi liked to have her rendezvous in this roundabout with its SAVAK headquarters in one corner.

"A woman blew herself up today, just round the corner from here, up Ferdowsi Street by the cinema" the grocer chatted. "Funny thing she was, her left hand was in plaster," the shopkeeper grinned and showed his tobacco-yellow very regular teeth, a glint of gold near the right corner. "I don't know how she managed to pull the pin out in time," the grocer added and made straight eye contact with Mostafa, looking for a reaction. For a second the image of the vivacious young woman he had seen earlier with her plaster poking out of the coat sleeve flashed across Mustafa. He nodded back at the shopkeeper without smiling. How did SAVAK know of the rendezvous?

*

It was mid-morning, and two men were walking side by side. A biting mid-winter breeze made both their faces glow. Anyone seeing them together would instantly know they were old friends. People who are close have a particular set of body languages, eye contact, facial lines, the way they move their hands, the space between, all speak of deep trust that only comes from love. Hamid and Mo'meni[10] were not only old comrades, but particularly close in the way they saw the world, their *Weltanschauung*, Mo'meni used to say. He was well read.

"We really must go to this meeting. It's going to be our last meeting and there are a few more things left to discuss," Mo'meni said in a voice that was a mixture of frustration and pleading. The two were on their way to see a comrade who was fairly knowledgeable about Marx, with whom they already held a series of meetings discussing theoretical issues.[11] "We will probably lose touch with him after this," Mo'meni added, hopefully, to clinch the argument. This was to be their last meeting. Hamid was silent. He looked pensive. They had been arguing about the wisdom of keeping this appointment since they woke up. "I know this guy is a risk, but we just have to do this last meeting to clear up a few points," Mo'meni had argued. As the chief theoretician of the movement, he was anxious to tie up a few loose points left over from their last discussion.

"After all, this guy has translated Marx's *Das Kapital*." Mo'meni finally said, "He ought to know what he is talking about".

"Then you will have to go by yourself," Hamid said. He said this and moved away from Mo'meni imperceptivity. It was a clear body language. "I don't have a good feeling about this, especially as this is a meeting about theory and not absolutely essential. If you are reckless enough to risk this meeting, then go on your own responsibility, but keep your finger on the grenade pin, just in case." The person they were meeting was a new member and who knows how careful he was with his security checks. Hamid was deeply troubled by the death of Bahman and the blows to the Fadai' in the Caspian provinces. They still did not know from where the blows had come. Ever since this morning, Hamid had felt uneasy about this meeting and he always listened to his instincts, it was the secret of his survival. He understood instincts as subliminal observations and thoughts, appearing to consciousness as a feeling. But they were more than a feeling, they were objective deductions. The two had argued before leaving but Hamid had allowed himself to be persuaded. That was out of character. But as they approached the comrade's house, something told him things were not normal.

"I don't really think you should go either," Hamid said aloud. "Theory can always wait when it is a question of life and death." It was the last time he saw his close comrade Mo'meni alive. A few minutes later he heard an explosion and later, mingling among onlookers saw the police carry Mo'meni's mangled body to a waiting ambulance, his beautifully ironed grey shirt now in bloody tatters.

Unknown to them a few days earlier the police had arrested the person they were about to meet and having squeezed out of him the agreed safety signals, were waiting to capture Mo'meni alive. As chief theoretician of the Fadai' his capture would have been a real coup for SAVAK.[12]

Hamid did not return to the house he shared with Mo'meni and phoned the others to vacate it immediately. They did but returned after two weeks when all looked safe. Hamid never used that house again.

Mostafa escaped to Mashhad and joined his comrades. He was killed in a shootout the following spring.

It was a bad month in a bad winter.

[1] Bahman Ruhi Ahangaran.

[2] A province bordered by the Caspian, to the north, and the Alborz mountain range to the south.

[3] Ahmad-Reza Karimi

[4] Bahman Ruhi Ahangaran joined the Fadai' in 1972 was captured on January 7, 1976, savagely tortured and died six days later in military hospital number 502.

[5] Shamsi (Faremeh) Nahani, born in 1949 in Tehran, joined the Fadai' while studying History in Tehran University and was put in charge of a worker's unit in Qa'em Shahr (formerly Shahi) that summer of 1975.

[6] Mostafa Hasanpour was the brother of Qafour Hasanpour one of the founders of the Fadai' who was executed after the attack on Siahkal.

[7] Zahra Agha-Nabi Gholhaki had joined the Fadai' three years earlier and had moved to Sari only 4 months before.

[8] Fatemeh Hasanpour.

[9] Shamsi (Fatemeh) Nahani.

[10] Hamid Ashraf was the leader of the Fadai' organisation and Mo'meni was its chief theoretician and at the time. They were sharing a safehouse in Kan Alley in Tehran.

[11] Fouladi, a translator of Marx's *Kapital*, lived openly.

[12] Hamid Mo'meni, the chief theoretician of the Fadai' was born in the village of Bidokht in Kermanshah Province 1952 and was killed on February 12, 1976.

Chapter 23

The ladder man

Fadai'

It was the first house in a blind alleyway off Behboodi *Street* in the capital. Opposite their alley, on the other side of the main road was a car park belonging to the ministry next door. But it was a mainly residential area. The good doctor lived there with his wife and two children. Behruz[1] would visit occasionally, usually without warning. They expected him without waiting for him. He knew it was safe when he saw a cloth hung by the bathroom window. Any cloth of any colour. He sometimes made and received phone calls from that house. The house of the good doctor, his wife's brother, was as safe as Behruz could hope for when you had to come to the surface to breathe. The underground ocean could be suffocatingly claustrophobic. The good doctor was sympathetic. More reliable than his own brother. Worked in a Lion and Sun clinic. A place for those who could not afford the paying doctors. The Iranian version of the Red Cross.

Behruz arrived at ten. A yellow-white kitchen cloth was hanging smilingly. He walked across the street, casually looked both ways, and rang the bell. He could have had a key but he did not want the good doctor to become compromised in case Behruz was picked up by the police. You had to think of everything if you lived underground. The good doctor's wife opened the door, small and thin and rather shy. Beautiful without being pretty. There was magnetism in her every move, totally uncoquettish. Sensual without being sexual. Natural. Behruz felt a deep trust in her. She could be relied on. Totally.

"Anything suspicious," he asked, after the usual greetings.

"No, nothing special."

"Keep an eye open please," Behruz said, as he always did, and went to the kitchen to pour a cup of tea from the samovar. There was tea all day at the good doctor's house.

Twenty minutes later Behruz left the house, looked at his watch, walked south towards the main street, stopped looked at his watch, walked towards the Shahyad monument,[2] walked for exactly 21 minutes, looked at his watch, crossed the road and took a taxi back to Behboodi street, crossed the road and did the same again walking towards Shahyad monument for exactly 21 minutes. Then returned.

When PM[3] was given this report exactly like I described it, he could not make head or tail of it. Ten days later Behruz arrived at the good doctor's in the early evening. The window cloth. OK. Bell. The good doctor opened. His wife came down to greet him. Smiles. Greetings. Behruz felt like home.

"Anything suspicious."

"No" she said and then added, "there was an old man checking the telephone pole. Three days ago. Nothing special." Her favourite phrase.

"How long was he there?" Behruz asked almost as an aside, as if he did not think the answer important. An old man. Must be safe.

"Oh. About half an hour. Forty-five minutes perhaps. Not long. Looked like he was checking the lines. Nothing out of the ordinary. Our phone keeps getting crossed."

"Keep an eye in case he returns. Can I stay the night?"

"It's your own house," husband and wife both said simultaneously. A very close relationship.

The phone rang at 2 am. He picked it up after two rings. He had slept by the phone.

"6 Shafi," the voice said not introducing himself and rang off. Was it Hamid, PM wondered?

Behruz woke up at 5, only needing four or five hours to be fresh. The good doctor was already up preparing tea. Behruz took a small cup, one of those with a thin midriff like a female waist, drank it, thanked the good doctor, walked out of the flat checking that he was not being followed. He had left the house at 5.30. It was twilight.

PM went to the home of the old man on the ladder with a large sum of money.

*

For some reason winter of 1976 in Tehran didn't smell like winter, at least not to Hamid. He had no time for scenery anyway, or for that matter the snowy white of mountains. It was a miracle he was still alive, or more accurately not so much a miracle than a combination of courage, quick thinking, alertness, agility, and of course luck. They said a guerrilla's life span was six month, roughly the same as a worker ant and less than a worker bee in autumn. But Hamid had outdone then all, slipped through every net they had thrown in his path, and still fighting in full command of the Fadai'. It was thirteen years and nine traps since he joined. No wonder his comrades called him "great" behind his back, though never to his face. He did not like that epithet. He would say it was good fortune, and attention to detail and constant vigilance that explained his extraordinary survival. And staying constantly fit. For him that was the simple logic of survival for the hunted, and he never lost an opportunity to pass on his skills. But few had that stamina and the attention to the minutiae.

The flat was on the first floor. He had lost count on how many houses he had changed. There was a window to the street where the lookout sat at night. You could see both ways. No need for lookouts during the day. Everyone living there was on permanent lookout. The two young boys occupied the room at the back with Ladan and Mahvash.[4] The men slept in the other room. The sitting room was divided by a curtain in such a way that a newcomer living behind it could access the toilet without being seen by the occupants, and to go in and out unobserved. The less information people had about the people coming and going the safer.

Safety. That too is the secret to survival. He never used the house phone. No one had his number. No one called. His was always a one-way communication only used for urgent business. He normally used a 2-rial-a-call phone booth. Today he had to meet Behrouz urgently as arranged. Something important was being planned. He got up at 5. Ladan brought him a glass of sweet tea and a piece of flat *taftoon* bread with white feta cheese on a plate. He normally made his own breakfast. She was wearing a loose baggy shirt with long sleeves hanging over a pair of somewhat baggy blue trousers. Socks, even in the house. Dress codes were strict. Was the aim of wearing contourless clothes a way of reducing sexual attraction in mixed safehouses? It was certainly practical, they were always dressed ready for escape at a moment's notice.

Hamid put on his brown shirt, tucked his handgun in his belt. Concealed behind the loose-fitting shirt hanging over his trousers. The sort of colour everyone wore. Nothing that stands out. Three cartridges. Checked they were full. Two grenades, one in each pocket. Best take three. Won't need the Uzi sub[5] today. Must go to the toilet. Always leave the house with an empty bladder.

"Back at 8," he said to Ladan, who went to the window to check the street. She could see both ways. He followed her and looked up and down the street from behind the lace curtain. Always retest the tested, was his way. Sometimes two people sat lookout. That way they could observe unobserved, as if they are talking by the window-sill. He looked in the mirror, checking that the dark mole on his nose was cosmetically covered and invisible. Final check.

He briskly walked down the stairs looking out of the large window that projected onto the road. Nothing suspicious. More stairs. He opened the front door, look again left and right and across the street. Not too obviously. No one was looking out of a window. A woman was walking across on the other pavement, middle aged with a loose scarf carrying a bag. Probably shopping. There were no shops on their road, only two-storied houses and a few with three. Both ends of the street were free. It was a perfect street for a getaway. He turned left, walked briskly to the next junction, turned right into a wider street, walked two blocks and was on the main road. He hailed a taxi going past. It slowed down as it approached and the driver turned to him. Jorjani Hospital, he said, and the driver stopped. He hopped in the front.

Always the front. Easier to jump out if needed. No passenger obstructing the door.

Behruz picked him up at exactly 6 in the street next to the hospital. A young man was sitting in the back. Greetings without names. They turned right into the main Damavand road and a man waved them down. Must be waiting for a taxi. The man saw the passengers and dropped his hand. They passed him and Behruz checked in the mirror. The man was hailing other cars. Must just be someone waiting for a taxi.

He wasn't.

Behruz knew the address on the other side of the city. As they approached, he turned into a number of side streets. Easier to be sure no one was following. They parked on a side street, got out, the young man took the wheel and they arranged when and where to meet and drove away. Behruz and Hamid walked to a two-storied house, Hamid regularly checking behind him without turning his head which could attract attention, using a tiny mirror he had fixed on a ring. It looked like a newly built house. The door opened as soon as they rang and a young girl with a grey scarf loosely on her head stood just inside the door. Waiting. They must have seen them approach. Welcome words. No names. They walked up some stairs and entered a room divided by a light brown curtain. You could see the creases. Must have been put up recently for us. A voice from behind the clean crispy curtain greeted them. No names again. No one had frisked them. There had to be trust.

"We would like to record the conversation and I will give a copy of each session at the next meeting," Hamid said and put an empty tape in the audiocassette player that Behruz had brought. Were the other side also recording?

"We have no problem with this," the voice said. He spoke fast, running his words into the next. His voice sounds like that of a teenager. North Tehrani accent slurring some of his words, especially the r's. Shall we start?

Hamid began with an explanation of the process that brought them here. He spoke of the split in the Mojahedin, making it clear that he was well informed about the radical change in their ideology, a significant section accepting Marxism. He spoke of the need to have a dialogue so that members

129

of both organisations could participate in the discussions through an internal publication. Hamid's voice was warm and friendly. Unhurried. As if he had pre-planned each sentence. He then went on to criticise the way the Mojahedin had split, in particular the fact that they had purged half their members. He did not mention the killings.

"Instead of expelling them when you came to accept a Marxist analysis of the world, you should have completely broken with them and come out under a new name," Hamid spoke, clearly enunciating his words. All the time picturing the face behind the brown curtain. His voice sounded older than the man behind the curtain. He looked at Behruz who nodded back. They were in agreement.

The curtainvoice argued with increasing agitation, as it justified the position their leadership had taken, his voice raised a fifth and the words ran into each other squeezing the space between. As if by compressing the wordless space you could squeeze out the uncomfortable facts, their conduct after the split. The voicebehindthecurtain was clearly unhappy at something. Was it their actions or the criticisms? Hamid calm, with a gently undulating pitch and clear word separation, was behaving as he would when in an operation. He never lost his calm, never panicked, never allowed emotion to take control. Life was a permanent battle that he would conquer by seeing it through. He was smiling.

After exactly two hours they stood up, said goodbye, agreed to another meeting walked downstairs, opened the door, looked up and down the street, walked to the next street corner. Looked again. Saw the young man in the car turn the corner, got into the car and drove off, checking the rear mirror every 10 seconds. Military precision. They drove through the streets towards the East again taking roads with little traffic. They were making sure no car was behind them for at least 5 minutes. The police often used different cars to pursue. And also taxis.

Hamid got off near the hospital, a brief goodbye, waited for Behruz to disappear, checked the road, walked back to Damavand street and took three taxis before reaching home. Before entering he checked the lamp post a little way from the house. The safety sign was there, as was the curtain. He went in.

Ladan and Mahvash had already eaten but the tablecloth was still there with his lunch. The two boys sat down with him as he ate. Like all the inmates in the house they admired him intensely but were not awed.

He did not miss his customary one-hour alone with the boys.

[1] Behruz Armaqani.
[2] Now Azadi (freedom) Tower.
[3] Quotes from PM (SAVAK agent Parviz Mo'tamed) is from an interview the latter gave to Iraj Mesdaqi in Paris after the revolution and published online. As noted in the Preface, PM's reports should be treated with utmost caution, it is full of unlikely boasts. He claims to have masterminded the phone tapping that delivered a severe blow to the Fadai' in Tehran.
[4] Ladan Ale-Aqa and Mahvash Khatami.
[5] An Israeli-built compact machine gun.

Chapter 24

The sighting

Fadai'

In the world of wars, lies become stories and stories become history. The dead don't write their history. The living, especially those whom history has swept aside, continue to embellish their lies, and most lies are not outright fabrications but a distortion of truths. In that way they may, in time, become believable. It is the truth we need to seek through the lies. And somewhere some truths are lost.

PM[1] went straight to the *Komiteh* from Jorjani Hospital. He could barely hide his excitement. He had seen Hamid and Behruz in the car. It was unmistakably them, he was sure. The two most wanted men and he had got the lead by tapping the good doctor's phone.

It was early morning. A few minutes later Azodi – the 'doctor' – walked in.

"What is it? Why are you here so early in the morning?" Azodi asked.

"As it happens, I wanted to see you," PM replied trying to remain calm while his heart was beating as if it wanted to fly. "I saw Hamid Ashraf." He couldn't hide his glee.

"What are you talking about?" Azodi screamed. Never any self-control, PM thought with disgust. Azodi looked exceptionally ugly. Perhaps it was the dryness of his skin which made him look like a desiccated mummy.

"Yes. I saw him drive past in a car with Behruz. And don't make such a fuss and pretend you're boss. This issue is way above your rank." PM hated Azodi the 'doctor', but not for what he was doing to prisoners. PM had no issue with torture, no matter how savage. To catch your enemy, you needed information quick before they had wiped out the leads. You did what you needed to crack them rapidly. No. This 'doctor' was erratic and emotional. Useless as a security officer. To kill under torture is an admission of failure. No. PM liked to use cunning and his brain to entrap. And the more you trap the better. It was war, as he saw it. You had to outsmart your opponent. Savagery was only useful if it gave results by destroying networks and the entire organisation. That was all that mattered. Individuals were mere casualties of that war. Collaterals on either side, he thought. The aim was to win. Killing your source of information under torture was poor strategy. Like a microbe that kills its host before being able to pass on to another. A useless act if the survival of your species depends on transmission. The effective bug is one that can pass from one person to another. Like measles. This Azodi just enjoyed watching pain. He was useless as a warrior in PM's type of war. And he gave himself airs. 'Doctor', indeed! Uneducated thug that he was. And now he was creating havoc.

"If you saw them there, why didn't you shoot them?!" Azodi kept repeating.

"Oh, shut up and get a hold on yourself," PM said, angry. "This sighting is not something we want advertised. If you have anything to say, say it to someone higher up." But Azodi was right, and PM knew it. This man, whose self-image was of someone far more intelligent than these mere interrogator-torturers, had missed a unique opportunity to capture or kill their most coveted catch by going to the meeting totally unprepared. What PM couldn't admit without losing face was that he was not at all sure he was going to see Hamid, or indeed anyone. A mere hunch had inadvertently proved correct.

They went to see the general in charge of the *Komiteh Moshtarek*.

"Why didn't you shoot him when you caught sight?" Azodi (Naseri) interrupted after PM had finished his report.

"Sadly, this head of the interrogation section does not have the sense to realise that I had only a small handgun with four feeble bullets. I wouldn't stand a chance against their machine guns. We need to find out where he lives. That is our goal. That's what we should aim for."

Who was PM? Who was this man working for SAVAK. He was an intelligence officer whose job was to piece together the bits of information that form a narrative that can trap or destroy an opponent. As a personality he was a functionary, a bureaucrat, a man of intelligence but lacking morals. He had no ideological commitments. What he was doing was a job. There was no emotion behind his work. You could call him autistic if that wasn't an insult to those with autism. Banal. As in Hannah Arendt-banal. Here was an Eichmann-like functionary, doing a job and doing it well, even ruthlessly regardless of cost. He was there to do a job, and he was cunning and resourceful enough to do it well. Unemotional. No respect for superiors he considered incompetent. Wanting to outsmart the smart. Devious. Competent and for that reason dangerous. In him lay a cruelty that was all the more savage because it was so abstract, so means to an end. He worked with vicious torturers and knew exactly what they were up to. Maybe even enjoyed it. Who knows how bureaucrats think? Banal and callous.

PM now had twelve safehouses in his net through phone tapping. It had been an arduous task and he had masterminded it, beginning with the old man on top of his ladder and the good doctor's house. That had been the weak link with Behruz's closeness to his family. He held his nerve because he wanted to nail the main prize, the elusive Hamid. No one must know of the operation, of the net until everyone was trapped inside it. He worked like a seasoned fisherman, never content with small fry. He wanted the king shark as he saw Hamid. The legend. The monarch himself had kept asking why this man Hamid had not been captured. That is how the good doctor had unknowingly spread the phone-net to safehouses in Karaj and Qazvin near Tehran, Rasht by the Caspian and Tabriz in the North-East, where Hamid had attended school.

PM wanted to trace Hamid's phone. He had even taken over the attic of the opposite house to the good doctor's and got a photographer working for SAVAK to take pictures of everyone who came and went out of the house. That is how he became sure that Behruz, recently released from prison, goes in and out of that house. They had over 150 men and women trapped in their net, knowing their name, face and even their voice. He felt good. But the king shark had eluded him. Hamid's was a one-way phone. He rang. No one rang him. And he never rang from a safehouse.

They guessed that Hamid lived somewhere in the north-east districts of Tehran. He had been sighted on more than one occasion there. He had to live somewhere nearby. They set up their snoop in Narmak central exchange in west Tehran.

The clock was ticking but the security men were biding their time to widen the net as much as possible. The monarch kept asking why this man is so elusive. Those at the top of the Fadai' had also sensed something was brewing. There had been no major raid on their houses or street clash for three months. The silence was eerie and worrying. The Fadai' leadership decided to organise an armed operation to test the water.

Then by a chance incident Hamid's hideout fell into the net[2] and SAVAK were not going to take any chances or waste any time. PM counselled waiting to trap more but PM was overruled.

It was mid-spring and the few streets with trees were emerald with sycamore green. It was a year since Bijan Jazani had been murdered along with 10 others in the hills above Evin. It was four months since the first wave of killings that began in the phone booth and the capture of Bahman in the winter. Ahmad, Changiz and others were still inside.

The second wave of killings began when the earth was being reborn.

[1] See preface on the reliability or otherwise of PM's report.
[2] Years later PM (Parviz Mo'tamed) talking in Paris claimed he had locked on to Hamid and was able to trick him into prolonging his conversation with Behruz by tapping into their conversation as if the lines had crossed. How that relates to finding Hamid's hideout remains a mystery. In any case it sounds unlikely that Hamid would be goaded into a long-enough conversation to nail him.

Chapter 25

The trap

It was the first day of spring and Iranians everywhere were celebrating *Eid Nowruz*. A new year had begun. It was March 1976. The previous *Eid* the Shah had shut down the two near-identical political parties that he himself had created and replaced them with a single party, Rastakhiz, the Resurrection Party which all Iranians were ordered to either join or pack up and leave the country. The Tweedledee and Tweedledum parties were supplanted by an empty balloon – one people, one party, one king. At a stroke, dissent, no matter how lukewarm was not just outlawed, it was wished away. Everyone was supposed to live happily ever after, just like one of those childhood stories. Reality was annulled by decree.

This *Eid*, the Shah went on to change the Iranian calendar. History was to start with the birthday of King Cyrus the founder of the Archimedean dynasty. History suddenly jumped 2500 years and the year 1355 became 2535. History too, had been annulled. "Rest in peace Cyrus, because we are awake" he had boasted at the tomb of Cyrus. I am the King-of-Kings (*shahanshah*), ruler of Iran, able to rub out history and dissent.

But the country was not all silence. What the Shah and SAVAK could not annul was the voice. No matter how hard they tried to squash that voice, it kept popping up. Across Iran, countless young men and women broke the silence with their bodies and died or ended up in his prisons. Yet the voice would not die, and more joined the battle. The regime, so focused on squashing the left, tried a new stratagem: why not channel the angry voice of the young, who were increasingly rejecting the silence of the never-never land, into the arms of the Marxist-hating Islamists. The Shah started to woo the clergy and encouraged them to rail against the "heathen left" and even provided platforms for radical Islamists thinkers like Ali Shari'ati whose anti-Marxist rhetoric was as strong as his vision for a radical Shia' Islam.[1] As it turned out, that was a strategic mistake. It allowed the mullahs to strengthen their infrastructure in time to ride the revolutionary tide that was already brewing and overthrow the Pahlavi dynasty three years later.

Meanwhile the Shah, in his bitter hatred of the left, wanted the thorn that was symbolised by the defiant voice of Hamid Ashraf and the men and women of the Fadai' and Mujahedin pulled out and destroyed.

*

Young Nasser[2] ran into the men's room looking extremely worried.

"Comrade Hamid, please come. Arzhang is late," Nasser said, looking up at him with eyes that had begun to shine with welling tears. Arzhang, the older of the two brothers, had gone out to buy bread. "He is always back on time. Something must have happened to him!" Nasser was clearly scared. It was not easy for a seven-year-old to live in hiding in a safehouse.

"Don't worry, the queue may have been long at the bakers." Hamid said calmly, but the boy was unconvinced. Normally his brother would return after 10 minutes, and it was already 15. He was scared. It was his brother he was talking about and having lost his oldest brother and father and with his mother in prison he suddenly felt vulnerable. Life was strange for the two boys living in a hideout with Hamid and four other adults in that first floor flat in Khayam Street in East Tehran.

"But he should have come back to tell us," Nasser insisted, and tears traced a path down both cheeks, passing pursed lips. He was only seven and living in hiding with no contact with other children is so stressful. "I know where the bakery is," Nasser pleaded, "please, please let me go and check." Hamid reached over and ruffled the young boy's curly hair. His smile seemed to calm the boy. He smiled back, sheepishly, almost guiltily. I must be brave, he thought. He was only a boy living in a purely adult world.

"I can go and check," Ladan interrupted. The boys were inseparable, like twins, especially now that their mother was in prison and their older brother had disappeared. They had totally absorbed the routines and dry discipline of the safehouse including writing detailed timed reports of all their activities during the day. They even insisted on eating frugally like the rest and protested when it was suggested they should have special fortified diets because they were growing. They saw themselves as part of the team – as fighters. You are forcing us to be bourgeois, the ten-year-old Arzhang had protested, angry and misty-eyed, at the suggestion in one of their nightly criticism-self-criticism sessions. It needed the authority of Hamid for the boys to accept having extra rations of milk. Life was very prescribed for these fighters. A self-imposed military discipline with ideological seasoning, bone dry and seemingly inflexible. Their survival depended on it and in the face of constant danger they were all adults, even the kids, with death never far in time.

Ladan heard the front door keep opening and closing. Nasser was clearly getting agitated and had slipped downstairs where he was checking the alleyway several times a minute. That was not a good idea as it might draw unwanted attention and Ladan was about to intervene when the doorbell rang. It was Arzhang with two *taftoon* flatbreads on his arm, still warm. He had been away exactly 19 minutes.

"There was a fight in the queue ahead of me, and the queue itself was long" he blurted out trying to pre-empt a telling off.

"You should have come back and told us" Nasser said with tears again rolling down his face. That night in the criticism-self-criticism session Arzhang was punished by banning him for one week from buying bread.

That was two days ago. This evening Hamid came back quite late. He went straight to the boys' room. He always dedicated at least an hour a day to playing with them. The boys loved him like the older brother that they had lost, or maybe a father-mother. The others heard them playing karate with Hamid, and laughter both childish and grown up. It was permitted to make a noise at that hour. The boys had become accustomed to keep relatively quiet during the day so as not to alert the neighbours. Boys of their age were meant to be at school.

Hamid looked thoughtful as he sat down to their ritual criticism-self-criticism session before they all went to bed. All the team were present, Hamid, Ladan, Mahvash Farhad, and the boys Nasser and Arzhang.

"Isn't it odd that we haven't heard from the police since those blows last winter" Hamid said and did not elaborate, but there was a barely perceptible wrinkle between his thick black eyebrows and a particular light in his eyes. There was a certain power in those eyes, as if they could penetrate walls.

"Yes, Ladan said in a soft voice, like she was talking to herself. "It is odd."

"That must be good. It shows they must be scared of us then." the younger of the boys announced and grinned.

Hamid smiled back at him and both boys looked up happy. What Hamid did not say was that he was planning some sort of operation to check the security of the organisation.

"Comrade," Farhad[3] whispered, shaking Hamid gently by the shoulder. Hamid was a light sleeper. Farhad was the lookout at that hour, around four in the morning. "I think we are surrounded. They are saying things through loudspeakers" there was just a hint of panic in that last sentence.

Hamid sat up and listened to the loudspeakers telling people in the neighbourhood to stay in their homes. Did it relate to them, he thought.

"I can't be sure it is about us, he whispered, there hasn't been any unusual activity around here, has there? Maybe there is another hideout nearby." Moving quickly, he woke everyone up. The boys too. Always think ahead. All the grownups prepared for a raid by the police.

He went downstairs and knelt by the front door, opened it a couple of centimetres and looked out from the lower part of the crack. A shot rang and a bullet hit the door above his head. It was close enough for him to feel the wind in his hair. There followed a volley of shots. He shut the door, bolted it, and made a quick assessment. They were surrounded on three sides, and their escape routes were blocked by armed men. He ran upstairs and gave the zero-zero signal and Farhad and Ahmad-Reza[4] started burning incriminating documents in the sitting room fireplace while the two girls began burning them in the bathroom. Bullets were flying everywhere and smoke was all over the flat burning their eyes. Part of the sitting room was on fire. Hamid, Ahmad-Reza and Ladan were at the window firing into the street when an old woman, the owner, ran into the sitting room, pale and terrified with her long uncombed white hair flying in all directions.

"What's happening Mr Mahdavi?" she shouted over the din in an unearthly voice, and then she saw the guns and shrieked.

"Don't worry mother, don't worry. It's war" Hamid replied in his calm voice, walked over, put his arm round her shoulders, led her into a back room and asked her to lie flat. Just then the old woman's daughter-in law ran in with a child in her arms, mother and child screaming,

"They are after us, not you, just lie down with Ra'najoon and keep your head down, you'll all be alright" he said and led them to the back room, and even though Hamid's calm voice did little to quieten the terrified young woman, she obeyed and lay down alongside her mother-in-law shielding the screaming child with her body, mother and grandmother whimpering. Hamid closed the door to the room, insulating it from battle and smoke. Everywhere was noise, noise of machine gun and single shots were combined with explosions outside and the crackle of the fire inside. One of the boys had been hit by shrapnel and was moaning on the floor by the sofa with his brother grouching next to him, deathly pale, deathly quiet and terrified. Hamid quickly looked at his wound. It was fairly superficial. Mahvash lay bleeding by the fire with a large gunshot wound to her chest. She was dying. He decided to make a run for it. He crawled to the petrified boys who had huddled in the corner in each other's arms, coughing in the smoke, hugged them each and told them calmly but firmly to stay exactly where they were until the shooting was over. He then turned to Farhad and Ladan who were at the window shooting out.

"I will throw a grenade ahead. Both of you follow me," he ordered. That was his way. Grenade in front and shoot your way out, throwing another grenade behind him to deter pursuit. And that is what he did, always clear-headed even under the most extreme circumstances. All three ran out, with Hamid in front followed by Ladan. Farhad was last. Ladan was immediately hit as she came out of the front door. Dead. Farhad climbed the wall on the other side of the alley into a neighbour's courtyard, and Hamid, who had stayed behind to cover him followed. Both the young boys were alive when they left.[5] Ahmad-Reza was already dead.

"My machine gun is stuck," Farhad said as they climbed down the opposite wall into an alleyway and Hamid let have him his Uzi forgetting that he had used it earlier and the magazine was half empty. The spare cartridge was on his belt. He was holding the Kalashnikov when he saw a group of soldiers at the end of the alleyway. He pulled the breechblock since it too was stuck. The soldiers had seen him and for a second froze as if mesmerised. He had become such a legend – like in films. Then instinctively they drew together. He fired his machine gun into them killing three and wounding others. Farhad got a bullet from behind and fell. There was no time to finish him off, as was their rule. Hamid ran, shooting and limping, and made it into the main street, limping all the way. A black Paykan car was passing by, and he stopped it at gunpoint. He had been wounded in the left leg.

"Forgive me sir," he said politely to the driver, a man in his late twenties, clean shaven and totally shaken, as Hamid opened the driver's door. Hamid spoke as if he had bumped into him in error. "I just have to...," he said as gently pulled the man from behind the steering wheel, who obeyed without resistance not understanding a word said to him, his body jellied into a robotic state. The poor man stood staring as if he had seen a ghost as did a group of armed soldiers who had just turned the corner as Hamid drove off. The whole episode could not have taken more than a minute but took a lifetime through perception.

Hamid drove towards another of their safehouses near the mountains north of Tehran. It had snowed the night before. It always snowed up there when it rains in the city. The air was crystal clear. Spring clear. As clear as his head. He thought of the two boys, their brother dead, their mother in prison, he felt for them just as their father would. Then he focused again on the future. Never dwell on the past except as a lesson for the future. As he turned a corner towards Pahlavi Avenue,[6] he saw a police car following him, pass him and swerved in front and blocked his path. Hamid braked, lifted his Kalashnikov and shot through the back window, swerved passed the car and sped into the next road. He had killed the Qolhak police chief and wounded two others in the police Paykan.

He had to change cars. Someone would have taken his number. His foot was beginning to hurt but the wound can't have been too big, he thought, as he hadn't bled much. His mind was clear. It took twenty minutes before he got close to the new hideout. He parked the car on a nearby road, went to a phone booth and rang.

"I am wounded on …. street. Can you come and get me" he said to the woman at the other end?

Five minutes later Saba and Abdol-Reza[7] arrived and led him to their house. The wound had stopped bleeding. It wasn't very deep. It must have been a ricocheted bullet that had lodged in the back of his left thigh. Saba cleaned it with alcohol, applied a tincture of iodine and bandaged it tight. Hamid wanted the bullet left inside. To extract it would need opening the wound and that would limit his mobility. He could run and climb quite well as it was.

They were having lunch when they heard the loudspeakers followed by machine gun fire and grenades. They must have known of this hideout as he was particularly careful that he was not being followed.

"Where is the escape route?" Hamid asked Saba. She led him to the small backyard, which they could access via a window from the kitchen at the back and from there on a ladder to a neighbour's roof and into another courtyard. They, two men and two women, managed to get down into an alleyway some distance away from the house. As they got to the entrance of the alleyway, they saw a group of armed men.

"Throw a grenade behind you," Hamid ordered and followed it by a burst of machine gun and then knocked on a door. A middle-aged woman opened the door one crack.

"My apologies. Quickly give us two *chadors* please" he said. He was polite but had already put his foot into the door and pushed it open as the woman stepped back seemingly paralysed. All four went in and closed the door. Then the woman saw the machine gun, blanched and was about to shout when Hamid put his finger on his lips. "Two chadors please, if you don't mind" Hamid repeated with a faint smile on his lips. She ran into the house and returned with two cotton flowered chadors which he threw to Saba and Nadereh, the two women in the group. Outside in the alleyway they shot another armed man and took his side arm, which Hamid passed to Saba who was unarmed, then ran towards the street with Abdol-Reza firing behind as they went. On the main road a police vehicle drove towards them trying to run them down, and Hamid fired again killing the driver and wounding the others. Another police car arrived but as soon as they saw the four armed guerrillas they panicked, got out and ran. Hamid jumped into the abandoned police car and drove back towards the other police car, got out, took the machine gun of the wounded soldier, and gave it to Nadereh and they drove away from the scene.

Shortly afterwards the two girls got out and made their way separately to a safehouse outside town. The two men drove toward Amirabad, stopped at a bakery on the way and bought a gunnysack in which they put the machine guns, then after driving a little more parked the police car, and stopped another vehicle which they took from its driver and drove to behind the university where they abandoned it. Hamid had told the owner where to find his car. There were risks worth taking.

They found their way to the safehouse in Akbar Abad and soon Saba and Nadereh[8] joined them. On the police car radio, they had heard radio chatter between security forces and that is how they got to know that most of their safehouses in Tehran and provinces had been in the net – through phone tapping. It had probably started with the old man on the ladder outside the good doctor's house.

[1] Shari'ati's weekly lectures in Tehran's Hoseinieh Ershad drew a large crowd of young listeners and his books were allowed to circulate at a time when the penalty of possessing Marxist literature was torture and prison.
[2] Nasser Shaygan Sham-Asbi aged 7 and his brother Arzhang aged 10 were

looked after in this house while their mother, Fatemeh Sai'di was in prison.

[3] Farhad Sadiqi Pashaki.

[4] Ahmad-Reza Qanbar-pour

[5] The boys were shot. SAVAK tried to make a propaganda coup by blaming Hamid in mercy-killing them. Even PM, the ex-SAVAK agent, admitted that they were alive when Hamid and the others left the house. Who killed them will never be known.

[6] Today's Vali Asr.

[7] Saba Bijan-Zadeh and Abdol-Reza Kalantari Nistanki.

[8] Saba Bijan-Zadeh was killed in a street ambush on February 26, 1977. Nadereh Ahmad Hashemi was killed three days later. Abdol-Reza was captured. He was with another Fadai' comrade who took cyanide and died but Abdol-Reza Kalantari Nistanki was captured alive and executed on March 9, 1977.

Chapter 26

The massacre

Fadai'

In his cell Ahmad had slowly morphed into an advisor with special knowledge of the kaleidoscope of interrogation techniques, their evolution, their strengths and even more their weakness. His pain was already part of him. Extreme pain is solipsistic, seemingly permanently imprisoned within your frame and incorporated into your very being, trapped, yet reluctant to depart, your existence inconceivable in its absence. Your thalamus, that rail junction of multiple neurones, begins a complex reshuffling and buffering that allows you to live alongside the pain. Like identical twins with differing trajectories but a common womb. The other twin would intrude into the conscious self with decreasing frequency. It never, ever leaves.

He became a listener and a guide.

Someone would be dumped in his room. Usually after the first interrogation but occasionally before. At first Ahmad had been wary of the second sort. A plant, maybe? But that would be probably too crude for a system becoming ever more polished at extracting information. Like a good psychiatrist Ahmad built on his innate ability to read minds, small nuances in the eye, pupil size, the congruence or discord between different parts of the face. The way the hands, and especially the fingers, moved, interlocked, turned to the world. The imperceptible sweat. The faint flush. A teacher of resistance was being trained on the ground in that sky-less cell. Some of the temporary cellmates

145

were a bit like a battery, glossy on the outside, but gradually emptying within. Others sometimes verged on the heroic. You learnt to recognise and predict. Ahmad himself was sealed up. They had got nothing out of him. Meanwhile, in the world that had a sky, high-ranking functionaries were working for his release. The *Komiteh* henchmen had left him, rotting they thought, in his cell, unsure of what to do with him. This man couldn't be that dangerous, Azodi, the chief inquisitor thought in his foggy head.

In the early hours of that morning he was woken up by another arrival. He pushed back sleep and sat up. His pain-twin poked at his still-raw, rough skin. He winced and hoped the newcomer had not noticed. The newcomer was young with a very boyish face, almost feminine. Big black eyes. Slight contrast to his rather light brown hair. Funny how genes get distributed, Ahmad thought.

Salam, sobh bekheir, they bid each other good morning. The young man squinted. Is he myopic, Ahmad wondered?

"*Khasteh nabashid,*" Ahmad said as if the young man had been toiling at something. Hope you are not tired - just a turn of phrase. He had used the polite second person pleural tense. "*Khosh amadi,*" he welcomed switching immediately to the second person singular. It was more familiar, more friendly. This young man had clearly not been interrogated, at least not recently. He had too fresh a complexion.

"He is dead," the young man said unexpectedly a little while later after a silent interval, "I meant Hamid is dead" he corrected himself, omitting the second part of Hamid's name, as if he was talking about a brother or cousin, or perhaps he wanted to leave an ambiguity in case he had blurted out too early. He fell silent for a moment to see the effect of his words. Or was it regret that he had revealed too much. You never know how the person you are talking to will react. The *Komiteh* cell is not a normal world and he had barely walked into this enclosed darkness. This must be his first visit. Or perhaps, again, he's a plant.

"I saw the house in Mehrabad Street where it all happened," he continued and again regretted his indiscretion. Then he saw Ahmad's feet and the next sentence came out calmer. "They killed them all in that house. All. Every single one," and his eyes misted over. How stylish his shirt was, even though it was torn at the sleeve.

Ahmad showed no surprise. He had heard of the massacre in bits via the wall-to-wall Morse messaging. But it was the regime who, drunk on victory, broadcast the news. Already the bloody purge in the Mojahedin following the breakaway by the Marxist faction[1] had handed a propaganda bonus to SAVAK. The subsequent countrywide attacks on Fadai' houses last winter culminating in the murder of the two boys and others in Hamid's safehouse in Kayhan Street this spring had delivered a severe blow to the armed struggle. And now this. A copy of the daily Keyhan newspaper with a front-page picture of Hamid's corpse and a fulsome report of the death of all the *kharabkaran*, saboteurs, had been handed to every prisoner. SAVAK was gloating in its victory. It was the only paper he was given to read during his entire two-year stay in the *Komiteh*.

"Did they arrest you in the street?" Ahmad asked, not entirely sure he would get a true answer. He was trying to normalise the flow of the conversation.

"No. I was having dinner in a relative's house when they raided the party. They arrested everyone who was there. They took us to Evin first but brought me here" he said. For some reason Ahmad's question seemed to have calmed him down. "I don't know why, but it wasn't my first time in Evin" he added almost as an afterthought. That was two days ago.

Our young man, and they were virtually all young, some very young, had been brought over to the *Komiteh* for further questioning. That was ominous. Even after your trial and sentence you were never truly safe. Any time they could pluck you from your cell, just as earlier they had lifted you off the streets or raided your house, and squeeze you like a tube of toothpaste, to extract a bit more information out of you. Our young man's name must have come up from some poor boy or girl under torture. It was an endless game of squeeze and resist, until there was no more left to squeeze, your information became stale, or they gave up on you. Our boy was somewhere in the middle of that journey. I misjudged him, Ahmad thought, he probably knows about me. That's why he was so open and abrupt.

A man of around 22, a student, he belonged to the new intake that had been attracted by the glamour of the street fights. The blows of last winter had drawn a huge number of new recruits to the cause. Most still raw and inexperienced, but romantic. Blood attracting blood. Our young man must be low on SAVAK's list. Why else would he be brought to this cell before his first session with the 'doctors'. Was he seriously interrogated in Evin when he was first arrested or was this to be the test?

"You saw them surround the area?" Ahmad asked, looking him straight in the eye.

"No, I wasn't there," he said and looked down with a flush. "Actually it was my brother. I missed the beginning but got there later, when I heard shooting. You see, we both live nearly. He told me they were shooting for a long time. They kept shooting for over 10 hours. He had a good view, my brother. It was terrible. They were all massacred," and the young man suddenly looked less secure. He had forgotten that it was his brother who was telling the story. I wonder if he might crack Ahmad wondered. You can survive the first blows when you are brought in for the first time. The adrenaline takes over, but being brought back again, knowing what to expect. That was more difficult. Did he actually have a brother?

"That's what they do, don't they?" Ahmad said reassuringly, referring to those massacred in South Mehrabad Street. "It's part of your everyday life out there," he clarified, "to die, I mean." What Ahmad could not know was that these were almost the exact words Hamid had earlier used to the good doctor in answer to questions about the perils of life as an underground fighter. The long-surviving guerrilla chief and Ahmad-the-sceptic had the same prognostic view.

Our young man was describing the attack in some detail, again as relayed by his brother, when he noticed Ahmad's frown. Ahmad was remembering his childhood friend in primary school. The two of them would spend the entire school break walking the yard and describing the latest film they had seen in intricate detail. Scene by scene. Some kids have amazing photographic recall. I climbed a brick platform by a door, the young man added hastily correcting his enthusiasm. It was as real to him now, as if he had witnessed it all himself. Helicopters too. Then deep blush. I was there, he said, and Ahmad understood.

Gradually the narrative was set, scene by scene. And as he talked, the young man gradually went into himself, building image by image. It was a film, and he was directing it. His voice, warm, animated, was like a narrator over a silent movie. He looked four or five years younger as he talked.

"One by one as they came out of the door shooting and were mowed down by machine gun fire. Grenades, lots of grenades exploding everywhere. None of them survived. Blood all over the walls. Broken glass, shattered windows. Then all went silent but they, those bastards, were so terrified, so terrified of the great comrade that they waited and waited. Once all the shooting had stopped, they waited for ages before they dared approach the house. They dreaded opening the door to the rooftop in case he was still alive." Ahmad listened without comment to the young man reliving the story of the death of the legend. He did not interrupt, even though he already knew. That was not his nature.

The young man did not know, but Hamid had tried to escape via the rooftop. A single shot from a sharpshooter, or from the helicopter that was flying overhead, had blown off part of his brain. Still SAVAK was unsure if it was Hamid Ashraf they had killed. Two people who knew him by sight were brought from the *Komiteh* to identify his corpse. It's him, he had said. He had recognized Hamid by his mole. It's him, she had said and recognised the mole, and the bushy eyebrows. And the fact that he looked so calm even in death.

Delirious with the joy of victory, they had, they thought, cut off the snake's head.

Out there, in the world where there was a blue sky with a few tearless clouds, an old man had passed by the house in South Mehrabad Street. The newly built, already shabby district was like a battlefield. The house was rubbled with bullets and grenades. It had been a new build in a new area near the southern perimeter of the airport. It was phoneless. Hamid had made sure of that. After the last blow all the safehouses they rented were without phones.

But SAVAK may have traced this hideout by getting all letting agents to report the names of whomever they rented. The only person Hamid could find who could stand as guarantor for this house was a semi-clandestine comrade who put his lorry down as security. Or maybe they got a lead by following some comrades who, using pseudonyms, worked in factories. Whichever way they found out, as soon as they knew Hamid was there, they had attacked. SAVAK were taking no chances. That is how the entire Fadai' leadership which had gathered for an extraordinary meeting to decide what to do after the police phone trap fell into a different trap.

The spring sun continued to shine in a sky with a few clouds that could not weep. On the surface a silent void with only the drums of death audible. Beneath, a generation silently wept and continued to resist and fight.

Two years later the Shah fled.

[1] See Chapter 24, The sighting.

Chapter 27

The end of an affair

Ahmad

Ahmad limped out into the light and was taken straight to hospital. Bit by bit his broken body was patched up by this and that surgeon or physician. The attacks of loss of consciousness that had begun in the *Komiteh* continued. Epilepsy, the doctors said. Jina stayed with him by his hospital bedside every night and most of the day. He was still having fits and was sometimes incontinent. He needed nursing, especially at night.

The weeks went by with a speed that belied the clock. It was early evening as the spring sun was sinking, throwing its clear light straight through the window. It flew over his bed and across the room hitting the opposite wall in a glowing yellow rectangle. How different the spring light is from the autumn, Ahmad thought as he looked out of the window into the clear evening light. The same angle. The same intensity but, oh, so different in colour. It is as if the city soot had shrunk to let the rays through. He shared it with Jina, sitting as she always did by his bed.

"Hello" Azadeh said as she walked in. She was holding Nina's hand. She had volunteered to look after her in the absence of her mother. The little girl let go and ran towards her father but stopped in her tracks as she reached the bed. Her big dark brown eyes with their fresh awning of black eyelashes flashed a combination of love and fear. She stood there not touching him yet wanting to touch him as if to see if there was a man, a father, there. Do I look unrecognisable, Ahmad thought? It wasn't her first visit. But every time it was like a first. She looked so fragile in that yellow light. The mandibular wires had been removed but left his face curiously lopsided. Nina was learning about life, a schooling before its time.

"Why don't you go home Jinajoon and let me sit by his bed tonight?" Azadeh said in a curiously altered voice. Coming from somewhere inside that she did not recognise. All this time she had been looking, searching for his eyes. An ache, as if a landslide of hard rock was compressing her chest. She found it hard to breathe. She had spoken with a voice that was not hers. A raging fire of rage was burning her, and her eyes let out a curious dark light. Jina looked up suddenly into her eyes and saw something. Ahmad looked through the mist that was always in front of his eyes and saw the dark anger in Azadeh's eyes and did not understand.

"No thanks," Jina said abruptly, her voice almost saw-like, looking straight back. There were no wrinkles around her eyes. Only a sudden resentment. "No, no. No need. I'll look after him, thank you" she added, and the light from her eyes changed colour, and turned towards Nina as she twisted her body away from the intruder.

Ahmad saw the exchange, saw the anger, saw the resentment, and did not see its source and a conflict rose in him that felt alien, but real.

"Why, that's a great idea," he said, while the image of Azadeh in that interrogation room when Azodi had brought him and exhibited his wreck as a lesson for the others from the theatre group came back like an apparition. She was there in that room when they sat his broken body on that stool that let out that fart-like noise. Like a statue on a plinth, or better a carcass hanging on a butcher's hook. Hadn't Azadeh witnessed his worst and best moment? He could not understand why Jina was rejecting this gesture of help as he saw it. He was angry. A different kind of anger to the two women. An anger of incomprehension that is all the deeper for that. So many shades of anger.

"*Nemikhad*," was all Jina could say, no need. The words had a finality. Contempt. Even hatred. Azadeh took little Nina's hand and walked out very slowly. As she walked through the door, they both turned and the four eyes converged on the bewildered and angry eyes on the bed and calmed him,

Azadeh's eyes pupil-wide with a nameless emotion. He saw through the misty film covering his eyes her bright green dress, tight at the waist. She walked out and her walk was defiant. As they walked through the door Azadeh noted that Nina had not touched her father. In those few minutes the life of four people changed. The sinews of attachment slowly melted into nothingness.

Yet he was unaware that something fundamental had changed. The past had a blue mist thrown over it. His future changed its trajectory. Two years of separation - he felt Jina's strangeness when he returned home. The other had infused sympathy into his body, and it had a healing effect. She had seen him physically crushed and defiant and through her wish to stay with him she had fashioned a new bond. The green dress and the memory of the wind on the stool were tied into a knot though he did not know it. Not yet.

And as he healed, the anger in him gradually morphed into sadness and pity and a feeling of hopelessness for all.

Chapter 28

The volcano

1977

The darkness over the country rapidly contracted, defrosted by the sun and the cries of people no longer afraid to cry out. Time slowly speeded up into a crescendo. Like a symphonic final movement. A slow but inexorable crescendo. The blackness began to glow in an iridescent universal love. Deep inside Ahmad, somewhere beyond access, two loves entangled like a multicoloured circus rope – so entwined that the human and the revolutionary love lost all distinction. But he was unaware.

That summer a number of intellectuals wrote open letters to the Shah, demanding a lifting of the stifling atmosphere. The Society of Lawyers found the courage to protest at the tortures committed by SAVAK.

The Shah, impervious to what was happening in the country, went ahead with the annual Shiraz Arts Festival where, oblivious to the growing influence of the Muslim clergy, the organisers, which included Queen Farah, allowed a Polish theatre company to put on an experimental play containing simulated sex in a shop window in one of Shiraz's busiest streets. Unsurprisingly it provoked a national uproar.

Schools opened on the autumn equinox. A new academic year and the streets of Tehran became a sea of school children. Some had absconded from school. It was time to rebel. A week later Tehran University campus witnessed the largest demonstration against repression.[1] The air in the capital was different. The autumn light seems to have acquired a spring of its own. Less yellow. Almost golden. The plane leaves seem not to want to fall. Summer was fighting to expand its light into rival territory. The light, and the distant bells of something better, vibrated in Ahmad's veins as if a torrent of blood was bubbling through them. Jina receded in a slowly escalating irritation as Azadeh dimly touched his inner core. The two women in his life were entering a tournament, with the object oblivious.

And he felt uncomfortable. It was the only time in his life when he felt he had lost control.

*

Sa'id the poet-playwright, had been released just after him, early in the spring alongside thousands of other prisoners. The Society of Writers had organised nights of poetry reading. The political air was lightening. There were to be ten days of poetry reading at the Goethe Institute in Tehran after a previous attempt in another venue had been interrupted by a hired crowd of thugs.[2]

On the fifth night, after four nights of relatively harmless words, Sa'id took the platform. What has become of my country? he sang, his voice slowly rising to a crescendo, his dark bushy moustache quivering.

What has become of my country?
  What has become of my country?

Where prisons are crammed with tulips,
  and dew drops,
  and survivors from mounds of martyrs
  now shed tears for charred tulips.

What has become of my country
  that flowers still mourn?
  The patient eyes of men are filled with tears,
  for so long.

The heart of love itself is fractured in the depth of prison,
  for so long.

From the crypts of captivity, we sang
  of the suffocating cage
  for so long
  that lacerating wounds block our throats.

Oh, the fist of revolution!
  The mighty fist of people!
  The fiery fist of the sun!
  What had become of my country?

And the Goethe institute erupted. Goethe, who witnessed 1848 revolution across Europe would have understood. The head of the Goethe Institute was far more cautious. He stood up and warned that things could not continue in this vein. But the tone had changed and the wild reception by the audience of anything that smelled of revolution set the pace. The writer Sa'edi and others went out to mingle with the crowd standing in the pouring rain. A fellow poet, Aslān Aslāniān summed up the days ahead:

  shab ast o chehreye mihan siaheh.
  baradar qarqeh khooneh,
  baradar kakolash atashfeshooneh.

(It is night and black is the countenance of my country / brother is drowning in blood / brother's locks are a volcano.)

The volcano, having spewed torrents of larva, finally erupted.

[1] Strike and bloody demonstrations in Tehran University, August and again

October 1977
[2] October 10-19, 1977.

Chapter 29

My Brother

Nayyer

My name is … let's call me Nayyer. It's close enough to my real name. I am going to tell you my story in my own words but since I am still alive and politically active it is best to be careful. All the other players in this story are known to me but at this moment in the story I am still a young girl waiting to welcome my brother coming out of prison.

Since the nights of poetry, we had spiralling cycles of defiance and death on the asphalt, when my country erupted in a cycle of demonstrations that were met by bullets followed, forty days later (the *chehelleh*), by another. That is how we commemorate our dead here. Then more shooting, more deaths leading to another *chehelleh* march and yet more deaths. IN between these we had the universities, factories and later offices in revolt. More and more people entered the revolutionary arena, until there seemed to be no one left to support the king-of-kings. It is as if the entire audience in the theatre of life had invaded the stage in solidarity with one another. All those boasts by the King-of-Kings, the "Sun of Aryans" as he liked to style himself, had simply gone off in a puff. The man who promised Cyrus he was awake, seemed to have been blown away by the cries of people.

*

That day the families of political prisoners, were having a sit-in protest on the third floor of the Justice Ministry. We were there demanding they release

158

our loved ones. Most other prisons across Iran had been emptied, so why not ours? Why not the prison holding my brother Mehdi[1] and all those others? We sat together waiting. With me was a young girl called Pari with whom I had shared a cell. I too had tasted a bit of prison earlier this year, although nowhere nearly as long as my brother Mehdi.

When night came and there was darkness everywhere after curfew time, the rooftops in every part of the city reverberated with slogans: *begoo marg bar Shah* - Say it! Death to the Shah! I loved that exhortation, that, 'Say it!', that urging of others to repeat after you. Whoever thought of that added bit, must have had vision. It made that slogan uniquely direct. It was like opening your arm and inviting everyone to join the revolution. It was as if the slogan was Cupid's arrow to the heart of the people. It wasn't directed at the king. Not directly, anyway. It was directed at me, and you, and her and him and them. At all those who were still bystanders. That was my favourite slogan. Somehow, I blocked out the Islamic ones. Join! Join! It said, and I loved hearing it, those dark nights. Those dark nights when the sky seemed to be dotted everywhere with stars, now that at curfew time electrical workers and workers in power stations were plunging the country into a nightly blackout. Somehow, with eyes no longer dimmed by light, the sky looked brighter, and the shouting rooftops seemed so much louder. So much more inviting.

The next day Azhaari, that general who had recently been made prime minister, went on television. "They're just tapes", he said pathetically, referring to the nightly rooftop shouts, almost pleading to be believed. "Tapes don't have legs, you four-starred ass"[2] people chanted back the following morning, marching in their thousands in almost every town and city.

Then the Shah fled the country, weeping like a homesick child.

Four days later, still in the ministry building, there I was, standing on top of the spiral stairs, waiting alongside my friend Pari. I saw him sprinting up the stairs, the garland of flowers round his neck, flipping about like it wanted to fly away, as he ran straight into my arms. The prisoners, once they emerged from Qasr prison had been met by huge crowds, tens of thousands, out to greet them by the prison gates. Our Bastille of the day. Someone had put a garland round my brother's neck. Such a delicious experience, that embrace.

I still taste it on my skin, my face my arms, my whole being. I think I squashed the flowers. There are moments that time cannot forget.

Don't imagine that it was always so rosy between us. When I was younger, he would push books for me to read. Not just that. I had to write my views on what I had read, in Farsi. But I can't write proper Farsi, I had protested. At first, he had point-blank refused to believe me, then slowly relented and had agreed for me to give him a verbal report. In Azari, our native tongue.

He was my teacher in life and struggle. I told him that, on the day we were arrested together. That was the last time I saw him. But I am jumping time and the writer likes chronology. Very conventional, he is. That was my brother who had taught me everything. With him walked out the last of the political prisoners in the Shah's prisons.

"Meet my brother Asqar" Pari said. I was so engrossed in my brother that all I saw was a head bent down towards me, two shiny eyes, a shy smile, and an outstretched hand. I still remember his hand felt warm and soft when he greeted me and said something about him and Mehdi being close. I must have said something in reply. The air around me was so full of my Mehdi.

That day I also saw Changiz for the first time, actually a blur of brownish hair on top of a reddish face walking up the stairs alongside my brother. Did we shake hands? Were we introduced? I don't remember. It was only when Changiz came to visit us at home before he returned to the province that I got to know him.

But something about Asqar, perhaps his luminous eyes, or his shy smile remained suspended in my deep memory. Isolated images sometimes hang around in memory and their meaning is only unearthed when we look back in time. Or maybe that is just a trick of the way we remember things that matter. But at that moment all I saw was my lovely brother after more than seven years separation, and that unforgettable hug. I was no longer a little girl, and my brother was no longer a Mojahed.

I was to meet Asqar a lot over the next months.

*

The monarchy, decapitated with the Shah gone, collapsed in a heap, but not before a final burst of brutality outside main gate of Tehran University with its four concrete pillars spreading upwards and outwards like the wings of two birds about to take off, the flying concrete acting a metaphor for the senseless slaughter of students in full view of television cameras, broadcast live to the nation.

Then, suddenly, all the pain evaporated, the air felt lighter and was filled with joyous laughter. Men and women danced in the street, in open lorries, in balconies. One man drove round the town, waving a one thousand toman banknote, the country's highest denomination, with the picture of the Shah burnt through, waving it out of its window like a flag of victory. All that blood had paved the way for the people to speak.

But they spoke in two voices that ultimately fought to the death. And as winter dissolved into spring,[3] hope sank in betrayal and morphed into resistance.

[1] Mehdi Khosrowshahi Baradaran. We met him in a prison cell with Changiz, Mamaqan and Mamali (see chapter 17, Mamaqan, footnote 40)
[2] General Azhaari, the prime minister appointed by the Shah to supervise the emergency military government that was imposed after bloody riots had got out of hand, was a four-star general. Street demonstrators chanted rhythmically: *azhaari-e bichareh; olaq-e char setareh; baz ham migi navareh?; navar keh pa nadareh* (Azhaari you stupid wretch/you four-starred perfect ass/still insisting it is tape?/tapes have no legs!)
[3] Horace Odes.

Chapter 30

Return to velayat

Changiz

It was a hero's welcome. The winds of revolution had crossed the air of even such remote provinces as Qareh Daq, a mountainous area close to the Soviet Union.[1] The *khan* had proudly brought his son back home after his four-year stint in prison. A hero's welcome. He was among the last set of prisoners to be released. Changiz, the Khan's oldest son minus a bit more of his distinctive hair, and with the faint blush now permanently entrenched on his cheeks, accompanied the old man everywhere. It was the end of autumn and the heavy winter snows had yet to descend, but a cold wind blew across from the north.

He had been away from *velayat* (home country) too long, but had not lost his humility, and that rare gift of being both a man of the people and an intellectual, but without the superstitions of one and the airs of the other. Despite his frail frame he looked, and presented, tall. Almost every day father and son were invited by someone. Everyone vied to play host to the old *khan* and his heroson. He brought light everywhere he stepped, was what they said behind his back. A secular saint.

That day, a week after homecoming, it was Günyaz, a distant cousin, whose name meant summer sun. He met father and son at the door. Tall, slim with a thick black moustache growing down both sides of his brownish lips and equally thick black eyebrow, it was as if a child was given a piece of charcoal and told to draw a face. Above, below and around the charcoal the skin had been well baked by the sun, like his name. Burning summer sun, solidified by winter frosts. His large black eyes lighted with delight as he welcomed his honoured guests. He took the old *khan's* hand in both hands and kissed him, hands first and then both cheeks.

"*Qædæmin mübaræk olsun!*" He welcomed in Azari and turned to face Changiz. Changiz felt the coarse hands, callused by sun and ice, as he squeezed them. Hard. Kiss and a long hug. They had been childhood friends though Changiz had later left for secondary school in Tabriz.

They walked across the courtyard and its single pomegranate tree, branches bending under the weight of a mass of autumn-red fruit almost too heavy for it to bear, and the small, blue-tiled central pond, up a few stairs onto a veranda, the old *khan* walking ahead, headproud. Two full length doors, each with two panels opened up to the veranda. The two panels of the left-hand door, painted light blue, now cracked and faded, met in the middle, surrounded by a wooden frame that was beginning to rot at the bottom. The top two rectangles of both leaves were replaced by glass. A cotton curtain, once white, blocked the view into the room. The other door led into the only other room. It was the home of a small landowner. You did not see the wife. Or children.

The men were sitting round the front room on small carpet-cushions. They had already stood up to greet the *khan* and the newly arrived guest of honour. Changiz counted seven men, some he immediately recognised. But not all. They were dressed in their best costume to befit the homecoming of the hero. Changiz blushed red as he greeted each one. Warm. They were offered seats at the top of the room, carpet-cushions slightly thicker than others. A cylindrical paraffin-oil-fuelled Aladdin heater, pale blue, well-worn, sat in the middle of the room and the men sat round it, like the rim of a bicycle around an axle.

A young woman came round from behind a curtain at the back of the room with a tray of *chai*, tea. She wore a long cotton dress, split to waist down the sides, emerald-green with olive-green plants with white flowers coming down in a vertical cascade that stopped mid-calf, beneath which you saw another cotton dress reaching to the floor with entanglements of brown and white patterns. Her jet-black hair was visible in front of a white scarf wrapped round her neck and fastened in front of her Adam's apple, as was customary in Azerbaijan. She had clearly put on her best clothes even if it was for a walk-in part. As she passed the *chai* round, starting with the old *khan*, she greeted the new guests without looking into their eyes. Changiz had been struck by the blueness of her eyes as she walked into the room. She must have Kurdish blood, he thought and got up to take the tray from her.

"*Salam*" he said going redder. Big smile. Bashful smile back, and her eyes remained hidden beneath her long black lashes. She gently pulled the tray away from his grip and moved round the wheel, then slipped back behind the curtain. A second round of tea and then a third.

One by one the guests rose to leave. Günyaz asked each of them to stay for supper but all but one refused, despite several pleadings. An old friend of his father, with a large head and a head-full of grey hair, which he had carefully combed back. The wife moved the Aladdin to the side and laid out the cotton *sofreh* in the middle of the room. They had sacrificed a chicken, something they would only do for a very honoured guest. They ate in silence using bread as a spoon.

Afterwards the wife, who would eat with the other women and children separately and out of sight, cleared the table and brought in another tray of *chai*. As she went through the curtain, Günyaz noticed that the cup holding the sugar lumps was empty. He called out to her to bring the sugar. Nothing happened.

"Maybe she had ran out" Changiz said in a quiet voice. "Don't worry," he said to the host, I like my *chai* bitter.

Ignoring him Günyaz shouted.

"Bring that sugar woman, do you expect the guests to drink the tea with my balls!" Changiz reddened, trying hard not to laugh. A cupful of sugar was placed on the *sofreh*.

The men went on chatting about the harvest. She came in and cleared the room, replaced the Aladdin, and went out by the curtain. A few minutes later they heard her calling her husband from behind the curtain. Loud enough for everyone to hear.

"*Aqa*, if you don't want to fuck me tonight, I'll go to bed then," she said in a firm but resigned voice.

Changiz smileblushed. Günyaz frowned, as if denied. Maybe we should go, Changiz thought. He looked over but the old *khan* was deep in conversation with the man with a big head topped by a combedback grey mane. They were exchanging something about wheat. He smiled at Günyaz and recalled a funny episode in the last year of primary school. Something about putting a snake inside the religious teacher's desk. He had screamed in terror and a wet area had appeared in front of his grey trousers. And spread. Probably the only trousers he had. Certainly, the only trousers that he ever wore to class. They never saw him again.

No one in the entire evening had asked him about life inside. Yet it was for them and people like them he had gone to Tehran to fight and depose the Shah. The job, now completed, he was back in *velayat*.

[1] Also spelt *Qaradagh* and known also as *Arasbaran* is a mountainous and forested area north-east of Tabriz and south of the river Aras.

Chapter 31

Homecoming

Ahmad

When Ahmad and his old friend Mehrdad arrived at the Bazargan border point in the afternoon they were met by a veritable cacophony of the rooks feverishly circling the bare trees beneath a cloud cast sky and crawing with a collective passion unique to rooks.

"There's our welcoming party, and they are already in mourning clothes," Ahmad sniggered, pointing upwards with his chin. Mehrdad looked at him and squinted. He too may had been seduced by the way the Islamists had taken over the revolution, slogans and all. Ahmad's lonely dissenting voice was lost in the euphoria of victory.

The two had been in Europe alongside Sa'id and others, writing about the revolutionary struggles, and raising funds for the Fadai' when the volcano erupted back home. Now they were entering the country with Khomeini now firmly in power and his first appointed prime minister, also named Bazargan, busy dismantling all the various spontaneous peoples' *komitehs* and *shoras* set up by revolutionaries. Declaring the revolution over Bazargan was urging workers to go back to their factories and offices, dismissing elected bodies (*shoras*) in universities and replacing them with his appointees. But a return to a new normality was not that easy and for a while a dual power existed side by side across the country, one demanding a return to what was before minus the Shah, and the other wanting to realise the slogans of the revolution.

For the latter the revolution was only just beginning. And in a multilingual country the various nationalities were unhappy with a return to yet another centralised government. Weren't they promised their rightful place in the family of nations that was Iran? And the new regime thanked the women who had fought shoulder to shoulder with the men and told to return home where women belong. That too would not happen.

Mehrdad[1] had been a counterintelligence officer in the Shah's army before he was arrested by SAVAK. Their friendship had formed in the dark basement of the *Komiteh Moshtarek,* binding them in an emotional cocoon. What the *Komiteh* had bound only death could part. Or betrayal, which was the same thing. In Europe the two, alongside Sa'id and more, had been busy building up international support for the revolution and gathering financial help for the Fadai'. It was in Paris that Ahmad wrote an article warning his fellow countrymen of the dangers of clerical rule, the first Iranian to do so. No one was prepared to distribute the article in the *Université Sorbonne Paris Cité* where the opposition to the monarchy had set up its stands. The exiled left, like the majority inside the country, had become mesmerised by Khomeini sitting cross-legged under the apple tree nearby in the suburbs of Paris, giving audience to whoever called and promising everything to everyone. Maybe they should have reread the story of Genesis.[2]

The two had entered the country by bus through its only entry-point, each with a Turkish *laissez-passer,* a small shoulder bag and a head-full of yearning. At the Bazargan border post they had to disembark and walk through a large, asphalted area teaming with people, nearly all young men waiting to cross. Ahead was a large white flat building looking squat-squashed under some invisible weight. They squeezed through a single gateway, like a human funnel, manned by two armed Turkish soldiers who would let through a few at a time, their faces expressionless, wax statues looking out at the sea of black hair moving slowly forward like waves on a river. They were armed with machine guns, US made G3 Mehrdad observed, which they held tight like they might go off. Or a sexual organ. The two passed a man sitting in a kiosk, perhaps a border police, who barely looked at their *laissez-passer.* Then a large hall empty but for a row of low tables and an officer sitting, bored, smoking in the corner. A custom hall? Whoever had squeezed in before the two had evaporated through a gate straight ahead with a cubicle, unmanned, leading into an almost deserted courtyard, another unmanned cubicle, another almost empty customs hall, a handful of Iranian border guards chatting oblivious of the traffic, and out into Iran. No one had bothered to ask them who they were. The rooks cawed and crackled as if in warning.

The noise of revolution had evaporated into the cloudy sky. But everyone started singing as the bus restarted. The singing began with *baharan khojasteh bad*, (Greetings to Spring)which had become an instant hit and icon of revolutionary hope,[3] and then went on to popular songs, old and less old. Mehrdad who had a good baritone voice started some Fadai' songs. Some who knew the lyrics joined in. The exiled left was coming home.

The bus was halted at a number of checkpoints on the road from the Bazargan border, through Maku and on to Tabriz. Checkpoints that were run by local boys wearing improvised armbands of different colours. Green, black even red. No one seemed to know what they were supposed to check. More an assertion that they owned the roads. The country. The future. That night in Tabriz they walked the streets looking for somewhere to sleep. No place. No sleep. No bus. All full. The entire country seemed to be on the move. Let's walk the 600 kilometres to Tehran, the two decided, and left just after dawn. February mornings are cold in the north, especially after a cloudless night. A bus stopped and picked them up some distance outside the city and they satdozed their way in the central gangway, interrupted by roadblocks every few miles. They drove all day and the driver discharged them some kilometres outside Tehran. He didn't say why. It was a moonless night and the distant light of the capital combined with the soot obscured the milky way, or even individual stars.

"We can go to my house, its empty" Ahmad said.

The sun had barely risen when his sister brought them the house keys. Then the negotiations. The local lads had set up a large barricade across the road right in front of his house. No one seemed to recognise him and there was no way they were going to dismantle their barricade for these two men with thick moustaches and a woman they claimed was the sister of one of them.

"Go to the neighbourhood *komiteh*[4] and sort it out," the self-appointed barricade commander, a young man barely out of childhood holding a Kalashnikov like he had seen in movies, commanded, then abruptly turned his back. It was important business, manning a barricade. Who knows what the counter-revolution was planning? The two men and one woman were lucky he didn't arrest them. Finally a kid from the neighbourhood who had gone to buy some bread for the barricaders' breakfast came back.

"Ali-khan," Ahmad called over, "*salam*, you know me, don't you? I've been away for a bit, been out of town. But I'm back now. Please tell them who I am. Tell them that's my house and that I live here." Ali, a boy no more than 13 or 14 with a down of bending hair on his upper lips and a lisp recognised the architect. A word with the barricade commander and they moved the barricade further up the road. Then a deep, dreamless sleep. All next day a stream of people he knew dropped in, some with jute sacs full of arms and ammunition looted from army barracks.

Those were exciting days. Suddenly everyone was free, and the exhilarations were hypnotic. The entire country suddenly woke up to the novelty that you could choose. You could choose who you agreed with, who you wanted by your side, and who not. Everyone was lining up, some joining groups, others rediscovering that their beliefs and actions mattered. And mingling among this milieux were the opportunists who were manoeuvring for power. The entire country was in a fluid flux. Those were turbulent days.

Then as the dust settled on the country the lines began to harden. Khomeini began the formation of the Revolutionary Corps, the *Sepah-e Pasdaran*[5] and meanwhile used street thugs which he referred to as the party of God or *hezbollah*. They were sent to break-up any gathering of opponents to the new regime. And there were a growing number of such opponents as the regime began to clampdown on all those revolutionary organisations it did not totally control. Gone were the independent factory workers' *shoras* who ran the factories after the owners fled the country. Gone were the university *shoras* elected by students, academic staff and office workers and who ran the universities. The various headquarters (*setad*) set up by political groups in universities were attacked by the club-wielding *hezbollah* and closed down.

But Iran is a multi-ethnic, multinational, multilingual country and many of these also set up their own self-organisations. After years of iron-fisted central control from Farsi-speaking Tehran, there were widespread demands for some regional autonomy. Among these the most prominent were in Turkaman Sahra by the Caspian, by Arabs in Khuzestan and in Kurdistan. Their suppression needed greater force than the club-wielding mob.

The next few months were hectic. Mehrdad became active in Fadai' headquarters, the *Setad*, set up by their student ranch, the *Pishgam*, in Tehran University's College of Technology at first and later Meikadeh Avenue after Khomeini's thugs threw them out of their Tehran University headquarters. The University that had played such a crucial role in the final months of the revolution was to become clerical territory. Or as Khomeini put it: 'the place is an expression of the unity-of-university-and-*rohaniyat*,' the clergy or more literally the 'spiritual men'. Already the two halves of the revolution were refining their lines of separation. Every day hundreds of people would pour into the *Setad*. Those were exhilarating days when the Fadai' grew into a huge mass movement with tens of thousands of supporters.

[1] Mehrdad Pakzad.
[2] The devil, disguised as a serpent persuades Adam and Eve to eat the apple of knowledge of good and evil. They were expelled from the Garden of Eden. God clearly preferred them ignorant.
[3] Arranged and played on improvised instruments by Esfandyar Monfared-Zadeh on lyrics and music by Keramat Daneshian (based on a poem by Dr Abdollah Behzadi, a Tudeh member, on the murder of Patrice Lumumba, the first president of Congo). Daneshian had been executed by the Shah and Monfared-Zadeh himself had spent time in prison. The song dominated the airwaves in the first exhilarating post-revolutionary days.
[4] *Komiteh* (short for *Komiteh-e Enqelab* or Revolutionary Committee) were set up by the revolutionary forces to supervise every neighbourhood. They were soon dominated by Khomeini's supporters. They should be distinguished

from the Shah's *Komiteh Moshtarek* we met above.

[5] *Sepah-e Pasdaran Enqelab Eslami,* to give it its full name.

Chapter 32

The lost keys

Azadeh

"I will get those keys. It's not that difficult," Azadeh said, almost casually, and they all turned round and looked at her in utter amazement. She had not said a word until then and had almost been forgotten by the men. "I think I know how to do it. But I need a couple of volunteers who are not known to the regime." Her mezzo voice was assertive, her eyes moist with emotion, her pupils dilated. There was fire behind the black pupils. She was smiling with confidence, and she spoke with utter self-assurance while a faint flush on her neck betrayed her bounding heart. They all looked at her and no one spoke for an eternity.

"How?" It was Ahmad who broke the silence. She had been looking into his eyes the entire time. She was talking to him. Only him. Her eyes gently morphed into victory with knowledge. He saw her for the first time, again.

The three men, Ahmad, his friend Mehrdad and FN had been sitting around the main table in the central office at the new Fadai' headquarters (*Setad*) deep in a heated, and at times angry, discussion over where the country was heading. Azadeh sat on a folding metal chair a little way apart, not taking part in the argument, but within earshot.

The new *Setad* headquarters was a large building, formerly belonging to SAVAK which the Fadai' had seized. The walls of the office were covered in Fadai' posters, stuck neatly and lovingly by a girl in her late teens, one of the student *Pishgam* members, unusually tall for an Iranian, and who was now busy tidying up some leaflets on a metal table at the far end. Where they showed between the posters, the walls were dirty grey, clearly in need of fresh paint. A large blackboard on the right facing the door was almost entirely covered by a zigzag of messages, memos, information, phone numbers, in white chalk. Above the central table was a large window, one of whose panes was broken and a piece of glass had fallen off, disappearing into history. The fact that no one had bothered to fix it was a mirror to the disarray of the regime's security apparatus as it neared its death. Now there were more important things to think about. Somewhere, the ghost of the old king and his henchmen still hovered over the building those early days. The men were deep in a heated exchange when a young Fadai' walked in, breathless. All three stopped talking when the young man came in looking agitated.

"They have got Haydar," the young man said in a croaky voice "and a few others too." He had to take a breath between each phrase. He was dressed in what had effectively become the unspoken standard left outfit of a loose-fitting grey shirt worn over un-ironed baggy trousers, with the optional short khaki overcoat on top. His face was tanned. Maybe he got it running a bookstand outside the main university gate.

"Which others?" FN asked and the space between his eyes and eyebrows widened. Close by, you would have seen the sweat on his forehead below his hairline. The fear in his eyes was genuine. As one of the few survivors of the original Bijan Jazani-Zia Zarifi group, he was now at the head of the Fadai' Organisation. Everything reflected on him.

"I don't know. I don't know yet. They were having a meeting in Haydar's house. I think Ali was there. And maybe Abbas. Perhaps others" the young man spoke in spurts. He paused, looking from one to another. While he was talking his voice had dropped a decibel. What he had just said was like dynamite. If the three had been arrested that was a clear signal that the standoff, the interregnum between the Fadai' and Khomeini's newly formed special militia, the Revolutionary Corps (*Pasdaran*) was over. All three were high up in the Fadai' command structure. It looked bad.

"It's worse," the young man took a deep breath and continued in a loud whisper, "Haydar had the keys to the stores with him." The news was already out before the sound waves had reached FN. What was he doing with the keys to the arms stores in his pocket Ahmad thought? The idiot!

"What was he doing with the keys in his pocket? That is so careless. So stupid. So utterly stupid" Mehrdad said. His voice had tailed off as if he was speaking to himself. Totally negligent. The idiots had abandoned even elementary security he went on muttering under his breath.

"That's enough comrade" FN said impatiently, fire was racing through his dormant veins, but he managed to continue in the same pitch. "It is not just the arms, they will tear the boys to bits. It was only last week that we assured the Bazargan government[1] that we had handed in all our arms." But the tearing up of the boys wasn't his main concern.

FN's hope of working with what he thought were the radical sections of the new regime was being ploughed into dust. They didn't know, no one around that table knew, no one must know of the weekly negotiations he was having with the regime through the Tudeh Party. Not just yet. He was moving them slowly, gradually, moving the entire organisation, now ballooned into a huge nation-wide entity, into a new understanding. These people needed to be goaded, guided, coaxed into reality. They still lived in that revolutionary cloudland. Only he, FN and a handful of others in the leadership, understood power. Real power. True, most in the leadership had apparently rejected the armed struggle in name. But the gun lingered with its romantic allure. All those interminable discussions in the various prison cells had finally thrown out the gun only for its barrel to re-emerge through the back window. They, this lot of ex-guerrillas and romantics, didn't understand where power really resides.

All these thoughts flashed through his head, just like the day he was having a car crash years ago, and his entire life flashed in front of his eyes. A particular look of superiority came over FN's face that struck Ahmad, as repulsive. Ahmad knew of the secret weekly meetings with the heads of the Tudeh Party through friends. He had been excluded from the conspiracy for good reason. He would have objected. But there was a long way to go before the conspirators could take the entire organisation with them.

And here they were, leaders of the Fadai', stupid enough to carry a bunch of keys in their pocket in a meeting of the leadership. Had they not learnt anything from the years of repression? Getting hold of the keys to the armed stores and the looming prospects of armed clashes in Turkmen Sahra[2] and Kurdistan, where the Fadai' had a substantial presence, would definitely put a torch to his plans. FN was an expert in hiding his intense contempt for the dreamers, nurtured by years of direct proximity in one prison cell or another. But not completely. Ahmad saw it.

"Don't worry about the 'how'. Just get me the volunteers and leave the rest to me" Azadeh replied to no one in particular in a way that demanded nothing but assent.

And she did just that.

*

She was carefully dressed for the occasion. She wore a long, loose, dark blue raincoat reaching down to well below her knee beneath which she was wearing black, loosely fitting trousers and elegant black shoes with only a hint of a heel. On her head a dark scarf tied beneath her chin half-concealing the grey shirt underneath. A few strands of hair were showing from beneath the scarf above her high forehead. She had the look of austere elegance. The two men were dressed in expensive-looking clothes, but without ties.

As Azadeh walked into the main office of Qasr Prison with the two volunteers slightly behind her, she saw two *Pasdars* (revolutionary guards) sitting behind the desk. One of them was reading a book – white cover with no markings. A remnant of pre-revolutionary clandestine literature. His lips were moving silently as he read as if he was trying to read it twice. The other was writing something in a large ledger. She looked around the room assessing the situation. It was a large room, unswept. The walls were grey and on one side, a large patch of brownish urine-like stain spreading downwards and forwards across the ceiling and down the wall. A leak from the floor above. To the right of the stain hung a picture of Khomeini with his long somewhat scraggly beard looking sternly across the room at a picture of an eternally young mullah with large black eyes and a round well-kempt black beard. It was the standard imaginary image of the Prophet's cousin and son-in-law Ali who represented the pinnacle of justice and resolve. The two photos looked at each other, arching the ideal to the real. Around Khomeini's picture the wall was paler. That's where the Shah's picture must have hung, Azadeh thought with a smile. It must have been larger than the Ayatollah's. The three had walked in through a door that faced the table. The *Pasdars* looked up as she walked in.

She looked back with her fathomless pupils. The veins in her neck had caught fire from the audacity of her mission. She walked up to the table, opened her handbag and placed a white envelope on the table in front of the *pasdar* with the ledger who looked at her with the greedy eyes of a purchaser. The other pasdar stopped reading, put a finger between the pages he was reading, and lowered the book onto his lap. He had a vacant look. He didn't see a woman, only another mother or sister looking for their son or daughter, perhaps.

"We are from the Human Rights Organisation", she said as she pointed to the white envelope on the table. As she spoke the vibrations in her veins spread up and down her entire body and as she was pointing out the envelope the fear inside her was set ablaze and the fire rose to her lips and eyes. A confident smile gradually spread across her whole skin, her whole body, and confidence slowly drained away from the man with the ledger. It was as if there was a quantum of confidence in that room that was slipping from one to the other.

"We have a letter from the Head of Revolutionary Prisons giving permission for this inspection," she started, and her smile broadened, and her eyes widened into certainty. "We are here to talk to the prisoners to make sure they are treated fairly." She picked up the letter from the table where it had been lying friendless and handed it over to the ledger-*pasdar*. It was a letter introducing her as delegate from *Kanun Vokala*, the Society of Jurists.[3] The two men stood beside her, sufficiently behind not to be prominent as she talked and close enough to prevent her from flying off. In turn they handed over a letter of introduction from the Human Rights Association, and a letter of introduction from the Association of Democratic Lawyers.[4]

She talked to the two men on the desk. She talked to the other revolutionary guards they went out to fetch. She talked to the head of the prison. And each time she became more forceful. More confident. And something about her eyes made them believe her. The dark depth of her pupil which radiated a threat that these men, who may have lived through blood and revolution, yet retained the innocence of not knowing, melted in credulity. None of them noticed her slight hyperpnoea. None of them understood the dilated pupils. That knowledge was to come later, if they survived.

They were led through a door behind the desk, into a large vestibule which opened onto the three prison blocks and two courtyards. They were led into one of the courtyards. They talked to the prisoners who were sitting huddled together in a corner. Thirty or so young men, waiting for their fate, arrested, but not yet interrogated. She talked to some, some alone, and walked out with the keys in her trouser pocket, smiling her thanks. The guards watched and saw nothing.

As she walked out, she turned round as if to say something, changed her mind, looked up at Khomeini's portrait, looked down, smiled, nodded and walked out with her two companions. The sitting guard at the desk looked at her, didn't know if he should smile back, blushed, looked down.

In the car she broke down sobbing. Uncontrollably. Bottled. Warm. Quenching the fire that was burning the walls of her veins. Slowly, gently the veins in her neck returned to the silence of peace. Those were early days of post-revolutionary confusion. Her nerves of steel had triumphed.

[1] The first post-revolutionary government appointed by Khomeini to run the country while the clergy organised themselves. Mehdi Bazargan belonged to the religious section of the National Front (*Jebheh Melli*).
[2] With the help of the Fadāi', the Turkamans, a Turkish-speaking minority living along eastern Caspian Sea, had occupied the large agribusinesses belonging to the Shah's closest allies and ran it in the form of cooperatives They had also created the Turkaman People's Political-Cultural Centre (*Kanun-e Farhangi-Siast Khalq Turkmen*). The new regime attacked them in the first Turkaman war in March 1979 which ended in a temporary truce. The second Turkaman war took place a year later and their leader, Tumaj,

was executed with three others on the order of *ayatollah* Khalkhali, at the time the topmost religious judge in the country.

[3] *Kanun Vokala* – the Society of Jurists – that had been prominent in the early period of the revolution. Not much later it was disbanded by Khomeini's followers.

[4] *Anjoman Hoquq Bashar* and *Tashkilat Hoquq-danan Democrat*, both soon to be disbanded.

Chapter 33

Moving south

Ahmad

It was a time of abandon. It was a time of exhilarating freedoms. It was a time of change. It was a time of chaos.[1] People owned the streets. The sky looked more blue. The winter was milder than anyone remembered. In those early days cars stopped at red lights uncoerced. Street cleaners cleaned unsupervised. The air tingled with liberation as if its molecules were oscillating with joy. Arms, even submachine guns, were put out for sale on the pavement, lying next to books. A friend would drive over with a van full of Russian vodka, now a banned item, and offer it for the price of a bicycle. There was no real government, especially when you moved away from the capital.

In Shiraz, a handful of university professors had taken over the television station and effectively governed the entire Province, especially at night when the mullahs shadowing them went to bed, not having figured out rotas. The TV station's phone was the only place people from the province could ring for help.

"Armed tribesmen have occupied a broadcasting antenna on such-and-such hill, what can we do?" We will call the gendarmes for you, replied the duty professor, and did.

"Our infirmary has no antibiotics," a voice from a provincial town. We will organise shipment from Sa'adi Hospital, said the duty professor, and did.

In the middle of the second night, Reza, the duty professor from the School of Agriculture was dozing by the telephone when he was woken from a dream he immediately forgot. The voice at the other end was that of an agitated and frightened young man. His incoherence and the poor lines made any understanding of what he was trying to convey difficult. The half-asleep professor only managed to catch the words "America" and "ship", before they were cut off. What was that poor boy trying to say? Something bad must be happening in one of our ports in the Persian Gulf, and the young man's terror leaped the distance, infecting the professor of agriculture. The phone rang again, then was discontinued. And again. The middle-aged professor was getting really agitated now. Things must be serious if the young man was so persistent. Slowly, like a jigsaw in a child's cupboard with several pieces missing, Reza managed to build a picture. The place was Bandar Abbas, and the young man was a conscript left to guard the naval base in Iran's main commercial and military port on the Gulf. All the officers, sailors and soldiers had absconded leaving the poor boy to guard the vast naval base. The young conscript had valiantly stood his ground when he had spotted two US warships approaching Bandar Abbas. He had frantically rang around but couldn't get through to the local army base, the main police station in the city, the gendarmerie or any other base in Fars province. Our duty professor was his last resort, and the desperate young conscript was clearly relieved to find someone who would listen. After ringing around frantically for an hour or so, Reza got through to an airbase in another province. "We will send a couple of Phantom Jets to scare the ships off," they promised. The warships were duly chased away.

That next morning the mullah on duty, *hojatoleslam* Movahed[2] arrived after a good night's sleep at home and Reza gave him a verbal report which he graciously accepted, and then handed over the control of the TV station and the Province to the next professor on the rota. That lunchtime, when offered two fried eggs on *taftun* flat-bread, Movahed graciously pushed it away. "It is not what the poor eat (the word he used for poor was *mostaz'afin*).[3] Bring me bread and cheese", he said and after a respectable few minutes, graciously consumed the two fried eggs and *taftun* bread. These were the new rulers, but had yet to learn how to rule. Such was the nature of dual power in those early days.

It was a time of heady freedom, a time of intoxication where the gap between desire and attainment appeared miniscule. Yet at that moment of cosmic exhilaration Ahmad felt suffocated by raw emotions. An overpowering need to escape from the possibility of closer human relationship, the glue of gloom slowing his very being. Unlike some who need closeness to navigate distance, he derived strength from solitude. Proximity to emotions ossified his thinking. Only with people who had intense empathy and a long, long history could he be himself. Otherwise, it was roleplay.

He escaped to his roots in the south, as far away as geography permitted. He handed the arms that had been delivered to his apartment to the Fadai' *Setad* or had them buried somewhere, gave over the place to his friend, Mehrdad, and went down to Abadan to join his childhood friend Mansur. There he reverted to the cloak that had served him so well in pre-revolutionary days, architecture, perfect as a front. He took command of the Khuzestan[4] division of the Fadai'.

Mansur was sitting by a desk writing in one of the two offices they had set up in Ahwaz and Abadan as cover. In his mid-thirties, Mansur, a poet, softly spoken, with bones of steel, a high forehead, curly hair, and unlike all the men we have met, our poet was unmoustached. A clean upper lip, hair-free, only because he had recently shaved it. Probably a poetic impulse. It was to grow back soon. It was mid-spring when Ahmad walked into the Abadan office grinning.

"Can you get hold of a van quickly?" he said. His grin turned into a sly smile. He had forgotten to greet.

"Now what have you bought?" Mansur said, knowing as only a close friend could.

"Oh nothing special. Only an entire warehouse full of printers, all 509 of them. Large printers, small printers, offset machines, everything. I bought the lot."

"What on earth are we going to do with 509 printers? Eat them? Export them? Have you gone mad or are you just shopping for the entire country?" Ahmad just smiled knowing that his childhood friend had already understood.

This was a spending spree that would have raised suspicion at any other time. But they were in the honeymoon period of virtual dual power. Semi-chaos above and semi-chaos below. There would be a use for them all. Between them they put together numerous print houses in the south, carefully camouflaged behind innocent looking offices. Being an architect had its uses. With Mansur, who spoke Arabic, they started two Arabic language papers. Then together they moved north to their childhood city-port of Khorramshahr. The next months were frantic with activity: organising workers in the oil industry, teachers in primary and secondary schools around Abadan, Khorramshahr and Ahwaz, studying conditions of the Arab minority, writing, organising. He was after all in charge of the largest Fadai' Organisation outside Tehran.[5]

Over the next year people gradually became disillusioned with how things were developing. The constant attack on any opposition to the regime, no matter how lukewarm, by street thugs, the compulsory *hijab* for women, the banning of music and videos, the expulsion of the left from the elected factory *shoras* (committees), the purging of thousands of teachers from schools, the purging of government offices, the attempts to purge the universities, the suppression of all national and ethnic self-organisation, and the all-out attack on Kurdistan, the daily experience of eliminating anything that did not fit the vision of the ruling clergy for the country.

Thus, the space slowly contracted, and freedom gradually evaporated. Within a year of the Shah's fall all political organisations were outlawed. The old *mulla,* Khomeini, went on television and threatened to erect scaffolds at crossroads across the country. The battle was once again being pushed underground, but the scales were still not as uneven as they would become later. Dissent was in the air.

Nowhere did the growing unease across Iran show itself better than when eleven months into the new regime the people went out to vote for the first presidential elections and cast their vote for Abolhasan Bani-Sadr who won a landslide victory over Khomeini's preferred candidate, Jalaleddin Farsi with, with just under 80% of the votes. Bani-Sadr attracted votes from most of the left and the democratic section of society as well as those who would have voted for the Mujahedin candidate whom Khomeini had earlier disenfranchised.[6] Six weeks later, in the first election to the *Majles* (parliament), ten percent of the vote in the capital was cast for left candidates. Asqar was one of the candidates of the left in Tehran and over 50,000 votes were cast in his name. That was before candidates had to pass through the ever-tighter ideological and loyalty sieve.

Azadeh joined them in Khorramshahr despite all his efforts to prevent this crack in his cocoon. Everyone else had insisted, oblivious to the roots of his objections. She had demonstrated her extraordinary ability in Tehran, and they needed her here. Everyone recognised her remarkable innate skills in creating opportunities. And she was very persistent. Grudging recognition of her qualities clashed with a rising aversion that he could barely conceal. An intense and evolving tension between attraction, and revulsion at his attraction, a tension between emotion and obligation.

After two weeks of living in the same house with her, he moved out. It was easier to prevent his shell cracking further if they lived apart. He moved in with Mansur in accommodation that they changed constantly.

The year was hectic. Printing. Sitting up till the early hours with Mansur, writing articles, supervising the numerous publications, organising workers, sympathisers, the Organisational outfit. They had to make sure their links with the printing press and with the Organisation were well camouflaged. This meant separating what was clandestine and what was open. It was a delicate task, forever evolving and metamorphosing, building barriers, walls to conceal, false floors - the semi-clandestine life was a living organism with a life and a death. Somewhere, always barely beneath the surface, hovered the entwining of attraction-aversion. It was a busy year.

Then Saddam Hussein attacked Iran and war broke out.

[1] *It was the best of times, it was the worst of times, it was the age of wisdom, it was the age of foolishness...* Charles Dickens, *A Tale of Two Cities*.

[2] In the Shia' hierarchy, *hojatoleslam* is one level below an *ayatollah*. You need to write a treatise approved by some learned clerics to become an *ayatollah*.

[3] Meaning the weak or the underdog which is how the Islamic regime prefers to refer to the poor or the working population, avoiding the word 'worker' which has class connotations.

[4] Oil-rich province in South-West Iran.

[5] At its height the Fadai' had over 2,000 supporters in the oil-rich province.

[6] The Mujahedin had grown into the largest opposition organisation in the country, though at this stage they preferred to bide their time and declared allegiance to the person of Khomeini. Their leader Masoud Rajavi was their proposed candidate for the presidency.

Chapter 34

War

Ahmad

Ahmad was working in his Ahwaz office when foreign troops crossed the Shatt-al-Arab river. Wartalk had been crisscrossing the airways for days, but the Iraqi invasion took everyone by surprise. It was the day before schools opened. The last day of summer. Autumn once more churning up the future. He set off for Khorramshahr immediately. Saddam's troops were on the outskirts of a city which housed the southern headquarters of the Fadai' with six or seven cadres and many hundreds of workers, teachers, students, women, unemployed, numerous clandestine networks, and countless secret printing presses.

The Iraqis had overrun the Ahwaz-Khorramshahr road but east of Karun River the road to Abadan was still open. He drove down to Abadan and stayed the night in a safehouse. Don't go, his comrades cautioned him. Obstinacy came naturally with being solitary. And confident. Over-confident? Maybe. Reckless? Sometimes. What he didn't put into words was a very personal concern. His stubbornness had an emotional core, he wanted to evacuate a childhood friend Hassan and his pregnant wife and bring them out to the safety of Ahwaz.

With him was a comrade belonging to the military arm of Fadai' who had seen training in Palestine. They travelled north in Ahmad's green Peugeot, one of the few moving against the tide of refugees coming the other way.

They arrived in the early morning as Khorramshahr was emptying. Mortars were exploding all round them, as far out as the first gendarmerie control post on the road from Abadan. People had piled whatever they could salvage on the back of flat trailers, once used to carry iron girders from the port, on lorries, cars, mule-drawn carts, or even wheelbarrows. But Hassan, the only friend close enough to his heart to be called *kakaye-man*, 'my brother', the man who had been central to his life, the man at the core of his first-ever interrogation, the same Hassan who was supposed to have passed on Mao's Little Red Book from the Chinese vessel, had already left, his house was empty and his neighbourhood was rapidly emptying. The Iraqis were hoping to enter an empty city.

Suddenly he felt drained. There could only be one *kaka* at any given time, and his *kaka* had gone without a trace. Iraqi mortars were pulverising his childhood memories. His childhood. His history. He began to walk the streets alone. The narrow alleyways were empty, and as he walked the deserted alleys of his childhood, those tiny fragments of memory that interact through time to become a narrative of a life blurred and all feeling seemed to slowly drain out of him leaving an expanding hollow inside. On all sides he was surrounded by dead birds. Had they died of fright or had they been poisoned by gas? An intense dejection overwhelmed him. Mudbrick walls protecting tiny courtyards had half crumbled here and there, exposing a tiny pond in the middle, an abandoned tin wash tub on its side with half-scrubbed clothes, soggy, the soap discarded in fear. Desolation had descended not just on Khorramshahr, but on Ahmad. A feeling of deep loneliness overwhelmed a man who loved being alone.

All day he walked alone, till dusk and darkness closed the window to memory. He entered an apparently empty house to find somewhere to stay the night. The owner must have been a civil servant, or a bank manager, someone who had spare money which showed in his choice of chairs. Perhaps he had built the house on inherited land, deliberately making sure that his wealth showed with just that bit more colour to the doors, especially ones the neighbourhood could see. It was visibly incongruous with surrounding houses, a house hopefully provoking envy for a successful man. He opened the refrigerator, and it was half pregnant with food. The owners had left in a hurry, they had not even folded the mattress, which still had the imprint of the human body it had lured to sleep. He smelt the smell of panic in the walls. On the doorstep an abandoned single slipper had flipped on its front, as if dead.

Out again in the alley a grey door opened and a little girl in a flowery white cotton dress ran out. She was barefoot and crying. She looked terrified. A woman, her mother perhaps, ran after her, picked her up in her arms, squeezing love to her breast, and sobbed. He walked on. A dark cloud of dust and smoke obscured the sun, glooming all that remained alive. Or even the dead. The once beautiful port was enveloped in the pungent smell of burning homes and date trees and burnt explosives. The only living thing that was not fleeing was the bougainvillaea, living and colourbright under the gloom, surviving the war in bright pink and red and white splashes, like coloured crepe paper. Maybe they thrive on explosions because they are not really alive. Only the dead can survive the carnage of their homes. Their neighbourhood. Their city. It was difficult to breathe.

Then he saw an old man sitting on a stone platform outside a house. A small house no more than three metres in width. He went over and sat down.

"Salam *amu jan*, uncle dear. What are you doing here, sitting alone?" he said lowvoiced, so as not to disturb the desolation. "Everyone has left. Why are you still here?"

"Salam *pesar jan,* dear-son," the old man said after a long pause, looking down at the uneven earthen alley floor. "Where would I go?" His voice was gruff from years of smoking. Or just wear. The words came out slowly, reluctantly, as if they too could not breathe the silent gloom. Weary.

"Have you nowhere to go?"

"No *pesaram*, my son. I have nowhere. Nowhere. There is nowhere for me. Nowhere." The last word came from a different part of his body. Slowly, in measured words, he unfolded his story. In short pieces, broken sentences, almost as if it was a real effort to expel the words. Deep emptiness between the sentences.

"Twenty, thirty years ago. I came here to earn some money. Put aside something. Save. Go back to the *velayat,* my province, Lurestan. Maybe find a wife. Set up a family. How can I go back now?" He paused long, breathing heavy with sorrow. Or just fatigue. "How can I return empty handed? I couldn't face the people. I don't have anything. I don't even have a gift for them. A whole life spent here, and to return empty handed? No. I'll just stay here and die."

A watery film covered up the redness of the white of his eyes. Then a teardrop slid down and rested on a round crater leaning on his nose. Ahmad only now noticed the potholes of smallpox that marked his age. And the shallow crater of *salak,*[1] with its uneven base dividing up the salty drop, as if to conceal its protest. He had survived a lethal disease to face this earthly devastation. Ahmad's tears spilled inwards.

It was a black day, he remembered, and there was a long pause in his narrative. He had walked his childhood alleys all that day and the next.

---

[1] Cutaneous leishmaniasis a condition caused by the sandfly, and very common in the Middle East.

Chapter 35

The man who trained in Palestine

Ahmad

Close to a bridge across Karun river, which the invading Iraqis had spared to allow their march to Abadan, the Pasdaran had their headquarters and one of the local Fadai' cadres had rented a home. It was a perfect hideout to set up a shortwave radio for news from across the country. Ahmad and some of his comrades he had met in the street crossed over the bridge to the right bank and stayed the night in that house. In their panicked retreat, Iranian troops had failed to demolish it.

Early next morning they walked along a wide avenue extending along the river for three to four kilometres, while mortars were flying death into Khorramshahr. Here and there Fadai' supporters had set up barricades, trying to boost the morale of the few people still remaining in the port-city. The army had abandoned the nearby garrison, leaving behind all its arms and ammunition. There were many abandoned vehicles which they started keyless, and loaded as much as they could in a few abandoned Peikan cars and pickup vans they found as well as Ahmad's green Peugeot. Ahmad was thinking of how useful they would be in the ongoing battle in Kurdistan.[1] All the while the sky rained exploding metal.

"Lets get everyone together and decide where we want to go from here," Ahmad said to a comrade. He sounded exhausted. His mouth was dry and he had not eaten for two days. At that moment the southern section under

189

his command was in utter confusion like the Fadai' everywhere. The entire Fadai' organisation had been caught off guard by the invasion at a time when they themselves were deeply divided about the nature of the new regime and their relationship with it - are they in opposition or an ally albeit with qualifications. It was difficult to formulate a policy when you were clashing with the regime to stop its assaults on every democratic gain of the revolution, including Turkaman Sahra and Kurdistan, and at the same time sidling up to the faction closest to Khomeini.

Gradually they collected most of the leading cadres and leaders of the southern sector but sitting down to meet proved more elusive. They would gather somewhere, an abandoned house, a courtyard, anywhere out of sight, but had to abandon because of that lethal rain. In one house, they had barely sat down when the walls of the adjacent room collapsed. They moved across to the narrow corridor but there too they were mortared and lucky to escape unscathed. In the end, they did not make any decisions but did find food in abandoned fridges.

Evening was drawing close when the group came to an abandoned street barricade opposite the city prison. The prisoners had all absconded and a single policeman was guarding the gate – a sad relic of duty. Ahmad and another comrade decided to stay the night sheltering in the barricade. He had parked his Peugeot with its boot full of arms in an alleyway nearby. It was too risky to drive at night. A shadow approached and he immediately recognised the tall man who had trained in Palestine by his droopy shuffling walk, Charlie Chaplin in a tall frame, his travelling companion. Ahmad beckoned him over. He grinned as he recognised familiar faces.

"Where have you been all day?" Ahmad asked more annoyed than curious.

"You wouldn't believe the incompetence," the newcomer said in a breathless voice, ignoring the tone of the question, and a huge grin spread over his unshaven stubble. "These guys hadn't a clue how to use an RPG7. Didn't have a clue in hell," he added and grinned even deeper into his ears. "I had to teach them." Ahmad noticed his unusually large head for the first time, made even larger by an untidy crop of dull-black hair that had not seen soap for days or perhaps weeks. It was a perfect target for a sniper.

"Which guys? What are you talking about?" Ahmad interrupted the man who had trained in Palestine. "You shouldn't have wandered off at such a time." He sounded like a schoolmaster.

"These guys are just boys, just boys. Little boys putting up a resistance against tanks and artillery. Pathetic they were. I walked in there and they didn't even ask who I was. Those boys manning the barricades, heroic, they were. Pathetically heroic. But I taught them how to fire an RPG" the newcomer was excited, ignoring the reprimand, and went on to describe, in minute detail like a storyteller in a *qahveh khooneh* coffee house, staccato, how he had walked over to the barricades manned by some local kids, heroically trying to stave off the Iraqi army. "I shot a tank," the tall man trained in Palestine added and grinned once more. Ahmad, who had been momentarily distracted by the man's shiny white teeth, suddenly felt a surge of emotion which climbed up his spine and ended on the crown of his head, as if his veins had backflowed. It was so unexpected and unprovoked he felt momentarily lost, like a child. It must be the emotional exhaustion and he tried to focus back on what the man who trained in Palestine had done when a mortar hit the house behind and all three ducked down into the shallow dugout behind the makeshift barricade. They are mortaring at night too, blindly. The man who had trained in Palestine didn't want to stop talking, deep in his story, oblivious to the outside world.

Ahmad had seen a cream Peikan carrying four *pasdars* moving up and down the avenue running along the river. It stopped in front of the prison and a *pasdar* leant out from the far window and exchanged some words with the policeman guarding the empty prison, then got out and walked casually over to the barricade. The guard must have said something about the three men hiding behind the rampart. Salam, he greeted. He was carrying the standard Kalashnikov, casually slung over his shoulder. He was a young man in his early twenties, unshaven as they all were, and a dark skin hinting that he was a local lad. He didn't look threatening.

"What are you doing here?" the *pasdar* said in a friendly tone and turned his torch on Ahmad. "Who are you, *to ki hasti*? *Esmet chieh*, what's your name?" he asked using the informal 'you', *to*. Was he chosen by chance or was there something in the body language that marked him? Ahmad winced in the light even though it wasn't particularly bright.

"I am local, from this town (*bacheh shahram*)" and gave his real name, his real address and the schools he had attended.

The other comrade was also a local lad, and gave his true details. He was in fact in charge of the city's Fadai' organisation. Then the torch turned to the man who had trained in Palestine and the *pasdar* began the same question but suddenly he stopped mid-sentence.

"Aren't you the guy who destroyed the tank with the RPG?" and before the tall man who had trained in Palestine could answer through his grin, the *pasdar* slid off and lifted his Kalashnikov. "Where did you learn how to use an RPG?" he asked in a different tone of voice. "Lie down with your hands behind your head! Don't move!" His comrades came over. Search their pockets! he ordered. One of them, a young man, probably no more than eighteen, reached into Ahmad's jean pocket and pulled out a long ribbon of paper.

"What's this?" the first *pasdar* said in a mocking voice, no, more like a triumphant voice, like the tone you use when you discover some kid in a hide and seek game. He waved the ribbon of paper in the air like he had just uncovered a viper's nest and killed the mother snake.

"Oh, nothing special. I wrote them down from the local radio news broadcast. For my own interest. I live here, as I've said. I need to know what's happening all around me, don't I?" Ahmad was calm. "Doesn't everyone," he smiled, and his smile was sincere, his pupils remained non-dilated. He hadn't technically lied. He had jotted bits of information about bombings and other acts of war in various parts of Khuzestan from the short-wave radio messages they had received in that safehouse opposite the revolutionary guard headquarters. For later use when he got back to headquarters.

They were transported in the back of a pickup van under armed guard, south to Abadan, and handed over to the *Sepah Pasdaran* prison.

[1] The demand by Iranian Kurdistan for autonomy was met with force. The Kurdistan Division of the Fadai' joined the two local Kurdish parties (Kurdistan Democratic Party – KDP, and the *Kumeleh*) in fighting back the attack by the army and *Sepah Pasdaran* on the Kurdistan Province.

Chapter 36

Abadan prison

Ahmad

It was the old SAVAK headquarters in Abadan, now transmuted into a prison run by the *Sepah Pasdaran*. There followed an amateurish interrogation, interspersed by amateurish beatings, to which Ahmad point-blank refused to reply. What right have you to question me, he repeated as if he was someone above questioning. The experience of the last days had ripped open his entire being, exposing the raw animal beneath. A dying childhood city whose very soul had fled drained his veins from those natural defence mechanisms time had hammered into our bones over millennia. The young *pasdars* were intimidated by the animal aura that arose from his eyes.

They took him into a room and made him stand beside what looked like a school desk. There was a large desk on the other side of the room, unoccupied and empty. A number of *pasdars* sat on a bench by the wall and a *pasdar* stood guard on either side of him. When the local religious judge, *hojatoleslam* Araki, walked in, all the *pasdars* stood up as they would for their headmaster. The white-turbaned *mullah* walked behind a large table followed closely by a small middle-aged man with a thin moustache, a caricature of a scribe, holding a folder tight to his chest. The *mullah* opened a thin folder which the little scribe had handed to him and held up the strip of paper. What is this? He said in mock-anger. To which organisation do you belong? He had the hoarse voice of someone with laryngitis. Same answer as before: I wrote down the news from radio stations. Why? For my own use. It's war and we are being bombed. I am recording it for myself, for my own use. Recording what's going on. Anyway, you have no right to question me. I'm a son of this town, this is my town. I was born here, went to school here and am now being bombed out of it, like everyone else, he added, his last word.

After rummaging for a few minutes in the folder, picking up bits of paper and looking them over front and back, without apparently reading them, he turned to Ahmad.

"You know the punishment for spying for the enemy," the *mullah* said, and waved him out. Pinkish lips, Ahmad noticed. Didn't look at all comfortable. Maybe he feels inferior with his white turban, not the black one that signifies direct parentage to the Prophet. Or maybe it is his vitiligo. In wartime a death sentence for a spy was routine. The whole thing had taken no more than a few hours. A mortar exploded somewhere close. As if on cue.

Separated from his two comrades he was led into a concrete courtyard, covered by wire netting and separated from the refinery wall by a netted metal fence that also acted as a corridor where the guards could go to their office block or exit through the main gate. With the wire netting covering the roof and side, it was like living in a chicken coop under a blackish purple sky raining the coagulated soot that had floated up from the burning refinery and congealed by the warm dampness of autumn. Everything around was black. Reality had lost its way. Very cinematic.

There were perhaps a dozen inmates, including an ex-SAVAK agent, a young Fadai' sympathiser, a middle aged man with leathery skin who had been picked up swimming across the Karun river and who refused to speak, a rotund Arab sheikh suspected of pro-enemy sympathies, an Arab youth who had pulled a knife on a *pasdar* for some unknown reason, a man accused of embezzlement married to a famous singer, a man from Abadan who had insulted Khomeini in a fit of rage, and one or two others arrested as Iraqi spies. Ahmad swiftly signalled to the Fadai' sympathiser, a small upward lift of eyebrows, to feign non-recognition. He remained aloof from the rest.

On that first day in the coop a *pasdar*, a young man as they all were, with a facial bristle that signalled his religious faith but made him look unwashed came up to him, his dark eyes smiling mischievously, and pulled him aside, out of earshot.

"My brother is one of your lot," he said in a rapid, almost inaudible voice that came from lips that hardly moved. He had a deep *bandari* accent[1] and an incongruously deep bass voice for his small stature which made whispering rather difficult. "They know you are here," he whispered, trying to dampen the resonating sound waves with his body. "It was me who told them. I can take messages for them if you want," and quickly suppressed a smile in case someone was watching. Ahmad looked at him, blank. This could be a trap, though if it was, it was absurdly amateurish.

The days rolled over under a rain of coagulated soot layering everything black-grey, echoing his own growing facial hair. The ex-SAVAK man, thin, with a thin face and a thin nose, sliding knife-like down the centre, highlighting his sunken cheeks, and thin lips, prematurely purpled by smoking opium came over. One look at Ahmad's bare feet had been sufficient to know its history. He sidled up. I only trailed people, he said in a voice that tried to please, replying to an unasked question. I was no torturer, the man continued arguing for a hearing. I had nothing to do with interrogations, absolutely nothing. Probably a regular opium taker, Ahmad thought and remained cold and silent. I have had some clean shirts sent in. I can let you have one, he offered. No thanks, Ahmad replied, the only words that he had said, and deeply offended the ex-Savaki. Ahmad also offended the man who had pulled a knife on a *pasdar* when he refused his offer of a blade to shave off his expanding mass of facial hair. He just wanted to be alone.

A day like yesterday. A *pasdar* called Ahmad's name and took him out into the adjacent grassy area, open to the sky where a number of tables had been set up under a make-shift awning with a few *pasdars* sitting or standing around.

"Sign this piece of paper" the *pasdar* said as he pushed a paper towards him. He was about to read what was offered when two mortars fell nearby and one of them hit the wire-mesh corridor. The *pasdars* immediately fell flat covering their heads. He stood indifferent.

"That's him, my husband!" A woman was screaming from where the wire-mesh corridor had once completed the chicken coop. "You scoundrels. You told me he is not here. There he is. My husband. There he is, you liars, over there!"

A woman expertly clutching a black *chador* under her chin which covered up her whole body like a tent ran across the trodden grass and threw her arms around his neck. It took him a second or more to recognise Azadeh. She had pushed open the mortar-damaged front gate and clamoured over the torn wire mesh. Where did she learn to hold the *chador* so professionally, not a strand of hair showing? And where did she get that shrieking voice, and he marvelled at the audacity of the girl? She had been outside for who knows how long protesting, pretending to be his wife. That girl has courage, he thought as a *pasdar* grabbed hold of her arms and tried to drag her away. She pulled her arm free with a jerk, adjusted her *chador*, turned round, and looked the *pasdar* in the eye.

"Would you be happy, brother, if a stranger tore your sister from her husband in this brutal way?" she said. The word brother escaped her mouth in a tone that mingled intimacy and threat. A strange pitch. Authoritative, leaving little room for dissent. The young *pasdar* blushed and retreated, confused, and stood with his partner watching from afar the husband and wife sitting side by side on a bench.

"We know of the death sentence" she said in a low fast voice, shielding the words with her *chador*, smiling all the while for the distant audience. "The lads have had a meeting. They have looked at the security of this place and it's really basic. They want to get you out." Short, sharp and very direct, pure Azadeh. He felt a sudden deep emotion that almost stopped his blood pulsating. A totally novel experience. Then the black-purple sky spread its blanket.

"No," he said, looking straight through her dark pupils. "I know how unprepared our organisation is. I am its architect. I created it and I know full well its strengths and weaknesses. We, our organisation I mean, are totally unprepared for the sort of circumstances facing us now. You try anything like that and the entire set up will be blown apart and go up in smoke, at great human cost, with hardly any effort by them. We will be annihilated, I better than anyone know how vulnerable to annihilation we are. No. Tell them under no circumstances are they to embark on such a mad adventure. It is a definite no, and that's an order." The last words were delivered in a voice that was soft enough not to be heard by the approaching *pasdars* but firm and clear.

"Stop acting the hero *(pahlevoon bāzi)*,"[2] was the last thing she said to him angrily, almost in desperation as they pulled her away forgetting that they should not be touching a strange woman. It was said loud enough to be overheard if the *pasdars* had not been deafened by surprise. They let go of her as if she was scorching coal. She made a move to kiss him on his cheek but changed her mind mid movement. She was unused to failure. A strange feeling of love and anger surged like a freak wave round her upper half bouncing against her inner walls, not settling. With those words was she mocking him or pleading. The blackness of her brown eyes rippled beneath the moistness. For a brief second he felt the closest he had come to longing. Then he blocked all feeling under soot. It was a final farewell. He saw his own corpse and it was emptied of love.

As she walked away the wave of emotion avalanched and tumbled downwards inside her plunging into her inner lake. Love and bitter anger at his selfishness tumbled in a jumble. He had elevated his freedom to die over her freedom to possess. Selfishness of martyrs who see only their own glory. There could be no understanding between these two versions of life. His last words were a smile that seemed to originate from some inner core and covered his outer skin, entire. Inside her, love burst into a self-destructive flame.

She hated losing, even to the dead.

[1] Coming from the Bushehr province along the northern border of the Persian Gulf.

[2] Literally 'playing the strongman'. Rostam, the legendary hero of the 8th

Century poet Ferdowsi's *Shahnameh* (*Book of Kings*) is the prototype.

Chapter 37

Khalkhali

Ahmad

"The *hakem sharr* is here" the young friendly *pasdar* walked over and whispered one afternoon emphasising the 'R' in a voice that was barely audible, virtually drowned in repressed tears. He used the word *sharr*, meaning evil rather than *shar'* (*sharia*) for the religious judge. "Khalkhali is coming to confirm the sentences. The death sentences," the young friendly *pasdar* added, louder. Ahmad looked at the totally distressed young man and smiled. Faintly. Ayatollah Khalkhali, the most senior religious judge notorious for his summary death sentences, had been chosen by Khomeini to ratify all death sentences passed by provincial judges to quash rumours that innocent people were being executed by inexperienced judges. His reputation for death preceded him. He had once said to a reporter that if he were to execute someone in error, it wouldn't matter, since the victim would become a martyr and go straight to heaven. He was, as the young *pasdar* said, the epitome of evil.

"You remember the clean shirt you offered me the other day." he asked the ex-Savaki man later that night. "Can I have it now please?" The same question for the razor of the knife-pulling young man. Having dressed for martyrdom, he spent the hours of darkness thinking.

Dawn was about to break and the first call to prayer, the *azān*, had just finished being wafted across from the local mosque when Ahmad was led out of the chicken coop under a sky that was purple-red and dark like a rotting carcass. Ahmad's shaven cheeks had bits of red showing here and there where the blunt razor had sliced the dermis. He wore a clean white shirt, like a death shroud. He was preparing himself. For some reason the image that kept popping into his head, in the way images just leap in uninvited, was El Sordo on the hill in Spain's Sierra de Guadarrama,[1] resisting and dying for a cause he deeply believed in, but fighting within a flawed structure, the inner world of images and dialogue, uncontrollable, but with their own inner logic. The young friendly *pasdar* led him out through the meshed corridor, through a wooden door into another corridor with a proper roof. A farewell look at the dark purple-red dawn sky. He looked like someone taking his pet lamb to be sacrificed. Ahmad probably did not even notice the tears in the young *pasdar's* eyes. Or maybe he did. No one really knows how another thinks. Do they even know their own dark caves? Not easy to penetrate the mind of someone else without contaminating it with yours. Images slip.

Along the corridor a row of men were sitting, leaning against the wall, head bent down in dejection. He sat down by the wall beside the two comrades arrested with him. Nodded recognition. No words. A comforting smile. Smile back. Resigned. The morning prayers over, he was the first to be ushered through a door into a large room. He had been here before.

At one end was a table behind which sat Khalkhali in a military costume several sizes too small for his huge bulging stomach. He looked ridiculous. Next to him the scribe. Opposite were several benches on which two or more dozen *pasdar* commanders sat. The young friendly *pasdar* took Ahmad to a bench that was at right angle to the others, sat him down, and returned to the door, standing with his back to the wall, eyes to the unswept floor. This was going to be a theatre of Islamic justice. Ahmad had an audience. He had always liked an audience.

"What have we got here?" Khalkhali started, getting up slowly, menacingly, theatrically, in his deep bass voice, almost fruity, a voice that was quite pleasant if you closed your eyes. "Let me see," he turned and looked straight at Ahmad. "What organisation do you belong to?" he said, holding up the strip of paper with a strange smile curving his thick lips. His eyes sparkled through his round black glasses, mischievously. He was comfortable, indeed overconfident in the role allotted to him, the butcher of the revolutionary courts. Ahmad looked at his round face, rounded more by the half-moon-crescent black beard acting like a picture frame going round to his black sideburns fronting a pair of large ears poking out below the other half moon-crescent made above made by the white cap that he sometimes wore instead of a white turban, sitting above a crescent of black hair showing below the cap. He did look absurd in his pompous gear.

Ahmad rose slowly and looked directly into the eyes behind the round black pair of glasses. He began what he had been rehearsing in his mind all night as the others had snoreslept. He spoke as if he was watching himself speak. Both speaker and spectator. He was wearing the armour of a mediaeval knight, the clean white shirt of the ex-Savaki man. It was a speech, not a defence. He liked what he was saying.

"I will not answer any of your police-style questions," he began speaking slowly, cinematically. Iranians love the cinema. "I have no objection to the judgement passed by the other court. Or anything you may decide here. I will not contest any judgement you make. But let me make it clear, absolutely clear. If there is anyone who can ask questions here, it is I. And it is you who has to answer for your deeds. Under no circumstances will I sink to defending myself against this absurd accusation of espionage. I will never submit to this absurdity. It is I who has to ask the questions. It is you who has to answer for betraying the revolution…"

"What are you saying? Khalkali interrupted him in a voice that appeared not to be his, completely taken off balance. "How dare you question my right? I represent the supreme leader, the Imam."[2]

"I have no objection to your judgement," Ahmad repeated for the theatre, bypassing Khalkhali. "I have certain principles and I will always remain true to them. But you! It is you who executed my comrades in Gonbad.[3] It is you. It's you who shot my comrades in Kurdistan, shot them while lying wounded on stretchers[4] before you who went on to execute thousands in that province who asked for nothing more than the right to order their own lives. It is you who has abandoned the revolution. It's you who has betrayed the revolution. It is you who has to answer to the workers, the poor, the destitute, those thousands whose innocent blood was spilt in a revolution that you have betrayed. I have remained and will always remain true to my principles. It's you who must answer for your deeds," he said emphatically and sat down.

"Me, killing people in Gonbad, what are you insinuating?" Khalkhali shouted, not really understanding what was happening.

Over the next 40 minutes or so Ahmad recounted the deeds of the regime in a voice that came out of some inner furnace. One by one, interrupted with increasing feebleness by Khalkhali. It was you who supported the Bazargan regime when they threw out and imprisoned shepherds from the pastures they had occupied. It is you who disbanded the factory councils the workers, workers who had given their blood for this revolution, had set up to defend their legitimate rights against the factory owners. Who is it that has betrayed this revolution? What did Bazargan say? He said, 'I asked for rain, and I got a flood'. What he meant by flood was the flood of poor people who were on the streets protesting. The very people who made this revolution. You have betrayed these people. You bombed the cities of Kurdistan. You crushed the Turkamans and the Arabs whose only crime was their wish to control their own affairs. I have nothing against you as a person. It is for what you have perpetuated on those people that you must answer.

One by one he described the deeds of the new regime ignoring the *mullah's* shouts and objections. The military attacks on Kurdistan and the execution of thousands of Kurds on Khalkhali's orders, the attack on the Turkaman cultural centre, the killing of Arabs in Khuzestan. The scenario had been turned upside down. Khalkahli was defending himself against Ahmad's accusations. Ahmad, ignoring the judge, was addressing the audience of *pasdars*. Every action has an image if you are a visual person. What Ahmad saw as he spoke was the figure of Fidel Castro in the Montana Barracks courtroom, the black and white image he had seen on the cover of the Pelican Book he had bought when in the UK. The Black and White image gesticulated and gradually melted into Eisenstein's *October*. Ahmad did not gesticulate. It wasn't his style. Once or twice he glanced at the door and saw the friendly young *pasdar* with tears running down his cheeks. The religious judge in his comic ill-fitting military gear and a few dozen commanders just looked on. They had become spectators in their own play.

The friendly young *pasdar* stood with his back to the door, hands pressing hard on the wood to stop himself from flying away, tears running down his cheeks. What were they seeing, these young eyes, innocent of life? There she was, the man-Zeinab in his improvised female costume standing up to the powerful, evil, Caliph Yazid,[5] defiant, radiant in her courage, the courageous sister of Imam Hossein, haughty, erect like one of those date trees that silhouetted the sky in his village back home. Then the image switched like in a dream; the courage of the woman addressing the Caliph merged into the image of the boy in his class. What was he saying? Something about injustice and slap came the hand to the left side of his face and he would not stop, standing, facing the teacher, another slap, same side, same defiant words. He, the teacher, went over to his desk and took out the cherrywood whipstick, the flexible wood making a whizzing noise as it flew through the stuffy air of that hot late spring classroom and landed, and he tilted it sideways just before the cherrywood hit the side of his face, moving away to soften the pain as he continued to look defiantly into the teacher's eye and repeated the insult. What was it? Protesting at some injustice or other, does it matter? Another swoosh, another avoiding move and the boy just went on looking through his watery world and repeated the insult. Again and again on the same side, head, neck, arms. Same side from the right-handed teacher. Then suddenly the teacher's face changed from anger to something indescribable, he turned, stormed out of the class, head bent. Worn out. Defeated. The boy too turned and sat down, and blood dripped onto his shirt that had not been washed for days, or weeks, looking straight ahead at some hidden horizon and tears. And the young friendly *pasdar* noiselessly cried for all those who had stood up for their beliefs, and for life that was not simple, and confused. Tears of pride in the resistance in all of history and of anger, and for his dead grandmother, and all who died and not known why.

Then suddenly Ahmad got up. I have nothing more to say, and walked over to the door. The young friendly *pasdar* looked lost and then, meekly opened the door and let him out. He cried all the way to the chickencoop.

The fellow prisoners who were sitting in a group, crowded round him in a circle. Ahmad spoke quietly.

"I'm a communist," he began, "a communist. That's what I have believed since childhood and still believe. For me communism is simply a fight for justice. Fight for justice alongside people like yourselves. Alongside ordinary people. Workers. People who struggle for a decent living. Alongside your sister, your mother, or that school kid. This court will probably confirm the verdict. I am not afraid to die. I have stayed true to my beliefs. Now let's play rock-paper-scissors," he said.

Till this minute he had never participated in their games. But there was no appetite for play. A gloom had descended on the soot-covered yard.

He did not sleep.

Life imposes its norms. War hollows out death of its fear.

Next morning the young *pasdar* opened the door to the enclosure. He was grinning. He had grown ten centimetres. You are free to go, he blurted so everyone could hear. The *agha* has pardoned you, he continued referring to Khalkhali. Set you free. You are free to go, and he went on to explain to everyone how Khalkhali had talked to the *pasdar* commanders telling them that he was setting him free because although he was an unbeliever and a *mortad*,[6] he was a man with a free spirit, a man who was *azadeh,* as he called it, free spirited. And Khalkhali, the country's most senior judge, would not soil his hands with the blood of a free-spirited man. That's what is meant by Islamic justice, he had said. True justice, Islamic justice, the young *pasdar* repeated proudly as pride shook away the creeping shame that had enveloped him yesterday and outflowed in a shimmering glow of relief through the wet film covering his eyes and spreading down his neck across his whole body in warmth and enveloping the world. His belief had been vindicated, he felt. Deep. Deep.

"Pack up your things," he said when he had landed back on the potholed concrete enclosure.

Ahmad rose and walked out with him convinced that this is a ruse to fool the others. That he was going to his death. He was waiting for death as he was led down the mesh corridor. He waited for death as he was pushed out through the main gate. He was waiting for death as the young friendly *pasdar* shook his hands and near-kissed him on both cheeks without touching lip to skin. He began to walk slowly eastwards down the road towards the horizon, yellowing in anticipation of the rising sun, through the smouldering black smoke that was arising from the refinery on his left, convinced that they would shoot him from behind. He turned left, walking towards Abadan still waiting for death at his back. Or a car to pick him up for his execution. He did not look back because he did not want to look at death. After 20 minutes he reached the deserted roundabout which announced the beginning of the city.

He then sat down and cried and cried and cried. The sun was desperately trying to pierce the smog.

[1] He fought to the death fighting Franco's fascist troops atop a hill in Hemingway's *For Whom the Bell Tolls,* chapter 27.
[2] Khomeini had been elevated to the exalted religious status of Imam before returning to Iran from Paris in the final days of the revolution. According to the Constitution, as the Supreme Leader, Khomeini had absolute power over both religious and secular society and all its institutions.
[3] Referring to the execution of four Fadai' cadres in Gonbad Kavoos, Turkaman Sahra Province (also spelt Turkmen Sahra) in the early days after the revolution, including Tumaj – see footnote 87, chapter 32.
[4] Khalkhali had ordered the execution of 11 Fadai' sympathisers in Kurdistan, some wounded on stretchers.
[5] According to Shia legends, Zeinab, sister of Hussein ibn Ali, a grandson of Mohammad and the third imam in the Shia' pantheon, who was martyred in the battle of Karbala by the forces of the Umayyad caliph Yazid (680 AD), was taken prisoner. Her heroic stance in the usurper Caliph's court is commemorated annually during the holy month of Muharram in religious street theatres, *ta'zieh*, where a man would act her part.
[6] An apostate, someone who had lapsed from Islam.

Chapter 38

The rider

Ahmad

He was like a man suspended in space. A deep sadness gnawed at his heart like a corkscrew. He had no words even for himself. He walked aimlessly, an hour or more, in a vacuum. The sun climbed through its ritual path, strong enough to penetrate the soot, and he just walked, dazed, unreal, without seeing, and then, all of a sudden snapped back into the world.

He changed three taxis to make sure he is not being followed, using destinations that took him to deserted parts of town, easier to see if you are being tailed. The man they had earlier considered a corpse knocked at the safe house. He was recounting the events in his customary meticulous detail when the 2 o'clock national news came on the radio. Everyone stopped to listen to the announcer.

"I am in *Mehrabad Airport*," the announcer said in a voice with a tinge of breathlessness that in a strange way combined the idea of excitement with the featureless deadpan delivery of a news bulletin. "We have an interview with *hojatoleslam* Khalkhali who has just returned from a trip to the south," the voice now became quasi-referential with a twinge of irony, perhaps? Maybe she too is in line for the purges to come. "You had gone to review some judgements in the Revolutionary Court in Abadan. What was the result?" She asked the question as if she knew the answer. Khalkhali rarely, if ever, changed death sentences.

"Yes, I was in Abadan. There, with the help of God I pardoned a man who was both a communist and an apostate. I did that because I judged him to be *azadeh*, noble and free. I released him and his two companions. This is the essence of Islamic justice. This is how Islamic justice works." The butcher Khalkhali, the *hakem sharr* (evil judge), as the young *pasdar* had called him, was speaking in his usual self-congratulatory voice. Listening to his own fate, Ahmad experienced a strange detachment. As if they were talking of someone else. Like one of the stories his old neighbour told the six-year-old Ahmad sitting on the steps outside their home in that port city up the road, now in ruin, the news item was detached from the now. Detached from reality.

That same night, Azadeh drove him in her 2CV *zhian*[1] in pitch darkness to Ahwaz. There he set up the regional headquarters in one of the houses which also housed a secret printing press, Azadeh, her sister and two married couples gave it legitimacy. Within a week or so an Iraqi bomb demolished an inner wall. They rented another large house for yet another regional headquarters. This time they found a house away from built up areas, away from bombs and surrounded by empty wasteland, except for a few neighbouring houses. An unpaved sideroad led up to the main road, a road that led to the oil company. This house felt more secure from Iraqi bombing but paradoxically also more dangerous as there could be no obvious escape routes. Once a week a courier would bring communications from the Secretariat in Tehran.

That day the courier was special. He was carrying documents from the Secretariat in preparation for a regional plenum to be held in their house. He carefully sewed the sensitive documents into the lining of his khaki anorak and set out on his trip. The bus journey was over 800 km long and he had to survive numerous roadblocks. Outside Borujerd, the *pasdars* stopped the bus and the passengers were asked to get out and line up. A *pasdar*, somewhat older than the others, walked past slowly, questioning a few in what looked like a random fashion. He made a cursory search of a young man's two bags and didn't find anything. He came to another young man who even before he got to him had started to fidget. Do you have a bag, the older pasdar asked politely. The young man turned deathly pale. Biology is sometimes so out of one's control. In his only bag, a well-travelled battered thing, they found numerous copies of a banned newspaper. He was carted away by two *pasdars* under armed guard and the older *pasdar* lost interest in the rest of the line-up. They must have had a tipoff. The bus had been stopped and had random searches more often than the courier had experienced in previous trips, although he had not been down this particular route before. In Ahwaz he spent the night in a safe house and warned them of the higher level of security. The war had made everyone jittery. He left early the next morning feeling more tense than usual.

As he was about to mount his motorcycle a sudden fear fell upon him, like a stone, as fears sometimes do. What if I lose my way? He was new to the area and had never been to the new headquarters. It was the kind of panic that gives no prior warning but seals fates. He made a tiny sketch of the address they gave him on a piece of paper, as tiny as his Bic-biro allowed, and shoved it deep in his trouser pocket in case he was stopped. Before mounting his motorbike, he had a last look at the address trying to memorise it and again carefully folded it and put it back in the bottom of his pocket with a few odds and ends that he transferred from his other pockets on top. Decoys. He was not good at memorising things, especially addresses. He rode across town passing a number of traffic lights all the time trying to picture the address in his head. He did remember, perhaps because he had committed it to paper. It helped visualise the journey. He rode not too fast, not too slow, taking care not to draw attention. When he turned into the main road that led to the oil company offices he felt an enormous relief. The rest would be easy. Riding down the main road towards the oil company, he recognised the left turning onto the dirt road and felt proud that he had remembered the map. It was late autumn, hot and dry, and the scorching summer heat had left a desiccated land on both sides of the road. As he was about to turn into the side road saw a car coming from the opposite direction. Should I risk it? Yes, I can. The thoughts were instantaneous. He revved up and swerved left. What he didn't and couldn't know was that embedded in the asphalt a single railway line crossed the road. And he failed to see the oil spill. He skidded on the metal and was hit by the oncoming car. Death was instantaneous.

Ahmad, in Tehran at the time, was informed of the missing courier, presumably arrested, and immediately rang Azadeh and asked her to call everyone and postpone the plenum. No one knew about the little sketch.

Since there was no identification on him, the young man's corpse was sent to the city coroner who after a few days, and when no one came to claim him, issued a death certificate. It was wartime and the city police had either not discovered the young man's home address or not bothered to contact it. The body was taken to the morgue to be buried in an unmarked grave alongside the countless other unmarked graves of those times. While stripping the young man's corpse, the man who washes the dead before burial, the *mordehshur*, felt something in the lining of his jacket, split it open, immediately recognised its importance and passed it on to the local *Pasdaran* headquarters. The security forces now had both the address and date of the plenary session.

In a carefully planned attack on the evening of the plenum, a team of *pasdars* surrounded the house and attacked at 2 am hoping to seize the entire regional committee. Disappointed, they arrested everyone in the house anyway, the two couples and Azadeh and herded them in the back room. Azadeh's sister was staying with friends that night. Not finding anything of note in their search of the house they started to dig up the garden. The house was relatively new, the pond had never been filled and the garden was bare. The pasdar commander and another were guarding and quizzing the prisoners in the back room when they heard an excited voice calling for the 'brother' commander. He ran to the window, saw the triumphant grin below and rushed out while the other *pasdar* walked over to see what was happening. Azadeh immediately understood that they had dug up incriminating documents.

"We are all new to this house, we know nothing about any hidden things," she quickly whispered to the two couples.

"No talking", the *pasdar* who was meant to guard them barked and walked towards them, menacingly turning his Kalashnikov as if to shoot but changed his mind. "No talking I am telling you, not a peep from any of you," he added in a less threatening voice. He was too excited by their discovery to have eavesdropped on what they had said, and he did not want to lose face by admitting his failure to guard his prisoners.

Back at the local *Komiteh* all five pleaded ignorance about the documents.

We are architects and had only recently rented the house and knew nothing about any documents, hidden or otherwise. They were convincing, and their interrogators were not that sophisticated. A slap here and a kick there. Azadeh was bailed when her sister persuaded the neighbours opposite, an Arab-speaking Iranian couple whom they had befriended, to leave the deeds of their house with the Revolutionary Court as surety. The others were bailed by their families travelling over from different parts of the country. Ahmad did not come back to that house.

That winter of 1980 was one of hope. The Iraqi advance had been more or less halted and the people, now over the initial shock of the invasion which had silenced all dissent, felt more emboldened. Though the purges in factories, schools and government offices had been mostly successful, in many universities the attempt to purge the faculty had met open opposition by the student body and stalled. There were street demonstrations in many cities and people were openly demanding more freedom. Everywhere you could see an air of optimism that the steady erosion of freedoms was about to be reversed. The winter and the following spring were the last months of optimism while the forces of yesterday and tomorrow manoeuvred towards their climactic confrontation. But those yearning for light were unready for a fight to the end and totally unprepared when darkness descended.

One sunny morning in June 1981 the country woke up to the news that a bomb had exploded in the headquarters of the *Islamic Republican Party[2]*building killing a large number of its deputies and many senior figures of government. Overnight the sky darkened. It was as if someone had pulled a roof across the sky blocking out light. A nationwide crackdown began, and in that dimness tens of thousands were arrested and the nightly execution squads dispatched hundreds. Among the dead were both of the man-and-wife teams of the Ahwaz headquarters, arrested and shot later that year. The buried documents came back to bury them. It was an unequal battle and freedom was suffocated.

Ahmad was driving when he heard of the execution of his friend, the poet and playwright Sa'id Soltanpour, who had been arrested at his wedding and later executed with seven others. The blow was severe. They had been like brothers, working not just in the theatre group but also later across Europe during the last year of the previous regime. Those were agonising days. He was emotionally shattered. He did not want to be there anymore. He did not want to be anywhere.

[1] A copy of the Citroen *Deux Chevaux* ('2CV') manufactured in Iran.
[2] *Islamic Republican Party* was formed immediately after the revolution in 1979 on the orders of Khomeini to consolidate his dominance on the revolution.

Chapter 39

The accident

Changiz and Shahla

Shahla was alone in that Shiraz basement, her refuge, sitting with a book open on her knees, drifting into thoughts of her two teenage girls when the phone rang. It did not normally ring during daytime. Her host, Abdi, was out at work. His young wife was at school. The others too had also gone to work. Few people knew she was there. She had left home in a hurry, as soon as their grandparents had come down from the capital to look after the girls, the day after her husband's arrest. Hers was a strange hiding place, where people constantly came and went. Abdi's sister, a doctor and her new husband had recently moved in. Both qualified at the same university where her husband taught. Then there were the friends. Abdi's friends, his sister's friends and her new husband's friends. People would drop in and out almost every evening. Not very private, that basement, but what choice did she have? There was no one else in town that would take her. The summer of mass arrests and mass executions had dried up old friendships. Her world had shrunk into its core.

Abdi's young wife had no friends to visit her. Her family lived hundreds of miles away. Abdi had married her only recently, a cousin from Abadan with an age gap, and she had to finish her schooling. But then Abdi himself was ageless, bubbling away with his latest enthusiasm. He had a brain that jumped ideas like a butterfly, with the same vivacity, agile, restless and ultimately homeless. Limping around with one leg shorter than the other, he bubbled

213

and joked Shahla's presence away. No one would dream of betraying her in this hideout.

All the guests knew Shahla's husband had been arrested two weeks ago. And in unison they all avoided the subject in conversation. Sort of an unspoken taboo. It was as if she was in mourning for a mysterious death, a private grief, to be tiptoed out of conversation. There is so little to say to someone who has lost a part of themselves. Words. Feeble tools. Really. How do you penetrate personal grief? Best avoid the issue and gently walk around it. Is it cowardice? Who knows? Let the griever grieve in the solitude of their grief. All that ritual surrounding death in every culture is just skirting death, whether by collective wailing, or forced gaiety. Surround the grieving person by noise, by bustle, and abandon them to work through real grief alone. All grief is a lonely process. Best to avoid the subject altogether.

Her friends in that basement and her friend's friends, did communicate. Communicated by acts, by looks, by touch, by smiles, by the changing tiny wrinkles that appear round the eye, or forehead. Body language. Rich in emotions, like poetry. Compacted. The eye has its own luminous vocabulary. But acts are more concrete, their message more direct, more brutal. Some friends, close friends, had pretended not to see her when they passed Shahla in the street. Others, like Abdi, not that close a friend, had offered her sanctuary despite the risks. People were strange. No ambiguity there. It was a time of social disruption. Outside that basement social ties were being unwrapped, crumbled and repackaged.

The day after her husband's arrest their parents had rushed down from Tehran to look after the children. Two elderly couples thrown together by someone else's love, now circling around in a whirlpool they did not foresee or comprehend. An alien world made real by the need to deal with it. A bit like finding dog shit on your doorstep. A son in prison? Isn't that where thieves and murderers go? A daughter in hiding, as if guilty of some crime, or God forbid, eloped. Revolutionary Guards roaming outside your veranda. It had all the unreality of the black and white films of their younger days. Foggy uncertainty ahead. Two retired grandfathers, two bewildered grandmothers, cooped together in a city with memories of gardens, orchards and laughing grandchildren. Now everything was foreign and cold. They coped through silence, miming their bafflement through doing. No words. No planning. Action without a verb. The two girls back from school would open the fridge and find it bursting with milk and meat and butter and bread. The grandfathers had gone out and shopped alone, without telling the other. Almost identical baskets. Food is a sharp echo of social background. Eating and feeding the children bonded them through their confusion. Endorsed and sealed their social ties. Wordlessly witnessing without understanding what had overtaken their world: *La Peste*.[1] Not read it.

During the day she was mostly alone in that basement, reading Romain Rolland's *L'âme enchantée* in Farsi.[2] Rolland took her into a world of love, torn from her when her own fathomless love was yanked away. Some days she went out to meet comrades for instruction or collect leaflets or the paper for distribution. That was dangerous work. Arrest would almost certainly be the end of her husband. And who knows what they would do to her. Why? She just did.

Every lunchtime she would sit glued to the radio's 2 pm news bulletin as they read out the names of those executed that day. His name was way down the alphabet and as they read from A downwards, she would almost wish the other letters would evaporate somewhere, and for the calm voice of the announcer to get to S quicker. She, it was a she, would read out the names in a voice without emotions, as she would football results, or reciting the *salavat* on a chain of prayer beads, as one light after another was extinguished for ever. She only half-heard the earlier names, but her heart began its pounding as the announcer approached S and then everything would go blank. How many wives, mothers, fathers, daughters, sons had stopped hearing at A or K? Or smiled at the end of the bleeding rosary, happy to be denied the name. Then, guilty for the named, ashamed of their momentary joy. Someone, somewhere, was screaming, and it echoed across hearts.

The voice on the other side of the phone was familiar, warm but strange. Changiz had never rung her number. You never trusted a home number. Must be an emergency, flashed through her mind.

215

"I have crashed the car," came the voice with its Azari inflexions. He had to repeat it again as she could not believe what she had heard.

"Where are you?" she stuttered.

"In the main police station," came the Azari voice, "they need to know if you gave permission for me to drive the car." He did not have a licence and she had no idea what his real name was or what name he had used with the police. It was the classical dilemma. In a revolutionary cell the less you knew of the other, the better. Of course, Changiz knew her name and everything about her in full. That was the nature of the relationship – the person in charge of the cell would come to her but she knew next to nothing about him. Not where he lived, nor his real name, nor if he had a brother or sister or even how old he was. But they trusted each other to the extent of trusting their lives to each other. And lending her car for God only knows what use. Weird thing this revolutionary trust until this trust failed – well you just died, under torture, or by the firing squad. Or in later years by hanging, which was cheaper. He was just a trusted man with an Azari accent and a smile that melted the heart. As close as a brother, and so far away.

She put on her best dark blue manteaux, her best dark blue scarf over her best dark blue trousers. She had to look like the owner of the Peugeot. Solidly middle class. She looked beautiful even in that bland uniform, her large hazel eyes and the outline of her face, the high cheekbones betraying some Mongol blood eight centuries ago, compensating for the absence of the beautiful straight black hair, now almost completely hidden under the scarf. She felt calm. She had always been calm in unusual circumstances. She had her smile. A smile that flashed across her face like the sun appearing from behind a cloud, warming the room or garden or the hill on which she was standing. A risk-taker she thought as she half remembered handing her pistachio-coloured Mini Minor to a policeman to watch over in the middle of Piccadilly circus when it stuttered and stopped, starved of fuel. 'Can you look after my car while I go and get some petrol, please?' she had said in her accented English, and smiled. An Audrey Hepburn smile, her friends had teased her. She had no driving licence and no insurance. Now, in another continent, she was off to disentangle a friend who was both very close and totally unknown.

It was a double act, a stand-up banter, an artistic performance on which at least three lives depended. Somehow, he told her what name he had used, and she concocted what relationship they had with one another, he with his Azari accent and rather outdated brown trousers and she in her elegant chic Islamist gear. The police officer must have guessed that things did not fit. There was something illicit going on and he could feel the chemistry between the two. Perhaps he thought they were having an affair. A Tabrizi engineer with a beautiful Tehrani. He felt the chemistry but misinterpreted its source, a chemical reaction between two thoughts that are close. Whatever came to his head he did not delve too deep. Maybe he too had his grudge against a regime that had deprived him of his secular pleasures, his glass of *araq* vodka, his glimpse of a shapely ankle. Only a few years ago he would have been respected, even feared. Now the police were reduced to traffic control and a few mundane tasks. The Revolutionary Guards, the *Pasdaran*, were running the show. This was no longer his city, to run as he desired. He belonged to the fallen regime and side-lined, a has-been. He let it go.

They walked out and she arranged for a garage to tow her car. Two years later with Changiz dead, executed sometime after his badly beaten body had been carried in a wheelbarrow and dumped in his cell, she was driving down-hill on a road covered with compacted snow in residential north Tehran where the roads were relatively traffic-free making it easier to ensure she was not being followed. But every time she touched the brakes, the car kept skidding to the right, veering dangerously close to parked cars. Changiz had skewed the chassis.

She could just see the sheepish smile of the brown-haired flush-faced friend from *Qareh Daq* with his deep Azari accent.

[1] Albert Camus, translated in English as The Plague.
[2] *The Soul Enchanted*, Farsi translation by Mahmoud Etemadzadeh.

Chapter 40

Is your brother home?

Nayyer

It's me again. Nayyer. That's what I have chosen to call myself, but I think I have told you this already. I'm going to tell you a bit more of my story because the telling is cathartic. But I won't tell it all. I don't want you to be numbed. Using a different name makes it easier to talk. Anyway, how can you tell the story of nine years of a lost youth in a few words? It is easier to tell it piecemeal. Easier in a book. You can read it whole if you speak Farsi, all three volumes of it.

Well, let me orient you. While Ahmad was having his *history will absolve me*[1] speech, I was running free. Those were exhilarating, intoxicating days, those early days after the revolution. I just can't find the right adjective. As if the sun was shining from inside my body. You felt so free. The future was so open. Open to possibilities, open to infinite hope. Everyone was suddenly young. Even the not so young grew young, like they had found that elixir of youthful vigour. There was a strange feeling in the air, how can I put it? as if the future was in the now. A sort of telescoping of time, yes, something like H.G Well's time machine, I'd read that, my Farsi was perfect now that I had been to university, I even had a go at reading *Das Kapital*, though to tell the truth, I gave that up real quick. Anyway, I thought, there are others who have read it and can explain to me what the great man had in mind, not that I needed an explanation. You could see the rot in the system just by looking.

And after all, if an entire population, give or take a handful, and oh, those villagers who still thought the Shah, now dead and buried, had given them land and it's only a matter of time before they could get something more than their subsistence out of it, yes other than the paid insiders and deluded peasants, the entire population had said a unanimous no to the pathetic king and his putrid system. If that was not living proof of the failure of capitalism, then what was? You really don't need proof for the sun.[2]

Anyway, I wanted to paint you a picture. An image of a time when all of us, all of us on the left at least, thought that all we had to do was to show people the light and they would follow that light, and not the darkness and superstition that these *mullahs* were pushing at them. We vetoed the absurd referendum Khomeini put to the people: choose between the Shah and an Islamic Republic. No other options. Hobson's choice and we, "the one-percenters", said no to that no-choice-choice.[3]

Then they came for me. It was near midnight, an autumn midnight. Slight chill in the air, cooling the fallen plane leaves. That summer of 1981 our sunny world had been shattered by mass arrests. A dark cloud, like those deep fogs I remembered from my childhood in Azerbaijan, blocked the sun. But we were still hopeful, still fighting. Don't fogs suddenly cease? Unpredictable in their suddenness to be, to the suddenness of not to be. And we weren't just a group of educated intellectuals. We had a real base in society. Had not my other love won over 50,000 votes in our only free election?[4] There just aren't fifty thousand educated intellectuals of the left in Tehran. It's simple arithmetic. Yes. Most must have been ordinary people, workers in the factory, people in the poor southern quarters of the city. Maybe the migrants. The marginals. The ones with no real jobs. I am digressing. It was near midnight and the bell rang. My sister picked up the intercom.

"I am a friend of your brother," the voice at the other end said.

"My brother is not home," my sister replied in a voice that said stop bothering us at this time of night.

"Open up immediately!" This time it was an order. Those days, hunters roamed the streets and stop-searched at random, raided homes at night.

Hunters were on the other side of the door. They must have my brother with them, I realised, and something emptied inside me. In a few seconds men armed with Kalashnikovs occupied the apartment. They started to rip the place apart and as there was nothing of particular significance, they just took some books and music tapes. I still remember a boy, no more than 16 or 17, who stood in the corner posing like something he had seen in films. Hips to one side, Kalash loosely held in his arms, finger on trigger, head tilted towards its tip. Classic Hollywood.

They took me. Why? I asked. You'll find out was the curt reply. Defend your principles whatever happens, my sister whispered in my ears as I hugged her goodbye. Those words stayed with me over the next 9 years.

My brother and his wife Nargess were in the Landrover when I was pushed inside. Eyes bound with a piece of cloth.

"Do you know them?" an armed *pasdar* sitting in the front asked.

"Does my interrogation start here?" I asked and immediately felt a sharp blow to the side of my head. "Of course I know my brother," I said, guessing that they must have known them by name to round up the family in this way.

[1] Fidel Castro's four-hour speech on 16 October 1953 in his own defence in court after he led an attack on the Moncada Barrack in Santiago de Cuba.
[2] The popular Iranian saying: *aftab amad dalile aftab,* 'sunshine came, proof of sun'.
[3] According to official report only 1% of the population voted against the Islamic Republic. The left boycotted the referendum.
[4] Election to the first parliament (*Majles*) where the Fadai' and their allies on the left obtained 10% of the vote in Tehran.

Chapter 41

The Barracks

Nayyer

What is there new to say about my initial interrogation in the old army barracks, *Eshrat Abad* barracks, turned into interrogation centres? They are all the same, give and take the individual taste of the individual torturer. The style was personal but the end result was the same. Pain. Some were clearly enjoying it, others as a duty, even religious duty, *taklif* as they liked to call it. That gave it gravitas and of course legitimacy. It's not my fault, it's not up to me, I'm just following God's orders, God's will, what Giordano Bruno called, before being burned at the stake, 'holy ignorance'.

This is it in a summary: sudden room changes in flexible spaces such as public baths now devilishly turned into packed human storerooms, with new arrivals added to all the time. Hanging over you the constant fear. The punishment rooms, pitch dark and so tight, so crowded, it was sometimes impossible even to sit. The wretched blindfold. The uncertainty. The utter uncertainty. The darkness. The dirt. The fear. No matter how brave you think you are there is the fear, fear of pain but also fear of helplessness, fear of the unknown, animal fear, of time being stolen from you. All time. You just don't know what the next minute will bring, the next door-slamming. New noises. No matter how good your imagination, you could never have pre-imagined the effect of a scream. The constant screaming of someone under torture. That terrifying pitch of a scream not out of fear, but of inhuman pain. You can't see them but they are there, under your skin, as if burrowed into you. Piercing concrete walls and steel doors right into your flesh, your essence, as if it is you who is screaming in pain, and fear. And of course, resistance. Heroic, at times suicidal, resistance.

Then there are such apparently mundane things like toilets and washing that can become torture, especially if you have a bladder infection as some of the girls had. They only let you use toilets once, or if you are lucky, twice a day. And try squatting on the toilet with legs and feet torn to bits by the whip. As women prisoners we also had to endure additional indignities, like having to wear the *chador* whenever we left our cells for whatever reason. And the curse of monthly periods. Virtually all interrogators and guards treated women as inferior beings. Even the women guards. And always hovering overhead, was the unexpected.

Once, outside our room, down the corridor, in the next cell, we heard the shrieking of a prisoner that seemed to be unrelated to any interrogation. Maybe she had done something forbidden. Whatever her offence the guard was beating her so savagely that he was panting, out of breath. We heard the sound of her head being banged against the wall which shook our cell followed by something heavy hitting the floor. It was heart-breaking to witness such an unequal battle, so inhuman, and be unable to do anything, even to protest. I can still hear those shrieks in my nightmares. My frequent nightmares. Nightmares of memory indelibly chiselled in your brain like a stone relief.

There are sad moments, hours when you feel sorry for yourself. Times when compassion and empathy crushes you. There were also good moments. Like the guard, we called Hassan Agha who used to bring us cigarettes, which we had to smoke on his morning shift, and once even a nail cutter and a comb from his home. Later my sister-in-law Nargess told me that he even arranged for her to see my brother. Once I managed to pass on a written note to my brother who was in a cell at the other end of the long corridor. I had found a cigarette wrapper under one of the blankets in our cell and using my hairpin wrote a brief note to him which I managed to throw into his cell when we passed it on the way to the toilets. I found his reply the next day on the same wrapper hidden in the toilet as arranged. I kept it for days, reading and rereading his neat handwriting reassuring me that he was fine. But then I had to destroy it for his sake. And mine of course.

I met so many girls, secondary school students 16 or 17 years old calmly talking of the death that awaited them. Asking to be remembered to their families when, never if, we got out. They passed on their life to the living. The guilt of still being alive drives me, now, every day. It will never stop.

Never.

Chapter 42

I'm in love

Shahla and Changiz

I am in love, he said and blushed. *Asheqam.* The word love sounded even stranger in an Azari accent, softening the *q* (gh) which moves from the throat to mid-tongue *g*. Closer to a kiss. Traditional Azari singers with their *falsetto* voices used the word as their name – *ashiq or ashigh* - lovers. There he was, tall, slightly stooped with his light-brown almost ginger hair so rare among the black-haired and the bald in that city. He too was beginning to bald.

That was actually not how it began. He had entered the veranda a little hesitantly. Normally he would bounce in. In a trot and a jump, like a six-year-old. But today he approached his age. What was his age? She never found out. Maybe 35 give or take a few years added on by the experience of prison, not once but twice. It was the same veranda overlooking the large orchard he had sat so many times breaking tradition and drinking wine. Those days no one on the left touched alcohol. It was taboo, bourgeois, not something a self-respecting communist would allow himself, even less herself. The left, stuck in its religious roots, still thought alcohol, and actually any luxury, bourgeois. But not Changiz. He had moved on. We had sat there, drank and reminisced into late as the gloom of dusk among the plane trees evaporated to embrace the beauty of the Shiraz night. Today was different.

"*Shahla joon,*" he had begun, his voice down a decibel, then a long pause. She heard a blackbird sing not far from her ear. It was late summer and already the plane leaves looked dry. It was their neighbourly blackbird's uniquely personal song, with a curious resemblance to a catchy tune in a popular song. Maybe the little blackbird had learnt it from a tape recording blowing out of the window of someone's house. Blackbirds are such mimics, Shahla had read somewhere. Only today the bird had dropped the second stanza. "You know, I have not really had much experience of life," Changiz had gone on, his voice almost failing to come out. She wanted to interject. Not much? He was so wise, so full of deep knowledge, so much older than his body.

"All those years in prison, you see I was just 17, just discovering myself when they arrested me. You know, they cut me a life sentence." That's the way ex-political prisoners talked – cutting a sentence, just as you would cut cloth for a suit. Or a bough. In a way it was a suite-of-sorts, of concrete and bars and walled courtyards. "And when I got out, I plunged again into revolution." Yes. He had helped create a whole new organisation in prison, with a refreshingly fresh look at the world, throwing out the cobwebs. And when the revolutionary tide released him alongside all the other political prisoners it was back to meetings, cells, organising, education, travelling, printing, talking, recruiting, talking, teaching, learning. All the things you did as a communist in the midst of a mass revolution. Anything but normal human relations. She was still waiting for the punchline. He was going to tell her what she had already guessed.

Asheq-e Khadijeh-am, I am in love with Khadijeh, but don't know how to tell her. Never learnt these things," and he blushed which with his balding ginger-brown hair and thick ginger moustache made his entire globe glow red. This boy-man who could talk deeply about dialectics, who in a few minutes could destroy an entire false argument, who had rescued Shahla in a single sentence from a conspiracy to side-line her within the group, and that, on his first week as their supervisor, was suddenly mute. Love seemingly had nothing to do with other more tangible human dimensions such as conspiracy, planning, organising, logic, persuasion, arguments, dissemination, deception, cunning, battle. This was a totally alien world to our seasoned revolutionary. There stood her tall friend who could conceive of liberating the entire human race, but was paralysed in front of a peasant girl, helpless.

225

Khadijeh had joined their group a few months before Changiz had arrived in Shiraz. She had been a student leader in Tehran University where she was studying in the Social Science faculty and, like hundreds of students, had moved from the much larger Fadai' student organisation *Pishgam* to join the new political organisation when it announced its existence with the dramatic call: 'The Revolution is Dead! Long Live the Revolution!'[1] She was introduced to them as an M. The rest of their circle were N. none of them had any idea what these lettering meant but somehow M was superior, more experienced, organisationally on a higher level than N. More trustworthy, or more likely better known to the M-givers. That is all they needed to know in that you-know-only-what-you-need-to-know underground cell. How did they fill the gaps from A to M? Shahla had thought and waved it away. There must be a logic somewhere. Not her place to question the battle-hardened comrades.

Khadijeh was well built, sturdy, in her mid-twenties. None of the team never saw her in any colour but dark navy blue with thick black stockings, occasionally with a hole or more. Changiz was the first to notice the hole and rebuke her for her slovenly attire.

We are fighting to make a more beautiful world, he had said in his soft fatherly voice, we are going to spread beauty, make beauty universal. There's nothing revolutionary in being shabby. Dress as well as you can afford. We want to help the working class elevate itself, not sink into its lowest denominator, he had added. That resonated with Shahla. This was such a refreshing contrast to the rest of the left that at the time felt and behaved as if a tatty dress draws you closer to the working class. Shabby and solemn. Once when she was behind a desk displaying political literature at the main university campus, she had burst out laughing at a joke. Shahla was so unselfconscious. An earnest moustachioed face next to her had turned round.

"Communists don't laugh loud comrade, that's bourgeois frivolity," he said in a voice that vibrated with superiority. Shahla did care how she looked. Laughter, joy, beauty is what we were fighting for in the republic of black and brown and tears, she wanted to say,[2] but chose to ignore the jibe.

"I will let Khadijeh know how you feel," she said to changiz, and a faint smile

226

flitted across her face. He knit his brows and seemed to sink into another world. His eyes, which she noticed for the first time, were light brown - why had she not noticed that before? - glowed and grew darker. It could have been the blood flow. She sensed that talking to someone closer to his age had done something, maybe strengthened his resolve. There was a long pause heavy with the stillness of expectation. "I think it's better if I do it myself," he finally said in a firm voice, and then dropped his pitch, "but you could drop a hint, no?" Maybe not that confident, then. She nodded and said something, the sort of non-committed jumble of words when you don't know what to say. He stood up abruptly, shook hands, kissed both cheeks, blushed and left. Dusk was rapidly descending on a lovely sunny day, like all the days that summer. He did not want to be caught in the house of a married woman after dark, whose husband was away in Japan, as he used to say. A week or two later they threw her and the girls out of the villa. That was the last veranda she ever sat on.

He borrowed her car for his mission. He obviously could not do this assignment in town. It may have had something to do with his father being a *khan* but life changing acts had to be done in the open, in full view of the hills and brown earth. Even though he was born in Tabriz, home had been *Qareh Daq* in Azerbaijan,[3] just south of the river Aras which divided Iran from the then Soviet Union. That was the river in which the writer of children's books, Samad Behrangi, the man who had written the *Little Black Fish* that had so influenced her and many children into radical politics, had drowned. Rumoured to be at the hands of the Shah's secret police SAVAK. And not far from the open spaces of the *Dashte Moqan* where Nader Shah Afshar had crowned himself king, even before Napoleon was born. Yes, he needed space to make his declaration of love. So, he asked Khadijeh to drive with him in the Peugeot on some pretext she never found out. Later he recounted the story with a twinkle in his light brown eyes.

"We drove up to the top of a steep hill not far from Shiraz. I stopped the car, turned round, and blurted out – Khadijehjoon, you will either agree to marry me or I will drive the car over the cliff with both of us inside. He must have blushed as only he could blush. Red and brown. And Khadijeh, normally so stiff, so reserved, had just smiled back. Did they kiss? She wondered but immediately dismissed – that would have been too bourgeois for Khadijeh, she was sure, but not for their Changiz. He gave a deep, deep laugh when he told her this story, no blushes this time. She imagined him in his off-white shirt and brown everything else, and she in her dark blue, thick socks, did they still have holes, and the obligatory headscarf of the Islamic Republic of Iran. Oh, why was I not a witness, she thought?

[1] *Rahe Kargar* was the first large organisation on the left to categorically oppose the nascent Islamic government as a betrayal of the revolution with the slogan: *The Revolution is Dead! Long Live the Revolution!* (Marx).

[2] Khomeini had preached: tears are good for the revolution.

[3] See footnote 117 Chapter 39, Return to Velayat.

Chapter 43

The village mullah

Shahla and Changiz

Now Changiz had another problem, a more intractable one. He needed to go to the village and ask for Khadijeh's hand from her father. He had no family in Shiraz. No one in his family had a clue where he was. He was here on a revolutionary mission under an assumed name, in charge of Rahe Kargar in Shiraz province and beyond. A fish immersed in another sea. Why they had sent him, so conspicuous in Shiraz with his distinctive hair, strange accent and up-down bumpety gait, Shahla never found out. She could pick him out in the crowd from hundreds of yards away as you could see his utterly distinct head bobbing up and down as he walked like a boat on a bumpy sea, the sun reflected on his bald patch. Those in Tehran, running the entire organisation, must have been short of able cadres. Changiz had been to prison twice, tortured savagely by the Shah and proven himself in the field. He was iron, tempered into steel, like the book Shahla had read as a child, the one by Nikolai Ostrovsky, that also had such an influence on their generation. He was like a colourful moth in the winter woods, conspicuously flashing colour to a predator state always primed to pounce. Darwin would have beamed with recognition.

He arranged to see her in town. After being thrown out of her villa, in her beautiful *baq* (orchard), and the spell in Ardi's basement, she had moved in with the girls to another friend's house. *Shahla joon*, can you come with me as my aunt? He so wanted to do everything right to make it easy for Khadijeh. They had talked it over now and decided to have a quiet wedding, but she wanted her family's approval. Where are we going, she asked, assuming it is somewhere in Shiraz? We are going to a village in Mamasani, deep in the Zagros mountain range. It was then that she discovered that Khadijeh was the daughter of a village *mullah* in the Luri-speaking region of *Kohkiluyeh* and *Boir Ahmad* province. It was also then that she had learnt her real name, well the given-name-Khadijeh part of it.[1] The family name remained cocooned. Her friend, who had difficulty in blending into the city crowd here in Shiraz, needed to convince a village *mullah* that he was a respectable engineer.

It must have taken huge courage and determination to have transformed Khadijeh, the village girl and daughter of a *mullah*, into the revolutionary girl in dark blue manteau and trousers and thick black tights, the revolutionary they had got to know. What to wear to the meeting asking the father for his daughter's hand, the *khastegari*, took a bit of thinking. Shahla had to be suitably auntyish, not too ostentatious, and fine to sit down on, or near, the floor. Unlikely to have chairs in a village in *Boir Ahmad*, she thought.

They drove in the Peugeot, her in a dark blue manteau and loose black trousers, the dark manteau and dark-coloured scarf a compulsory uniform for women in the Islamic Republic, he in his best brown suit, his hair carefully combed back. He looked so unlike the Changiz she knew. Despite his lack of worldly experience Changiz straddled two worlds like a seasoned tightrope walker. Shahla, who had straddled two continents and two cultures was much more rigid in her behaviour. She knew nothing about his family and with her immutable Tehrani accent, not a trace of Azari anywhere in her, even though she had done some schooling for one year in Tabriz, what if someone in that household would spurt out in Azari?

It was while driving to the village *mullah* that she had also learnt Changiz's name, that is his first name, but still no surname. That would have been too adventurous. Until then she had known him by his *nom de guerre*. It was a gesture of trust, but also a huge responsibility. Will she keep his secret under torture – a question everyone in her position constantly asked themselves. She drove the Peugeot through the unpaved, narrow, winding alleyway full of stones and potholes up a hill. A dry ditch had been meanderingly cut through the middle of the path by the annual spring rains making driving even more treacherous. Will I, won't I, hit a mud wall? They arrived unscratched but a little sweaty outside a dull green wooden door dug into a wall. She noticed that the wall was higher than the surrounding houses. For a second it gave her the strange feeling that the *mullah* was running a prison. But they were going to ask for the hand of his daughter and thoughts of prison vanished.

They knocked and a woman of undefinable age in a black *chador* opened the door. From her eyes, Changiz guessed she was about 35 or so, maybe an aunt. they walked across a yard with a small pond in the middle. The blue ceramics reminded both of them of their grandmother's house. The water was clear. No fish. No sludge either. They must have changed the water in anticipation. A few red geraniums still remained in the patch of garden, not really well kept. Not dead-headed. They were ushered into a room, low ceilings, whitewash over mud-brick wall, a small empty vase next to a picture of Imam Ali in a small alcove on the opposite wall. Otherwise, bare. Nice carpet, probably locally woven. They all got up when the guests entered, young men, older uncles, a few women in black *chador*, the women and men on opposite sides of the room, and the *mullah* himself, thin, wrinkles around his eyes, barely a smile. They were both city people. Worse, from a distant part of the country. Peasant suspicion was added to the Lurs' historic suspicion of Turks.[2] Both were ushered to the top of the room where honoured guests sit on the carpet with cushions leaning on the wall, Changiz next to the old *mullah*. Khadijeh entered bringing the tea wearing her usual dark blue manteau over baggy trousers, thick socks, and scarf. She looked nervous. A flush of red had squeezed a thin film of sweat on her brows, and upper lips. She must be sweaty under her arms, Shahla thought. Here she was no longer the courageous revolutionary, but the oldest girl of the village *mullah* being given away in marriage.

Many years later she tried to recall their trip to the *mullah's* house through the grey cloud of time. This is how she remembered it:

The family only spoke *Luri* and Khadijeh had to translate. Whether my Tehrani accent, so distinct from Changiz's Azari, was even noticed I have no idea. Yes, he's an engineer, I lied, and I'm a distant aunt, speaking for the family, sadly he has no other relatives down here, its war time and Tabriz, at the other end of the country, is a world away. Then came the thorny issue of the *jahazi* (dowery) given by the bride's family to the groom, and the *mehrieh*, a sum of money the groom pays to the bride. We wanted a nominal sum and manoeuvred them into agreeing by using war-austerity as an excuse. The old mullah looked unhappy but resigned. It was not a good time to look unpatriotic, especially in front of an engineer. Who knew what government links he may have. Then came the time to celebrate the contract: everyone took a few of the customary *noql*, a sweet given out at weddings and other celebrations. A sudden strange feeling of lonliness came over me. Those were the same tiny twirly sweets, with its chalky-white cover wrapped round and embracing a fresh-green pistachio core that were also passed around at my wedding. And now he, the love of my life, was in prison with an unknown future. Then back to the present, an *estekan* glass of tea, and another, and for some, a third and time to leave. By the door everyone seemed happy. The men shook hands. The women kissed. The mother smiled, the aunts beamed, I must have smiled back. Changiz grinned as he said goodbye to his new father-in-law. The old *mullah* looked serious but reconciled. Khadijeh stood around not knowing where to put her hands. Then a sudden gust of wind blew dust in our face.

The two travelled back to Shiraz, the first hour in total silence. Then out of the blue Changiz blurted out, "you don't really know you love someone until you say it in words, not really" he was thinking aloud. "There is a magic in language that transforms the nature of feeling". There was a long pause in which neither spoke. "I think words themselves are alive, with a life of their own, like living people" another long silence when the only sound was that of the moving car over a deserted landscape. He was back in the hills above Shiraz.

"You won them over," she said, breaking the silence. "You won them while speaking in a foreign language. How the hell do you do it? You just sounded as if you had always been part of the family."

He smiled and blushed. "It was your smiling presence, your winning smile, which made me, and made them, feel at home," he replied, and she did not believe that. He had a way with people.

Once, over an extended lunch with a group of *ashiqs* in Tehran, most of them working as painter-decorators, Changiz had recruited everyone to his organisation by just being himself. Among them was a staunch Fadai' who had defended his beliefs with particular vehemence. In the end, he too succumbed to the Changiz charm. Or words. Or humility. He was like an Old Testament prophet gaining a following wherever he went and whoever he touched, spanning class and education as few people could.

A year later the newly married couple were dead. Their badly tortured bodies riddled with Kalashnikov bullets. Separately, but together in death and truth.

[1] Khadijeh Arfa', though the team knew her until then by her pseudonym.
[2] Also spelt Lor. For relations between the Lurs and Turks over the centuries, see: *The Lurs of Iran* https://www.culturalsurvival.org/publications/cultural-survival-quarterly/lurs-iran

Chapter 44

Evin

Nayyer

And then they took us to Evin from our barracks and the colour changed. On route we were made to sit on benches running along the sides of a covered box at the back of a vehicle. Peeping furtively from beneath my blindfold I saw my brother Mehdi and his wife Nargess, a few others and two guards on either side with submachine guns pointing at us. After what seemed like an eternity, they opened the back and ordered us to hold on to the person in front. I managed to get hold of my brother, who was wearing a green woollen pullover I had given him. We managed to exchange a few words.

"Be careful here," he said in his warm voice that tore into me. "They bluff a lot. Don't be fooled by them."

I said what had been rolling around my head for days.

"You were my first teacher and will always remain my teacher." I knew in my heart this would be the last time I would ever talk to him. It was my farewell song.

We arrived at the second floor of the building and entered real hell, one that I had not, and could not have imagined. Made to sit, back to the wall in a passageway, blinded by the cloth wrapped round our eyes, we heard screams, coming from every room, criss-crossing the air as if I was sitting in the middle of a large echo chamber, or a cave, with the screams of the damned bouncing off every wall, noises that were amplified in the absence of sight. I was sinking, I was drowning in an ocean of pain.

"Stop! Stop! I can't take any more," a voice shrieked, a voice so young it had not had a chance to grow, and the swish of a whip through the air was deaf to her plea. A woman was begging for water in another room. Bloodied feet were visible from beneath my blindfold. Then a sudden sharp slap on the face or head from a passing guard with their bare hands or a biro, preparing me, softening me, pounding out any thoughts of resistance. I could feel the fear bubbling in my veins. I was on fire from fear.

Someone kicked me. Gently. It was an old man with a pot on wheels. Come girl, come and eat, he said in a tender voice. He led me to a room where I was allowed to take off my blindfold. There were women everywhere, many only old enough to be at school. Most pale and petrified. I looked for Nargess but couldn't find her. I saw a woman of around thirty with a large bruise on her swollen face. She wasn't eating. Every once in a while, she would bite her lower lips as if she was trying to control herself. I saw that her feet were bandaged to the knee in a dirty bandage. I smiled at her. She returned my smile, but the bruise stubbornly refused to smile back. In the next few days Sepideh and I drew closer together.

Our room was watched over by two penitent prisoners, *tavvabs*[1] as they called them. They carried their invisible badge of penitence like an hidden badge of honour, a key to escape hell. I'll tell you about them later because now I have to help Sepideh wash and use the toilet. She had felt unclean for ten days, she told me in a voice that betrayed a self-loathing. As a real believer, being unclean, *najess*, made her prayers worthless. She was unclean and she hated herself for not being able to rid herself of all that *nejasat* (uncleanliness). She reminded me so much of my grandmother and her obsession with cleanliness.[2] This was no obsession though. Sepideh could only crawl, and having to squat in the toilet and wash yourself clean afterwards, well that was a nightmare.

On my way back from the toilets I saw a young woman in a yellow-tinged overcoat arguing with a bearded man leaning on a door threshold.

"I don't believe in God," she was saying in a firm voice, "these are what have made us humans, tool-makers," she added, waving her hands at the man. "These hands are the instruments of creation."

"*Bichareh*, you stupid wretch, don't you see that everything was created by God. Everything. Even wretches like you." The guard was angry but defensive. I must have caught them in the middle of a long discussion.

"I didn't say God does not exist. I simply don't need him to create me." Her voice was firm. From where I was sitting, I could not see all of her, but the girl in the yellowish overcoat just grew and grew. "I can understand you might need some explanation for your existence, but I don't. I just don't. We became what we are because we could make tools, and we could make tools because we could do this," she must have brought her thumb and index finger in apposition. "I see no need for a creator. It's all here in the flesh. In this world. In evolution…."

"You stupid misguided idiot. You stubborn fool. It was God that made your hand possible, a God that created *Adam* and then *Havva* (Eve) from mud. People like you deserve to die. There is no place for dregs like you on this earth." He said angrily and walked off muttering something that sounded like *astaqforellah*, God forgive me! Suddenly I felt toughened by her outspoken courage. Her daring, and audacity had clearly unbalanced the guard. He had never seen someone who questioned the very core of his beliefs, especially a mere woman. He did not know how to respond. He hadn't even slapped or kicked her. He just walked away. Later I got to know her well. Suzan had been a nurse and her courage was infectious. Always smiling, always helpful, this rather short but beautiful woman was a rock on which, for the next few months, many of us leant and drew strength.

I was standing in a queue for the toilet when I saw him from the corner of the blindfold. My brother was sitting beside a column, waiting to be interrogated. Two men were standing over him. One was the Chief Prosecutor, Lajevardi, now in charge of the prison system across Iran and responsible for organising the nationwide system of torture.[3] Lajevardi was whispering something in the ear of the other man. The man turned to my brother.

"Do you know brother Lajevardi?" The man asked.

236

"Only from a distance. We were never in the same prison. He was in Mashhad and I in Shiraz." His soft but firm voice, that had been echoing in my head all these days, rippled through me. I loved that calm, clear voice, words delivered as if he had all the time in the world. They were talking of the Shah's regime when both were prisoners of SAVAK. I wanted to touch his face, hold him close. Real close. I yearned and yearned and let that yearning flood my inner being.

How the world had changed only to remain the same. Former prisoners torturing former fellow-prisoners, now their captive. Yesterday the two were distanced by prejudice and hatred, when Muslim prisoners refused to sit at food with fellow-prisoners from the left who they considered *najess*. Now the two were in the immediacy of a savage intimate embrace.

[1] *Tavvab* – literally penitents, are fellow prisoners who had agreed to cooperate with the prison authorities, from running the day-to-day affairs of the prison, to betraying former colleagues in prison or outside on the street, to spying on fellow prisoners, to participating in interrogation, torture and even executions. Over the next years they would be important tools in the hands of the regime to break the opposition. Self-hate made them even more vindictive toward those fellow-prisoners who had not cracked-up. We will meet them a lot.

[2] *Najess-pāki,* the art of avoiding uncleanliness and keeping your body clean of impurities like urine, blood and faeces is fundamental to *Shia'* practice and a favourite topic for many a clerical dissertation.

[3] Lajevardi was the universally feared chief prosecutor of the Islamic regime, in charge of all prisons. As a former prisoner of the Shah, he knew many of the older generation of political activists personally. He had a deep hatred of the left and the Mujahedin that dated from those days when they shared a prison. Now he was the architect of the systematic torture and use of the penitent *tavvabs* to break prisoners.

Chapter 45

My Interrogation

Nayyer

We waited in that cell for our turn to come, a wait seemingly without end. Walls were dirty grey in that windowless room when I first arrived, but as day followed day and the wait stretched into the ever, I began to see fleeting images and colours in the grey. I had deliberately not eaten for some days while waiting for my turn. Someone had said that if you are weaker, you lose consciousness quicker under torture. Anyway, it was impossible to sleep with all the screaming and lashing. One woman screamed all night and when she was brought back into our room the next morning, she had a mess for legs. Another night the whistling sound of the whip flew over from the same direction, all through the night, but not a sound from the couch-bound victim. Who was this hero? Perhaps it was my brother. Or were they flogging the dead? I used the brief moments of mealtimes and toilet to get to know Suzan, the nurse, better. It was impossible not to admire her courageous stance. Even some of the guards were overawed. They would argue with her over her beliefs and even allowed her to help with the bandaging of legs. Once they took Suzan to her home hoping someone would call or ring. For the 24 hour she was there she engaged the *pasdars* in ideological debate. They shot our lioness that autumn.[1]

At that time Dr Sheikholeslam, an orthopaedic surgeon and fellow prisoner was the only trained doctor in Evin. He was allowed to operate on prisoners, but only if they were not earmarked for execution. For those without hope, he was only permitted simple bandaging. I saw one such person they called Massoud a few times on my way to the toilet, lying unconscious on the floor in the corridor or on a bed. One day the guards found him dead by a wall.

There were some creepy anomalies in that strange world. A boy of seven or eight used to bring us water and take on other small tasks for the prisoners. His father had previously been in charge of Evin. His grandfather now looked after him and was given some menial tasks in Evin prison.[2] What kind of people exposed a child to such scenes?

What kind of people would allow a child to witness the torture of their mother? I saw Setareh fleetingly in a corridor with her young son. Years later, in another prison, she recounted her story, reluctantly, in bits squeezed out like thick glue. Her newborn son was with her for two years. There they were, in that corridor, for months and months, months when the little boy believed the world was the blanket on which they both sat and slept day and night. There, on that miniature blanket-world, he sat, hour after hour, days without daylight, not allowed to move. Or roam. A dystopian universe where, blanket-bound except when he helped his mother crawl to the toilet holding on to his tiny body, his innocent eyes were seeing men and women, without eyes. He was her eye. He was her crutch. Setareh's unbelievably penetrating eyes, large like that of a doe, were closed to light, day and night. Beautiful? Maybe. But mesmerising they certainly were. Her executed husband was buried in the backyard of their home, denied burial in a public cemetery, whether Muslim or non-Muslim. He was a non-person even in death.

*

Then, after five days my turn came. You can't remain on edge for that long and the terror had already blurred round the edges and gradually become less terrifying. Narges, my sister-in-law had been through her interrogation and was sent to the prison block. They led me to a table in a room facing the wall, and I was writing down my answers on a piece of paper when someone hit me hard with a truncheon from behind.

"Why are you hitting me? I am answering your questions" I protested.

"Just making sure you know where you are," came the reply, as if I did not know which hell I was in.

"Write down everything. Every dirty little thing you have done. All the filthy acts against the revolution you have committed." His shouts sounded more like barking. The walls amplified all sounds which were further magnified through my emotions. No one is normal under a threat that appears to have no end, a menace that seems to spread beyond a horizon, into an infinite uncertainty. Space and time lose their natural relations. You float in a world where nothing is real, and all reality eludes understanding.

Every few minutes I felt something hard hitting my neck and back. A reminder, for what needed no reminding. All around me were faceless voices. I was not allowed to turn round. Close by, a young man was tearfully describing his activities at school in minute detail, utterly terrified. It did not stop them hitting him with something hard, cutting off his narrative with a thud and a shout. The voice of another girl at the other end of the room was telling, no beseeching, her torturer:

"That newspaper is not mine. It's my brother's."

"What about that bottle of wine we found in your house? Is that your brother's too?" There was no sarcasm in his voice, just naked menace.

"Yes," I heard her say almost under her breath. "That's my brother's too." Then what sounded like a slap followed by the sound of something metallic hitting the floor. Had the blow toppled her and her chair?

When I finished writing I put down the biro. A hand snatched it. It was then that I saw how dirty the walls were. Human stains of indefinable origins. A few minutes later the blows rained down, hard, really hard like nothing in my memory store. Automatically I stood up shrieking from pain, protecting my face. I heard myself calling my mother, involuntarily, like a child. After a while he stopped beating and threw me out into the corridor.

All around I heard the sound of interrogations. It was a woman's voice, high pitched and piercing: Untie me, she was pleading. Please, please untie me. You want my husband. I will take you to my husband.

"Now you are coming to your senses," a man's voice said and then the sounds of chains rattling.

"I'm sure my husband will come for our child. He loves his child."

"You stupid wretch. Why did you disgorge children if you planned to plot against the revolution?"

"It wasn't my idea. My husband wanted kids. It wasn't mine. I swear to God I was against it. I really was." I can still hear her voice. Such despair, trailing, fading away down into some deep well. I later learnt that they took the severely beaten and battered woman home and stayed there for some days. The husband never came. I don't remember what happened to her. Her name too is gone. All that remains with me is her voice, an echo of utter despair.

A few hours later I was taken back to the same room. It was now less crowded. They sat me on the same chair and told me to place one hand above my head and the other behind my back. Now hook your hands together, the man ordered, but my hands would not link. An excruciating pain, like an electric current, shot through me as he pushed from above and below and brought my wrists side by side and shackled them. He took off my watch. Pain gradually spread from my arms and shoulders to the rest of my body. I was set alight, burning in an inferno of pain. It must be like that when they burnt people at the stake. Time moved slowly, extremely slowly, childhood slowly, and every few minutes the interrogator would give a sharp blow to my elbows. It was as if a sledgehammer was crushing my body. He moved me to another chair. I was now facing the room. Maybe he wanted to see my facial expressions. I lost track of time, but the room was now empty except for interrogators coming and going. An intense thirst came over me and I asked for water. I'll fetch you the toilet ewer, the man sneered, and this insult momentarily eclipsed the pain. I remembered the last words of my sister, 'hold to your principles whatever happens'.

A man came in and all the interrogators stood up. From beneath my blindfold I saw the edge of a *mullah's* cloak. They called him *haj-aqa*.[3] Later I learnt he was the notorious gun-toting *mullah* Hadi Qaffari.[4] Who is this? He asked. Her brother was a guest of yours, a man's voice answered. So this *mullah* was present when they tortured my brother. He may even have participated.

"Where have you hidden the arms," the *haj-aqa* asked, using a different

241

voice? "Tell us and I will instruct them to free your arms." Was the question directed at me?

"You clearly have no idea about my dossier," I said unable to suppress a smirk. "There are no arms. I don't believe in arms."

"You'll rot away like this here until you confess," he said and left the room.

"You shameless slut. You laugh at *haj-aqa*," my interrogator said, slamming hard on my arms. Some time later as I was drowning in pain, he asked me if I would agree to an interview in front of cameras. Who am I to go in front of cameras, I managed to reply, I haven't done anything to confess.

They picked me up, laid me down on the floor, on my stomach and a *pasdar* sat on my shackled hands. Someone stuffed a dirty rag into my mouth, and someone started whipping my feet. Involuntarily I withdrew my leg and screamed through the rag a scream that was like an animal. They put a blanket over my head and the man sitting on my back put his hand over my mouth and face and pressed down. I felt I was about to suffocate and struggled to free my mouth. Then I don't remember anything. Starving myself must have worked.

When I woke up, I heard a male voice shouting, shame on you, cover yourself up. They unlocked my arms. Lifeless arms. Cover yourself you shameless slut, came the order. The men who had assaulted me so brutally were now concerned about my modesty. With great difficulty I pulled up my *chador* and blindfold. My arms were not mine. I could not sit and had to sprawl myself on the corridor floor. I heard a man tell me to get up and walk on my feet. I can't. Don't you want to reduce the swelling on your feet he asked? I can't. I'll do it tomorrow, I heard myself say through a mist. No one was whipping me now. He took me to the women's room and gave me a glass of water. I will come for you tomorrow to go on with our talk. Tomorrow was years away. I fell asleep. There is such a thing as pain fatigue. It was daytime when I heard my name. It was the same interrogator. My heart sank, but he had come back to return my watch. The cell walls were grey.

A week later Golnaz another severely beaten girl and me, hobbled blindfolded, carrying one another across corridors, across the courtyard, feeling the cool autumn air on our face, then through what smelled like the dispensary where we saw more torn up people, where Golnaz was slapped hard on the back of the head because old-man-Kachuhi who escorted us had spied her pointing with her chin at a boy lying half dead on a wire bed. Here even porters dabbled in torture.

"Passing on information, eh?" old-man-Kachuhi sneered and hit her again where there was pain, then more pain climbing stairs, agonising pain, shared pain, dragging ourselves through some interlinking rooms and we arrived at a closed metal door. A hand without a body reached out taking special care that prying male eyes do not see the owner of that hand, took some papers from old-man-Kachuhi, maybe read it, then the body-less hand reappeared and we were pushed through to the women's block. I had kept my promise to my sister. There had been no tears. You don't cry for yourself. Tears came later.

[1] Suzan Nikzad was executed in the autumn of 1981 accused of working for the Fadai' Minority.
[2] Mohammad Kachuhi, in charge of Evin, was shot by a *pasdar* early that summer during a mock execution of political prisoners, probably in error. The boy's grandfather continued to work in Evin taking prisoners from here to there.
[3] Referring to someone who had completed the *Haj* pilgrimage to Mecca. A polite form of address.
[4] Hadi Qaffari a well-known militant cleric who often carried a pistol stuck in his belt.

Chapter 46

The split

Ahmad

The war was ravenously chewing through a generation that threw themselves at its jaws on their way to paradise, somewhere in the nowhere. The prisons were devouring the other half of the same generation who had thrown themselves into the battle for a paradise in the here and now, in the somewhere. An umbrella of fear and unease half-blocked the sun. The sky no longer shone. Men and women became numb. The country was in deep gloom.

Moving house to house in Ahwaz, Ahmad became increasingly anxious for the safety of the large number of activists, young and old, under his responsibility.[1] Through that murky mist he saw clearly the mortal danger hanging over them unless they drastically changed direction and made a fundamental tactical retreat. The Fadai' Majority, having shed its most impatient militant activists in a premature split,[2] was now drawing ever closer to the Tudeh Party and through them to the brutal regime that was overseeing the bloody repression.[3] Once the flirtation morphed into a decision to merge with Tudeh, a second split became inevitable. Ahmad and those closest to him set about gaining the support of almost the entire organisation in Khuzestan province, a significantly large section of the Fadai', for the rupture. He returned to his father's house in Tehran to help finalise the matter.

Autumn 1981, nature hovering between death and a future rebirth, an autumn a year and a lifetime ago, when the town of his childhood was ravaged by war, when death from mortars and the firing squad had briefly hovered over his head, followed by a spring when hope had appeared as light peeping over the horizon only to be devoured by the darkness of mass arrests and executions, and now another autumn and the challenge of managing an orderly split in an organisation to which he had devoted a life. With a small group of comrades, he was going to organise a rupture. An orderly rupture. Lessons learnt from the earlier chaotic premature split of the Minority Fadai'.

Then came the day of the Plenum. The provisional central committee, made up of many Fadai' veterans, were gathering in a secret location, a house on the foothills of the Alborz mountain. It was approaching the end of winter and in the lower slopes of the mountain already the signs of the coming spring were visible on some trees. As he approached the house, having parked some streets away, he momentarily had that squeezing feeling of longing he experienced every spring, a very primitive feeling of yearning, like some awakening primordial urge. He squashed it and rang the doorbell.

Discussions began in the early morning. It was not long before he felt alone in that smoke-filled room of many men, and no women, and where he was the only non-smoker. By mid-morning he realised that his vision of a decentralised, less venerable organisation was shared by a bare handful.

He had come to that vision meticulously, painfully, studiously, almost like a detached observer. For months he had closely observed the growing control of one faction of government over the machinery of state, the judiciary, the closure of opposition presses one by one, wave after wave of arrests. He had read every newspaper he could get his hands on. Listened to every debate in the *Majles* parliament. Followed all the major speeches in the Friday prayers.[4] Made notes, tabulated, configured, examined and re-examined, synthesised. This is what he had always done. This is what he was good at. Tabulating. Putting side by side apparently unconnected bits of information. Looking for patterns. A hypothesis forming. Then going back critically to see how the hypothesis functions, explains and predicts. Always refining. Always questioning. Always moving. It was a mind that proved highly successful in predicting. A mind that had difficulty with the more abstract emotions of love, especially the possessive nature of some love.

"We are under threat of annihilation, he told the gathering that afternoon, in an increasingly exasperated voice. He felt suffocated. We should abandon the top-down model we have been following. With death and dungeon hanging over us, the only logic is to make our organisation much less vulnerable, shielded until such time as conditions change. Our current policies are inherently doomed. That's after all what has brought us to this room. That's why we decided to split. We have watched as this regime we are ostensibly supporting, cuts away with stick and sword all the freedoms we won through the revolution. One by one. Cut by cut. Cutting away chunks from our organisation, bit by deadly bit. Cutting off the freedoms we, the people, have given so many lives to win. It is as if we, all of us who believe in liberty, in justice, in a fairer society, one that does not exploit the labour of others are being sliced to near-death, before what I have no doubt will be a massive and bloody final deadly crackdown. The writing is on the wall and our organisation has chosen to close its eyes to the tiger in the room, saying 'God willing it's a cat.'[5] If you agree with the picture I have portrayed, then let us look again at the entire project. If what prompted us to organise a split are those policies of Tudeh that have turned us into near-passive observers of a looming catastrophe, for us, for them and for freedom and democracy in our land, then let's work out a different approach. Let's question everything. A sudden cough interrupted his speech. Choking, he sat down. Maybe it was not just the smoke that was suffocating him.

It was yet another theatrical performance. He thought theatre. He lived theatre. He should have been a playwright. He was. Author and actor in the theatre of life where to fail was fatal.

By the evening it was clear to him that the majority in that room had no problem with the policies advocated by the Tudeh. Only of being identified with its name, a name that in some minds carried with it a history of shameful capitulation or even betrayal.[6] One or two people spoke in his defence but it was clear that most had made up their minds: Tudeh's policy, purged of a name.

Very early the next morning, before anyone was awake, he left for his father's house, leaving behind a brief note:

If the sole purpose of our gathering here in the Plenum was to continue with the Tudeh political line and merely avoid the stigma of its name, I would rather have gone straight to Kianuri himself.[7]

It was perhaps the briefest piece of writing he was ever to do. A theatrical full stop to twenty-four hours of bad theatre.

As he emerged onto the road there was a heavy downpour. The kind that softens you up for the coming spring. He pulled up the collar of his coat. He heard a harsh rattling sound coming from above. He looked up. A large number of black crows were kwarcking and clicking and circling the two plane trees on the pavement on his side of the street, winter-bare against the early morning greywhite sky. Nature was speaking. They had warned me before. Creatures inside him were kwarcking, echo-like. No content. No depth. Not exactly foresight. But a foreboding.

A sudden deep melancholy enveloped him like a cave. He felt totally alone, unable to breathe from anguish. How could they be so blind? How could he have misjudged his closest friends? He walked fast, nearly slipped on the wet pavement, drove to his father's house soaked to his undershirt, undressed, thought of showering to wash away the anger, changed his mind, not eaten for 24 hours, only bitterblack tea, turned on the samovar, electric now, not like when he was a child, had a piece of *sangak* flat-bread[8] and white cheese, left half of it on the plate, lay down on his bed, and closed his eyes where he saw the crows circling round the near bare trees. Now they were silent.

The plenum suspended, the Secretariat came over to persuade him to return. They argued till lunchtime. In vain. He had made up his mind. Adamant. He resigned. It was a personal decision, he said. Theirs was no longer a vehicle that he felt comfortable in. But he kept his relationship with some old comrades. He would meet Mansur the poet and Mehrdad weekly. A few others close to him also left, just like Ahmad, without fuss. Time was coming to the boil.

A year later, just months before leaving the country, he wrote to Mehrdad. All the evidence points to the same conclusion, he wrote in his precise architectural handwriting. The regime sooner or later will deliver a final savage blow to the remaining left-wing parties that are hanging in there by a thread, he wrote, and expanded on his reasons for predicting a savage final assault on civil society. I recommend that, until further notice, those who are well known to the authorities leave the country by whatever means they can. All relations between cadres and sympathisers should be suspended forthwith. In particular, the publication of the official newspaper should cease immediately because it leaves such a visible footprint behind as it moves from writer to printer to distributor to reader. Split the entire organisation up into independent self-contained cells until the time those outside the country can come up with a way of creating horizontal links that are less vulnerable to attack. He was in effect asking the entire organisation to suspend all activity until some safer model could be found in keeping with the worsening atmosphere of terror.

Some who read the letter accused him of cowardice. He has lost his nerve, they sniggered. A few months later, he was on his way to his weekly meeting with Mehrdad. Houshang, a friend not known to the authorities, usually walked ahead to check the safety signal before he met up with Mehrdad, a precaution they had devised to avoid ambush. The look on Houshang's face as he returned said it all. The safety signals for the first and second rendezvous point were missing, Mehrdad, the military counterintelligence officer turned revolutionary and his close friend, had been arrested. He was later shot.[9] Mansur the poet, and childhood friend, committed suicide some years later in exile.

Even though Ahmad did not know the extent of the blows to the Fadai', he had been out of the organisation for two years, he knew that some in the current Central Committee knew his home address. Always prudent he moved out of his current home, just in time, another chance decision that saved him. Life is a series of lucky escapes, until one day that fails. Life is merely the postponement of death.

[1] With almost 2,000 men and women, it was the largest sector identifying

with the Fadai' Majority.

[2] A year previously, in 1980, in what Ahmad (and many others) considered a premature split, the minority of the Fadai' Central Committee split to form a separate organisation, the Fadai' Minority, leaving behind the Fadai' Majority.

[3] Since the revolution the pro-Soviet Tudeh party had followed the lead from Moscow and supported the Islamic Republic regime.

[4] Friday Prayers were an important weapon for the *mullahs* to pass on their centrally co-ordinated message to the faithful.

[5] *Inshallah gorbast*. A popular saying in Farsi.

[6] In particular the perceived failure of the Tudeh Party to fully support the popular nationalist prime minister Mohammad Mosaddeq who was overthrown by a CIA backed coup in 1953, turned a significant section of the population against the Tudeh Party. See *All the Shah's Men*, Stephen Kinzer, Wiley & Sons, 2003.

[7] Tudeh Party leader.

[8] Typical large Tehrani flat bread baked in an oven covered with hot stone pebbles.

[9] Mehdad Pakzad having endured severe torture without cracking was executed on 26 June 1985 in Evin.

Chapter 47

Aubergine stew

Jina

Over the previous year Ahmad had lived with 11-year old Nina and Jina on the top floor in a duplex apartment in a multi-story block. Living as friends. Separate bedrooms. Separate bathrooms. Almost separate lives. But they eat together as a family, if they were home. Azadeh had gone to Paris a year earlier. The apartment block was one of Ahmad's own development. Below, on the ground floor, he had set up an architectural office and was working there on a project with a married couple, both of whom were also architects.

"We should leave the country too," he said one day when they were having supper. He had long wanted to leave. There was nothing more he could do there.

"No, Ahmadjan! No! I won't. I just won't," she said softly, without looking up, almost as if talking to herself, and took another spoonful of rice with a small piece of lamb and aubergine. They were having *khoresht bademjoon*, a dish of boiled chicken and aubergines, taken with rice, his favourite. Whoever came home first would cook. This was her turn. Her voice, low in volume, was laced with an anger that was entirely new to him. He put his spoon down.

"But why?" Ahmad said, taken back by the blank refusal. She usually listened to his suggestions. It wasn't as if she had been unaware of what had happened to him. Or of his reasons for quitting the Fadai'. "I don't understand why you threw out my suggestion without at the very least asking me why I am making it. You know I never do anything without carefully thinking it through. You rejected my suggestion ..."

She lifted her head and looked him straight in the eye, interrupting.

"I am through with following you everywhere. I am done with it. It is as simple as that. You can go if you want. You can take Nina too if you want. But count me out. I am staying. I'm staying here in Iran. In Tehran. I'm going nowhere." Her light brown eyes had looked straight into his. Pupils dilated. He was struck by how deeply penetrating her look was. She was not particularly beautiful, but those eyes were razor-like in their penetration. Today.

"Look, let me make myself clear," Jina continued in a voice that came from somewhere bottomless with a history. I have followed you everywhere. I followed you to Rasht, leaving my family. Do you think they were happy to see their daughter go off to an uncertain future with a man who had spent a year in *Qezel Qal'eh* prison? I did it for love. Then I married you, even when I did not believe in marriage, because that would make your camouflage more secure. I did it for love, a love that I don't think you ever understood. Raw love. A living, heart-wrenching, squeezing, terrifying love, the sort of love that stops sleep, and when finally dreams come, they come in flashing waves of light zigzagging like coloured thunderbolts, pouring downwards in gushes of uncontrollable emotion that wakes you up in sweat and anguish and longing. And longing." The last words were barely audible.

"I didn't really have a voice in our life," she went on in her normal voice. "Did you ask me when you just walked out of the Gilan project, abandoned it on a momentary decision to prove your honour, and sulked in the apartment for six months? It was a heroic stance. It was. An honourable stance, showing your disdain for worldly things. You defended a defenceless underdog. I liked it. I approved and said nothing. But I was denied a voice in that heroic, honourable, principled stance. Did you think I might object, or did you simply not even consider that I have a stake in this enterprise?

And now. Do you realise, I have not had a voice in this narrative? Have you considered that? Have you for one minute given any thought to that? Actually, all the women in this narrative have walk-on parts. Except Nayyer,

251

who I wish I had met. But then, she wasn't part of your story. She took up her own story. Have you even noticed that I have been given just a walk-on part? Even in this story, I've been all but voiceless until now. I want my narrative. Anyone reading this story would just see me as a blur. I know that is not what you wanted. That is not you. You do, you did, love me in an abstract sort of way. But that love was also a walk-on part. A peripheral part of the narrative, not unlike Rosencrantz in that Hamlet our theatre group put on, and SAVAK banned."

"I did, l do, love you" Ahmad interjected but immediately regretted having cut into her narrative. Into her voice.

"And then there was your friend," she continued, not having heard or ignoring his interjection. 'I tolerated your friend Azadeh imposing herself daily more and more in our life when you were in the *Komiteh*. And then in the hospital. Perhaps I am being too harsh. She was my friend too and it was a comfort having her. And afterwards. I did it because I trusted your judgement. Your logic. I must have been imagining things, I told myself. But she kept drawing closer and closer. Using Nina as a bait. I watched you taking the bait and I ignored it because I trusted your good sense. I sat by you in that hospital bed, watching you squeezing the pain inwards, trying to put on a brave face. To project that image of a stoic. Do you imagine I did not feel that pain in every cell of my body? And that woman tried to insinuate herself between our pains. To squeeze herself in that sea of pain that bound us together. And you didn't understand. You, who are so observant of the world around you, just did not see the wall she was creating, splitting our pain by an invisible barrier, masquerading as compassion and friendship. But even when I left you, I stayed with you. I joined you in Ahwaz after you rose from the dead. We heard and felt the bombs together. We changed houses together. I even ignored the other woman and her sister sharing safehouses with us. It was expediency, a cover, even though her aggressive presence pained me deeply. We saw the arrests of our friends together; we felt their deaths together. We were together while not being together. Friends, not lovers or…. or a married couple. But together because we had a history."

Nina sat beside her holding her spoon half filled with food, listening, not comprehending the words, not all, but totally following the storyline. She put her spoon down, muttered something neither heard and left the room. Neither noticed. Jina went on in a calmer voice, as if travelling inside.

"Don't misunderstand me. I loved you even when I had lost you. I always knew that you did not reciprocate that love. I don't think you have ever known the kind of love I am talking about. Of course, you have loved. Of course, you have. You are loving all the time. But it is a different love. They say God created the cat so that man learns to stroke the tiger. My love for you is like a love for a tiger. A tiger masquerading as a cat. So I stayed with the tiger, but kept my distance. You don't stroke a tiger every day. We remained friends. I like that, though deep inside I hide my old feelings. You who saw all feelings never saw mine. Never.

But leave with you? Leave the country? Leave my parents, my job? This is where I draw the line. I didn't follow you outside the organisation. I wasn't particularly active, but it gave me an identity. I know what I am, where I stand, what I have fought for. I won't jettison that for a nebulous idea. You can go. Yes. You can even take Nina. But I am staying. That is my final decision."

She sat silent. Eyes lowered, Absorbed. A cloud of thought soaked her. She was no longer living in his world.

Ahmad got up. Silent. Walked to the kitchen and came back with two glasses of tea in a silver *engareh* holder. He placed one on her right with two sugar lumps next to it. She always used two. He sat opposite her at the table and slowly drank his tea. No sugar.

She drank her tea, got up and took her plate, barely touched, and walked over to the kitchen. All the time Ahmad had watched. Watched her light brown eyes that were fixed on him turn inwards into a world of memory. Memory and images. I'm like a monk. Or a nun. I'm married to an idea, his inner voice whispered. You. You Jina, don't know, you will never know the nature of the pain that is not physical, the anguish of suppressing love, denying desire again and again. You will never know the singleness of the vow that drives me. You cannot understand a weakness, my weakness, which cannot simultaneously love a woman and fight. You cannot imagine the energy the battle takes from one. It leaves no room. Like a nun married to an abstract idea. I am that nun, that monk. I bear the pain. My pain and your pain. What I have done to you is nothing short of murder. I know I have done it. I detest myself for doing it. I had no choice in doing it. It is in the nature of this battle.

He was suspicious of emotions while simultaneously mesmerised by it, the hey-ho of love and attachment. It is in that contradictory limbo that human love tried to walk into his life. No wonder it failed him and her.

He said nothing. There was nothing to add. Nina's name was in his passport, and he would take her if he left. But he stayed on. He stayed on in Iran, watchful and observant in his own unique obsessive way. And he stayed on with his family.

Chapter 48

The old dispensary

Nayyer

Our new home had the surreal name of cellblock 240, after its internal phone number. It had once been the infirmary. Entering it after that infernal Dantean passageway felt like I had gate-crashed into a treeless walled garden with trees made of steel and brim-full of people of all ages, school-age to the truly elderly. The air was stale. We were free to walk in the walkway onto which the cells opened. I quickly learnt the reason for opening the cell gates was to allow them to squeeze more prisoners into the available space. The cells, five by five metres each, were populated way beyond capacity. Our room was already brim-full of about 100 mostly middle-aged women, there on charges of political or economic 'crimes'. They weren't too pleased that a couple of young extremists, as they saw us, had cramped their already intolerably cramped space.

"*Khanum* Alizadeh,[1] for God's sake don't send us more!"

"*Khanum* Alizadeh, there is not even room to breathe…!"

"*Khanum* Alizadeh, we don't even have room to sit. We are up all night…!"

Immediately after settling in, I joined the toilet queue, refusing the offer to jump it because of my injuries. It gave me time to survey my fellow prisoners. I found my sister-in-law Nargess and a few old friends from outside in the room housing the left. It was even more crowded than the one I was assigned. I decided to sit with them at mealtime. The girls took turns to spread the mealtime spread, the *sofreh*. Two of us would share a plastic plate. Beside each plate, the girl on the labour-rota[2] would put a piece of bread and then divide the food with particular precision: today a small piece of butter with one teaspoon of jam. That first meal was the most delicious prison food I had eaten. I noticed some girls eating separately. They are from the Tudeh and Majority Fadai', my friend explained, they don't mix with us 'counter-revolutionaries'.[3]

When evening came the loudspeaker announced that the *Hosseinieh[4]* is open. At that time going to common prayers was not yet compulsory. Some of the girls went off because of their belief and others because it gave them an excuse for an outing. A few of us seized the opportunity and gathered in one of the cells where anyone who had a voice, sang and the rest of us joined in wherever we could. A few girls improvised a comic version of an interrogation with the 'prisoner' trying to outwit the interrogator. I hadn't laughed so much for a long time. I forgot the feel of the stinking heavy air, and the pain. Next day they called out names for transfer to *Qezel Hesar[5]* prison. We all sang *mara beboos* (kiss me), a song of farewell by a father, about to face the firing squad in the previous regime, to his daughter.

And so the days went by. Each afternoon we would gather near the entrance to greet new arrivals. They kept arriving like an unending stream. It was refreshing to see fresh faces, but it put increasing strain on our limited resources. And they were truly limited. Since the amount of food delivered to the cellblock was unchanging our portions inevitably shrank and shrank and shrank. We were chronically hungry. There was also the issue of two tiny toilets and a single sink for the entire cell block. We started queuing in the morning to get in by about lunchtime. When the corridor could no longer accommodate the queue, we introduced a numbering system. You took a number in the morning and again after lunch. Of course, those with wounds or bladder problems were given priority but many refused to take advantage of this and suffered in silence.

And then there were the showers. At first many of the girls were too shy to take part in communal showering. You see, five of us had to share the shower at any time. But soon dirt and grime overcame coyness. The frequency of showering also shrank with the rising number of inmates. And we just got better at speed bathing and speed toileting. As time went on the lack of sleeping space became a real issue. Even utilising every available space, including the passageway, we had to resort to sardine-sleep, sleeping on your side, no turning, no bending of knees. Some girls had to squeeze under the beds. The space below the three-tiered beds was so low you would have to somehow wriggle out if you wanted to turn. Those of us with leg wounds were allowed to sleep by the wall. That way there was less chance of someone stepping on your wounds.

Suzan, the courageous nurse in yellowish overcoat I had met earlier in the interrogation centre, arrived and brought both joy and nursing classes, showing us how to change bandages, how to massage wounded feet to speed up healing (one hand in front, one hand behind, from toes upwards) and how to massage heads to soothe headaches. Then one day her name was called. She stood up, smiled, no individual farewells, and walked through the gate fist clenched: 'goodbye kids. Hoping for victory' was the last word we heard and a smile that I still see in the sky, like that of the cat in Alice in Wonderland.[6]

*

Waiting as we did, every afternoon by the gate to greet newcomers, I spotted Sima-D, an old friend, and was shocked by how thin and worn out she looked. She saw me and with her eyebrows signalled that we should not acknowledge each other. I had known her for years and we had been mountaineering[7] together. That evening, in a corner, away from prying ears, she explained.

Mine is a lost cause, she said, and her eyes misted over. She looked so sad, so desolate. I don't want to cause you trouble, she continued in a voice that seemed to disappear down a well inside her. Please leave me to my fate. She looked as if she was already on the other side. It's fine, I reassured her. Our acquaintance is quite natural. I still see her faint smile, unbelieving, but calm.

She had been betrayed by her group's supervisor, arrested with her cousin and despite the fact that they knew everything about her, was tortured anyway. Later she introduced me to Nahid-M who had, unknown to me, already been in our block. Both had stood firm in their beliefs under cross-examination. One of the interrogators wanted to have an ideological debate with Sima-D.

You go and sort out the economy, she had replied, you can keep your ideology. Both their names were called out on the loudspeaker one day. We went out to the tiny yard to spend the last minutes of her life together. There was a drizzle and she, from the Caspian provinces, loved the rain. We shared a cigarette. I remember the strong smell of burning cooking oil coming from the nearby kitchen. Tomorrow's food. She spoke of her lifelong devotion to the Fadai' cause and wanted people outside to know that she had stood firm by her beliefs, if ever I got out alive. The thought of such a spirit being snuffed out tore my insides. Just then Nahid-M appeared at the door to the concrete yard.

"Do you have a tweezer?" she asked Sima-D, grinning.

"What on earth do you want a tweezer for? Sima-D said.

"I want to look good going to my death." Sima-D took a tweezer out of her bag and passed it over. They looked at each other and a smile of understanding passed between them.

Both went out smiling, hand in hand. They did not want a tearful goodbye. Both were sure that victory is close.[8] Look after my cousin, was Sima-D's last words to me, but the cousin wanted to be left alone. I went back to our yard and watered the concrete with my tears.

*

Then personal tragedy struck. They had called Azar out that afternoon, and later asked for her belongings. One of her friends turned to us with tears in her eyes. They are going to execute her, she said, and that night the sound of the fusillade followed by the single shots were like hammers on my head.[9] Without thinking I began to hum a tune (*morgh sahar*, the dawn bird) that this shy, quite girl had sung for us the night before in her heavenly voice. Azar herself was that dawn bird, the bird that mourns at dawn and stokes your broken heart.

Then they called Nargess to take a phone call. A phone call? At that time? I tried to see it in a positive light. Maybe her family had used some influence or other to get to talk to her. You are being naïve, my friend said. I was being naïve. A few minutes later Nargess came back distraught, beating her head and repeating over and over again: They killed him, they killed him.[10]

My brother, my teacher, the closest person in the world to me was dead. We fell into each other's arms. The girls finally managed to calm her down a little.

"They passed the phone to me. He was saying goodbye. Goodbye for what I shouted. I am being shot in an hour, as an ex-prisoner in the Shah's regime. He was calm. Like describing a trip somewhere." She went silent and hushed us to silence. At 8.30 we heard the fusillade sounding like the crumpling of an iron mountain. Then the shouts of 'death to communist, death to *monafeq*, *alah-o akbar*, Khomeini our leader…..'.[11] We counted 86 shots. There were 85 people accompanying my brother. He was not alone. Between tears Nargess asked, what do you think his last words were? He probably sang a militant song, I replied. I think he was teasing one of his companions, his wife said. He probably was. Another young girl, from our block was among the 86. She too was a nurse.[12]

He was dead and I was still alive and there was relief and there was guilt and there was grief, and the air became putrid again.

I took a sleeping pill and dreamt a poem. My dead mother in a blue silk dress, the dress my sister had worn to her wedding night. Blue was my brother's favourite colour. She walked smiling and behind her the guests were smiling too. Floating somewhere vaguely were my long dead father and uncles.

Blue is the colour of the sky in its boundless dimension.

Blue is the colour of the ocean whose far shores you cannot see.

Blue is the memory of my brother that for me is infinite.

And his smile,

Which too was blue.

[1] The (female) *Pasdar* in charge of the cell block.
[2] *Kargari*: the name given to fellow prisoners on the prisoner-organised rota for cleaning, sharing out of food and other menial tasks for that day or week.
[3] The Fadai' Majority's and Tudeh's support for Khomeini did not stop the regime from arresting them. Officially they blamed their arrests on rogue

rightist elements within the regime. They were ostracised by fellow political prisoners.

[4] A place for holding religious ceremonies and public prayer.

[5] Prison in Karaj, a city west of Tehran (see later chapters).

[6] Suzan Nikzad was executed in the autumn of 1981.

[7] Political activists would go on group mountain hikes as a way of creating group solidarity and to be able to hold group discussions without attracting the attention of the security police.

[8] Sima Daryani and Nahid Mohammadi were executed on 29th November 1981 accused of being members of the Fadai' Minority.

[9] Azar Latifi was executed in December 1981 for supporting the Fadai' Minority

[10] Mehdi Khosrowshahi Baradaran, executed autumn 1981

[11] The standard chant of the *'hezbollah'*. *Monafeq*, hypocrite, a name given to the Mojahedin because ostensibly they declare themselves to be Islamic but sow dissent among the faithful.

[12] Farah Ne'mati, accused of being a Mujahedin supporter.

Chapter 49

My first Eid Nowruz

Nayyer

I met Shohreh on the first day I arrived in Cellblock 240. I knew her from my days in the real world. She seemed so cheerful with a permanent smile that added to her amazing beauty. She came from a prominent family with a long history of opposition to both the Shah and current regime. A first-year student of mathematics, she was arrested while walking in the street. Someone may have pointed her out, or she was followed, she did not know which. When a delegation of two bearded men had come to talk to us prisoners, introducing themselves as representing *ayatollah* Montazeri,[1] they had made a special note in front of her name. When asked why she was here, she had replied that she was taken as hostage to her father, a well-known figure in the bazaar and the religious community. The next day she was taken for interrogation.

I forgot to say that some weeks ago we had been moved to a different part of the building, on the floor above the ground floor, not only with no access to the courtyard, but no view of anything but a bit of sky, our windows being painted over, and we were locked in our cells all day except for three very short toilet breaks. Although we were less crowded, this was additional punishment.

It was late afternoon when Shohreh came back limping. She grinned when she saw that rather than cooped up in our cells we were roaming the corridor, everybody looking remarkably happy. What happened, we both asked simultaneously? Lots of girls had gathered around to hear Shohreh's story.

"You go first. How come they left the cage doors open?" she asked.

They just did it, one of the girls said. A guard just opened the cell gates at around 10 and walked off without saying a word, I added. It wasn't toilet time, a voice over my shoulder said. We were all stunned, I added, we couldn't believe it wasn't a trick. After weeks of utterly miserable existence in the cramped cells and with only very limited toilet time, to be let out seemed utterly weird. We had poked our heads outside, unbelieving, but there were no guards anywhere to be seen. They had just opened the cages and let us out, as simple as that, totally arbitrary.

"They must have just got fed up with locking and unlocking the cages day and night and of all the grief us bunch of girls gave them, one of the girls added with a giggle." Shohreh had just smiled listening to us girls ranting on. And you, what happened to you we finally asked?

"Oh, nothing much" she said in her mellow voice and her large deep black eyes shone wet with laughter. It turned out she had been whipped badly and hung for a few hours by her wrist. So that was why she limped.

That night the girls decided to celebrate our new liberty. We all squeezed by the wall creating room in the middle of the cell for the dancers. Some girls were trying out regional dances. Shohreh insisted on joining them when they were doing a harvest dance from the Caspian province of Gilan. They taught her the moves and she learnt fast but she was a terrible dancer. One of the girls shouted:

"Shohreh-*khanum*. A dance is not a keep fit exercise, it needs a bit of finesse." But she persisted and danced away, well, more like she was doing her work-out. Then I noticed the stiff movements of her arms. She must have been in a lot of pain, despite her smiles. A week later she was called to court. She came back pale. What happened, we asked. She had heard two of them at court whispering to each other, this one is for execution.

That night I asked her, she was so close to me, what it felt like knowing you are condemned to die. Her reply took me by surprise.

"It isn't the execution and death that is the issue. I just would like it to be delayed, even if it is for an hour. I just love these girls and enjoy so much being with them." She could have been talking about a party.

A few days later they called out her name during lunch. She blanched, got up quickly, put on her *chador* and grabbed the headband to cover her eyes, as if she was in a hurry to leave. Some of us got up and followed her to say goodbye. She turned back at the gate and waved at us. She did not want to leave a tearful image. That night, around 8 or 9 pm, we heard the firing squad, as we did most nights. The barrage of lead stopped the beating heart of our Shohreh and there was an explosion of tears through the entire block of 600 prisoners. The girl with big black eyes and short curly hair was loved by everyone.[2]

She joined others in her family: Her sister Zohreh had been killed in a gun battle with the Shah's security forces. Two of her brothers, Hossein and Mohsen were shot and killed in two separate operations by the Islamic regime during the bloody crackdown on the political opposition in 1981.

*

This chapter was going to be about the celebrations of *Eid*. But I keep digressing into friends lost. Anyway, I really have to tell you about the boy-man on the bench. I am trying to tell my story, at least parts of it, from memory, and memory is bitty. Bits of memory interrupt the flow and insist on communicating, on being. I do envy those who have a narrative memory. Ahmad does. Don't you think? That boy-man insists on being and I must try to bring him into being.

One day my name was called over the loudspeaker and my heart sank. A feeling of terror chased up and down my entire being, but after a few minutes I managed to lock it in a box. There were several names called out that day on the loudspeaker. We put on our standard *chador* and blindfold and started walking in line. I took hold of the *chador* of the girl in front. I had an intense urge to talk, you could speak softly covering your mouth with the *chador*, but I couldn't be sure who would be listening, there were so many *tavvabs* snooping around.

Let me just digress and get the *tavvabs* off my chest before I tell you about the joy of *Eid* and the boy-man on the bench. The *tavvabs*, a religious term I detest, were really quite sad. That is, if they weren't so pernicious. So malicious. Anyway, the term means someone who has repented – performed her or his repentance, their *towbeh*. They were penitent for all the 'sins' they had committed, by which they meant the 'sin' of opposing the regime. But of course, you had to show your penitence. How would the jailors know you are penitent unless you showed it, and continued showing it? And in this parallel universe, that meant helping out with the running of prison, snooping, spying, reporting misbehaviour, getting confessions, helping out or even taking part in torture, witnessing and in some cases even actually performing executions. Not only was the *tavvab* emptied of every moral or ethical or even emotional ties with everything they loved or believed, but they had to fill the empty space not just with the hocus pocus surrounding religion, but also all the savagery of a political prison that was run on ideology. They had become a singularity, crushed and subservient.

Sometimes the *tavvabs* would do what the interrogators could not bring themselves to do. One mother told me how she was arrested by one daughter and whipped by another daughter. Such was the depth of depravity some penitents were sunk to. They were penitent for the crime of being human. Of being a person. Of thinking. *Homo sapiens,* recast as a non-human creature that rejected its own past humanity, its every memory, its very being – now an un-human. And of course, some were executed when they had used up their usefulness. How could the regime trust someone who had so betrayed all they believed in, including their humanity? Some after release returned to their human form, as if they had been under a wicked spell, but carried the ignominy and stigma for years.

Anyway, back to the narrative, we found ourselves sitting in a corridor head down for a few hours. In the room behind me I could hear the swish of a whip but no scream, no shout, not even a whimper. Who was this hero? I would so much like to befriend her or him. I tried to lift my head to look around beneath my blindfold, but a fist came down hard on my skull. Keep your head down, you! It was a woman's voice. A *tavvab*?

Someone led me into a room and ordered me to sit on a stool. I could still hear the swish, but now close to me from inside the room, when a voice told me to take off my blindfold. A bearded man with a camera was facing me but I automatically looked over at the swish. A man, a young man, maybe a boy, was strapped down on a wooden bench and a *pasdar* was straddling the bench facing backwards beating him with a whip, sweat running down his face and wetting his yellowed-white vest - he had had to take off his shirt. Was he too hot? He was panting from exhaustion. And frustration? No sound from the youth being ridden.

Look at me, the bearded man barked and I heard the camera click. I was led out, and soon was back in the cell. I had met my hero. Who he was I never found out. I so wish he survived. When I returned, a cloud of gloom was hanging over everyone. They had taken some girls out for execution.

*

And then spring came and *Eid Nowruz*[3] - a new day and a new year, my first in prison. That year the spring equinox was at two in the morning. The evening before the radio had announced the arrest of a large number of Fadai' minority leaders and supporters. We were just recovering from the two girls among us, taken for execution when that news came, but we wanted to celebrate *Eid* and celebrate the dawn of spring come what may. The girls had prepared a series of sketches and some choral pieces. Earlier that evening we laid out the *haft sin,*[4] a spread consisting of seven items whose names started with an 's', which we had to somewhat improvise along with a painted fish, cakes made from sugar and bread, we had a few dried fruits which we set down, and right on top of the cake a red star made of bread dough.

The theatre groups would move from room to room performing their sketches, some quite satirical and political. Then we sang, in groups and individually, songs that reminded us of the outside world, of the mountains, of the jungles, of the days of hope, of freedom, and of our loves and wishes. When the equinox came many sat quietly travelling inwards to their home and their family. I spotted my sister-in-law Nargess sitting alone, tears running down her cheeks. I sat beside her, and we held hands, silent, our imaginations soaring outside the cage.

Next morning, we went on our visiting tour, that's what you do in a real-life

Eid. You start your visits with the seniors in the family and then everyone else, family, friends, neighbours. That's what we did here, starting with the oldest inmates. Until lunchtime the entire cell block was a mass of moving women going from one room to the next. We then made three concentric circles in the passageway and began group singing, stamping our feet in unison with the beat of the militant song *'bar pa khiz'* – arise! Even our recluse, *Haj Khanum*, the old lady who had made her home underneath the stairway and spent her days in prayer joined in, smiling and stomping. It was the most exhilarating *Eid* I had celebrated. Ever.

Later in the year when the anniversary of my brother's execution came we had to cook up a ruse for a gathering. I hit on an idea. Since Nargess, his wife, was so often ill, why not feign sickness as an excuse to visit her? And so we did. There she was sham-ill, prostrate in her cell and they came, almost the entire cell block. Many girls brought cell-made cookies. Others, little flowers or red stars made of bread dough. Some were more lasting. I remember an embroidery with trees and a field and a girl with her hair blowing in the wind. Another, a small fish carved on a small stone. Fish is a symbol of freedom she said in such a way that the snoopers could not hear. These became my treasure until the guards raided our cell in our next home, *Qezel Hesar* and took everything away.

Then one day they called Nargess and me. We had been waiting for this. Neither of us had been through a proper interrogation yet.

[1] At the time Montazeri was the officially designated successor to the Supreme Leader, Khomeini. He was later deposed from this post, ostensibly for objecting to the massacre of political prisoners in autumn 1988. (see Chapter 68)
[2] Shohreh Modir Shanehchi was executed on January 6, 1982. She was a supporter of *Rahe Kargar*, one of the four main left wing organisations (see footnote 42, Chapter 17, Mamaqan and Appendix 3). Her father Mohammad

was a refugee in France at the time of Shohreh's arrest and execution. During the Shah's regime he had given sanctuary to a number of persons who now occupied prominent positions in the current regime.

[3] Iranian calendar starts with the spring equinox. *Eid Nowruz* is normally celebrated for 13 days. It's a real spring festival with numerous customs relating to life and rebirth such as the *haft sin* (see below).

[4] Literally 7S: seven edible things beginning with an 's' sound are displayed on a tablecloth alongside a mirror, painted eggs, a goldfish bowl and a spring flower, such as a hyacinth. *Eid Nowruz* is a pre-Islamic celebration of spring, as old as Iran's history.

Chapter 50

Second interrogation

Nayyer

Summer was coming to a close, you could tell because the light we saw through our small windows was yellowing. We had not seen a plant for a year, since our arrest. I said goodbye to my cellmates. Who knows? They might send me to another cell or even another prison. One of the girls, we had become really close after a year of sharing a cell, walked me right up to the gate. We hugged tight and long. I heard the angry voice of our guard behind me.

"It's this disgusting love of yours for one another that separates you from God. Stop slobbering over one another and turn to God." We ignored the jibe and just hugged. I doubt if she would have understood deep human emotions.

After hours of waiting blindfolded outside the gate a male guard came for us. I had to follow him by holding on to the end of his biro, there being no touching between sexes, except of course when they slapped, punched or kicked you, with Nargess behind me, holding on to my *chador*, like the procession of the blind I had seen in some etching or other.

They walked us through what was probably a corridor. Must be the present dispensary, it smelt of alcohol, or some other medical smell I thought, then more corridors. The thought of more torture just grew and grew. My heart was beating fast, and I could feel the sweat soaking my hair and on my neck under the *chador*. Finally, we were led into a room. I was separated from

Nargess and told to sit on a stool. What felt like fresh air was stroking my face, an eerie sensation after this gap of time, and not a sound of whipping or screaming to be heard. Then I recalled one of the girls telling me that torture took place in the basement of Block 240, noise-proofed by a thick iron gate. Imagining the screams rather than hearing them just made them even more terrifying. We live through our imagination.

Take off your blindfold a man's voice spoke with a strange accent and even stranger timbre, croaking like he had something stuck in his throat. In front of me stood a bearded man in a black shirt and black baggy trousers. There was something in his eyes, the way he was looking at me, that made me shudder. I pulled my chador tight over my face. Covering my fear with a black cotton shield.

"It seems you have learnt modesty," the bearded man in black said in the same croaky voice. Sneering, eyes looking straight into mine with that same repulsive look. I am a student priest, he went on gruffly, this isn't my job. Creatures like you have forced me to come over and help out. Then he pushed a piece of paper in front of me on which he had scribbled a few questions in a child-like handwriting in red. Was he a student? Which school did this creature go to?

"We know who you are. Write down all your activities." These were the exact words my first interrogator had used. Clearly went to the same class. "Have you been abroad," the weird-voiced man in black asked? No, I replied. "If you lie to me I will send you to *ta'zir*" - that is religious-speak for punishment, read torture. It always reminds me of Orwell's newspeak. I had read Orwell's 1984, obviously in Farsi, before the revolution thinking it was a perfect description of the Shah's regime. These savages who had hijacked our revolution, the revolution in which both my brother and I and so many others had devoted our lives, were better experts in sanitising words. Without another word my bearded man in black turned round and walked out through a door.

Meanwhile another interrogator grabbed the sheet of paper from one of the two boys who shared the room with me. He glanced at it briefly, too brief to have read anything, and started to kick and punch the poor lad.

"Looks like you aren't going to behave without a good thrashing are you," he shouted and dragged the boy to the door by his collar. In his excitement he had forgotten his religious-newspeak. They are taking him to the basement, I thought and shuddered. A sudden terror gripped me. I saw pain as if it was something solid. You can't run away in a prison, locked into your dread, claustrophobic dread. I felt totally alone.

For the first time I looked around. Why had I not done that before? I must have been so focused on what was going to happen to me. Maybe a year in prison had softened me up. Who knows how fear develops? It feels like it evolves somewhere inside you, creeps on you, silently, surreptitiously, then suddenly in giant waves, overwhelming you, freezing your thoughts, channelling everything into a narrow tunnel to be released in an explosive torrent that envelopes every cell in your body, an upsurge that blows away your will. Or, if you are fortunate, simply withers away. The incubating foetus in an egg growing into a terrifying monster bursting out of its shell, overwhelming you, robbing you of the ability to think, or simply just folding inwards, shrivelling, no longer threatening your being, leaving you, the person, back in control. I worked all this all out some years later, a kind of retrospective introspection plus lots of observation. Anyway, I am digressing.

The room we were in was actually a partition in an open courtyard and you could see the cloudless late summer blue sky above. And what a beautiful blue. More blue than all the blues I had ever seen, intense, transparent and shiny. Yes shiny, the blueness just shone like a gigantic lantern, lighted from an invisible energy, and so free, and that feeling of freeness was infectious. That tiny square of a visible sky, so immense at that moment, was free and its freedom calmed me, and the calmness penetrated my fears. I looked sideways at the remaining boy in our room and gave a short cough. He looked over and smiled. In a few minutes I found out that he had been arrested on his motorbike the day before and they had raided his house and taken his wife. He was worried about her. Then I heard footsteps and quickly went back to scribbling on my question-answer paper.

"I checked and you are telling the truth." The bearded man in black said in his still croaky-weird-otherworldly voice. He must have verified it with

Nargess. I felt even less scared. The fear evaporated like sweat. This interrogator of mine was an amateur and I wasn't going to be intimidated by his extra-terrestrial croak or his lascivious looks.

After a lunch of bread and white cheese, I was led back to the grilling room and this time the bearded man in black started to kick and punch me as soon as I arrived. Someone must have spoken to him. I opened my mouth to protest. I'll hit you even harder if you utter a sound. When he shouted his voice sounded even more unnatural. But somehow the croak had flown away.

That afternoon they took me to another open-air cubicle. I got the feeling I was not alone. I peeped from under the blindfold and saw that there were four girls but no guards. I pulled up my blindfold and told the girls to do the same. There is no one here, I whispered. The place was filthy. I started to clean up the place. How long have you been here? one of the girls asked, looking surprised that I was cleaning our cell. One year, I said. So, you are a veteran, another said. They were all wearing their outdoor clothes, obviously newly arrested.

"I heard they strip girls and torture them," one girl said, so pale, she looked like she was going to faint. Torture, yes, I said but I haven't heard anyone being stripped naked. She seemed relieved. She was clearly more afraid of nakedness than torture. I was arrested with my husband, she went on. It's all his fault. He's to blame. I have nothing to do with his politics she said in a voice that was bitter and verging on tears. Then she went silent. She was young, and rather pretty with big black eyes that seemed to be perpetually asking why on earth she was arrested. She looked so innocent. Angelically innocent. After a while she opened her purse, took out something. They must have brought these girls straight here and not even bothered to take their belongings. She was looking at a photo of a young man. Wistfully. Lovingly. I recognised the face. It was the boy I had talked to.

"I was with him this morning," I said. Is he OK? she asked, anxiously, pleading for reassurance, her black eyes even larger through the watery film that was quickly covering it and spilling down the side of her nose. Yes, I replied. Fine. He was fine, I repeated and touched her arm.

Later that day they came for me and took me through that iron gate of the basement and I entered hell again with its echoing sounds of pure pain. But all the rooms of that inferno were occupied. After a few hours of screams and the sound of the whip ripping the air and hitting raw flesh, someone pulled me away, roughly, and the long walk back to my old cell, blindfolded, holding one end of a biro. No explanation. Not a single word exchanged. My courage was not going to be tested a second time. Not yet.

Back home everyone wanted to kiss and hug and then questions. Later Nargess came in walking with difficulty holding the wall. Someone had whipped her, 60 lashes she had counted, without asking a single question. She had no idea why they had beaten her. And anyway, she knew nothing of any importance to them, and her husband, my brother, had already been executed a long time ago. She knew nothing had been whipped and I escaped with a few punches. Hell is mysterious.

Later that month I went to court. The *mullah*, the judge, refused to listen to anything I tried to say in my defence. I was given three years. I did not know at the time of the mathematical, or perhaps algebraic mystery, that in this parallel universe, three means nine.

Chapter 51

Flies

Nayyer

In the faraway days of freedom, in summer with its hot dry days and cool nights we would take our cotton mattresses up on the flat roof of the house, spread them on wooden beds and sleep the night under the open sky. Indoors, the watercooled air conditioning was noisy and made everything damp. But Tehran nights were cool and quite pleasant if you could ignore the hooting cars. Then dawn would come, and the sun woke up the flies and gave them a pestering energy. I would slip down beneath the sheet just leaving the tip of a nose out in the fresh air and the pesky creature would find that tiny spot among the sea of sheet and blanket. These penitent fellow-prisoners, the *tavvabs,* that buzzed around our cells were like that fly. There was no way of escaping them. No matter how many times you swatted, they just came back. They liked to torment flesh.

It became increasingly more difficult for those of us on the left, segregated in our room, to maintain friendly contact with the rooms that housed the Mojahedin.[1] The *tavvabs* followed the official line that we on the left, as non-believers, were unclean, *najess*. Anyone from the other rooms caught talking to us were warned against associating with us unclean infidels. We, however, continued to visit room four belonging to older, religious inmates.

I had not seen my friend Goli for nearly a year. She had needed an operation for the wounds on her leg and afterwards was shunted around before ending

273

up with us. We were so happy to see each other, but it was not the same cheerful Goli I had known. There was a deep gloom in her intelligent eyes. She had aged.

"I saw his body, she whispered, they took me to see his body and she could not go on with the tears lumping in her throat. It was her husband's body she was taken to see, and memories of my own brother flooded me and we cried and cried in each other's arms. Goli and I used to walk together hand in hand in the corridor and a *tavvab* would walk behind us, brazenly listening in. Pesky fly but far more pernicious. They warned us a number of times about our friendship and even reported us to the *pasdar* in charge. Some nights we would sit around and a few among us with a voice would sing, mournful songs, happy songs, revolutionary songs. Those loathsome *tavvabs* would interrupt our singing by marching *en mass* past us shouting slogans against counter-revolutionaries. Nobody forced them. They were doing it to ingratiate themselves with the guards. And they would snitch on us. Omnipresent flies with the vileness of flying snakes. Or scorpions.

Sometimes we would hit back. We were ostensibly *najess*, unclean, so water became a weapon of war. While they, the *tavvabs*, were going through their ritual washing in preparation for their five-times-a-day prayer, the *wuzu* or *dast namaz* as it is called, we would pass them by with dripping wet hands and 'inadvertently', splash unclean *najess* water over them, and they would have to go through the entire washing ritual once more. And change clothes. Then there was the 'missing link', a nickname we gave one of them with a face like a monkey, and every time we passed her one of us would say 'they have found the missing link' and giggle away. She never discovered why we laughed. Caging brings out the best and the worst in the caged.

But it wasn't only the ever-present pests that made prison life even more unpleasant than it needed to be. There were those in our own room, fellow prisoners, who drew endless lines in the sand, creating walls within walls. Since we pooled all our money and resources, we would end up in never-ending pointless arguments about what to buy from the prison shop. Such was an interminable debate about watermelons. It has no nutritional value someone argued, a frivolous bourgeois pursuit another added. We ended up not buying watermelons. Worse were the boycotting and the isolating of fellow prisoners. Many of the girls boycotted prisoners with Fadai' (Majority) or Tudeh Party backgrounds because they had supported the regime.[2] It didn't seem to occur to them that they were fellow inmates, suffering the same deprivations. It was particularly cruel, as it came from people who had once manned the same barricades.

Ostracism also spread to behaviour some saw as unacceptable. Friendships were quick to develop in that cramped environment and even an hour of closeness was enough to generate deep and lasting friendships. Empathy quickly morphed into comradery and even love and devotion. Sometimes it may have gone beyond deep friendship. Such was the rumour being spread about two young schoolgirls whose closeness was interpreted as unacceptably close. They were not only shunned by many of the girls, but the rumour was passed up to the guards and the two girls were separated into different cell blocks. Prison conditions not only bred closeness but also flamed bigotry and intolerance.

But let me not exaggerate. The overwhelming experience was to counter evil with love. Among them are my room mates Maryam and Shohreh-S.[3] I had become friends with Shohreh-S, this gentle silent girl with such a deep melancholy in her eyes. Her face reminded me of the image of the woman adorning the cover of Maxim Gorky's novel, *Mother,* her young face prematurely aged by a sadness, the source of which she took to her grave with her. It was that sadness that drew me to her. She had been arrested along with her husband and his sister. The two had fallen in love in university, both students of computing. The other girl, Maryam, had only been in our room for four days. She was in the infirmary to have the deep wounds in her legs treated when they called her name. Maryam was taken from the infirmary to her death without returning to the cell. The words of Shohreh-S, her face as she described her deep love for her husband, is yet another image engraved in my memory. He too met his death at the same hands.

Shohreh-S brought light into our lives. She would tell wonderful stories; she could be side-splittingly funny and she had a heavenly singing voice. For her birthday, the girls decided to make her a present, an embroidered painting where we all contributed, even if just one stitch. It represented an imagined landscape in Khuzestan, with a clump of palm trees, a girl riding a bicycle, her dark hair blowing in the wind. It was an image she had conjured up of her youth in one of her tales of reminiscence. Her own hair was long and beautiful even in the darkness of our cell and despite the constant battle to keep ourselves clean.

I was not present when they took our Shohreh-S and Maryam to their execution.[4] Shohreh-S had been given her sentence a year earlier and no one knew why it had been delayed. The light that she brought with her was so brutally extinguished.

I had been moved to another prison, a larger hell. The hell of *Qezel Hesar*.[5]

I need the distance of time to talk about that experience

[1] The *Mojahedin-e Khalq*, the largest opposition group to the Islamic regime were ostensibly muslims with some borrowing from Marxism and Maoism.
[2] As mentioned, in the early years, the pro-Soviet Tudeh party backed the Islamic regime for being anti-imperialist and the Fadai' split on the same issue (see chapter 46, *the split*). Most of the rest of the left, in addition to the Mujahedin, opposed the Islamic regime and were savagely repressed. In those early years Tudeh and Majority members and sympathisers were sporadically arrested and even executed, but their turn for a total crackdown came two years later in 1983.
[3] To be distinguished from Shohreh Modir Shanehchi, see chapter 49, My First Eid Nowruz
[4] Maryam Fatemi and Shohreh Shirzad, supporters of *Peikar*, were executed in early March 1982. After the revolution *Sāzmān-e peykār dar rāh-e āzādī-e ṭabaqe-ye kārgar* – Organization of Struggle for the Emancipation of the Working Class (Peikar for short) had become the second largest oppositional organisation on the left (after the Fadai' Minority).
[5] A prison in Karaj, a city west of Tehran, the largest prison in the country.

Chapter 52

Qezel Hesar

Nayyer

It was a bus ride to the nearby city of Karaj and we could take our eye-blinders off and peak through the gaps in the curtains that blocked the outside and it was early winter and there were real trees with real snow on its branches and real children returning from school and real life was going on and somewhere inside me a cry of anguish flared and a cloud of sadness constricted my heart and then without warning the river of life began to flow through me and washed away my tears, and there was calm.

We arrived at this vast new place, and were marched down a long corridor, long enough for a *pasdar* to pass us by on a bicycle, and we kept on walking in what felt like a never-ending corridor to the large square area they called the *hashti*. We were lined up and a girl, another prisoner, took our details and wrote it down in an exercise book. Then a large man came, scruffily dressed in camouflage khaki and heavy boots, gave a cursory look at the list, turned to us with impudent, savage eyes.

"So, this is the new bunch of refuse they have given us. Another lot of wretched counter-revolutionaries. We know here how to deal with scum like you. We will either squash you into a human being or send you to hell. None of you will get out of here alive without repenting. You will either repent or you have me to face. Every one of you. This here is no hotel, this is *Qezel Hesar.*" As he talked he walked along our line looking us up and down one by one, stop in front of one girl or another looking them straight in the eye and poking them on the head as he continued his intimidating monologue. He seemed to pause over ones with blue eyes or who wore glasses or were small in stature or who looked up at him defiant. There was a young flunky following him everywhere and every once in a while saying something derogatory, provocative, about one or other of us, ingratiating himself in a sickening sycophantic way. Then the outsized man abruptly turned round and walked away. We had met *Haji*.[1]

"Follow me," he ordered, and we walked more corridors and came to a curtain. When he pulled it back, we saw the bars and beyond it the cells.

"This is Block 4," *Haji* Rahmani said, "and across the way is Block 8. You all have heard of punishment Block 8," he added and smirked. We had. "That is where you end up if you misbehave," he said and walked off shuffling.

Now if you wanted to cast a figure that fitted a coarse crude cruel foul-mouthed lumpen-like loathsome figure to run your imaginary prison, someone to encapsulate the epitome of an ogre or a monster, you couldn't find anyone better than *Haji* Davood Rahmani himself to fill that role. He was a natural bully, with his swanky arrogant shuffling walk, his large corpulent figure, pot-bellied, the way whatever he wore, *pasdar* uniform or whatever, simply cried on his body, his voice, at times mocking and others threatening, sometimes theatrical at others bellowing like a trumpet, the way he talked using gutter language, and his leer, at once crude, leering and brim-full of hate. That was the man who would make our life miserable for the foreseeable future. If this description sounds melodramatic to you, reader, that is exactly how I remember this misogynist brute. But there was to be a brief respite.

We entered our cellblock, General Block Four (*Band Umumi Chahar*), through a large rectangular area that was the *zire-hasht,* leading into a long corridor with 12 cells on either side, the larger cells at the beginning and smaller ones at the end, the large ones holding three three-tiered beds. I was taken to my cell by Zohreh, a girl I had known since she was first arrested. She had that look of terror on that very first day I met her which never left her. Zohreh was to slowly walk down the steps of penitence, first by betraying her parents.

Her mother, who shared a cell with me, confided to me once that she was terrified of her daughter. Zohreh was to sink further into the quagmire of collaboration, to become one of our main tormentors. But I am jumping ahead.

After the deprivations of Evin, having space, plentiful food, a relatively well-stocked prison shop, a courtyard that was large and where we could play games with our self-made ball and ropes, and adequate showers, sinks and toilet facilities was simply wonderful. After the chronic hunger of Evin, we now had food brought in a large pot on a trolley and received by the *kargar* of the day and distributed to each cell according to the number of its inmates. The trolley was pulled down the central aisle surrounded by shouts, jokes and laughter. The girls had nicknamed it the *karevan-e shadi* (caravan of happiness). We even made tea in a large tin can using the initial hot water from the tap when it was heated up for the showers, loose leaf tea we bought at the shop and an army blanket to cover the can. It did smell of sheep and the army blanket but delicious still. This place was not as bad as they had scared us with.

The first shower brought back memories of my childhood and of public baths. The air was steamy, and the girls were scrubbing themselves frantically outside the shower cabins and took turns to go under the shower. One girl was sweeping the water into the drain with a broom while another girl we had put in charge of baths, nicknamed 'Farah the bath tender',[2] would call out time when our group's 20 minutes were up, echoed by the sweeper. Each batch of us girls had 20 minutes to wash and shower. That first morning they let us out into the open-air space, and I looked up and saw the expanse of blue sky after 18 months of semidarkness. It was like being reborn.

"We'll have flowers and vegetables there in the spring," a girl told me and pointed to a ploughed area at the back of that large courtyard, now covered with snow. I looked up again at the sky and saw pigeons and crows flying free in that cloudless sky. The air was clear. It must have rained recently. As my eyes came down they fell on the watchtower and the walls surrounding our courtyard, topped all round with barbed wire, and I returned to the real world.

"*Ya allah*," came the brusque shout and we all frantically rushed to put on our *chadors* and sat down in our cells. *Haji* had entered our block. This was the first time I had seen him since arriving here. He walked slowly from cell to cell carefully scrutinising each inmate. Then he came to our cells at the end of the corridor. I sat, scared, with my eyes lowered. They had warned me that *Haji* did not like being looked at in the eye nor did he like to be called by name – *Haji* or *Haj Aqa* was all that was permitted. Then I looked at my cellmates and some were brazenly looking up at him and I felt ashamed of my fear. He looked at each one individually pausing over those he knew personally making some menacing remark. Then he walked away. Later the loudspeaker announced that all left-wing prisoners were to present themselves in *zire-hasht*. You have one week to denounce your heathen views, or your place is in punishment Block 8. After discussion about 40 or 50 of us refused his demand and were transferred. Nargess, my sister-in-law, decided to stay, she was too ill to stand more punishment. The real world had caught up with me.

What happened next was a series of happenings melting into one another, each more difficult than the last – I had begun another voyage into an unpredictable world of torment.

*

The first thing that struck us when we walked through the gate of Block 8 were clothes. Masses of clothes. Clothes hung everywhere, every railing covered by bits of clothing hung out to dry from floor to ceiling. For a second I thought I had entered a second-hand clothes shop. Someone must have climbed up the poles like a monkey to hang them that high. The damp air hung over a narrow central corridor with cells on either side, each 1.5 by 2 metres with a single three-tiered metal bed topped by a tiny window covered by wire mesh. In between were plastic and cloth bags hanging from anywhere they could hang. They contained the belongings of each inmate. The cell walls were all but invisible in this tangle of colour. There was very little daylight and precious little space for air. This new home of ours was cramped. The girls crowded us, the new arrivals, and I met a few old friends, and we kissed and hugged.

Haji came the next day and selected a few girls who had renounced their previous views or political group to be transferred to Evin and then another line up for transfer to *Gohardasht*, a nearby prison.[3] We had heard that conditions there were far worse than the punishment block here with prisoners isolated for months on end in solitary confinement and not permitted to make a sound. Even a cough or sneeze or rustling of plastic bags was punished with severe beatings, the whip or a stay in the doghouse with room only to squat, a veritable cage. Us new arrivals were assigned to three cells that were to be locked up to be let out three times a day for food and toilet. Ours were the only locked cells. There was to be no courtyard outings. When our belongings were delivered after a few days it was clear they had ransacked them and removed all handiwork and other signs of independence.

But soon I realised that despite the cramped space, the dark, the damp, the fact that virtually all of us developed skin conditions, the absence of any real medical support, the scanty food, the severely limited access to the prison shop, and being locked up, I preferred this to our previous home – it was *tavvab* free. And anyway, things were daily worsening in Block 4. New transfers from our old home spoke of stepwise restrictions there – exercise of any kind was prohibited, all handiwork was banned taking away the only important pastime of the girls, no one was allowed to share goods or permitted to shop with someone else, hitting mostly those girls without visitors. But although we too were given the same orders, who listened? There was no *tavvab* to snoop.

Once we settled in there were new people to get to know. There was this dignified old woman in her sixties, rumoured to be related to the old *Qajar* dynasty, which ruled Iran from the late 18th Century to after the First World War, and her thirty-something daughter, a writer. Both were highly educated, and it was unclear why they were here. Both had stood their ground and were open about the fact that, although they were Muslims, they did not believe in an Islamic government. When *Haji* confronted them for their views, they said they believed in parliamentary social democracy which left our big-bellied jailor looking baffled – he kept on repeating the word under his breath, clearly the first time he had heard it. The two were respected by us girls and while they both seemed to prefer their own company, and chose to live in the corridor, they were very welcoming to questions about literature, of which they both had a deep knowledge. The daughter spoke both French and English and would help us with our foreign language learning. The mother also interpreted dreams.

Among us we had a girl who was only 14 when arrested and had served her prison term. She was given the choice of recanting her views in a recorded interview before being let out or staying here which she repeatedly refused. She was transferred to Evin and at some later date her videoed interview was broadcast in the closed-circuit TV. Some among us called her a traitor. I found that judgement absurdly harsh. She had served her sentence for a year in a punishment block with honour and wanted to go back to life and school. Prisoners could be cruel to fellow prisoners. We learned the hard way to soften our judgements.

Then *Eid* came, my second, and we went out of our way to celebrate it with our truncated version of *haft sin*,[4] our dried-flatbread-and-ground-sugar cake and even our own red fish made from bits of cloth. The two tiny children among us had never seen so much colour and joy in their short life. Soon both were one-year-old and we put up a birthday party and dressed them in tiny regional costumes cobbled together from any bits of coloured cloth, string and lace that we could find in our sacs and a few months later they were handed over to their grandparents. Both mothers agreed that this was no place for kids to grow up. We missed their cries and laughter and nonsense chatter. The mothers missed much more.

It was spring and if you sat on the third tier of the bed and pressed your forehead on the wire-mesh window you could see the spring flowers growing on the waste ground by the kitchen. If you got there early before the kitchen let out its pungent smells, you might even smell the new grass and hear the crickets and the sound of the waste water pouring out of the kitchen sewage could be a mountain spring. I let my imagination fly free.

[1] *Haji* is someone who had made the pilgrimage to Mecca. It was the name the girls in *Qezel Hesar* were told to refer to the prison governor Haji Davood Rahmani. Rahmani had a particular hatred of women who, according to numerous testimonies of survivors, he could not imagine as anything other than as sexual partners for men. In his view all the girls who entered politics were inherently predatory and there for sexual reasons.

[2] Farah Vafa'i (nicknamed *Farah Hamoomi*) was executed during the 1988 massacre of political prisoners.

[3] Prison in Rejai' Shahr an area north of Karaj

[4] See chapter 49 'My First Eid Nowruz'

Chapter 53

Haji Rahmani

Nayyer

Haji walked in. Twelve names. What for? We did not know. They didn't come back. Not for another year and a half. Had they been sent to *Gohardasht* as punishment, we wondered? No. They had been kept for months in a toilet and regularly taken out for a beating or the lash.

Haji again. The *tavvab* in charge of our block had complained. What was it this time? Apparently, we had not returned to our cells in time, we had argued the case of a girl with bladder problems who needed the toilet urgently. We were lined up against the wall in the *zire-hasht*. *Haji* started with the first person. Curses, the fist, the boot. Then my turn came. I felt his boot between my legs and suddenly I was airborne and then felt a hard blow on my head which had hit the wall and I nearly fell but managed to regain my balance. Once he had dealt with the entire row he walked out. I felt I was bleeding. How long were we to stay like this? My legs and back hurt. Every hour or so I switched feet to ease the pressure. Occasionally I would rest my forehead on the wall but would listen carefully for any footsteps to avoid another beating. We were allowed to sit down to lunch and supper and that made the following few hours more bearable, but that night was a nightmare. You had sleepiness added to fatigue. Your only wish was to lie down, even for a minute. We weren't allowed to talk but occasionally managed to whisper to our neighbours, enquiring how they were coping.

All night I heard the moans of mother Soheila. She had bad sciatica. Next morning, she could take it no more and sat down. A guard came over and savagely beat her up. An hour later she sat down again and again, kicks and punches. The third time they let her be. Later that morning we had just had a brief respite during breakfast and were using the few minutes of toilet to exchange a few words when we heard *Haji* shouting and cursing. He was roaring like an angry bear.

It was mother Soheila pleading. "What have I done," mother Soheila kept repeating and the beating and kicking continued. She was lying on the floor when *Haji* found a crate, placed it on her back and sat on it with that huge bulk of his.

"*Haj-agha* she is sick. You know she is sick." But he just ignored our pleas and sat there, smirking. Anyone who had protested, later tasted his fists and boots.

The second night was truly unbearable. I could barely keep my balance and only survived when I remembered what mother Soheila had gone through. The nightmare ended on the afternoon of our second day. This was *Haji's* normal way of punishment in *Qezel Hesar*.

Some faced punishment daily. Marzieh, a young girl who suffered from intense bladder irritation, endured her torment daily, day and night. No sooner had they locked her in the cell, and she would have another desperate urge to pass urine. No amount of pleading could persuade the guard to let her out. She would writhe with pain until the next break. One day she developed total urine retention, her belly swelled like a pregnant woman and she was in such agony they had to take her for catheterisation.

*

That summer about seventy people were brought over from Evin and the atmosphere of our cellblock changed. These girls arrived high spirited and defiant. They were not going to submit as easily to the bullies in charge of our cells. We were political prisoners and prisoners have rights, they argued. They would be brisk with the *tavvab* in charge of our block and openly confronted *Haji*. Prison rules should not trample our core beliefs. They refused to attend the forced indoctrination sessions or listen to the videoed interviews with fellow prisoners. Until they came, we would just sit through these sessions passively, pretending to listen, busy with our thoughts. They wanted our boycott to be official. They also wanted to make their refusal to pray official. While few of us on the left actually prayed, they wanted us to make this our right. I, and a few others argued that our resistance to the authorities should be comparable to that of other prison inmates in *Qezel Hesar*, in other words passive resistance, and moreover, isolated as we were from the rest of the prison, and the balance of power being what it was, to enter into open defiance would only spell major climb downs down the line.

"Would you have stood outside a police station and openly cursed the Shah," one girl argued? But we were a minority and could not convince the rest. In the long run they were proven right and standing up for your right to dissent became the norm in the prisons, but not without many more of us cracking in the interim under the mounting pressures. The suffocating atmosphere of prison and our total lack of understanding of democracy and all those artificial ideological barriers between groups made it difficult for the majority to predict the difficulties ahead. No one could possibly imagine the tortures awaiting us, from which only a few, a tiny few, would come out unscathed.

Meanwhile we needed to cope with overcrowding. Our tiny cells now had to cope with 20 or more prisoners locked in our cell for the night. This is how we did it: Five slept under the bed with only head and shoulders poking out and with no possibility of movement, the first and second level beds we gave to a few who were ill and on the top tier four or five girls slept with their legs dangling over the edge, resting them on our improvised bed extension – a rolled-up chador, one end attached to the window above the bed and the other tied to the bars. That still left three or four people who slept sitting up squeezed in the tiny area between the gate and the bed. We took turns to rotate our sleeping places. One night I got thirsty and got up to ask one of the girls who was not locked in their cell for water and when I tried to go back to sleep the three girls in their slumber had filled my space. Rather than wake them up I just stayed standing the rest of the night, one foot on the floor and the other on the railing. Our cell gate had a small opening, presumably for passing food in without needing to unlock. Someone came up with the idea that maybe the thin ones could squeeze through at night when the guard retired to her room. One very thin girl managed it. A second one tried and got struck by her buttocks. Pushing and pulling from both ends worked. Both had a good night's sleep at the end of the corridor away from the main gate to the cellblock and prying eyes. I too was thin, I tried, but my head was too big.

One day in late summer they suddenly stopped locking us in without explanation. We later found out that this was in anticipation of a visit by a senior *ayatollah*.[1] We were even allowed weekly courtyard outings. On that first outing we were so excited we made one hell of a noise playing games. The guards ordered us back to the cells prematurely. Some obeyed but others argued. Suddenly *Haji* turned up. He had a habit of picking up whatever was at hand to beat you with and this time it was a broom. The sight of that fat man chasing the girls with a broomstick round and round the yard was so comical it provided a source of laughter for a long time.

But times became less funny. We had been in *Qezel Hesar* for some weeks, and now about 40 of us were taken away, mass punishment for us non-Islamic prisoners refusing to sit through one of their interminable religious talks. It went like this: One of the girls belonging to the left, who was on duty for that day's *kargari* (work-rota) refused to put the carpet out in the corridor for inmates to listen to a videoed interview. We, on the left, had for some time boycotted such shows. But usually that day's *kargar* would put the carpet out for those who had not joined the boycott.

"That's not my job, do it yourself," she told the *tavvab* in charge. She would not budge. A couple of Mojahedin prisoners, who had not boycotted the talks, took the carpet and spread it outside. This was the first time there was discordance between the left and the Mojahedin.

That same night *Haji* stormed in with a horde of *pasdars*, dragged us out one by one, lined us up and started beating us with sticks and boots. Stop hitting, someone shouted, and the chant was taken up by all of us. The protest was answered by more beatings. They beat us until there was no strength left to protest. The corridor was littered with sticks broken on our heads, arms and back. Some of the girls were taken to *zire-hasht,* that is what we called the vestibule as you entered the main gate of the cell block and made to stand all night. They returned in the morning badly bruised and some seriously damaged. A few days later *Haji* came and took twelve girls away; to where we did not know. That evening I too was taken with others to *zire-hasht.* We were not even given time to dress properly. We just grabbed any *chador* we could over our flimsy clothes. I managed to grab two plastic slippers, one red and the other black. They lined us up in the corridor facing the wall, blindfolded, and if we as much as whispered beat us.

"Are you OK?" A stranger's voice whispered in my ear. I didn't answer, as I didn't recognise the speaker. A few seconds later I heard the voice asking the same from my neighbour and when she answered pulled her out and gave her a good thrashing. They took us out and packed us in the back of a lorry. Were they taking us to another prison? But after a short trip they stopped outside another building. We were clearly still inside the *Qezel Hesar* compound. They lined us up and a *pasdar* walked from one to the next beating with a thick stick. Any protest only prolonged the beating. One of the girls was struck for nearly half an hour. I couldn't help but admire her resistance; she remained silent under the blows. They made us stand all night and whoever faltered was beaten, like the girl somewhere down the line who I found out the next day had dared sit down.

It was dawn when they took us to a room. It would have been visiting time today. What were they telling our poor visitors? The room was filthy, tiny and windowless, with a few soiled army blankets in one corner. We set about cleaning it. There was no provision, no soap and no sanitary towels so we had to cut ribbons off our clothes. Every day *Haji* would come with a whip and punish a few of us at random. The days went by very slowly as there was nothing to do so we began learning poems that some of the girls knew by heart. I still remember bits of the poem *Ebrahim Dar Atash* (Abraham in the fire) in praise of the epic of resistance in Vietnam by Ahmad Shamlou.[2]

After a few days we were transferred into another room, equally tiny, but with a window to the small garden and a tree. Oh, what a bliss it was to see the yellowing leaves of autumn. And stars and the moon. There was a single toilet for us all and a sink with cold water. It was cold and we were in our flimsy summer clothes. We were totally cut off from the outside world, but we divided ourselves into three groups and took turns to exercise. And to walk we stood in a circle and took turns to walk around that circle. Food was the leftover from other cell blocks and we were perpetually hungry and cold. It was a constant battle to maintain our strength that cold autumn.

One day one of the girls heard a muffled noise while in the toilet and by putting her ears to the wall discovered that it was the television coming from a room nearby. The sound was so faint as to make it difficult to distinguish the words, but you could follow the headline news. That was how we heard the news of the invasion of Grenada.[3] We didn't know any details, but I sympathised with the feelings of the people of Grenada. It must have had something to do with freedom if the Americans were snuffing it out.

It was not all camaraderie, though. Among us was a girl who knew French and some of us were keen to learn. Teaching had to be done by word of mouth and declining French verbs was difficult without seeing it on paper. One of the girls had smuggled a couple of pencil buts in her chador. But sadly, the majority opposed us using it to learn French. Learning a foreign language was a 'liberal' pursuit to be shunned by hardened communists, they absurdly argued. Those of us who disagreed were boycotted. Prison life, sometimes, creates its own fragmented prisons. Here we all were, facing an uncertain future and a miserable present and yet that was apparently not enough to draw all of us closer. The ideological walls remained insurmountable.

But there was also beauty. Deep personal attachments formed. That's how I found my two children, two very young girls who attached themselves to me like their mother. They would cuddle up to me at night whispering,

"*Khalehjan*, auntie dear, can we visit your house?" One of them would whisper and I could feel the shuddering of her body against mine.

"*Khalehjan* can you make us one of your lovely cakes?" The other little girl would interject.

"*Khalehjoon* it's so delicious can you teach me how to make it? What about one of your delicate cream cakes?" And so it would go on, imagining their future, picturing the visits they would make to each other's homes, imagining tasting my cooking and eating my superb cakes. They dreamed their childish dreams. Until one day *Haji* came for us. Our real nightmare was about to begin.

I narrated what I am about to tell you to Asqar one summer afternoon in a faraway place at a faraway time. I told him as we walked side by side on the green grass edge of the walled garden, with the summer birds and insects of East Germany listening in. I told him what I am about to tell you in one go and made that man with his light brown eyes and greying moustache and hair, still handsome after all these years, cry.

[1] Ayatollah Ardebili a senior cleric.
[2] One of Iran's greatest and best-known modern poets.
[3] October 1983 US President Reagan ordered the occupation of the tiny island of Grenada.

Chapter 54

The gavdooni (cowshed)

Nayyer

Blindfold off we saw ourselves in an area that was probably below the *zir-e-hasht,* which we later came to call the *gavdooni,* the cowshed. It was just as dirty with large worms squirming in corners in the dirt. There was dirt everywhere. We set about cleaning and spread the blankets we had brought with us on the floor. It was beginning to look like home, despite the cold and the damp. It was late autumn and we still had only our summer clothes. We were always cold. They had promised to bring our clothes and we waited in the cold and nothing came. They did, however, give us some soap, toothbrushes, and cleaning material. Food ration for our *gavdooni* was meagre and we were perpetually hungry and our strength was slowly ebbing away in the cold and hunger, like a leak. They wouldn't let us wash the pots in which our food was delivered because we, as heathens, were unclean and they would not be able to use them for anyone else. To them the left was untouchable, except of course with the whip and stick, and fists and the boot. This was our additional burden to bear, added to the one of being a woman in this strange universe.

We had barely settled in the cowshed when *Haji* stormed in, picked out some of the girls, and slapped and kicked them out of the door. We heard their screams as the beating continued outside and then there was silence. The same thing happened the next day for another group of cell-mates. We didn't know where they were being herded but experience had taught us that it would be a hell worse than the one we were in. Then our turn came.

They led us to a room and we were made to sit down in a row facing forward, with *chador* and blindfolded, a metre apart. You could not see but you heard the breathing of the person on either side of you. There we spent all of that day in total silence without being allowed to move or talk. The *tavvab* Zohreh, named after that hot inhospitable planet, Venus, with its sulphuric acid rain and oppressive atmosphere, paced up and down behind us like a guard dog, whip in hand. We sat there immobile and silent all day, all night, and the next day. Slowly it dawned on me that this was to be our punishment, to sit like a statue all day, everyday, immobile and mute, unable to communicate with anyone. You could predict all the other torments, but this was something new, unimagined. Unimaginable.

Every morning at 6 we were called to sit up looking straight ahead. And if you didn't sit up immediately the whip made sure. At 10 at night, you were ordered to lie down, again failure to immediately carry out the order was a taste of the whip. We were not allowed to talk or take off our blindfold even for meals which we took, sitting, facing forward, not permitted to turn left or right, or straighten your leg; you sat immobile like a statue. Zohreh hovered over us, vigilant, an animal in human skin. All we heard was a deathly silence punctuated by swearing from Zohreh and the male *pasdars* if they caught anyone pretending to be alive. And the screams while someone was being whipped or punched and kicked.

I kept thinking how long this was to go on. Would it be days, maybe a week, or would it be without end. On the third day when the order to sleep was given, and what a relief that was to the stiffened muscles of your leg and thigh, to stretch your numbed thighs and legs, to wiggle your toes, to feel the ground, I felt the softness of a hand touch mine. I recognised her because *Haji* had beaten her that day and I heard her protesting, '*Haji* I haven't done anything'. Our cold hands spoke: I am worried, what about you? We knew what we were doing was dangerous and any second Zohreh might catch us touching. So we separated after a second or more. Just touching a friend was so calming, I slipped into a deep sleep. An hour or more later I was woken up by Zohreh's swearing. Two of the girls were pleading, we haven't done anything, but Zohreh was beating and cursing. Had they done what we had done and touched hands or was it just Zohreh ingratiating herself to the guards? Two *pasdars* ran in hearing Zohreh's swearing and she pointed out the two, who were taken out and severely battered. I lay there helpless in that darkness where night and day could only be distinguished by whether you were sitting or lying, where fear was clawing into your every organ, and time stood still, listening to the torments of the girls. The two girls were ordered to stand all night long and when *Haji* arrived the next day he ordered them to be lashed. One of the girls who was being whipped more severely pleaded to *Haji* to stop the whipping. She had something to say to him. They took her away and I don't know her fate after that.

One day *Haji* after having whipped me and some others said something strange. "You are going to have your own beds" he said and followed that with a peculiarly strange laugh, as if he was letting us into a secret. The serpent had dangled the apple and for a brief moment we fell for it. A few hours later we were ordered to get up and stood against a wall. For the next few hours we heard the sound of hammering close by. They were constructing our 'beds'. It must be some kind of torture with nails. Were we to be made to sit on a bed of nails, like the Indian fakir? What did our own demon have in store for us? The hammering stopped and an eerie silence followed. Each of us was struggling with our imagination.

I was kicked into a rectangular wooden box that was to be my bed, my sitting area, my whole existence, a collective burial in a dark silence, confined by a coffin without a roof. When I sat cross legged in our tomb our knees touched the sides, and when I lay down my feet touched the bottom. There was no back wall so that Zohreh could monitor all our movements. We had been entombed in open coffins.

Days went by in total silence as we sat immobile like a mummy, no light, no sound, a true graveyard. The silence of death. We had been assigned to be a living corpse. The seconds went by very slowly. Time stood absolutely still, like the silence that surrounded us, only to be broken by cursing and the screams of girls being slapped, punched and whipped. There we sat immobile, looking straight ahead into a black void, in total silence, our *hejab* worn at all times, day or night, and the blindfold even though there would have been nothing to see. In the middle of the night male *pasdars* would sometimes walk in, silently, having taken off their boots so they could come by stealth. Were they afraid of disturbing living death? You could hear their breathing and you felt their presence. One night one of them came and stood over me. I could not see him in my blindfolded darkness but felt his presence. I held my breath, terrified. What did he want? He stayed there for some time, immobile, and then left just as surreptitiously as he had arrived.

We were allowed the toilet three times a day and only for exactly one minute. Zohreh timed it, like some kind of sports trainer, and pushed the curtain aside with not a second to spare. I used that minute to stretch my squashed muscles that seemed not to belong to me. I had developed severe constipation and my buttocks hurt constantly with bearing my weight. Sitting. Sitting. Forever sitting. At mealtimes we put our plate behind and Zohreh would splodge in the food. Yet meals were moments of bliss in that monotonous world of the living dead. Eating slowly was such a pleasure. I yearned for tea and when Zohreh brewed some for herself the smell was mesmerising. One day I heard her say, I have some spare *chai*, who wants it. I was tempted but thought she was laying a trap. Apparently one of the girls had put up her hand and I heard Zohreh mocking her, and I felt so ashamed for her.

After the first week when I lived five minutes at a time to make time contract, I learnt to fill out time by trying to recall the past. Reconstructing memories. Scene by scene like a movie script. And live the present by trying to imagine what my loved ones were doing. I tried to be aware of time, of the days. I tried many times to compose stories, but I could not finish any of them. It was difficult to concentrate for long periods. Best to allow imagination to flitter. But how big was my store of memory and imagination. What would I do when that store dried up, when imagination flew away into the darkness. One day while eating my spoon struck the wooden partition. I heard my neighbour answer back. From then on, we communicated during meal times. I wish I knew Morse then, but we managed to create a limited vocabulary by trial and error.

Haji would come in everyday whipping his whip in the air. He would find any excuse to put one or more of us to the lash. It was his way of dehumanising us, and perversely humanising himself. What went through that misogynist monster's head? That day it was Parvin's turn. Her voice was unmistakable.

"*Haj Agha*," she was saying between swishes of the whip, "I didn't talk. Believe me I did not talk." There was no pleading in her voice, none at all! She was emphasising her points, as if teaching him to become human. From what I knew of her she would not lie. She never lied even to her enemies. She would remain silent. But she never lied. She had not spoken with her neighbour, that I was certain from her words. That protest was against the unfairness of her punishment on top of the unfairness of everything else. Parvin was not cowed, just indignant. And angry.

One day we heard the sound of men talking. It was Lajavardi, the man Khomeini had put in charge of the country's prisons. What they were doing to us was not an individual decision by *Haji*. We were not alone. It was not the whim of one local monster. It was national policy. I shivered.

Fifteen days later I was taken to Evin to face further interrogation. The nightmare of my living coffin was over before my sources of life had been drained out. But not for the other girls. Day after day, week after week, month after month. Ten months. A lifetime for time to stop. How can I convey the experience of perpetual darkness in the light of day? Not just blackdark but silentdark. A world without sound, without light and without movement, without humanity. A world that was still and dark. It was a death which hovered over you because you were not dead, your nerves desperately trying to fly, to move, to dream, to live outside you, outside this darkness, outside these coffins. To flee this death. And then, more darkness and silence and everything still, but for your heart that went on beating and beating and beating, and you didn't know when it too would cease beating. After the second month, one by one the girls cracked and agreed to be interviewed on television, where weeping uncontrollably, they admitted to crimes, to lust, to being worthless, begging for forgiveness. These interviews were broadcast on the prison closed circuit television for those still in their coffins in the cowshed. Sometimes *Haji* would bring the actual wrecked girl to tell her cellmates in person of her repentance. Those broken souls were also emptied of whatever information they had so preciously guarded in the initial interrogation sessions. Some would denounce brothers, mothers, cousins, friends, fellow prisoners. They were emptied of everything that made them human. *Haji* was making them in his own image, but without his power. The nightmare lasted 10 months for some but did not end when they were transferred to block 3 in *Qezel Hesar*. That was where all those penitents were housed, and where the spying, and the reporting continued. *Haji* had forbidden them to talk to anyone in the prison-block, even to people sharing their cell.

They were not to tell of their experience. They were silenced inside and outside. They were to be ghosts that walked and talked but did not exist as a person, just a shell.

Chapter 55

The caretaker

Ahmad

The arrest of such a close friend as Mehrdad, the ex-army officer, hurt him deep. The fact that he had predicted it, the fact that Ahmad had warned him, the fact that Mehrdad knew the danger even without having to be told and yet was still happy to take the risk did nothing to lessen the pain. Ahmad had lived while so many close friends were dead. Zia was dead, Abbas (*amu palang*) and Aziz were dead, Bijan, who he had only really got to know the few weeks they shared the large cell in *Qezel Qal'eh* was dead, Sai'd the poet-playwright was dead. He felt the guilt of living. But Mehrdad was a particularly close friend. Their friendship went back half a lifetime, from the infernal cells of *Komiteh Moshtarek,* and now he too was arrested and would almost certainly be shot. And here he was still practising as an architect. And although he was no longer a Fadai', he saw himself as nothing other than a revolutionary.

As a species we live with one foot in this world and one in an imagined magical non-world. And the two worlds coexist in the same brain. Maybe magical thinking was necessary for our survival. Isn't that how gods, and devils, fairies and *jinns*, and Mount Olympus and hell and heaven and all the other entangled magical stories became deeply embedded in all our cultures? At one end some of us have belief in the soul, the afterlife and unbaptized babies living in limbo in perpetuity, and at the other, some can ignore the reality of an earth burning up in front of their eyes even as it threatens their very own existence or that of their offspring. Some can simultaneously believe in the immaculate conception, ghosts, the curse of number 13, or the prophet Mohammad's ascent (me'raj) into heaven[1] and simultaneously work as an architect, chemist or develop a vaccine. Facts and observed realities dissolve in a sea of wishful thinking, if not outright denial. Is it not magical thinking that allows some to appear as superhuman saviours in the eyes of others? How else are we to explain the concept of a Hitler or a Mahdi or one or other populist leader. And when some of us discarded these unreal worlds and unlikely idols, did we not replace them by other utopian hopes and dreams? Wasn't the idea that the physical sacrifice of a handful of men and women was enough to blow down the walls of the Shah's militarised citadel equally magical thinking? And wasn't it magical thinking that kept Mehrdad in his ultimately doomed stance. As a species we are poor at predicting the future and compensate by using our imagination to fill in the potholes of knowledge to create a narrative that may or may not have any relation with reality as it unfolds. It becomes a matter of chance - the future as a hit-and-miss affair.

But Ahmad lived in the real world, he thought, and it is best to be prudent. He understood that you can see what is there if only you looked. That same day of Mehrdad's arrest Ahmad and Jina vacated their flat on the top floor of the apartment block in the Vanak suburb of the capital, leaving everything behind and moved into a rented house next door to an old lady who had been like a second mother to him in the past. But Nina continued to attend the same school. One morning, soon after moving to their new house, Nina was walking aimlessly in the school courtyard during the break. Those days she often preferred to keep herself to herself. Like all children she understood things better than grown-ups gave credit. She was aware of the dangers and that her parents were different from her classmates. Her expressive large shiny dark brown eyes had been witness to her father's pain and wizened face.

That morning in the schoolyard she spotted a girl who lived in their old apartment block, the one in Vanak they had just vacated, talking to a group of other girls, her pigtails bobbing in excitement as if she was describing some adventure. Nina moved closer to catch the thrill.

"They came in the middle of the night and woke us all up," the girl with the pigtails was saying breathlessly. "They knocked on our door and threw us out of our flat right in the middle of the night. They did. They threw out everyone, everyone in the building, every single one, from all the flats. Some of them, the men, were still in their pyjamas. It was just so funny." She had a strangely grown-up voice for a ten-year old.

"What did the invaders look like," one of the girls interjected?

"Men with Kalashnikovs of course, who do you think I was talking about?" the girl in pigtails said, as if that happened every day to her. "*Pasdars* in full military uniform with machine guns." And she flipped her head back as if to say what a stupid question and her pigtails flew in unison and touched in mid-air as if clapping. Then she saw Nina and abruptly stopped and gave her a sheepish look. One of the other girls looked over, hostile. Nina walked away. She had never got on with that stupid neighbour anyway. Vindictive thing. Jealous. Jealous of my nice clothes. And of baba and mum. Everyone knows my baba. And mum too. Anyway, this raid couldn't have anything to do with them. They weren't living there, were they?

Who knows why she told the story to her mother? Life is made up of good and bad chance events. They were in the kitchen and Jina was making her favourite omelette for Nina.

"You know that stupid girl, the one who lived on the second floor," Nina said out of the blue, "the one who giggles all the time, well, she was saying they, I mean the *pasdars*, searched everything in our old house, top to bottom, and when she saw me coming, she just stopped. She gave me such a funny look mum, as if I had done something bad. She just walked off holding hands with another girl without another word to me. So mean. I never really liked her."

She was there to hear the news and she was there to convey the news. Two life-changing chance events. Life, revolving round chance and choice.

"It was Lajevardi himself leading the posse," Houshang, the childhood friend who had brought back the news about Mehrdad's arrest, said on his return from the fact-finding mission to the Vanak apartment block. Houshang knew some people in the block of flats and had gone over to investigate what had transpired without raising suspicion. "The chief butcher was there in person. He went over with a huge force. You must be quite a prize," he said with a wink to Ahmad and Jina. "They searched both the upstairs duplex and the ground floor office and took everything away, documents, books, papers, everything. Everything," he emphasised unnecessarily.

"Bisharafha,"[2] Ahmad said knowing that they had ransacked his life's work. Whatever happened to the downstairs couple? Were they also arrested?" He was now really anxious.

"No. No. You just have to listen to this," Houshang said, animated. "It's a great story," he said and stopped abruptly. "Give me a nice hot cup of tea as a mojdeh, a reward, and I'll tell you." They did. "Remember the caretaker, the man you asked to be caretaker," Houshang said and put a large sugar lump in his mouth, moved it to his right cheek with his tongue and took a sip of tea. You could see the lump poking outward from his clean-shaven cheek. He was a thin man.

"Yes. You mean Agha Reza?" Ahmad interrupted, not really reassured by Houshang's calmness. "Did they take him away with them too? But why would they do that? He works with the local Komiteh.[3] Aqa Reza was one of the boys who worked on the construction of this block. I asked him to stay on and take care of the building. He was such a reliable guy. And his brother too, they were both good honest people. I gave him a small flat to stay with his wife and children. They wouldn't take him away for being a caretaker. Both him and his brother had joined his local Komiteh. That brother of his had also worked on the site when we were building. He is a pasdar in Lurestan now. Why arrest Aqa Reza, an insider?"

"No, no, he's fine," Houshang said, having patiently waited for Ahmad to tell him what he already knew. He was used to Ahmad's ways. He took another sip of tea. The lump on his right cheek was distinctly smaller. "Just listen to this. Last night Lajevardi pulls this guy aside and says: 'do you know who I am?' 'Of course, haj-agha, who doesn't know you?' 'Does the guy who lives here on the top floor flat have any visitors?' 'No haj-agha, he never had any visitors to my knowledge. *Agha mohandess*[4] had no visitors.' 'Do you know where he is at this time of night?' 'No *haj-aqa*, I have no idea, absolutely no idea.' 'Do you know where any of his relatives live?' 'No *haj-agha*, I don't.'"

"He lied," Ahmad smiled. He knows my father's address. He knows it perfectly well. He once bought a sheep from Lorestan as a present." As Houshang was telling the story a sly smile had gradually spread over Ahmad's face and his eyes began to shine. Jina, who had sat rigid on the edge of the dark green sofa, also moved back and leant on the backrest. This story was going to have a happy ending.

"Anyway, listen to his *artist bazi,* his playacting, your caretaker's amazing presence of mind." Houshang spoke fast with shining eyes. Reminded Ahmad of when as children they recounted to each other a film one of them had seen recently. Scene by scene. Storytelling as cinema. Like the cutting room. "This morning Agha Reza was watering the flowers on the front porch when he saw the husband-and-wife architects get out of their Peikan on their way to work in the office," Houshang went on with his story. Each sentence was imperceptibly faster than the one previously uttered. "Your caretaker looked up, saw them, and just turned the hose towards them, pretending to wash the pavement, stopped them in their tracks, went up and muttered under his breath. 'Four men are in my flat, four in the flat upstairs, four in your office. Tell the *mohandess* not to show his face here again'. Then raising his voice, he spoke so that everyone could hear: 'These tyres of yours, they are just totally gone. They're useless. Haven't you noticed? They're gone. They're totally flat. They're no good.' Your two architect friends just stood there looking at our caretaker, not really taking in what's going on. Your caretaker walked over to the back of the parking lot, walked back with two tyres. One in each hand. 'Open the boot', he said aloud, and dumped the tyres in the boot. 'Off you go and get them changed,' he said with a smile, having shook the hand of the husband." Houshang ended his story, gave one of his deep bass laughs and noisily drank down the end of his tea. This last sip would be bitter. The lump of sugar had long melted. But it would sweeten up in the stomach, too late for the taste buds though.

Ahmad just shook his face in amazement. Lajevardi had stolen his life's

301

work. All the work he had done in the shantytowns, the expanding slums that encircled the cities, all his research on the small towns and villages across the length and breadth of Iran, a life's work of scholarly research. All gone. Removed to oblivion. Would they have any use for it? Would they understand it? They were only detailed notes. Not yet organised into a coherent narrative. All this flashed through his mind in a split second, as thoughts do. He shrugged, as if to say to himself that it did not matter. But it did. It was a much bigger blow than taking his money or flesh. It was his legacy.

The architect couple lived not far from the office in Vanak. Ahmad drove straight to their house in a white Peikan. He rang their door. The wife answered and blanched the colour of the Peikan.

"Come in and just leave your car." She was worried the car had been followed. The house was large. One of the older houses in Vanak. They told him the story as they took him to the back courtyard, which had a door to another alleyway.

"That *sarayedar* (concierge) is a jewel. He saved our lives," and they re-counted the tale from their perspective. Such quick thinking. So resourceful. And yet he was one of them, the wife said, one of them she repeated as if she was talking of another race. Houshang drove round the back with his car and took Ahmad away through the back door.

"Go and don't even think of looking back," the wife said with tears in her eyes. "Don't fret about us," she added, "we'll be alright. We will." She didn't seem sure. When it became clear over the next few days that no one seemed interested in the Peikan, Hooshang came back and drove it away, and sold it. The two architects never went back to that office.

Over the next few days *pasdars* raided Ahmad's sister's house, who had prudently gone to stay with another relative. Their parents had already returned to Yazd, and Ahmad stayed with a distant relative, an ex-Tudeh member, who was involved in theatre in days long gone. It was time to plan an exit out of the country. But first he had to make a trip to Yazd to say farewell to his parents and get a replacement birth certificate.

He needed that to have a passport under an assumed name.

[1] Me'raj (or mi'raj) is when Mohammad is said to have ascended to heaven from the Temple Mount one night in 621 CE.

[2] Literally: people without honour, here meaning shameless or base.

[3] Neighbourhood Revolutionary *Komitehs*. See footnote 86, Chapter 31, The Homecoming

[4] Literally engineer. A polite way of calling anyone in any kind of higher education.

Chapter 56

Choices

Nayyer

I am entering a period I would rather skim over. But that would mean being untrue to truth. I toyed with the idea of writing it in the third person, but that too would be skirting around truth. I would like to live through the experience with you, just as I remember experiencing it.

I'm back in Evin and a merciless sword of death is hanging over me. That's what they told me. Despite having already received a prison sentence, the prosecutor has demanded a death sentence for me, unless, of course, I change my stance and stop my obstinate belligerence and agree to confess on camera. I'm in a turmoil of indecision. All alone with my thoughts and fears I'm torn between emotions and between the different paths I should take. Should I just give up and surrender, as so many around me have done? Or should I go on defying them and take the consequences? Whichever I choose, I know the road is going to be littered with agony and pain. Give in and I would fall into that bottomless pit of misery and self-loathing. I would be extinguished as a person, like a lamp without light, just as I had witnessed all around me. And if I resist, I will need to prepare myself for a life of pain without end. Am I ready for that? Am I really strong enough? Anyway, who can predict the outcome of a battle that has no end in sight under such an imbalance of forces? Given its random ups and downs, would my life in this cage still not end up in total surrender at some future date, a miserable, wretched subjugation? Or would I still be standing on my feet despite it all? How can I possibly, honestly, predict the 'me' in that future time? These are thoughts that I just can't push away. I battle within myself, fight and fight and the doubts just pile up. I need to trust myself, but can I? I have witnessed those rare trees that did not bend against the storm. I have already told you about some of them. There were many others that bent and swayed this way and that, but still remained rooted. But what about my tree? How strong are my roots? Agonising doubts bubble up. This is a battle that I have to face, alone. To look deep into myself, looking for strengths and weaknesses. And I will make mistakes, but I must, must retain my light.

I have been in prison for two years now and survived interrogation, the cowshed and the coffin. Now a new challenge is thrown my way for which I am ill prepared: they call me to a debate. I am brought face to face with one of the leaders of Peykar,[1] one of the largest organisations of the left. This once figure of strength and militancy had capitulated and is now being paraded in front of cameras like a prize bull to debate handpicked inmates and use his reputation to break them intellectually. I'm in a largish room with grey walls. They sit me down by a table. It all looks so calm and professional. A video camera is looking at me and through me. Today's debate is conducted under the auspices of a young interrogator. What am I doing here? What is their plan for me? I don't want to get sucked into philosophical arguments that are way out of my depth. I must somehow avoid this alien territory. Best to lead him onto the realm of social justice, I'm thinking. Wasn't that why I entered the struggle in the first place? I hear myself asking:

"Do you think this regime is capable of giving social justice?"

"This is forbidden territory," the young interrogator interjects. "You just added another nail to your coffin." He is sneering. I hate that flaunting of power. It makes you feel so helpless. You aren't even allowed to choose the subject that may determine your fate. The discussion thereafter goes over my head.

We're back in the confined space of my cell. It is my world. Curiously, I feel safer in this space. No one is trying to crush me, to catch me out. I think I have accepted my fate, and my probable death, but I'm terrified of dwelling on it. I push it back to where you lock-up fear. I walk up and down, seven steps one way, wall, seven steps back, wall, avoiding stepping on my two cellmates, one a *tavvab* and the other a mother of a young child outside. Past events in my life keep roaming round and round my head, randomly focusing one minute on some bad memory or other and then, suddenly, I'm overwhelmed by images of that deep love I had discovered before walls and cages separated us. It is like switching reels. Seeing him, his gentle forever-smiling light-coloured eyes in that orchard again where we declared our love for one another. I am looking at the row of poplar trees with their white trunks reaching up to the sky. Like hope. An intense longing squeezes me. A longing to touch him, to walk beside him, to hear his voice. Tears I cannot control are rolling down my cheeks, wordlessly. I am crying inside and out in silence. How can I explain it, all those memories, like an expanding balloon, all that emotion, whirling, seeking desperately my inner strength, looking for that courage that is rooted in love? Then all of a sudden, the balloon bursts, leaving a void. I feel empty again. And afraid.

Days go by. Debates. I cannot recall how each one went. It's all a blur. Am I navigating that labyrinth well? What do the words they are dragging out of me mean? They are digging at my most vulnerable spot. How am I doing? I don't really know. I have no means of measuring success or failure. Then back in my concrete castle. The pressure mounts. Gradually, over the days and weeks, those images that normally make up memory, images that were once happy, beautiful, ones where life shone in pleasant flashes of imagery, that memory-telescope to the past which normally singles out the happy moments has swivelled away. Now when I look back, the images that appear are all dark. Joyful ones have almost all been blacked out. Only scenes of sorrow, scenes of pain, of failure remain as my constant companion now. Isn't that switching from happy to sad memories not typical of depression, or times of stress? That's what a medical student friend of mine once told me. In times of stress, of depression, that memory-telescope switches and the past, instead of lighting and brightening the present spreads shadows of doom, she had said. She was right, my friend. How right.

I decide I just can't face the debates anymore. A strange foreboding is overtaking me. Where are these ideological debates leading? What do they want from me? What trap are they laying? I am too tired and too weak to fight back. They are exhausting me. I can't go on being on my toes all the time, constantly alert to their traps. I must get out of these debates somehow. I tell my interrogator that I am unable to participate any more. To my astonishment he doesn't insist.

It is night time and they call me for questioning. They are calling for me most nights now. I am led to the main corridor of 209.[2] On one side you can see the interrogation rooms. On the other side a number of gates with metal bars that lead into corridors with cells on both sides. I can see all of that from under my loosely worn blindfold. At nights prisoners are hung from these bars by their arms. When those hanging prisoners hear us coming through the sound of our plastic slippers that we deliberately drag on the floor, they would cough or change feet, making human contact. Every time I pass these hanging men, most were men, a guard is always with me, and I don't dare look up and see their faces. But I feel their presence. I know that others were also hanging in the basement, some tied up so high their feet could not touch ground.

Back in my cell I jerk up repeatedly from sleep and remember that within a few metres of me, my fellow chained are leaning on one foot or other aching for a moment's sleep. I feel their pain. The same pain I have experienced with the ghapan (steelyard), a pain that twists through you and overwhelms your entire being, and that eternally stretching time. Time without end as if it too wants to savour your torment.

Tonight I am waiting for a long time in the corridor, and I suddenly feel an intense cold. I had never felt so cold in my life. It is as if the winter cold has touched hands with the freezing pain of those suspended in that corridor. My bones are aflame with freezing. I am shivering from the cold in my summer clothes and the presence of all those bodies hanging from metal bars. They sense my cold and cough and cough in sympathy, and I drag and drag my slippers in response. It is a dialogue of freezing pains. The interrogator comes over.

"Why are you shivering?"

"I'm cold."

"Don't you have clothes?"

"No. Most of my things are left behind in *Qezel Hesar*."

"Why don't your family bring any?"

"How would they know where I am?"

"You can have visitors from now on," he said. A sudden joy comes over me. I had lost hope of ever seeing them again. I forget the cold.

"But they don't know where I am."

"You can phone and tell them." It is as simple as that. A power that is as absolute as it is arbitrary. Or maybe just the chaos of hell.

He allows me to phone. I do. I dial my sister. It is the middle of the night in the real world, and I have woken her. On the other end is a voice that has the softness of a caress. It is magical and I am floating with emotion. All I can do is cry and between sobs and asking about the family, manage to tell her about the visit. Oh I do wish time would stop and let me savour the caresses of her voice. You stopped when I was sinking in pain. Why not now. Why not! Hurry up and finish your phone, the guard keeps saying with increasing exasperation and I continue talking to the world beyond the cage. It was heaven talking. Time is so cruel.

Finally, the day has come. Today is visiting day. Visits for someone who shares a seven-step-cell with two others has two rewards. I will once again see my loved ones, and on the way there, I might get a chance to exchange a few words or a furtive hand-squeeze with fellow prisoners in other cells.

My sister looks as anxious as the day they took me away. She looks even more anxious when I tell her I am about to go to court again. I am separated from the world by a double wall of glass that blocks all human sound, and we talk through a phone that crackles with eavesdropping. But the double-glass seal is totally powerless in stopping the communication of two hearts that beat to the same tune. I hear myself asking the same questions, how is this aunt or that uncle or that niece and nephew, and in between reassuring her, while all the time our eyes and our whole body speak a different language, conveying a stream of emotion and understanding, but also our unknown stories across that glass seal. Our language is one of love that goes beyond kinship into an emotional unity which is nourished by viewing the world through the same lens. I say nothing of my terrors and my doubts, and her eyes talk back by seeing into me and my doubts and understanding and her eyes reassure me and give me hope and strength, while all the time our lips are talking about the mundane. And suddenly the ten minutes are over, and the crackling phone is silent. I leave the visitors room strangely fortified by her eyes.

I see Fereshteh in the visitors' cubicle next to me. I haven't talked about her before. We had been together in the cowshed where she had shown great courage. We had been very close. Our parents had also become friends outside the walls. After the phone link ends, I have a few moments and a chance to ask about mutual friends.

"How did they bring you here?" I ask quickly. How are the girls?

Her silence baffles me. She had been the most audacious among us. She averts her eyes. Then I see the tell-tale ultra-concealing *maqna'eh* head covering under her *chador* and a small rosary that she holds in a reverential way, not the way many of the girls do when they use it as a plaything. I look through the glass and see her mother tearfully trying through gestures to ask me if her daughter had changed.

Her daughter has changed. Here is the girl who had stood firm under torture, who always addressed the interrogators brazenly, a girl who had called her husband, who had capitulated early under torture, a traitor. That girl had agreed to all of *haji's* demands. Even to co-operation.

"I don't know," Fereshteh says bruskly after I ask several times. She lies. The cowshed had tamed the wild beast.

[1] *Sāzmān-e peykār dar rāh-e āzādī-e ṭabaqe-ye kārgar* – Organization of Struggle for the Emancipation of the Working Class (Peykar for short) was

a Marxist offshoot of the Mojahedin Khalq. See chapter 24 when Taghi Shahram, one of its leaders, meets Hamid Ashraf for discussion after their split. Shahram was executed in July 1980.

[2] Evin's different sections were known by everyone by the internal telephone number. 209 was the main interrogation block.

Chapter 57

Apathy

Nayyer

After much self-struggle I have decided to pray. It is happening insidiously. An intense feeling of apathy is slowly overtaking me. A feeling of hopelessness. Cooped up in that small cell, waiting for the next interrogation on which my life hangs. New prisoners come and go, young women, some lost and bewildered not knowing what to expect, others, veterans of prison, totally broken, pathetic, praising their captors for saving them from themselves, like the two young women who just arrived. They tell me about the workhouse, the *kargah*, where they worked twelve hours a day without pay, working away their sins, where everyone spied on everyone. That was the first I heard of the workhouse. The two are taken away after a couple of days. Maybe they were put in our cell just to break us. I begin to dread being sent to the workhouse, to feel lost in clouds of doubt. I am slipping bit by bit, one small step at a time.

That first step is when the *tavvab* in charge of our cell block orders my cellmate and me to get ready to go to the overnight *komeil* prayer.[1] I do. In the past I had point blank refused, but now a real fear of the future and of myself weighs heavy on me. It's just a pretext to get some fresh air, I rationalise. But what next? Where and when do I apply the brakes? I should save my energies for larger battles, I tell myself. But was this just an excuse? I hadn't seen the sky for several years or felt the wind on my face. Going to that prayer session means having a long walk over the hill, with the Evin valley below us.

Is the reward worth the price of submitting to a night of tears, wailing and mumbo-jumbo? Listening to weepy prayers begging forgiveness from God. I am no stranger to this atmosphere of repentance. Lajevardi and the prison authorities have repeatedly drummed into us how the entire society outside is against us. How we have sinned.

Alone and vulnerable, I am open to such insinuations. And the more friends fall into that cesspool, the more exposed and lonelier I feel. News after news narrows the space that was me. Someone I knew from *Qezel Hesar*, we had been in the cowshed together, is brought into our cell. I ask after the two young girls who used to cuddle me at night as they would their mother. All night long in the intense cold of the cowshed I used to feel the shaking and shivering of their bodies as they pressed themselves either side of me. We had lost touch when they put me in the coffins.

"*Haji* had saved them," the girl says. Her words whip me like lash. I feel even lonelier. I had loved those girls.

Now I pray. I can only call that surrender. I had done the same in Cellblock 4 in *Qezel Hesar* but prayer was compulsory there. There is no direct compulsion here, only a choice between life and death. I have been told that if I stood by my beliefs, I would probably face death. But my dossier is such that by adopting a less belligerent posture my death sentence could possibly be commuted to a long prison sentence. Right or wrong, I choose to live. Yet these days, I hate life. Every time I bend in prayer, I feel wretched. Once my praying was reported to the interrogator, they left me in peace. For a time.

I see old friends, some shattered, others not, and what they have become pulls me this way and that. One old school friend I met on the way to the visitors' hall, now thin with lines on her face, her old jolly self lost somewhere on the way to here, is now in possession of new truths. She's a stranger to me. Later I see her helping out with interrogations. Another friend from *Qezel Hesar* has not capitulated but tells me that the girls back there had agreed to minor, pretend, retreats. Seeing her pale thin face, a reminder of the coffins, yet still with spirit intact gives me some hope. Above all there is

Nasrin,[2] a friend from outside, bravely standing up for her views in front of a crowd of watching prisoners. Her courage gives me heart. They had added religio-political conversion through debates, to the whip and other physical torments to crack us. They don't just want my information. They want my very essence. The me in me. Would I be a Nasrin or join the hundreds of innerless, faceless wrecks?

Now my interrogation starts in earnest. They want information that is years' old. They accuse me of things that I know nothing about. They pretend they had arrested my sister and her testimony contradicted mine. I deny everything but her arrest hurts deeply. After my brother was killed, she is the closest thing to me. It turns out to be a lie. I understand that much of my dossier is related to my behaviour in prison. There it is, noted down in elaborate detail. I become ill both physically and mentally. I withdraw into myself.

My current cellmate, a really caring girl called Nahid, is at a loss as to what to do. She is young and has only recently been arrested. She was about to be married to her fiancé. It was a love match that her parents had initially opposed, but finally acquiesced. Then he was soon arrested and spent two and a half years in prison. It's his turn to wait for you, I had said to her jokingly. While in the confined world of a cell, good and bad feelings are usually shared, I choose to travel my pain alone and Nahid, helpless in how to help, leaves me to myself. Self-hate and a hatred of a life without any hope are strangling me. I detest life but fear death. I want to die, but somehow in a natural way. I don't have the courage to commit suicide. Am I making sense? I have hardly eaten without going on a hunger strike. But, over time, I have collected and carefully hid away some sleeping pills. I didn't have any special plans for them. I just horded them. I don't recall consciously planning anything. Last Friday Nahid went to the *komeil* prayer. I felt too weak to follow her. While she was waiting by the door to be let out, her medicine bottle was in a corner, winking at me. A thought suddenly occurred to me, as if someone was talking in my head. How easy it is to cut my wrist with that glass! But when they opened the gate to let her out, she bent down and took the bottle and left it outside the door. She told me later she had guessed my intention.

That night I took all my pills. I didn't have enough to kill me, only enough to pull me into a deep sleep. I slept for 12 hours, then vomited followed by another deep sleep. I woke up retching. My stomach hurt like it was about to explode. Nahid kept banging on the door, but no one came to let me out. I fainted and then woke up vomiting. Nahid kept knocking hard on the cell door until, finally it was opened, with Nahid's help I put on the *chador* and blindfold and clawed my way to the infirmary. I passed out again and woke up with an infusion in my arm.

On my way back from the infirmary I saw two *pasdars* dragging a man past the metal bar gate that led to the basement of hell. His feet were bloody and dragging on the concrete floor. For a second I saw his face. He looked like the dead. His eyes were half open on an ashen face. Maybe I was looking at death itself. But that vision did not faze me. Death had already shown me his face.

Then a woman is brought into our world. She smiles. Her beauty is stunning. With her is a small child. She wants to play. She wants us to be a donkey or a lion. She needs toys. She needs smiling company. That little girl gives me a new life.

I had to relearn to love the beautiful and that child directed me back to love. And to life.

[1] An all-night lamentation usually performed on Thursday evenings
[2] Nasrin Baqai', was executed with her husband Hossein Ghazi in the spring of 1984. Both were members of the Central Committee of Rahe Kargar.

Chapter 58

Safety pin

Nayyer

"Your belief is your own responsibility," I said with a voice trembling with anger as she led me out of the interrogation room. "But don't play around with the life of your old friends and other prisoners. Protect your honour!" It was a sudden burst of anger at seeing an old friend turned inquisitor.

I was in yet another interrogation, one in a chain of interrogations whose absurdity and utter futility wore me down. A hand put an album in front of me, belonging to 3 years ago. "Identify anyone you know," the female voice spoke from behind me. Something told me I know her. It was her tone of voice. I skimmed over the first album. She walked in front of me to hand me another. I saw a girl I knew well and had greatly admired in *Qezel Hesar*. She had spent months in the punishment block at *Gohardasht* prison too. She was a model of resistance. Now she was working for the interrogators. It hit me like a blow to the back of the head: she was probably one of those who had helped populate my dossier with reports of my past obstreperous behaviour.

I could not get her out of my head. Later I found out that although she had agreed to work with them, she did not behave as a *tavvab*. Then one day, during one of the sessions, I brought up the shortage of dried milk for our little child.

"That is none of your business," my interrogator said and walked out for a few minutes. I bent down and picked up a safety pin on the floor. I had had my eyes on it since entering.

"We will be sending you to the open cell block tomorrow," he said on his return.

"Thanks," I said. The word had slipped out without me.

"Don't you dare say anything there about your experience in *Qezel Hesar*," he said. "Don't forget we follow your every move." Then, as I was about to pass by him, he stretched his hands out. Give me the safety pin, he said and there was a note of victory in his voice. And utter contempt. Something in me collapsed. A feeling of wretched helplessness gripped my inside. I had never felt so alone. I tried to conceal my agitation as I unfastened the pin and put it in his outstretched hand. I could not suppress the tremors in mine.

"This worthless piece of metal is only of value in a prison where humans are denied even a minimum. Like this puny thing I can use to hang up a child's nappy to dry," I said in a voice that was alien to me, groping to regain my dignity.

"You could have bought it from the prison shop." That sickly sneer again.

"If we could, we would have done it already," I said, gaining my own voice and trying to push down my inner anger, anger at myself for laying myself open to humiliation.

"Then having it in a cell must be illegal." He was savouring his victory.

"Not really. We were allowed them even in *Qezel Hesar*." Even in that rat-hole, I wanted to say. I swallowed. He let me pass.

When I got back into the cell, I wanted to tear something up. I was trembling uncontrollably. I had allowed him to get the better of me. The humiliation of being caught out, like a petty thief, stayed with me for months. That is how fragile you become. Little things tear you up. But I had survived the ordeal. I had bent here and there against the hurricane, but I had kept my roots. They had been dug deep by my brother.

We celebrated my last night before I left the interrogation block. That night all my emotions took on a bright colour. The family had sent in some clothes, among them was a beautiful white shirt that I later found was sent by my love. I wore it on top of a pink pyjama top my sister had sent, saying bright colours will remind you of nature. That night the cell was swirling in delirious emotion. We put a few pieces of bread on a plate. Dissolved a few days' sugar ration in red plastic cups and warm water. Twirling. Dancing. Kissing. Apologising repeatedly for I don't know what. Kissing again. I told them I loved them. Hugging, kissing first this then the other again. I felt drunk. I wanted to dance all night. The little girl slept.

Chapter 59

Walls within walls

Nayyer

My new world was one where the walls were invisible. Groups lived separate lives in the same room. By the right wall the *tavvabs* sat, by the left wall the left, and facing me by the back wall, the Mojahedin. Where do I sit? Where do I fit? I chose the left wall, sitting somewhere between the Mojahedin and the left. Soon I moved closer and joined the left. But there too I saw invisible walls. Soon after the revolution the left had split into those that supported the new regime, albeit with qualifications, and those who vehemently opposed its attacks on democracy and inexorable path to a religious dictatorship. The Tudeh had from the beginning sided with the regime and the large Fadai' organisation had split along these very lines into a Majority, who joined the Tudeh and supported the regime, and a Minority, who opposed it.[1] Now the left wall of our cell mirrored this division with the Fadai' (Minority) and other groups[2] who opposed the Islamic regime shunning the Tudeh party and Fadai' (Majority) who they saw as appeasers who had betrayed the revolution. On the back wall sat the Mojahedin, the largest opposition group in the country, who stuck close together. And something new for me, the banned religious group, the Baha'is[3] who were on the whole older and who maintained good relations with the others. Floating above this maze, there are the ubiquitous *tavvabs* needling, obtrusive, and like tics, sticky and difficult to avoid. It was strange getting used to the

318

peculiarities of these separate drops of oil, floating on the same vessel.

There were *tavvabs* everywhere. Swarms of them, more brazen, now actively proposing new restrictions to the prison guards. Making statues from bread paste or scratch-painting on bones were now banned. Prisoners who did not pray were not allowed to wash up or do any tasks that needed water. They were unclean and 'wetness' would pass on their uncleanness to the pious and clean. They could only do dry cleaning jobs, like sweeping and dusting, so they did not pollute. They were untouchables.

I saw a young girl who had been with me on my first days of arrest, her face still beautiful, now without its brightness. What was once a cup full of joy and defiance had been drained of her very being. Torture, like a hole, had leaked her spirit, her zest for life, drop by drop, emptying her of everything that was her. That, now empty cup, had become a cruel and vindictive individual who made life hell for those under her command, not even sparing her old teacher who shared her cell. She would have loathed or pitied the person she had become when that full cup that was her was still full. I wondered how she would feel once she was back in the real world. Can she ever regain even a shred of her humanity?[4]

*

The story of children in captivity is simply sad. Cheshmeh was a 9-months old girl born in prison. Her mother was tortured savagely while pregnant with her and she had little hope that little Cheshmeh would make it. Her name, meaning a spring, was so appropriate to her clear large green eyes that sparkled like a mountain spring. On her chest her mother had stuck a sign 'don't kiss me' so kissable was she. If even half the 250 fellow prisoners kissed her, she would melt. Her mother, who was faced with the choice of a death sentence or release on condition she did an interview repenting her past, tried to keep herself separate. She had refused the interview and did not want to make life more difficult for others who may suffer by association with her. She would wake up before everyone else and wash and clean Cheshmeh's nappies and clothes so as not to unclean the pious. She did not pray so was unclean. Her little girl had body excretions, so she too was unclean. She would not accept help. Her husband, whom she loved with passion, had been executed. She too awaited death. Maybe the little girl felt her mother's anxiety. Cheshmeh with her beautiful eyes was always irritable. The *tavvabs* treated her mother with particular brutality.

One day they took the two away with all their belongings, and a gloom descended on the block. What did they do with our little mountain spring? Much later we found she had been released. She had relatives high up in government. The news made the *tavvabs* particularly angry and the rest of us jubilant.

There were between 10 and 15 children in our cellblock. The oldest was 6. She put her name down like the grown-ups to take turns in what we called *kargari* – feeding and cleaning the block. It was quite a challenge to keep the other kids occupied. We made balls and teddy bears from cloth but that did not satisfy their constant curiosity. Some of the games they played mimicked life inside. They would lead one another blindfolded holding a stick or pretend to ride the only car they had ever seen in their short life – the minibus that took us to the visitors' section. Life was tough.

Being in prison is like being locked up in a moving train. People walk in and out of your space. You make friends, some intensely, deeply passionately. They would be gone and re-join you in a different space, not just older but transformed into a different person inhabiting a fast-ageing body. Nothing is static, except restriction, narrowness, and at times, intense loneliness. Mother Rezvan, was a middle-aged woman who kept herself to herself. She was probably there as a hostage for her daughter and son-in-law who had gone into hiding. In the middle of one night the girls found her hanging in the showers. For weeks she had secretly made a rope from the plastic bags our bread was delivered. A deep gloom hung in the air for days. Mother Rezvan slept next to my school friend Goli. Her feet touched Goli's head. It was Goli who gave me the details in tears. She, like many in her room, had nightmares for weeks.

That Ramadan for the first and last time in my life I fasted, even though I secretly broke it here and there. And I hated, still hate, myself for doing it. I felt I had betrayed myself. I have never condemned anyone who had succumbed to this or to prayer, but even now I have not come to terms with the inner feeling of wretchedness and self-contempt. That inner battle persists to this day.

Then something unexpected happened.

[1] See Appendix 3 for details of the main political groups operating inside Iran before and after the revolution.

[2] These included the Paykar, Rahe Kargar and a number of small Maoist groups.

[3] The Bahai' religion was banned in the Islamic Republic as heathens not deserving the protection of the Islamic state. Bahai's were ordered to convert to Islam or face death as apostates. Christians, Jews, and Zoroastrians, as 'People of the Book' were permitted to pursue their practices provided they paid the special Islamic tax (*jeziyah*).

[4] An attempt to explain the mind of someone who became a *tavvab* after the experience of the coffins, and afterwards, has been published (in Farsi) – Homa Kalhor, *A Coffin for a Living*, Independent Publishers Network, 2020, ISBN 978-83853-562-9.

Chapter 60

The pool

Nayyer

"Everyone prepare to leave, with their plate and spoon!" It was the loudspeaker. What was going on? There was total confusion in the block, then a rumour: we are going to a picnic. A picnic? We who hadn't even been allowed into the courtyard. It must be a trap. What was the trap? Some decided to stay.

"Leaving the block is compulsory," the loudspeaker barked again, as if it read minds.

At the height of a 40-degree summer heat Evin's cooling system had broken down. With over 30 girls in a confined space of my new quarters, for weeks we had felt suffocated. Protests to the office were dismissed; the cooling system everywhere is down, they said. The last three weeks had been torture. Some had even pulled back the fitted carpet and slept on the somewhat cooler floor.

It was in the midst of that heat-wave that I had my second court hearing. I listened in that stifling courtroom with my heart beating to the list of accusations, many relating to reports of my disobedience in various prisons, hunger strikes, messages sent outside, some accusations which had not even come up in the questioning. At the end the prosecutor had asked for the death penalty.

"What have you to say for yourself?" The presiding *mullah* asked emotionless. Tears welled up. How do I defend myself? I felt so helpless, so alone. Suddenly the sound of the *azan*, the calling to prayer, boomed over the loudspeaker.

"Return to your cell. I will call you back," the *mullah* said. I was taken out and an intense feeling of absence came over me. I was alone in a totally unequal battle. I felt a deep despair. Back in the cell, talking to my friends and playing with a little girl who had adopted me, gradually my head broke through the cloud, and I was back on earth. I was playing with the little girl when the loudspeaker barked, calling us to prepare to leave, with our plate and spoon. It was a really strange order.

We left with *chador* and blindfold, walked the blind-walk, a hand on the *chador* ahead, down Evin slopes, past the central building, turned right near the visitors' hall, entered a wooded area and after a hundred metres or so were told to stop and take off our blindfolds. The place was like an adult playground, with climbing ropes, a metal climbing frame and obstacle tunnels. Perhaps a military training ground. There was even a swimming pool. With real water.

We were so excited we didn't know what to do. Running around, climbing the ropes, the metal frame. One or two were brave enough to jump fully dressed into the water. I too joined in. A *tavvab* girl joined us as well. She was a very good swimmer and started teaching us how to swim, seemingly oblivious of who she was. We were no longer unclean and *najess*. Even Rahimi, the female *pasdar* in charge of our block stood by and watched us smiling. After an hour I got out and stood in the sun to dry my clothes, but that wasn't going to work. So, I undressed under my chador and sat wrapped in it. Others followed my lead. We all looked strange.

Lunchtime came and they ordered us to put on our *hejab*. The van with the food arrived. That too was unique, a plate full of *lubyapolo* (rice and haricot). We even had watermelons for dessert. Dessert! That was the first time in three years. Our little 3-year old was delirious with happiness that day. After lunch some lay in the sun. I put on my clothes which had dried, and with a few others explored the surroundings. No one was hindering us. We walked.

In one corner was a glasshouse full of flowers which we knew the *tavvab* boys cultivated and the prison authorities sold to visitors. We too could buy them and present them to our visitors but were not permitted to take them into our cells. Once we realised no one was stopping us we walked into the dense woods. The rustle of the trees, the sound of a stream nearby was simply intoxicating. For a second I thought of escape.

"They won't let us escape so easy," a friend said aloud, clearly thinking the same thoughts. The Evin walls with their guard towers were at the end of the woods. I remembered seeing the wall from the hills above Evin in those days of freedom.

Then back to the stifling heat of the cells and being *najess* unclean again, a bit like switching a light off and another light on, with a duller hue, where even children were segregated into clean and unclean. I went to room six which we had nicknamed liberated territory because it was devoid of *tavvabs* and exercised and sweated profusely in the stifling heat.

The next day, on television, we heard Lajevardi boasting of his services to the Islamic Republic and especially in Evin where prisoners even went out to picnic! Now we understood.

But, regardless of Lajevardi's machination, it had been a blissful day for us.

*

The light was yellowing. Autumn yet again and the second anniversary of my brother's death. It was always autumn. Everything bad happened in autumn. Last year I spent autumn in *Qezel Hesar's* cowshed wishing for a miracle. I had felt the autumn wind on my face when they arrested me. The leaves must be yellowing now. You could look out of a small window when you climbed to the top bed, but there were no trees so I could not see the yellowing leaves. Yet you could feel autumn from the pleasant cooling air. Some nights I would look at the sky, lighted by city lights, thinking of birds flying and the bustle of the world outside, and I would block out the noise of chatter and hubbub of the girls below and fly to the love that I had left behind, a love that was now only a memory in those autumn nights, a sweet memory that gave colour to the greyness of prison life, colours of blue, green and red, colours I loved, colours that described and even more, stirred up emotions.

With the coming cold came the debates about closing or leaving the window open. I was indifferent. For me the painted window, the paint scratched away by the girls earlier to let in light and let out communication, was a gateway to dreams of my love at night and watching my friend Goli in the courtyard in daytime. Goli was my closest friend before my incarceration, and we shared a cell for a short time. Now, once again we were separated. She had signalled to me that she had been given 5 years.

One day when prisoners returned from *Hosseinieh*[1] they found one of their girls missing. Had she been abducted on her way there or back, like what had happened to another girl two years ago? That other girl had been pulled aside by a *pasdar* from the end of the line on her way to the *Hosseineh* and raped. She had come back in tears. The authorities had promised to punish the *pasdar* but being blindfolded she could not identify the rapist. Was our girl also raped? The prison loudspeaker called her name out a number of times. Finally late that night she turned up. Apparently on the way back she had been peeping at the Evin valley under her blindfold and got left behind. A *pasdar* had found her wandering aimlessly and ordered her to return to her cell immediately. Being new to the prison she had lost her way and was captured somewhere else and accused of trying to escape. The new prison chief had finally intervened and had accepted her explanation and severely reprimanded the errant *pasdar* for letting her walk back alone. We laughed and laughed.

She had been free for a whole afternoon.

[1] A place of enacting religious pageants and of prayer (akin to a chapel)

Chapter 61

Respite

Nayyer

My name was called over the loudspeaker. Must be my sentence and my heart raced away. They put a paper in front of me and ordered me to sign: seen and noted. I was given ten years starting from the time of my court appearance. The three years I had already spent there floated off, like smoke. I signed, relieved that I was to live. Get used to prison life, my friend told me back at the cell. Get used to prison life I told myself back in the cell. My sister was devastated when I told her.

Soon a few of us who had received their sentence were shipped back to *Qezel Hesar,* the home of the cowshed. Yet another parting from newfound friends. *Mother* hugged me. *Mother,* the woman who refused to be identified with any of the prison groupings; who kept a good relationship with me; who had defied the ban by the politicals of buying watermelons on the feast of *yalda,* the longest night of the year, in itself an exceptional concession by the guards; the woman who had taught me so much about tolerance and patience, hugged me and whispered in my ear:

"Look after yourself. Try to be above the petty divisions of prison." It took me many more years to absorb all her lessons into my heart.

Back in *Qezel Hesar* it was unrecognisable. The gate to block 7, which was given over entirely to the prisoners from the left, opened into a large area

326

known as *zir-e hasht* (literally under eight) which led to a wide corridor with 12 small cells on either side, each with a three-storey bed, and shower and toilets half way down. The brightness and cleanliness startled me. Fereshteh, my neighbour in the coffin, was now the *tavvab* in charge of the block and detested all political prisoners, particularly those who had stood firm on their beliefs. But you have met Fereshteh already with her ultra-concealing *maqna'eh* headgear and prayer beads baffling her tearful parents on the other side of the glass partition at visiting time.

Not all gloom, though. I was reunited with Goli and the world opened up. Before I had settled, my old spoon-knocking neighbour banged the lock on the main gate to draw attention.

"*chadors* on," she bellowed.

It was the new prison governor Meisam. He wanted to hear our grievances. The brazenness of the demands made by the inmates was shocking to my ears. Things had certainly changed since the days of *haji* Davood Rahmani.[1] Slowly the story of what had happened to my fellow inmates in the cowshed unfolded. A tiny few survived intact, well almost intact. Some like Banafsheh had endured the entire ten months and survived.

"Most of the girls in the cowshed gave in," she told me in her quite voice. Banafsheh had always been cheerful, full of jokes, always modest, without any pretensions. Even now, with her face prematurely aged from her ordeal, she retained her good nature and sense of humour. She brought me up to date. A, one of the oldest and most respected of prisoners, had one day suddenly started to laugh out loud, loud like guffaws. Her laughter had gradually turned to tears. Loud wailing tears. She had then suddenly stood up and started praying. Right there in the coffin. Praying. Another day another veteran, S, stood up in her wooden box and shouted at the top of her voice

"I'm a Marxist. I want to defend my beliefs." *Haji* took her away and debated with her.

"What?" I interrupted. "Since when had *Haji* known anything about Marxism?

"Oh, you have no idea what the prisoners had taught that monster," Banafsheh replied with a smile. "Anyway, you're lucky you didn't hear her interview. It was broadcast over the loudspeakers."

"Why? What did she say?"

"She cried and cried. Before I was 'nothing', she said. I wasn't human. I was base. I had animal-like passions. She kept repeating this between tears. Sometimes she could barely make herself understood through her tears. It was pathetic. She kept asking for forgiveness for her satanic sins. When later on they brought her back to the cells she wore a white chador praying all the time. She would stand in the courtyard looking up at the sky with both hands in supplication begging forgiveness. It was a pitiful sight. She even changed her name to a religious one."

As Banafsheh spoke, the image of S shortly after her arrest, always wearing short tight clothes that stood out in prison, came to me. She had heard of her husband's execution a year after her arrest. Banafsheh went on and on recounting the tale of this and that girl when Sima, another one of the cowshed inmates came over.

"Why on earth are you telling it all in one go on her very first day?" she was addressing Banafsheh. Sima was a modest girl, and her modesty was central to her strength of character. She too had resisted to the end.

"No no, I want to hear the whole story," I begged. "I want it now. I have been waiting a year to know what happened to those poor girls I left behind. I won't be able to sleep unless you tell me."

How did it end? I finally asked. Here Sima took over the narrative. It was the change of leadership. The new governor. The change was sudden and unexpected. They hadn't taken down the coffins and he was taken to see them. The coffins were still being used with living corpses still there. He took photographs and sent it to *ayatollah* Montazeri,[2] she said in her gentle voice, not looking you in the eye. That was her way.

"They say Montazeri had cried when he saw the pictures. He said it is torture, which is prohibited in Islam."

I laughed at this. What about the steelyard (*ghapan*) and the lash? But of course, I forgot. They are not torture, but *ta'zir* (Islamic chastisement)!

"You wouldn't believe it, but when Meisam, the new governor, told us that what had gone on was pure torture, some of the girls stood up in protest.'

"No *Haj-Aqa*! What was done to us wasn't torture. It was a blessing to make us human."

Giti, was a living symbol of the cowshed's 'blessing.' Day or night you would find Giti sitting quietly under the bars of the entrance area. Immobile. Head down drifting in some inner world. I never saw her talk to anyone. She would only go to the toilet when everyone was asleep. She never took a shower. Even when they left it empty for her.

"Microbes are a necessity of life," she had once said. She, a student of psychology in an earlier life, remained immobile, as if the coffins were still there, living with her microbes.

I was still grappling with my inner turmoil. My praying had become more sporadic. There was a war raging within me. Every time I prayed, I saw someone turning away from me. But is that what they actually did or was I merely externalising what was an inner conflict within myself? I felt disgusted with myself. A part of me wanted to cast off this pretence. Another part refused to bow to peer pressure. A battle was being fought inside me between self-pride and self-hate. I wanted to give up the pretence but on my own terms. Conflicted with these contradictory emotions I became more and more irritable. I took it out on those closest to me. Only my dear friend Goli, stood by me, taking the snubs, caring for me. Those days of inner loathing, even the love that had kept me company my entire time in captivity, was pushed aside. Later I felt ashamed of my behaviour in the face of her generosity. Not long afterwards I gave up praying for good.

Another spring and several visits by regime dignitaries. The inmates had lost their previous fear and started demanding their minimum rights as a prisoner. After a struggle we got our way and were given a capsule of gas and a large pot to boil our clothes in order to kill off a skin fungus that affected all of us. We got warmer water to shower and antifungal cream to use on ourselves. We looked strange with our boiled clothes, crumbled and totally changed in colour. But the wretched fungus was gone.

Mona, the youngest in our cell, loved to draw. They had allowed her to keep the book that taught drawing. One day she asked me to sit for her. Halfway through I suddenly lost consciousness. Panic. Infirmary. A needle in my arm. My portrait unfinished, a perfect mirror of the fractured nature of life in prison.

I had fallen asleep when I was woken by the sound of music, birds chirping, the sound of a running stream. Was I dreaming? I opened my eyes. All the girls were sitting watching the television with open mouths. On the screen there was a cartoon. A fluffy dandelion seed was moving from branch to branch playing a melodious flute. The leaves danced to the tune, a nightingale echoed back in response. The dandelion's flute stood by a bud. Slowly the flower opened, and the flute bowed and moved on. Oh, we all wished it would never end. Mesmerised. The chicken wire window was full of faces looking out. I went to walk in the entrance area but that too was full. I felt suffocated. I just wanted to fly in a field or meadow. The walls were all closing on me.

Then I saw the silent Giti, the human stone, sitting in her navy-blue manteaux and scarf, looking down on the bare floor. Alone in her own world.

Maybe one day I will become like her…

[1] Davood Rahmani (Haji) the ogre of *Qezel Hesar* died at home in 2021. He was never punished for his crimes.

[2] Montazeri was the designated successor to Khomeini. At this time he had been put in overall charge of the prison service, replacing Lajevardi, and was responsible for the relative easing of prison conditions for a time before the massacres of summer and autumn 1988. He was summarily removed from his position as Khomeini's heir by the Supreme Leader Khomeini himself and put under house arrest. He had raised some objections to the 1988 massacre.

Chapter 62

Bus ride to Yazd

Ahmad

One last look in the mirror to check his camouflage, and a friend drove him to the bus depot. Tehran, late night and in the winter rain, was relatively quiet. He was on his way to Yazd to bid farewell to his father and mother but also, try and get a copy of his birth certificate which he could alter to conceal his real identity. The bus left Tehran and entered the nearby city of Qom without an incident. The passengers had settled back for a bumpy snooze through the desert as the bus left Qom. It had been an uneventful trip so far. The bus was warm.

Just outside the city the bus stopped. Two men wearing *pasdar* uniforms stepped up. One of them, a young man with a thin growth of short cropped facial hair, as if it had never seen a razor, climbed up and stood beside the driver, looking down the aisle into the full bus. Ahmad was sitting on an aisle seat just over two thirds of the way down on the right, pretending to be asleep. He had shaved the thick black moustache, removed his glasses and changed the style of his hair. It is amazing how much fiddling with a few strands of hair can achieve to alter a face. At least that's what the mirror on the wall had told him. The early winter rain that had soaked him when he boarded at midnight had stopped soon after they left the capital. It was after 2 am. He had dried out in the stale warm bus air, thickened rancid with breath, cigarettes and sweat.

The older *pasdar* blocked the door with his body, curving out his paunch, while the young man began walking down the aisle. Slowly. Stopping at each row and carefully scrutinising every passenger in turn. Left and right. As he walked past, he brought with him the smell of the cold air. He walked to what Ahmad guessed was the back of the bus, walked back and stopped at his side. He touched Ahmad's shoulder gently and said in a soft voice.

"*Haj-aqa.*"

Ahmad opened his eyes and breathed in. This *pasdar* was very young. A short lad, his head barely above the sitting man he was addressing.

"*Befarmai'd?*" Ahmad replied, meaning what can I do for you?.

"Where are you going?" the young man said using the polite form of language you use for a respected person. He spoke with a soft, almost boyish voice with a twang of menace.

"I'm going to Ardekan."[1]

"And what is the purpose of your trip?" Still a polite, soft voice, each word clearly enunciated.

"To visit my mother."

"Do you have any identification?"

"Yes. My driving licence." And he took out his licence from the top pocket of his shirt and handed it over. The boy-soldier studied the card carefully, very carefully, looking back and forth at Ahmad's face. His skin had a strange yellow tinge.

"Let me see, don't you have your birth certificate?" He said looking intently into Ahmad's eyes.

"No."

"Any other ID?" He was sounding less polite.

"Sorry no," Ahmad said trying very hard to sound normal.

"What are you taking with you?"

"Just a few souvenirs for my mother."

"Do you have any pamphlets, newspapers, or explosives?" he said, all the time staring into Ahmad's eyes.

"I don't think such jests are very appropriate," Ahmad said reprovingly. My sac is up there. You can check for yourself. He was beginning to feel uncomfortable.

"I will, don't worry. What is your job?"

"I'm an engineer."

"What kind of engineer?"

"Architect."

"Where do you live?"

"Tavanir," he mentioned a borough he had once lived in.

"Where in Tavanir?"He couldn't remember the alleyway's name. Maybe it did not have a plaque, or maybe it had fallen off. He had changed houses so often they were somewhat of a blur. Memory can play tricks, especially under pressure. Was the house really in an alleyway? What if it was on the street? And suddenly a number of houses merged in a jumble in his head.

"That alleyway sloping down towards the park", he improvised. The lad clearly knew the area. He nodded as if he understood and went on.

"Where is your office?"

"Ahmad remembered that a friend had an architect's office in Lalehzar street on the third floor. "It's on Lalehzar," he said after an imperceptible pause.

"Where on Lalehzar, further up from Cinema Asia or below?"

"A building on the corner of Lalehzar and Manuchehri streets. Third floor." Sounding exasperated but with increasing fear. I must not show my fear he kept repeating. It was getting more difficult to answer in a relaxed neutral way. The young man clearly knew the area well and was not entirely happy with the replies he was receiving. He just stood there and stared and stared. Ahmad had to summon all his powers to remain calm. He started bringing up images of Nina and her childish talk. The other passengers had all woken up and some were fidgety. The atmosphere was becoming tense. The young man walked slowly down to the door, turned round and just went on staring and staring down the aisle. Then he turned and walked out and closed the door.

"*Salvaat*,"[2] shouted the driver as soon as they were a distance from the roadblock, and the entire bus burst into the ritual chant, *alaahom-a sallé ala Mohammad va aaleé Mohammad* filled up the air, up pitch and down, like a huge sigh. Then he put on a cassette and the wonderfully deep voice of Delkash flooded that space,[3] his way of showing disgust at the behaviour of the *pasdar* and his sympathy for the intimidated Ahmad.

He arrived uneventfully in Ardekan just after sunrise and took a taxi to his father's house that he had never previously seen. It was at the end of a narrow *cul-de-sac* alleyway and took ages to find. That same day they drove to a neighbouring town, Meybod, where his father had an acquaintance in the Registry Office, to obtain a copy of his birth certificate. He needed that to modify his name and use it to get a passport to leave the country.

On the way back with the new birth certificate in his pocket they saw his mother walking out of the alleyway. She was wearing a white chador with a pattern of small flowers, the sort you wore around the house. She was signalling a quick exit.

"Walk on without stopping," is what they heard, and walk on without stopping is what they obeyed. A block away she caught up with them and they got into the Mercedes Benz 72 belonging to his father.

"A man on a motorbike arrived at the door with two *komitehchi*," (man from the *komiteh*) his mother said in a voice that was fast moving from anxious to relieved. "We heard that Ahmad *aqa* has come home and came to greet him, they said. Which Ahmad are you talking about, I said to them? Your Ahmad, one of the *komitechis* replied. Oh, I said. Well, our Ahmad hasn't come home. He isn't here. *Ravi Sunni bood*"[4] implying whoever informed you was mistaken.

The family drove to Yazd and Ahmad stayed on with an uncle. How to get back became a dilemma. Two weeks later he decided to risk flying back. Yazd airport was fine but at Tehran's Mehrabad airport he entered the arrival hall and was confronted by three or four groups of *pasdars* and among them perhaps some *tavvabs* minutely scrutinising every passer-by, every passenger. It was like walking through a tunnel of death, three times or four.

[1] A small town on the road to Yazd in central Iran.
[2] *Salvaat* is a salutation regularly used by Shia' Muslims to reaffirm their

belief: 'O Allah let thy blessings be on Mohammad and his progeny'. Here, it was a sign of relief and thanking Allah for seeing them through this ordeal.

[3] A much-loved popular singer. Listening to a female voice was forbidden in the Islamic Republic. That particular cassette was a defiant gesture.

[4] Literally: the narrator was a *Sunni* – reflecting the deep animosity and disagreements between these two major branches of Islam.

Chapter 63

City of stones

Nayyer

The sounds triggered a memory of a childhood trip to Maraqeh, my aunt and uncle by my side, that I had suppressed. There, on the dirty grey wall of the *qahveh khooneh* (coffee house) we had stopped to rest, hanging slightly askew was a painting in garish colours with images of the damned being tortured, creatively, gruesomely, sickening to the child's eyes. It was a painting of hell. My young eyes had seen and recoiled. I could not finish my fried eggs, which I loved so much. Why did tired travellers need such a visual jolt? Now I was hearing that same hell floating up from the depths.

From time-to-time tears and wails had wafted upwards from the bowels of the concrete building. We knew that down there, in cellblock 8, was now home to *tavvabs,* some of the girls I had shared a cell with a couple of years ago. They had been subsequently transferred to Gohardasht to experience its vicious solitary punishment. The wails, rising like steam from the witch's cauldron, were howls from the pit of hell, tears of the living dead. Listening to the rising pain in *Qezel Hesar,* I felt my heart constrict as if it was threatening to beat no more. We had watched those girls, clad in their black *chadors* in airing-time sitting silently in a corner of the courtyard, or shuffling alone, not communing with anyone. Now we were informed that ten of us were being sent down into that pit. Why we were singled out, was a mystery at first, but single out they did, and no protest, argument or pleading would change their decision.

Nothing, not even the rising howls of torment had prepared us for what we saw when we entered block 8. There the girls sat, with their black scarves, blank, vacant look, silent. No words exchanged. No sign of recognition from girls I had known so intimately. Here was the silence of death. Not just a stone here and there, but an entire city of stones.

Our group was split up and scattered across the rooms. I entered a room of ghosts who only became animated that night, a prayer night. What started as a slow whimper became a wail, a howl of misery from within punctuated by sobs and tears. A wail like that of a mother weeping over her child's grave. All their suffering was distilled in those bitter tears. I spread my bedding and crept under the blanket but could not block the sound. The pain penetrated the hands that were blocking my ears. I wept silently for their tragic destiny.

Over the next days I watched *Haji* Davood's creations in horror. It had been drummed into those poor girls that laughter and joking was a sin. Months and years of indoctrination had convinced them of their sinfulness. They had lost the ability to communicate. Even talking to cellmates had been forbidden. That habit persisted even now that restrictions were removed. They turned inwards into a world I could not possibly know. We had been transported to a town whose inhabitants seem to have ossified into sculptures of desolation.

Those first days, all of us found it difficult to eat with the ghosts. They saw us as something unclean. One or two broke their silence and vehemently protested at our arrival. We, the ten of us, took our meals in the corridor. We were unclean, as were three among them who did not pray. They too were shunned like lepers. Yet, bizarrely, the three girls who were highly educated, ran classes for the stones which many, to my surprise, attended, then once outside of class pushed them away as unclean! We showered separately, cleaned separately and ate separately.

A few of us went to the office to complain and demand that we are sent back to our original cells. It transpired that they had brought us here to bring some life back into these living corpses. This was part of the reform plan of the new management.

"You created this mess, clear it up yourself," one of the braver girls told the deputy governor who had come to hear our grievances. He reddened and swallowed his anger.

"Take these whores away from us," one of the ghosts shouted to the official. The feeling of rejection worked both ways.

"We brought you here to change the environment and make it like other prison cellblocks," the deputy governor insisted, almost pleadingly. "You can live here any way you want. No one should be permitted to insult you."

Finally, the management relented, and we were returned to the world of the living. What would these ghosts do if, or when, they are returned to the real world?

*

The day came when I was split from my friends and sent to cellblock 3, the same block that had previously led to our sojourn in the cowshed and beyond. I walked in with great trepidation. There would still be many girls there who had experienced the coffins. What was the atmosphere going to be like? I walked over to the last room along the long corridor that began with a wide area – the *zire-hasht* – head bowed. One or two girls greeted me, but my response was cold. I didn't know what to expect. News of my coming quickly spread and a few old friends came to visit. I had expected excuses of why they had cracked. Instead, they asked me if I wanted tea. I was taken aback. Tea? Now? It was daytime on the first day of Ramadan.

Little by little I learnt that despite the damages, many of the girls had survived almost intact. The cellblock was far less crowded than before. I shared a bed with another girl, taking turns to sleep on the floor. Soon she left and I had my own bed. The more relaxed atmosphere had also disoriented the few *tavvabs* there. A few began to quietly recant a second time, blaming false promises.

My prayers became very sporadic. Here most of the girls on the left also prayed. Now that I was neither under pressure from the guards to pray nor from my cellmates to stop praying, now that it was up to me to stop, I did. I felt immensely better.

One day that autumn of 1984, I was taken up to the governor, Meisam, who told me I am free to go home provided I repented. I still had nine years of my sentence to serve. They had offered me freedom, but at a cost. I refused. Many scolded me for my stubbornness. So many of the prisoners had given a cursory message of repentance and walked free. But my sister understood and encouraged me. They reduced my sentence to 3 years but I knew that was just a number. It meant nothing.

My refusal was final.

Chapter 64

Ozra

Nayyer

My apologies. I have been ranting and reminiscing in an endless string of memories. You do that when you are in a cage, especially when alone in a tiny cell. It is so easy to go inwards and lose yourself in memories and emotions. I mustn't let my story last as long as my prison sentence. I don't want to lose you but am trying to weave in the story of the thousands who shared my life. They all deserve to be remembered, even fleetingly. Such was Farzaneh Zolfi who survived seven months locked up in a toilet. There were so many others, some I got to know personally and some through others. I'm going to jump about for a bit in spacetime. In a way that is how my own prison life was. You were moved into one cell, you made new friends and you were yanked away to another cell or another prison, to start again somewhere else. There were other times when you yearned to be taken away somewhere, anywhere other than where you were stuck. Life was a zig-zag of experience, a world whose best descriptive adjective was unstable, and perhaps even more accurately, unpredictable.

"This is not *Qezel Hesar*," the ugly man said, "that break is over. This here is Evin," he stressed the name and I saw a strange thrill in his eye. He was truly ugly, with his bristling facial hair, black peppered with white, unwashed unkempt hair standing up here and there, and a huge nose poking out aggressively as if to devour you. There he was standing erect like some demi-god in his shiny green *pasdar* suit. He was really ugly. Maybe I saw him as ugly because his ugly reputation had preceded him. His brutality. The way he made sure he was there whenever there was a whipping going on. It was late spring in 1985 and the year-long breathing space of *Qezel Hesar* had come to an abrupt end. We were back in Evin, and Evin was harsh.

We walked through one of the four doors leading from Evin's main 216 corridor to the women's block, down the stairs of cellblock 4, and for a handful of us, into room number 7. What hit me was seeing girls lined up along the wall with a look of utter hatred. Now I understood what Mojtaba[1] the ugly *pasdar* in green had meant when he sneeringly talked about the end of time-out. We were the unlucky ones banished to the room of the *tavvabs*. Not your ordinary *tavvab* but a bunch of girls who had truly cracked. Earlier in another prison they had pretended repentance while managing a secret Mojahedin organisation within the prison. When all this came out, they had to endure months of intensely savage torture in front of each other, followed by the coffins and more torture. This group had lost any semblance of being human. Here was a new breed of *tavvab*. They had not turned to stone. We were trapped in a cage of ferocious animals.

"We don't want to be in the same cell as these *tavvabs*," we protested vehemently to the guard in charge of our room.

"You are just going to have to accept the rules here," she said curtly, but then softened her voice and promised to enquire higher up.

Those first days I spent my entire time in the corridor, only going into the cell to sleep. We ate separately and we gave up on drinking tea when the *tavvab*-girls stood guard over the flask making sure we don't pollute it with our unclean hands. Once again we were the untouchables. Worse, I overheard one of them telling another we deserve to be lined up against the wall and shot or strung up until we are dead.

From day one Ozra refused to sleep in her cell, room 4. She took a grey army blanket and lay down to sleep right there, in the corridor. I'm not going back in there with those animals, she said. One *tavvab* girl grabbed her by the hair and dragged her in and locked the cell gate. "This slut deserves to be hanged," she shrieked with a voice full of loathing, and nearly strangled her, but Ozra was adamant. She sat upright for hours by the gate and as soon as it was opened took her blanket and went right back to lie down in the corridor.

"No one's going to make me stay in that rat hole," she kept repeating. "No one!" A number of *tavvabs* pounced on her, beating and kicking her. Mojtaba, the ugly head *pasdar*, appeared.

"What the devil is the fuss about?" he shouted in his gruff animal voice and not waiting for a reply began laying into the poor girl. After he finished with her, bleeding from nose and mouth and cuts here and there, she crawled into room 2, *tavvab*-free room 2, and refused to budge. Little by little the rest of us joined her. She smiled a triumphant smile as the last of us entered room 2 with our belongings. As her lips parted for a smile a trickle of blood rolled down her lower lips unto her shirt. That triumphant battered face is another image that will remain with me till, finally one day, all memory fades.

In the end the guards gave up trying to force us to stay in our designated rooms, but they continued to deliver our food to the rooms we had been allocated. After ten days or so they gave up on that too and delivered our food to room 2. It was a victory which we would never have achieved without Ozra's courage. And determination. We were *tavvab*-free, a small, liberated zone inside that prison. It was paradise.

*

The next two years moved through time, sometimes rapidly and at others as if time was frozen. I remained troubled by the way we prisoners persist in creating our own prison inside prison, like a Russian (matryoshka) doll. Separate communes, boycotting this or that political group, this or that prisoner, drawing imaginary lines that became insurmountable walls and mountains, splitting us up into smaller and smaller groups, fighting battles of long ago, creating pain and loneliness. They defended their own narrow interpretation of the world as if they were terrified that it might be blown away in the wind. I began to understand their terror at stepping beyond those imaginary walls into a world they may not be able to control. I tried to stay out of this added hell, maintaining cordial relationships across the barriers, across the imaginary walls, across historic splits and divides. It was difficult but I persisted to the very end.

There were not just the walls that needed conquering. There was also the utter boredom of sameness. Living close with someone for month after month in a space which shrank with time, we emptied each other's heads. Each of us became like a book you have read over and over. You not only know the plot, you know the next sentence. Then there is the irritation of being cooped up with someone you had developed a particular dislike to. Rational or irrational, you sometimes just took a dislike to someone in the same way you developed strong bonds, sometimes too strong, with someone with all its heartaches and ups and downs. Imagine seeing the subject of your irritation day after day without being able to walk away. The aversion simply grinds into your soul and trying to hide it makes it even worse. You just long for relief and being moved somewhere else becomes a dream. But moving too could be a mixed blessing. Simple things like abandoning your secret hiding place where you hid your most precious possession. For me that was my booklet of poetry which I had compiled from memory or from others reciting. It was there I discovered the Palestinian poet Mahmoud Darwish writing about prison life and the Turkish poet Nazem Hekmat – how did his book of poems actually get inside?

One day they suddenly told us to wear our *chador*. I panicked. It was a search with no warning. Quickly I stuffed my booklet of poetry in my stockings. When the *Pasdar* started to search me, I feigned ticklishness once she reached my belly. She thought I was hiding something there and took a long time feeling around. When she got to my legs she skimmed. After almost freezing to death in the icy winter winds in the courtyard we were returned to our cells to find the place in utter chaos with all our belongings strewn about. But I had saved my treasure. Most of the few other books had been confiscated.

*

Then back to Evin for another cursory court, repent and set yourself free, refused, ten plus three, minus the six I had already served, you do the maths, me, resigned, didn't really think I would ever get out of this place anyway, ever, get used to it, reproached by family and friends for my doggedness, maybe perceptions outside had softened, 'but I can't accept their inquisition' I said, maybe I was just stubborn. I had to be punished.

Months in solitary again where the silence of being alone is like being blind. You become intensely sensitive to noise, to movement. Every sound is amplified. You listen for whispers, for the different sound of slippers to tell you which *pasdar* is doing what. In that tiny space, one and a half by two metres, the hunter-gatherer in you wakes up. You search for prey. What's being exchanged between *pasdar* and prisoner down the corridor? You become like that nosey gossipy old woman of lore. Who is doing what to whom? You expand your world through your senses. You live in your head.

In that tiny cell I spent hours thinking of the man I love. A narrative developed around him, an almost mythical figure that more and more became my own creation. My love. My personal love, an ideal of love, wild open spaces, birds in flight, wind, the bright light of spring, colours, holding hands, poplar trees swaying in unison by the wind as they reach up for the sky and sun, all intertwined in a narrative that time embellished with detail. Would he, could any mortal being, live up to dreams? At visiting time, I had written on the palm of my hand: 'I am not alone, he is always with me'. Then I saw tears well up in my sister's eyes and I regretted writing it. What they didn't tell me is that at every anniversary of our love he wrote a long letter to me, in his beautiful prose, and equally beautiful handwriting, and sent it to my sister. My sister kept them stacked away in a secret hide out for when I will be released. Asqar had managed to escape arrest in time and was now in Europe. She did pass on some of the clothes he also sent.

*

Then, one day, and another move, I walked out of the cell that was my new home into the open sky, walked down some steps and into my past, into the same courtyard I had occupied another world ago, now a little larger than the one I remembered, the same porch and below that, the same playing field. Memories flooded over me. I had spent the last months of the old regime here, in that cell with its courtyard in what felt like a lifetime ago. We had been playing that day when the loudspeaker announced the names of those that were to be freed. Only eleven of us were left behind. Tears of parting. They had walked out and were met by a huge crowd who all wanted to kiss them and lift them up. Then our turn came. And then my brother's.

I sat down on a platform on the porch. Everything was spinning inside me. An old mate brought me tea; some were looking at me with sad eyes. They thought I had become mental. The outer wall of the yard had been pushed back and a number of ancient plane trees and a tiny stream, previously outside the walls, were now inside our enclosure. In the afternoons a trickle of water would pass down the stream and we would paddle with bare feet to cool down. It was my first real tree I could touch, with leaves I could see moving in the wind and cool moving water I could feel and hear since my arrest 6 years ago, excepting the 'picnic'. The water had flowed down from the foothills of the Alborz mountains and still retained that memory of freedom. It was still cool. Yashar, a little boy with the blue-green eyes the colour of the sea, would paddle in this stream. How he and the little boy Rowshan would suffer those days when the guards punished us by closing the yard. One day Yashar put on the beautiful clothes we had sewn for him and was handed over to his grandmother. Little Rowshan, was left alone and sad among a large family who treated her according to their own needs. Rowshan's childish needs were secondary, and ignored. At this stage, with the Iran-Iraq war in a stalemate and the opposition all but annihilated, the future looked hopeless for us. Most of the prisoners had sunk inwards into themselves. The children in captivity were now no longer seen as children in need, to be nurtured, to be taught what it means to be human, to be loved for simply being, but became an appendage to the needs of the girls, each entangled in their own demons and cocoons. Later both children lost their fathers in the prison massacre.

*

Thinking about the distance of closeness reminds me of our jogging ritual. Here distance was disciplined into a jogging ritual that was a mirror to prison life of those days. Every afternoon as the sun started to climb up the back wall, we would run with military precision and in strict order in the yard. Groups differing in size, some only three, two or even one, would run in unison, a fixed distance apart, like an invisible bar. If one group overtook another they would settle again with the same distance. Here the invisible walls existed but were now mobile. An hour of organised jogging in distinct groups. The distances were real. After so many years the invisible walls had solidified into normality. The prisoner lived with these distances, ate with these distances, did cleaning duty (*kargari*) with these distances, read newspapers with these distances, talked, or ignored one another with these distances. Distances day and night. It was not just political affiliations that decided distances. There was no clear logic to the groupings. People would create their own distance, or not, according to their own interpretation. Their own construct. Some lived and ran alone. It was impossible to question the motives. At times it led to isolation and isolation in prison can be devastating, something I only understood slowly, perhaps too slowly. From day two, I too was running in unison, in a grouping, observing the distances.

For me though, the greatest distance came in the convoluted depths of my memory. Every spring, in remembrance of that spring day he and I had spoken of our love for one another, I created my own personal ritual. It was a celebration of our love, and memories, and bonds, and hope. I would shower, if at all possible, put on something new if at all available, and walk alone, anywhere, even the corridor if nothing else was there, living and remembering those moments of perfect love. He walked alongside me, as he had done in that in that *baq* (orchard) holding my hands, the new-born leaves rustling in my eras. In that world of pure love I was no longer a prisoner. Every spring, as nature renewed its compact with life, I too renewed my vow with him. Love freed me from the walls, the bars and the suffocating loneliness. And if a smile came to my lips, I would not suppress it. I was inside myself with my own love, with him at my side, holding hands. My own rite of spring.

[1] Mojtaba Sarlak

Chapter 65

Parvin

Nayyer

In this life to die is not new,
But also to live, of course, not newer
Russian poet Sergey Yesenin just before his suicide.

Maybe these words of the poet, at that time circulating among the prisoners, affected Parvin more deeply. After a very long gap we were once again bombarded with another chain of public confessions, this time of leaders and cadres from left groups. There were no hiding places from the sound waves emanating from loudspeakers at full volume and flooding our entire space. No escaping these one-sided and slanted polemics whose principal aim appeared to be to discredit the left groups and in particular individuals who had not cracked under torture. This was sometimes cleverly done by innuendo. Our jailors had become quite sophisticated with time, though few of us fell for such ruses.

I actually liked to listen to these 'debates', even though I boiled with anger much of the time. They would sometimes quote large chunks of literature to support this or that view which I gulped up like a hungry wolf. We were starved of books other than those on Islamic philosophy, except of course for a few that had been smuggled in somehow and were almost tattered from being passed around. Or hand-copied. And we also had each other's memories of books that we had shared with our cell-mates. One of the girls had a photographic memory of the texts she had read and which she had recited for us almost verbatim. Years later I saw the film *Fahrenheit 451*, and it took me back.[1]

When we were preparing to sleep, I saw Parvin rummaging on top of the cupboard. Must be looking for a piece of clothing or something, I thought. Then I saw her with her bath bag about to go to the shower room. The water is cold this time of night, I called out to her. She mumbled something that I didn't understand and walked away. She had been acting strangely all day, strangely distant after someone in the debate had said something about her husband, Mehran, almost as a throwaway remark. In the middle of a wide-ranging criticism of his organisation's policies and strategy he had suddenly introduced a sentence that had little to do with the argument he was developing. He had been in the same cell as Mehran in the summer of 1983, he had said, and found out that Mehran, one of the leaders of his organisation, had identified the voice of two of his fellow leaders for the interrogators.[2] I was sitting next to Parvin, and saw her going deathly pale. Parvin was Mehran's wife and had always been intensely proud of his reputation as someone who had not divulged any of his extensive knowledge under severe torture. From that moment on she just closed up and no amount of joking and clowning by me, or a number of her friends, could get any response out of her. For the first time she did not sit with us to eat. She just sat, leaning on one of the metal beds, mute, unresponsive, motionless, and without any outward sign of emotion, as if she had been petrified.

"Come and eat" we coaxed, "today's soup is absolutely delicious," we lied but she did not hear. One girl got up and took hold of her bowl and tried to put a spoon of soup in her mouth, but she just flicked her head irritably like a baby does and spilt the soup on her dress without reacting. After supper she sat watching the television without seeing as if she no longer lived in this world. Afterwards she went over and helped another cellmate do some sewing in total silence. It was so unlike the friendly Parvin who was friend and mother to most of us.

I followed her to the showers without knowing why, I just felt uneasy about her behaviour, and saw her go into a cabin and close the door. Probably gone to wash her underwear, I thought, but did not return to my room. A couple of other girls also came and we loitered around brushing our teeth for a very long time, waiting for her to come out. I smelt the lime of depilatory powder[3] but thought nothing of it. Most of the shower cabins were occupied and clearly the cold water did not deter those wanting to get rid of a bit of unwanted hair here and there. But time dragged on, and I became anxious and knocked on her door. Parvin came straight out and without uttering a word went to her bed and pulled the blanket over her head. Minutes later I heard her sobbing quietly and went over and looked under her blanket. She gave me a look of pure hatred and pulled the blanket back over herself. I had never seen such a look of hate, and from someone with eyes as kind as Parvin's. Then she vomited and the sharp stench of lime, arsenic, acid, and bile exploded in our room. What have you done? I screamed. I didn't know what to do. I just yelled and yelled, and a number of girls ran over. Then I remembered someone who had a supply of anti-emetics. I ran over to her room and shook her awake.

"Give me some of your anti-sickness pills," I said in panic.

"Why? What do you want it for?" She was an argumentative girl.

"Just give them, damn you. I haven't time to explain," I said, exasperated by her calmness. "Parvin is vomiting all over the place. Just give them!"

"Why is that girl paying attention to the rubbish that comes out of that damned loudspeaker...?" I cut her short.

"This is no time for stupid polemics, just give the damned pills and shut up," I said, now almost shouting, and immediately regretted my words. I found Parvin squatting by the toilet retching. The entire place smelled of lime. How much had she swallowed? We rummaged in the bin and found the wrapper. It was empty. We banged and banged on the main door until a *pasdar* opened. She didn't believe us and had to see for herself.

"Stop wasting time, this is an emergency. We must get her to the infirmary now! Now!" I was now hysterical. Parvin had run back to the shower cabins and closed the door holding it inwards with all her might. When we managed to wrench it open, she clutched the pipes with both hands. One of us fell on

349

her knees and begged her to let go. She just clung on looking at us without seeing. Then Mehrangiz just walked over and with one blow on her wrist released her hands. Someone put the *chador* on her and Mehrangiz gripped both her hands tight as they approached the steps. Parvin just looked in a strange way at them as if she did not comprehend what was going on. Then an argument with the *pasdar* who refused to let Mehrangiz accompany her to the infirmary. Another girl, *chador* and blindfold already in place, just walked over and took Parvin's by the wrist and pulled her away, leaving the stunned *pasdar* helplessly looking on.

Next day was visiting day. Do we tell her family? Hours of agonising debate. She is still alive and it is her right to decide her own fate, some said. But the family also has a right to know, others, including me, argued back. In the end the second wave of prisoners going to the visitors' hall simply went ahead anyway and leaked the story to the family.

Next day I went to the office to ask how she was. Jabbari a *pasdar* was there.

"What is this Parvin, Parvin thing everyone is asking? That trash is dead" she said, mockingly and grinned. I lost all control.

"You bastards killed her. Parvin was a sister to me. She was my life. You. You stupid, evil bastards killed her," I was shouting and didn't care. Screaming, just saying anything that came into my head. Then they fell on me. I don't remember anything except the rain of blows from all sides on my head and body and the noise of broken glass. I saw a *pasdar* pulling Jabbari away. I returned back to the cell bruised and swollen.

A day later we heard that she had been transferred to a hospital outside, in the capital itself. We began to hope, even though a doctor, a fellow prisoner, thought the dose and the delay in treatment were bad omens. She died two or three days later. The entire block went into mourning. We decided on a protest hunger strike blaming the prison for her death. But even here each group or commune chose to do their own strike with their own declaration. Even what to do with the food we were refusing to eat was the subject of interminable debates. Our disjointed prison experience would have been funny if it wasn't so heart-breaking after such a tragic blow to our entire community. Parvin had been a mother figure for many of us, loved by all.[4]

350

[1] A film by François Truffaut. In a world where all books are burned, a secret group formed where each individual memorised a book and would pass that on to their offspring.

[2] Mehran Shahabeddin, was a Central Committee member and responsible for organisation in Rahe Kargar, (see footnote 42, chapter 17, Mamaqan and Appendix 3). After the revolution it rapidly grew to become one of the most influential left organisations in the country. He was executed in 1983 having withstood savage tortures.

[3] A mixture of lime and arsenic called *vaajebi* is traditionally used as a hair remover in Iran.

[4] Parvin Goli Abkenari was born near Anzeli in Gilan province in a politically active family. She was active in Rahe Kargar and was arrested along with her husband, Mehran, her brother Ruzbeh and a sister. They had only been married 40 days. Mehran and Ruzbeh, who became close friends in the Shah's prisons, were executed after severe torture. Both had gone to their deaths with their secrets intact. Parvin committed suicide in Evin on December 6, 1987.

Chapter 66

Bazargan and beyond

Ahmad

Leaving the country was no longer a choice. Even vehemently reluctant Jina was persuaded once a roll call of close friends disappeared into the Islamic inferno. Then it was a question of a chain of contacts: a colonel in the passport office who got him a new pass, with his new name, both Jina and Nina as companions, a couple in a second car driving ahead to check out the dangers ahead, a friend of Jina in her birthplace, Urumieh, on the shores of the salt lake with the same name, who had a friend in Bazargan customs with links to the border guards on the same crossing Ahmad had taken with the now dead Mehrdad four years, and half the book before, the promise of a safe crossing using a break when the *pasdars* go off to public prayers, a stay in the friend's house in Bazargan, man, wife and child sitting dawn to dusk for a week ready to leave, dressed and packed ready to depart at a moment's notice, conjuring up conversations with their hosts, then a dash, two border controls to navigate, municipal police (*Shahrbani*) and *Sepah Pasdaran*, the *Sepah* away talking to God, the municipal policeman, a mere wink and a smile, enjoy yourself (*khosh begzareh*), he winked a second time with the other eye and beamed, then navigating the Turkish side, the friendly customs official taking their dollars and some gold coins they had bought, passed it through a small window separating the two countries that they collected on the other side.

The whole thing was B-movie-unreal.

Just then Ahmad saw two brothers he knew from his time in prison in the old regime. Both were now working in one of Tehran's *komitehs*. What were they doing there? Did they see him? If so, they failed to recognise the moustachioless man. What a difference these landmark facial features make to your appearance. Almost miraculously the bus to Istanbul had just three empty seats left. He handed a cassette to the driver to play. It was a *bayat-e turk*. He could not hold back his tears. B-movie.

Within a month Ahmad was in Paris and mother and daughter in the US. Azadeh had used her connections to get him refugee status in a mere three days and had rented him a house in a Paris suburb. She later gate crashed into that house. Three years later and a turbulent relationship with Azadeh, what may once have been something masquerading as love became a battle for possession. A question of ownership. Not of things but of the person. But years of living inwards made Ahmad non-possessable.

"I have always got what I want," she once blurted with angry eyes. "You are the only thing in my life that denied me that," she said, almost spitting the words, and she was not wrong.

How do you describe the unique road to a failed relationship? As that Russian hermit-sage wrote a century earlier, all relationships break down uniquely. What goes on in their head is churned through so many mutations in its journey into the world that it ultimately translates into something uniquely personal, and probably false. One can only ask questions. Why had he not confronted his feelings earlier? Perhaps his weakness, his total inability to express his true feelings, taking the national trait of *ta'arof* [1] to an absurdity, wanting to always project an image of benevolence. Who knows how either side saw the relationship? Perhaps it was doomed before it started. He felt trapped. She felt betrayed. There could be no dialogue, only war. His weakness, his inability to say no and hurt someone's feelings, boiled inwards until it burst into a volcanic no. She, with her total belief in herself, which at times took on the appearance of recklessness, never forgave him for the denial. It was now a film noir in the hands of amateurs.

I met him for the first time outside Tottenham Court Road underground station.

[1] A very Iranian custom to offer or say something without really meaning it. The recipient is meant to recognise and differentiate *ta'arof* from a genuine offer and politely turn it down.

Chapter 67

Joy of spring

Nayyer

That year, 1988, the spring equinox was at 2 pm. Mother and Roqiyyeh, who had always walked through the invisible walls, led the way to a joint celebration of *Eid* and for once the absurd barriers were blown away. It was my seventh *Eid*. Most of us showered and put on whatever unworn clothes we had. At the moment of equinox we all ran out into the corridor and embraced. Suddenly I felt Parvin's absence, as did her close friend who I saw sitting in a corner quietly weeping. A momentary gloom and then it was our turn to use the courtyard. I ran out the moment they opened the gate, suddenly feeling claustrophobic within the milling crowd of girls. A basketball was lying around. Perhaps it had belonged to cell block two. Within minutes we had two teams. Giggles and shouts. It was sunny and pleasantly warm. Exhausted after half an hour of vigorous ball play, we turned to a vaulting game. More giggles and shouts. We had almost forgotten what it meant to have fun. Then the last rays of sun jumped over the top of the wall, and we sat down to sing. Someone from cellblock one sang back, and we moved closer to the wall. Fazilat[1] from our side sang songs of spring in her angelic voice and was echoed back by the invisible voice inside. Our laughter and singing had brought a momentary cheer to their ever-gloomy block, Mona, our artist who was in their cellblock told me later.

Then back to normality. The Iraqis were daily targeting Tehran with rockets.

I heard the explosions and through the narrow gap between the two metal bars on our only window, which I could access by squeezing between two beds and climbing to the top, I had a view of the sky and parts of Tehran, and a young boy on a roof flying his pigeons from a small coop. I watched them circling up and up into the sky, higher and higher, free, and then spiralling down to their boy-master. Occasionally I saw a plume of smoke rising from some house or other. The television news was full of boastful claims of victory, but our visitors told us a different tale. The city was in a panic, they told. Those who could leave had moved north of the Alborz Mountains, or to another town or village or even camped in the desert. The daily sirens did the talking. I saw an Iraqi plane dive down towards the city one day followed by an explosion not far from us. We were hastily herded back into our cells.

Earlier, Hossein Zadeh, the prison governor had called us prisoners one by one to his office, men and women, asking our views on religion, the Islamic Republic and Marxism.

"You can say whatever you like. The air is heavy with democracy these days," he mocked. He had a sickly-green grin. "But we'll see about that," he said, looking straight into my eyes. The menacing look passed over me, undeciphered. I had seen it so many times. We shall see about that, he muttered, this time to himself. We did not take his not-too veiled threats seriously.

When Ramadan came round that spring, a month into the new year, some of us decided that, since we were not fasting, we would not take the early morning *sahari* pre-dawn meal and unless they respected our rights and fed us as before at breakfast time, we would go without food all day until the *eftari* meal at dusk. After many years of prison, they should respect our minimal rights, we felt. We made our demands in writing and the authorities simply stopped bringing the morning *sahari*. One meal a day it was.

A day before Ramadan there had been a major reshuffle. Some Mojahedin prisoners from cellblock one, all carrying either a life sentence or were under a death sentence, were taken to solitary and the remainder redistributed around Evin. There was an even greater reshuffle on the male side. We heard they had completely emptied *Gohardasht* prison, in the outskirts of Karaj, from female political prisoners. We tried, but failed, to see a pattern.

I had slowly, emotionally, matured over the last few years. My old friend Goli had been transferred back from *Gohardasht*, but she had lost her old joyfulness and zest in the collective punishments out there. I no longer felt possessive, no longer felt jealous when I saw Goli, through my tiny window to the courtyard, in an intense relationship with another inmate, Setareh.[2] Whenever she was with Setareh, Goli smiled and laughed and that made me happy too. They were now so close that they dressed identically, like twins. It was sometimes difficult to distinguish them. Such deep relationships were not uncommon. You needed to hang on to something to maintain your sanity, be it belief or love. I too developed intense relationships.

We laughed, we giggled, we loved, we lived, we learnt from one another, we leant on one another, we grew in one another. It was not all gloom. It was not all pain. It was a university that had no visible end, but a university of women who shared a past and shared a present and did not have a visible future. Pain, separation, disappointment, and even death hung over us, but so did deep friendship, love and a shared experience that tore into the very essence of what it means to be human.

One night I counted three separate shots, a few seconds apart, after a burst of machine gun fire. Three prisoners from the left, shot.[3] Even then none of us had any idea of the deep crevice ahead.

[1] Fazilat Allameh, Mojahedin, was executed late summer 1988.
[2] We last saw Setareh lying helpless on a blanket in a corridor with her small son helping her to the toilet. See Chapter 45, *My interrogation*.
[3] Sa'id Azhang (Tudeh) and Anushiravan Lotfi (Fadai' Majority) were executed that night, Spring 1988.

Chapter 68

The cull

Nayyer

That summer the cull began.

The two o'clock news on that hot July day was brief and unambiguous. Iran had accepted UN Resolution 598. Khomeini had drunk the poisoned chalice, as he put it. The eight-year war was over, but no one was celebrating. In our coop the air weighed heavy with doom. It felt really suffocating. Rumours were circulating that the Mojahedin had crossed the Iraqi border, armed by Saddam Hossein.

A few days later all visiting was stopped until further notice. Never before had they stopped visits for the entire prison and across the whole country. Then newspapers stopped coming and a few days later they took away the television. We were cut off from the outside world, effectively sealed off. Entombed.

But we needed to breathe even if the air you breathed had the smell of death. I was teaching English to one of the girls I think, sitting cross-legged, our only book in English open in front of us when the loudspeaker called out the names of three Mojaheds. They stood up, went over to their corner for their chador and blindfold. One of them looked over to us with an eerie smile escaping from the corner of her mouth, as if she was unsure if that was the right reaction. A strange feeling of trepidation passed back and forth between us, but we didn't walk over and say goodbye. None of us really understood what was happening. Maybe we thought they would be back. But they had packed their belongings. Maybe they are being transferred to another cellblock. They said nothing. They had been told nothing, but that was not unusual. Then why didn't this feel like previous partings? Somehow more permanent. They left and we went back to our lesson. On the surface nothing had happened. Nothing had. Except for that foggy fear in the air.

Over the airwaves, the ubiquitous loudspeaker was relaying the Friday prayers. Words. Words. Words of hate. Words of how they had crushed the invasion and destroyed the Mojahedin. A prominent *mullah* was shouting into the microphone: …that woman, one of these *monafeqin*,[1] blew up a hand grenade in her face so we wouldn't recognise her filthy, ugly face. I pictured him gloating, his beard bobbing, his face contorted with loathing, ugly, cruel. I felt nauseous.

Then another group was called out. Where to? We still didn't know. That afternoon the courtyard was unusually subdued. No walking, no chatter, just whispers, when one of the girls who had been taken away that morning entered the yard. I saw her run to her friends who were squatting in a cluster in the far corner, her black *chador* flying behind her like the wings of a raven. She had pushed back her blindfold onto her forehead, and you could see her terrified eyes from the far end of the courtyard and physically see the terror spreading out of those eyes and enveloping all the others. A few minutes later she was called away again. Was it some technical error or had they deliberately brought her back to spread fear? Her story froze us.

That morning after leaving us they were taken to a place where a large number of men and women were waiting. Waiting to be seen by a judge. They were asked a few simple questions. Which group do you belong to? What do you think of the Islamic Republic? What are your views on the *velayate faqih*?[2] Their replies were written down. These questions, they were assured, were for the purpose of organising a pardon. They were then led one by one in front of a judge who asked a few more questions and wrote down his judgement there and then. If you said you were a Mojahed rather than *monafeq*, no further questions were asked. From there they were then taken to another place. Some were told they are being transferred to *Gowhardasht* prison. They even showed them a piece of paper as evidence. Only a few fell for that story.

I still see the look of abject terror in those light brown eyes, showing so much white, as our messenger was led out.

The cull had begun. Some nights, in the middle of the night, we heard shots. Most were just strung up. Cooped up in our corner, no papers, no television, no news, we had no idea of the extent of the slaughter. We sat there numbed. Few talked and when we did it was in whispers, as if we were in hiding from death. Did anyone know what we were going through? From the crack between the iron bars, the only window to the world beyond, I saw balloons being hoisted over Luna Park. It was the International Exhibition, now back in Tehran after the ceasefire. The young boy on the roof was still flying his pigeons. They flitted up and free and down to their cage. I had watched my pigeon-boy going through his routine, day in and day out for weeks since I had moved here and discovered my sliver of a window to the world. Now even the sky seemed to be dark-blue or was that just my imagination. Life was normal out there. Did anyone care?

Months later those of us who had survived pieced together what had happened from our families. Through the summer and autumn, they, our families, had besieged the prisons every day, in every city, every town, across the country, morning to dusk. Then, after weeks and weeks of anxiety, of fear, of dread, of frantically running from one place to the next, they had been handed the belongings of their loved ones. All jumbled up. The butchers must have just thrown everything in a pile and just picked bits and pieces at random. Some just had a sac thrown over the wall into their courtyard. None of them ever saw the bodies of their sons, daughters, husbands, wives, grandchildren, their loved ones who were buried in mass graves. How many had been massacred? There are no records. At least 3,000. Maybe 12,000. Only history will know.[3]

From our small corner they took every single Mojahed woman. The last group were brought back. There were simply too many people waiting to see

360

the judge. They were given a form to fill. Questions about their views and of the prison. They too were told it is for the purpose of seeing whom they could pardon. By now no one fell for that lie. For days they waited out their fate. Maybe there was a glimmer of hope. Every time a *pasdar* appeared my heart would sink. Then the moment came. As they read the names, one person was left out, Mahin Qorbani. She was left behind. Anxiously she walked up and down. Why had they not called her? She was a veteran of prison and had spent her entire time here in punishment cells. She had lost her belief in the Mojahedin and had drawn closer to the left but, not wanting to openly break with her old friends, had kept herself to herself. White strands had appeared in her hair and her young face had prematurely aged. Now her loneliness was more intense, the guilt of not accompanying her former comrades on their journey. She decided to protest at her exclusion if her name is not called over the next few days. It was. She ran to greet death with a smile. True to her name, she was yet another *qorbani*, (sacrifice).[4]

[1] *Pleural of monafeq*: A derogatory term used to refer to the Mojahedin, meaning someone who creates dissension and splits among the faithful (*ummat*). It is often translated as hypocrite.

[2] Article 5 of the Constitution, gives the Supreme Leader, at that time Khomeini, absolute control over all religious and civil matters in the country. The *Vali Faqih* has the last word on everything.

[3] The figures range from over 2,500 according to Amnesty International to 33,000 given by a defector from the regime after the 2009 Green uprising. The true figure is difficult to know as many were executed in Kurdistan and Baluchestan and other provinces and buried in mass graves. A report, which is widely accepted to be near the truth, puts the number as 12,000. See N. Mohajer, 'The Mass Killings in Iran', Arash 57 (August 1996 in Farsi): 7, quoted in Abrahamian, *Tortured Confessions*, (1999).

[4] Mahin Qorbani was executed in 1988. In Farsi Qorbani means sacrifice.

Chapter 69

Death by instalments

Nayyer

One day while we were sitting down to lunch, they came over and put two questions to us: 'Do you pray?' 'Will you interview on camera?' One by one we put down our spoons and said a resounding no to both and joined the queue for death. The two who had said yes did so with such anger that the man from the judiciary doubted his ears. Our group had shrunk but on the surface prison life went on as normal. Classes every morning, promptly at 8, like school. Enforced silence after lunch. Cleaning and tidying schedules. Surface calm. Then night and ghosts of darkness. Sleep broken up by cries and shrieks or just the subdued moan of someone's invisible dream. We would jump and seek the terror, breaking her nightmare with a glass of water. And hands. Holding hands. Then back to normality.

Life outside was also back to normal. I could hear the shrieks and laughter of children playing in the Luna Park, or the pigeon boy's birds spiralling daily above the roof. I would watch the dusk covering my city between those bars. The large balloons of the now resumed International Exhibition, one of them with the British flag, floating upwards reaching for the sky and mountain. On Fridays I could see lines of men and women climbing the foothills of Alborz, like we did all those years ago. Did the outside world know what went on here? Did they care or were we outside the focus of caring? The forgotten generation? With so much happening in the world, the miners'

362

strike in England, the Sandinista peace talks in Nicaragua, the Farabundo Marti Front fighting in El Salvador, the Palestinians still struggling for their rights, had these and more exhausted the attention span of the people who are fighting for human rights? Were we still in the human orbit? In those moments I felt desperately alone. Rightly or not, I felt totally abandoned by the world.

The judiciary closer to home had not forgotten us, though. Every once in a while, they would come and ask questions that required only a yes or no. Do you pray? Will you face the camera? Another time they took all the lifers and interrogated them for hours before returning them. They too had introduced themselves as the Committee of Pardon.

We got hold of a cutting from a newspaper smuggled in from cellblock two, where they were now allowed, and read that the spokesman of the Supreme Judicial Council, after some colourful insults to communists had said that 'after the *monafeqin*' it's the turn of infidels, meaning us on the left, and asked for the 'maximum punishment'. We read this and fought inwards to disbelieve our eyes and push it aside.

It was early August, and the summer heat was at its suffocating peak. A Bahai' woman was brought to our cell. She described it to us, but we did not believe her until news from cellblock two confirmed it. This is how the ritual went for communist women who did not pray. The judge's sentence was a clear choice: die under the lash or pray.

Starting at dawn with the sound of the *muezzin*, the cell door would open. The prisoner would be taken to the corridor and laid out on a bench. Five lashes. Back to the cell and the next cell door would open and the ritual repeated and the next and the next …. Then it would start all over again after the noon call to prayer, again at about 4, then again at 8 and the last one at about midnight. Twenty-five lashes in five instalments, day after day, till death do them part.

At the beginning Mojtaba, the ugly-green *pasdar*, did the whipping by himself. Locked inside their cells, the girls would hear the whistle of the

363

whip tearing the air and the squeak of the bench when the whip whipped round the body of their friend. Later other *pasdars* joined in, male and female. They even forced Yousefi, an old woman, overruling her objection that she doesn't know how to wield the whip. Whipping the infidel to make them pray would take them closer to heaven.

The turn of our block came. They called out seven or eight names, all either Tudeh or Fadai' Majority supporters. We said our tearful farewells. They came back before noon. They had each been called into the judge and asked, 'are you a Moslem?' and 'do you pray'. One by one they had replied in the negative and had been sentenced: death by flogging or contrition. All of them had there and then declared a dry hunger strike. That was unbelievably brave. The flogging was to begin that same noon. They took them away.

From then on, every time we heard the voice of the call to prayer, we would freeze in our steps imagining the screech of the whip through the air. It was the waiting between the lashes, they told us later, which was agonising. And sleep deprivation. They could not sleep at night. The time gap between the last and the early morning was only about three and a half to four hours. So, they tried to catch some sleep between dawn and noon, a longer respite. A couple of weeks later they came and took another group, but they were brought back that afternoon because their turn to see the judge had not come. The next morning, they dressed waiting to be called but no call came. So, it went on for a few days. The girls would put on their best clothes and wait. One of them with a sense of humour shouted: "Hey, *pasdar* what happened to our whipping?" Finally, they were called. It was September when schools start and she jokingly quipped as she left: "We are off to school *bacheha*, we'll either pass or fail."

Time slowed right down. While we waited anxiously for them, each of us did something to distract ourselves. One made a carpet trellis between two bed posts; another patiently designed a complex pattern for knitting. Two of the girls insisted on sewing a dress for me out of a pair of trousers. There is no way you can get enough material from that for a dress, I said, but they went ahead anyway. I had to stand still for an hour every day as they moved the cloth this way and that over my body. In the end the dress was a real misfit. We read and re-read the only book we had, *Les Misérables*. Then someone suggested we recite from memory a book we had read. Laleh had an amazing memory and could recite in detail a book she had read, not just recite but retell it in a most engaging manner. That is how we listened to Aleksey Tolstoy's trilogy *Road to Calvary* and later Romain Rolland's long novel, *Jean-Christophe*, in her warm mesmerising voice every evening, like Scheherazade in the *Thousand and one Nights* with the same threat of doom hanging over us.

And daytime we joked mostly about the whipping.

"I will tie a pillow to my back and pretend I am a hunchback," one said.

"I have made a shield from tin cans. When the whip hits it, the twang would make them thinks they had done a good job," said another.

"They only whip girls whose parents are Moslem," another interrupted. "Otherwise, you are not a *mortad*, an apostate."[1]

"That's, good" I said, "I will tell them my parents were Marxists." The girls were shocked. "Don't worry, I added they are both dead and cannot be whipped."

"But they may ask you about your grandparents," another quipped. I hadn't thought of that. Then I had an idea. "I would tell them they were utopian socialists!" I replied excitedly.

In the corner of the courtyard Sharareh was worrying with a friend what would happen to Eshrat who was one of the longest *mellikesh* prisoners, someone who remained locked up despite finishing their sentence.

"How could she inject her insulin in such circumstances?" Eshrat had diabetes. Roghieh, who earlier in the year had organised the *Eid* celebrations, was passing by and on hearing their concerns burst out laughing.

"Let me tell you a story," Roghieh began with her customary broad grin showing her uneven teeth. "There were once a couple who couldn't have children. One day they sat down and started a game of imagining. Let's imagine you are pregnant, the man said. She nodded and saw her tummy grow and grow and grow. I'm going to give birth, she replied, and went silent. A few minutes later she cried out, look! nine months and nine days and nine hours have gone by, and I am really big, and oh my God, I am going into labour. He looked over with a serious look. You gave birth to a girl, he said. What shall we call her? Safieh is a nice name, he said. And Safieh she was, and Safieh grew and becomes a beautiful young maiden, and a nice man comes asking for her hand, and they have a big marriage and invite everyone from their village and the twin village up the hill, and very soon Safieh becomes pregnant, her belly grows, and then, nine months, later she suddenly bleeds. Just bleeds and bleeds. Safieh is on death's door. Both parents start wailing, and beating their head and their chest, crying, 'woe onto us if Safieh dies, woe onto us…' They were laughing so much we all went down the courtyard. Laughter forgets pain.

[1] In *sharia* law, apostates, Moslems who had renounced their fate, deserve death

Chapter 70

More names

Nayyer

I woke one morning to someone crying, a cry like the voice of death, like something emanating from an inner hell. Tears of despair, an infinite rope of pain twisting through that putrid air of despair. The cry came from below us and tore into me. There was such pain in that cry. It was Nazi, I later found. For days her back had born the whips until the never-ending pain became unbearable. She capitulated and with a few others was taken to cellblock one, immediately below us. At each prayer time, a *pasdar* would stand by the door of their cell and watch her pray, five times a day, witnessing the crushing of her spirit.

Ozra, the feisty girl who had, way back in time, refused to sleep in the same cell as the *tavvabs* and stubbornly slept in the corridor,[1] resisted for thirteen days, then found a way to cut her wrists. They stitched her at the infirmary and the next day resumed the whipping. After a few days she too gave in. For some years Ozra had been put under particular pressure by the security chief of Evin, Zamani. He had singled her out, maybe because of her forceful defence of her beliefs, or perhaps because of her stunning beauty. He had resolved to crack this arrogant young woman, first through debates, and when she had realised the trap that was set for her and refused to cooperate, through repeated whipping and solitary confinement. And now the five-a-day whipping schedule. Like many others Ozra stopped praying

367

the moment the pressures were lifted.

Mahin had been alone for years. She had borne ten months in the coffin without cracking, but afterwards she became a loner. She would eat alone; she would sit by herself and after a while she stopped talking. She was in the cell next to mine and whenever I went there her silent presence was like a scream and shamed me in my chatter and laughter. She never protested. Never. Nothing made her happy. Nothing made her sad. She just sat withdrawn, as if all emotions had melted away out of her. Sometimes I would doubt if she was aware of what was going on around her. But she saw. You could see that in the anxious looks in her eyes that bloody summer. We worried she might commit suicide and would watch her carefully. If she did not come out of the shower quickly, someone would go in on some pretext or other. If she locked herself in, they would climb the next cubicle. A number of times they stopped her cutting her wrist. At her last attempt, she pulled her cut wrist away angrily. They were forced to call the *pasdar*. They shouldn't have but there was no choice. She killed herself in the infirmary. They killed her. The beautiful face of Mahin Badui'i was a silent scream.

There were many others. Ra'fat, with her blue eyes framed by her pale childish face, took hair removal cream and died. She had been one of those Mojahedin who had pretended to be a *tavvab* while secretly smuggling news of the prison out. Her second interrogation had unbalanced her mind. She kept herself separate. Most of the time we would find her in the shower room, her trouser legs rolled up, washing herself or a dish. Her brother too had hung himself in prison.

Then the news came that the head of prison had been changed. Forutan was back. For two weeks they had not taken anyone to the kangaroo court. Then they brought our girls back, walking skeletons. For 22 days they had borne the lash and continued their hunger strike, only ceasing when they had a period. Two (Mahtab and Nadin) were no more than skin and bones. In the last week they were unconscious and were woken up by kicks and the whip. In the final days they could not walk to the corridor and were whipped in their cell. Mahtab could not remember anything of the last days. When asked, do you pray, she could only manage a lifting of her eyebrow. What hurt most was the intense thirst, she said. The dripping tap in the cell winked at her. One day she woke up soaked in water. Had she drunk or was that perspiration? One night she had heard a male voice from above singing the beautiful song, 'elaheye naz'. Was this a hallucination? Was it real? But hearing it reassured her she is still alive. How powerful the urge to live is in humans.

But Soheila never came back. There was a rumour that one of the girls had hung herself. Was it Soheila? I never found out. Maybe she had died under the lash. Her mother, once visiting resumed, kept asking about her. Her sad, thoughtful, tender face remains with me. Our Soheila had cried for hours in silence when Parvin had committed suicide.

Names, names, I have to remember their names. I am living. I can talk. I can write. I can record.

Must remember.

More names.

All their names.

Must remember.

Must talk, must recall, must record. They all deserve to be remembered. Their names, for ever…

[1] See chapter 64, *Ozra*

Chapter 71

Epilogue

Nayyer

It was early October when the *pasdar* of our cellblock collected the phone numbers of our family. Visiting was to resume. It signalled the end of that summer and autumn of doom. Then the extent of the horror opened up to us. The first visitors were in tears, begging us to compromise, not to throw away our lives unnecessarily. Every day for three months they had been knocking on this door and that door trying to find out our fate and left empty handed. Now they gave us the names. Every girl that came back from the visiting hall came back with names. They couldn't have killed all of them. But names. More names. An endless line of names. They were throwing the belongings, all jumbled up, one by one. In some provinces just throwing the sac over the wall into their courtyard. One by one, names. As the girls came back more names.

- They delivered Shahla's things
- Belongings of Zohreh's husband
- Fati's brother.
- Effat's husband.
- Nazli's brother.
- Maryam's husband
- Farideh's husband….

- They returned Farah Vafai's things
  - Shurangiz Karimi's
  - Mehri Ghanatabadi's
  - Zohreh Haj-Aghai'...

Each name was a blow in a suffocating silence. We asked each other how it was possible. Then more names

- They have also given Leila Hajian's
- And Ghamar Azkia
- And Effat Khoi'
- And Maryam Talebi
- And Farzaneh Zolfi, the girl who had been locked up for seven months in a toilet.
- Also Soheila Rahimi...

On and on like the line up to hell. You mean we have to believe that they had murdered everyone that went from our cell block and cell block one? I told myself there must be some still alive somewhere. After all, why kill Fatemeh? She was only a child. A mere supporter. And disabled. She had already finished her prison term. She had just married. She was like my little sister, my daughter. I used to teach her English. Could they have murdered this little angel too? I told Goli she must be lurking in some corner. They can't have murdered her. They had. And all fifty Mojaheds from our cell block, and another 200 or so from cell block one and two.

We learnt later that they had been hanged. The Mojahedin who answered the question 'what charge?' replied Mojahed and not *monafeq* were sent to their deaths immediately. Some, like Ashraf, were beaten before being hanged. Fazilat was lashed prior to being strung up. One of the prisoners in cellblock two had seen her husband and two other girls with their *chador* wound round their necks hoisted up. It had been their turn next, but they had been returned to their cells. She had agreed to anything they demanded.

They asked communist prisoners if they were Moslem. A no or ambiguous answer was a death sentence. In *Gohardasht*, after the cursory court they went to join the line on the left. While waiting to be executed they saw a *pasdar* with a wheelbarrow full of prison slippers. They saw Naserian walking around a

371

lorry with a disinfectant spray. They used cranes for hanging. They drove the Mojaheds by lorry loads and hanged them on cranes in batches while the others watched. A prisoner saw a huge pile of brown and grey plastic slippers outside a door. Another looked into a hall and saw dead bodies hanging by dark-blue plastic ropes from hooks like butchered meat. They piled the dead in large containers perched on trailers, normally used for carrying dead meat, to be buried in unmarked mass graves.

We did not cry. Even those of us who lost a brother or husband did not cry. Thereafter you did not hear any laughter or happy games. A cloud of doom and guilt descended on the survivors of the cataclysmic deathstorm. The guilt of staying alive. A guilt with which I will have to live until my turn comes.

When I finally got a visit, my family begged me to stop my obstinacy and not waste my youth.

"Just sign the damn thing. It is only a sentence. They will do it again. They will kill you. They will." They begged, they cried. Just sign. No one outside cares anymore. They will understand, everyone's family begged and cried. You stubborn idiot, Naserian sneered, we can kill you anytime. And the prison authorities bullied, threatened, and sneered and some were incredulous at our attitude.

They are heathens, one *pasdar* said to another outside my cell. It was her only explanation. That's what heathens do, incomprehensible, irrational, evil.

Slowly some of the girls made some minor concessions and went out. I didn't. Two grey years. And six months in solitary again. There was nothing to recant. They had taken my youth, my joy, my enthusiasm. But they could never take my spirit. Nor my love. He was with me when I was happy, and he was with me when I was down. He was with me when I was in that cold, dark, solitary, dirty, tiny room, freezing the winter months. He was with me in my less cold, solitary cell with a window to the sky. He was with me back with others, locked up, counting the minutes they would let us out to the toilet, bladder squirming with urgency. He was with me when I embroidered with coloured thread from some cloth or other a lake with a bird flitting upwards from the reeds towards the sun whose rays came down towards me reflected on the water. He was there. Everywhere.

I got out two years later. They gave me a home visit, a leave. I never went back. I had not signed.

Chapter 72

Walk in the paradise garden

Ahmad saw them walking hand in hand. They were walking on the periphery of that garden. A large lawn separated them from the others signalling that they wanted to be alone. After 11 years. Asqar was walking with his head lowered as if he was trying to catch every word she was saying before it escaped into the air. The early morning summer air was pregnant with life but the two walked as lovers everywhere, oblivious to the sounds of the living world. They gave the impression to Ahmad of talking love. He turned away not wanting to disturb their compact even through the waves of seeing. Then he saw her face as she turned and knew.

Ahmad is right. It was not about love that I was speaking to my Asqar, though love was enveloping us. I was talking about *Haji*. And Asqar knew about the *gavdooni*. Everyone there knew about the cowshed, the *gavdooni*, the room below the *hashti*, the vestibule. It is like knowing about pain. It was like knowing about the trenches. It is like knowing about hell. But here was someone in the flesh who had been to hell and had come out talking in a soft voice. You could not talk in a loud voice about the place where the only sounds were of whip and shouts. Where the only movement was that of the boot, or the whip or of pain. Where the only light was inside you. I was telling him of the *gavdooni* and as I was telling him tears were dripping down his cheeks onto his clean blue collar and into his open shirt watering the few strands of dark black hair I saw poking up, trying to breath the clean morning summer air in that place east of Berlin where we had gathered for a congress and where I saw my Asqar after nine years of prison and two years of trying to get out of that country that had swallowed my youth. My eyes were dry. The subterranean ocean of tears had dried up long ago. I needed the rain of love to replenish it. And to tell the tale of how a generation of hope and love had been squashed. This is what I told my Asqar.

Some of the girls stayed the full course. The full ten months. All were damaged permanently. Some committed suicide. Few could create a lasting relationship with another person. The cowshed had taken away the thing that makes us human, our social nature. A few remained human.

Nayyer walked and talked and all the time she looked straight ahead at some other world, eyes dry, mouth dry. She did not see the stream of water pouring out of Asqar's light brown eyes, trickling down his cheek, watering his greying moustache and then dripping like an icy stalactite, on his blue shirt. Salty water was carrying a message to a distant sea. A message where love and anger, circling one another in a dance to the death, was trying to message someone who was not there but who may listen, someday, somewhere. Anywhere.

As she spoke the ghosts and screams escaped into the air and spread until they filled all space and all time, and as they stretched love, that too became fragmented in memory and both bound and separated the lovers, and us and bound us and separates us and all that will come after.

*

Ahmad walked silently on that yellowing grass. That was the moment he knew that, like the hermit Miron's prayer Gorki's grandmother recited in the kitchen, the road ahead for mankind was endless and what he had to say, and what he had to do was also without end.[1] The oak tree would grow from a sapling to a forest and the tasks at hand would remain unfinished.

And the birds sang their songs of seduction. And the earth rolled along in its perpetual motion through space oblivious to the beauties and pain.

[1] Maxim Gorki, *My Childhood.*

Appendix 1

Glossary of Farsi words

ab-enbar basement water storage

ablamboo squeezed pomegranate, the juice is then sucked through a hole

akhund another name for a mullah, a Muslim cleric

amu jan uncle dear

aqa gentleman, sir

araq Iranian-made vodka

artist bazi clever manoeuvring (slang)

asheqam I am in love (*ashiq = in love*)

astaqforellah God forgive me (Arabic)

bacheh child

bandari relating to the ports north side of the Persian Gulf

baq orchard

befarma'id greeting, welcome, come in

be vallahe swear to God

bichareh wretch, hapless, poor

bi dar-o-peikar without restrictions

chai tea

chai khooneh tea house

chador shapeless piece of cloth covering entire body but the face

Eid Nowruz Iranian new year starting with the Spring equinox.

engareh metallic holder for tea glasses

enshallah God willing

estekan small tea glass

Fadai' Organisation of Peoples Fadai' Guerrillas

haji someone who had performed the Haj pilgrimage

Hakem Shar' religious judge

hamvelayati someone coming from the same provinces

haft sin decorative spread for Eid, containing seven edible items,

halabiabad literally 'tin town' – shanty towns encircling cities

havakhori open air exercise breaks in prison

hejab (or hijab) *compulsory* covering of hair and other exposed parts of women

Hojatoleslam Shia' priest – one level below ayatollah in the clerical hierarchy

Hosseinieh chapel-like, for prayer and sermons.

jenayat murder

kaka brother

Kanun Vokala Society of Jurists

kargar worker – in prison it was the name of those on the cleansing rota

khanum Mrs or Miss

kharabkar literally: saboteur, the term used for Fadai' and other groups

khasegari asking for someone's hand in marriage

khasteh nabashid 'hope you are not tired' – a common way to express sympathy

khoobi, khooband you/they are well (question-answer to 'how are you?')

khoresht bademjan aubergine (egg plant) stew made with lamb or chicken

khosh amadi welcome

komeil prayer an all-night lamentation usually performed on Thursdays

korsi quilt covered brazier used to sleep under for warmth in winter

kor a religious term for enough water for purification

lubiapolo dish made of rice and haricot

madar mother

maqna'eh a particularly concealing head covering only showing the face

mellikesh literally: nationalised – nickname for those kept in at end of their sentence.

mirab person who controls the sharing of water

mohandess engineer

Mojahedin People's Mojahedin Organisation of Iran – founded in 1965

mojdeh good news

monafeq "hypocrite" – used for Muslims who sew division among the faithful

mortad apostate

muezzin the person who calls out to prayer

Muharram the first month in the Islamic year and of mourning for the Shia'

nahr stream, brook

najess unclean (in a religious sense)

nalbeki saucer

nan berenji rice cookies

Pasdaran Revolutionary Guards (made up of pasdar)

pasdar revolutionary guard (singular)

pashur a ditch encircling house ponds, allowing overflow to drain offprint

paroq a haunt, place that someone frequents

Paykar the name taken by the Marxist (Maoist) split from the Mojahedin

pesar son

pesaram my son

Pishgam the student organisation of the Fadai'

qahveh-khaneh coffee house, frequented by people for tea, smoke and food

qahvehchi someone who serves in a tea house (*qahveh-khaneh*)

qalyan hookah

qannadi patisserie

qanat underground aqueducts - conveyed water over long distances

salak cutaneous leishmaniasis

salam greetings

salvat Islamic salutation to God, the prophet and his offspring

samovar a kettle-like device for making tea – originated in Russia

sangak a flat bread baked on hot stones in an oven

saraydar concierge

Sepah short for *Sepah-e Pasdaran* – Khomeini's Revolutionary Guards

Setad headquarters

shahrbani municipal police

sharr evil

shirinee cookie

Shoraye Enqelab Revolutionary Council – the highest state organ after the revolution

sofreh tablecloth, spread on the ground in more traditional homes

susul commonly used slang for spoilt upper-class men and women - haughty

tabrizi poplar tree

taftoon oven-baked flat bread

taklif religious duty

ta'rof the Iranian habit of repeatedly offering something or complimenting

ta'zir Islamic punishment

tavvab penitent (in the religious sense)

velayat province

Velayat-e Faqih rule of the jurisprudence – the Constitutional article that gives the Supreme Leader absolute power in the Islamic Republic.

vozu ritual washing before daily prayer

Yalda Night longest night of the year – celebrated in Iran from pre-Islamic times

zire-hasht an area just inside the main gate of every prison block

Appendix 2

Selected names

pn = pseudonym

Main characters

Ahmad (pn) Architect, revolutionary – exiled
Azadeh (pn) lawyer, friend and briefly lover of Ahmad – exiled
Changiz Changiz Ahmadi – executed IRI summer 1983
Fakhri (pn) Ahmad's uncle
Jina (pn) Architect, married to Ahmad – exiled
Nayyer (pn) political prisoner – exiled
Nina (pn) Daughter of Ahmad and Jina – exiled
Ra'na (pn) Uncle Fakhri's wife
Shahla (pn) 35-year old woman whose husband was in prison
Tal'at Ahmad's sister

Ahmad Chapters

Aqa-Reza Caretaker to Ahmad's apartment bloc in Vanak district of Tehran
Hassan Hassan Atarifard, childhood friend, deceased
Hossein-the-poet *(pn)* Friend from Khorramshahr, poet, manager of Rasht office
Houshang Close childhood friend from Khorramshahr
Mansur Mansur Khaksar, childhood friend, poet, Fadai', exiled, committed

suicide

Mansureh Mansureh Kaviani, childhood friend

Mehrdad Mehrdad Pakzad, ex-army counterintelligence, Fadai', executed June 1985

Rahim (pn) Artist, theatre director and writer – exiled

Reza Reza Kianian, part of Sa'id Soltanpour's theatre group

Sa'id Soltanpour Poet, playwright, Fadai', executed Islamic regime June 1981

Sara *(pn)* The family's choice for marriage

Sia Siaksar Berelian, set Tehran University Chancellor's car alight, exiled

Yashar (pn) Playwright and director – exiled

Changiz Chapters

Khadijeh Khadijeh Arfa', wife of Changiz, Rahe Kargar, executed 1983

Mamaqan Abdollah Afsari, founder of Rahe Kargar, executed IRI May 1983

Mamali (pn) Artist, ex Rahe Kargar, - exiled

Mehdi Mehdi Khosrowshahi Baradaran, Nayyer's brother see below

Nayyer Chapters

Asqar Asqar Izadi, Nayyer's love and future partner

Azar Azar Latifi, Fadai' minority, executed December 1981

Ashraf Mojahedin, whipped before being hanged in summer 1988

Banafsheh Survivor of 10 months in the 'cowshed' and 'coffins'

Cheshmeh Baby in prison with her mother

Eshrat Fellow prisoner

Farah Farah Vafai' nicknamed *Farah Hamoumi,* executed summer 1988

Farzaneh Zolf Locked up 7 months in a toilet, executed summer 1988

Fatemeh Young Mojahed, finished her sentence, learning English, executed 1988

Fazilat Fazilat Allameh, Mojahedin, lovely voice, executed summer 1988

Fereshteh A friend from the 'Cowshed' days, later a *tavvab*

Giti Victim of 'coffins'

Goli Close friend from before prison

Golnaz Met during initial interrogation

Laleh Fellow prisoner

Mahin Qorba Mojahed, executed summer 1988

Mahin Mahin Badui'i, survivor of 'coffins', committed suicide 1988

Mahtab Survivor of the five-times-a-day whipping

Maryam Maryam Fatemi, Peikar, executed March 1982

Marzieh Girl with bladder irritability

Mehdi Her brother Mehdi Khosrowshahi Baradaran, Mojahed, then Rahe Kargar, executed 1981

Mehran Mehan Shahbeddin, ex-SAVAK prisoner, CC Rahe Kargar, executed 1983

Mehrangiz Fellow prisoner Evin prison

Mona Artistic cellmate

Nadin Survivor of the five-times-a-day whipping

Nahid Cellmate, takes care of Nayyer after her attempted suicide

Nahid-M Nahid Mohammadi, Fadai' minority, executed November 1981

Nargess Nayyer's sister-in-law

Nasrin Nasrin Baqai', Central Committee Rahe Kargar, shot with husband 1984

Ozra Feisty prisoner in Evin

Pari Asqar's sister

Parvin Parvin Goli Abkenari, wife of Mehran, Rahe Kargar, suicide Dec 1987

Raf'at Committed suicide after five-times-a-day whipping

Rezvan Middle aged prisoner, hanged herself in prison

Roqiyyeh Fellow prisoner Evin prison

Sepideh 30-year-old woman severely tortured

Setareh Met during initial interrogation

Sima-D Sima Daryani, friend from outside, Fadai' Minority, executed Nov 1981

Sima Survivor of 10 months 'cowshed' and 'coffins'

Sharareh Fellow prisoner

Shohreh-M Shohreh Modir Shanehchi, Rahe Kargar, executed January 6,

1982

Shohreh-S Shohreh Shirzad, Peikar, executed March 1982

Soheila Soheila Rahimi, mother with sciatica, hanged or hanged herself in 1988

Suzan Suzan Nikzad, Nurse fellow prisoner, shot in Autumn 1981

Yashar & Rowshan Two children in Gowhardasht prison

Zohreh *Tavvab*, particularly vicious

Shahla Chapters

Abdi *(pn)* A friend who gave her sanctuary – exiled

Fadai' Organisation

Abdol-Reza Abdolreza Kalantari Nistanki, executed SAVAK, March 1977

Abbas Abbas Surki, *(amu palang)*, Fadai' founder murdered by SAVAK

Ahmad-Reza Ahmad-Reza Qanbari, died in pólice raid 1977

Aziz Aziz Sarmadi, founder of Fadai' murdered by SAVAK

Bahman Bahman Ruhi Ahangaran, died under torture by SAVAK 1976

Behruz Behruz Armaqani, died in shootout, May 1976

Bijan Bijan Jazani, historian, founder of Fadai', murdered by SAVAK

Farhad Farhad Sadighi Pashaki, died in police raid 1976

Fatemeh Fatemeh Hasanpour, suicide y grenade, 1976

FN Farrokh Negahdar current Chairman of Fadai' (Majority) – exiled

Hamid Hamid Ashraf, head of Fadai', shot in ambush with 11 others, 1977

Ladan Ladan Ale-Agha, died in police raid, 1976

Mahvash Mahvash Khatami, died in police raid, 1976

Mehrdad Mehdad Pakzad, ex-military intelligence, Fadai' leader, executed IRI

Mo'meni Hamid Momeni, chief theoretician of Fadai', suicide by grenade, 1976

Mostafa Mostafa Hasanpour, killed in a shootout, 1977

Nadereh Nadereh Ahmad Hashemi, died in shoot out February 1977

Nasser & Arjang Nasser and Arjang Shaygan Sham-Asbi, young boys, killed in shootout

Saba Saba Bijan-Zadeh, killed in shootout February 1977

Shamsi Shamsi Nahani, suicide by grenade, 1976

Zahra Zahra Agha-Nabi Gholhaki, executed SAVAK

Zia Hassan Zia Zarifi, founder of Fadai', murdered by SAVAK

Regime functionaries (Shah and Islamic Republic)

Azodi Mohammad Hassan Naseri, Chief interrogator

Forutan Yousef Forutan, New head of Evin

Haji Davood Rahmani, governor of Qezel Hesar prison, torturer

Jabbari Senior Pasdar in Evin

Javan 'doctor' Parviz Bahman Farnezhad, Interrogator, Evin and Qezel Qale'h

Hosseini Mohammad Ali Sha'bani, Interrogator Komiteh Moshtarek

Hossein-Zadeh Mohammad Hossein-Zadeh Movahhed, Administrator Evin 1980's

Kachuhi Father of ex-Evin chief Mohammad Kachuhi who was shot by a Pasdar

Khalkhali Senior Religious Judge, notorious for giving out death sentences

Lajevardi Head of Iran's prisons, architect of systematic torture and *tavvab*-creation

Meisam Reformist governor of Qezel Hesar replacing Haji Davood Rahmani

Montazeri Ayatollah Hosssein Montazeri, designated successor to Khomeini

Mojtaba Mojtaba Sarlak, Pasdar in charge of Cellblock 4, Evin

Mostafavi Mostafa Hirad, Interrogator Evin and Qezel Qale'h

Naserian Mohammad Moqise'i (Naserian), head of Gowhardasht Prison.

PM Parviz Mo'tamed, ex-SAVAK agent, interviewed in Paris

Rahimi Pasdar (female) in Evin

Saqi Ostovar Ayub Saqi, sergeant, torturer, in charge of Qezel Qale'h

Teymoori Sergeant, torturer at Qezel Qale'h

Zamani Chief of Security in Evin

Appendix 3

Main opposition parties and groups to the Shah and Islamic Regime

Tudeh Party: formed in 1941 and became one of the largest official communist parties in the Middle East. Tudeh, with its trade union base and having infiltrated the armed forces, played a major role in the nationalisation of the Anglo-Persian Oil company during the premiership of Mosaddeq and was highly influential in the intellectual life of the country. After the CIA-organised coup in 1953, the party, including its extensive network within the military, was all but destroyed inside Iran and its leadership was exiled to the Soviet Bloc. After the Sino-Soviet split in 1956 the Maoist faction split calling itself the Revolutionary Organization of the Tudeh Party - later renamed Ranjbaran Party. During and after the Revolution, Tudeh supported Khomeini and his regime until it, in turn, was brutally suppressed by that same regime in 1983.

Organisation of Iranian People's Fadāi' Guerrillas (OIPFG) – Fadāi' for short. Created in 1971 after the amalgamation of two guerrilla groups following the attack on Siāhkal police station. It suffered a number of near lethal blows from the Shah's SAVAK but survived to emerge on the eve of the revolution. After the Revolution the Fadāi became the largest left organisation in the country with tens of thousands of supporters. The occupation of the US Embassy by the Islamic regime caused the Fadāi to split in 1980 into the

Fadāi (Majority - so called because it included the majority of the Central Committee) which allied itself with the Tudeh Party and supported the regime, and the Fadāi (Minority) which continued in opposition to the regime.

Fadāi (Majority) supported the Islamic regime alongside the Tudeh Party until 1983 when it was suppressed along with the Tudeh Party. It consistently mirrored the Tudeh line. There was a further splits in the organisation in 1980 and 1981

Fadāi (Minority) after the split with the Fadāi (Majority) in 1980 went underground, but fought alongside Kurdistan Democratic Party (I) and Kumeleh in Iranian Kurdistan. In the rest of Iran, the Fadāi (Minority) suffered severe blows in the bloody crackdown of 1981-3.

Organisation of Iranian Peoples Mojahedin (PMOI) created in 1965. It initially had links with the religious section of Mosaddeq's National Front (Nehzat Azadi). It espoused a revolutionary interpretation of Islam, strongly influenced by the Shi'a thinker Ali Shari'ati, but also by a Maoist version of Marxism. It joined the armed struggle after the Fadāi' attack on the Siāhkal police station in 1971. In 1975 a large section of the Mojahedin converted to Marxism and emerged after the Revolution as the Peykār Organisation. In the aftermath of the Revolution the Mojahedin became the largest opposition group in Iran. While initially supporting Khomeini, they prepared for an uprising and suffered severe blows in the crackdown of 1981.

Peykār (full name: Sāzmān Peikār Barāye Rahāi' Tabaqeh Kārgar - Combat Organisation for the Liberation of the Working Class) originated as splinter group from the Mojahedin (1975). Originally known as the Marxist Mojahedin, it adopted a Maoist interpretation of Marxism, and was strongly opposed to the Soviet Union. In 1978, on the eve of the Revolution it adopted the name of Peikār. After the Revolution Peikār became the second largest left organisation in the country, after the Fadāi'. Under the blows of the regime Peikār imploded and many of its activists and cadres were executed or imprisoned.

Rāhe Kārgar (full name: Sāzman Kārgaran Enqelabi Iran - Rāhe Kārgar - Organisation of Revolutionary Workers of Iran - Rāhe Kārgar). Originally created inside the Shah's prisons by a number of cadres from various opposition groups, both Marxist and Islamic, who had escaped execution. It was formally launched in 1979. Rāhe Kārgar was unique in that it rejected the reformism of the Tudeh, the reliance on the armed struggle of the Fadāi' and the 'third worldism' of the Maoists. It attracted members from many opposition forces and rapidly grew to become the third largest force on the left with an influence on the radical left far wider than its numerical strength. In 1982-3 the Organisation, including large section of its leadership suffered under the blows of the regime who were either executed or received long prison sentences.

There were a number of other, mainly Maoist, organisations also active in Iran after the Revolution.

Regional and National Organisations: The above list excludes the two mass Kurdish parties that are active in Kurdistan - Kurdistan Democratic Party of Iran (KDPI-I), a mass party created in 1945 with a social democratic ideology with particularly strong base in rural areas of Kurdistan and another mass party, Kumeleh, created after the 1979 revolution and developed a strong urban base. Both were, and remain, predominantly Kurdish organisations. In 1983 Kumeleh merged with the Communist Workers Party of Iran. Both parties have experiences splits in recent years.

About the Author

The author is a medical doctor who trained in the UK and went back to Iran to teach in Shiraz (formerly Pahlavi) University. He participated in the revolution that overthrew the Shah and was later imprisoned by the post-revolutionay regime for his defence of freedom. After release he returned to the UK to work as a medical doctor in the National Health Service. He is now retired.

He has published an autobiography: Sliding into Revolution, Lulu Press, 2022

Also by M.S.Kia

Sliding into Revolution
A doctors memories of life, love and revolution

This is a worm's eye history of the Iranian Revolution in the eyes of a participant, a doctor and university teacher. This is a story of the crucial role played by those whom the ultimate victors have tried to erase. This is the story of the democratic forces of the left, who helped ignite the revolutionary fire.

Even though the Revolution in the end disgorged an autocratic theocracy, the Islamists were not the only participants nor necessarily the inevitable winners.

Reflections on life and love
Collection of poems (in preparation)

www.ingramcontent.com/pod-product-compliance
Lightning Source LLC
Chambersburg PA
CBHW030030030726
47500CB00001B/42